UNEXPECTED EDEN

UNEXPECT EDEN

LEXI POST

Acknowledgments

For Bob Fabich whose confidence attracted me from the very first. For my sister and best friend, Paige Wood. She's always there when I need her.

Thank you to Carol Webb of Bella Media Management for all her advice and fast service. A special shout out to Nova for inspiring Wally. And thank you to my critique partner, Marie Patrick, for making me a better writer. I couldn't do this without her.

Author's Note

Unexpected Eden was inspired by Emily Dickinson's poem, *Come slowly, Eden!* This poem was first published in 1890, four years after Dickinson's death and titled Apotheosis by two friends who edited her collection. This title is interesting in that it refers to the change of a human into a god or it can refer to the best example, such as the best example of a poem. Since Dickinson was a recluse and single her whole life, her poems that contain veiled references to passion, such as this one, can be fascinating.

What if the secretive Dickinson purposely disappeared from her writing desk to visit another planet by the name of Eden? Would her poetry then mean something else entirely? Would *Come slowly, Eden!* take on another meaning, such as the transition of a woman from Earth into life on another planet? Or perhaps the way in which she needed to adjust, or needed to be taken—slowly?

Apotheosis

Come slowly, Eden!
Lips unused to thee,
Bashful, sip thy jasmines,
As the fainting bee,

Reaching late his flower,
Round her chamber hums,
Counts his nectars—enters,
And is lost in balms!

Chapter One

Jahl sat naked on the floor of the stone storehouse and grinned as the unbreakable infragilis vine binding his wrists split in seven places and fell into his lap. His captors were naïve to think they could hold him, but then again, as former rulers of Naralina they were probably ignorant of many things, including the fact that he and most of his men had portal chips like them.

He stood and stretched his legs. As much as he wanted to further explore Haven, he had to leave. The two leaders of Haven were getting too close in their interrogations. He could withstand the force of Wareson's air blasts, but Nassic's ability to make him tell the truth had already revealed more than he'd planned. They now knew Loraleaf existed, though they had no idea where it was and that was something he couldn't afford to reveal. Too many men lived in Loraleaf and he refused to put them in more danger than they were already. His three nights of investigating the Haven compound had yielded much and he would be satisfied with that… for now.

Scrat, he'd forgotten to cover the surveillance eye. He scanned the storehouse and noticed a bag of dried gourds. Perfect. He used his mind to overturn the bag and send it up to cover the eye. One of his men's reflection abilities would have been better, but Jahl had to use what he'd been born with, even if his father thought his ability useless.

He turned to the wall behind him and focused. The stone moved aside allowing him to pass through. Once outside his prison, he allowed the stone to return to its normal configuration just as he had the past few nights. No need to leave any clues behind. Luckily, his captors had been too distracted by their new mate to spend any length of time with him or they may have remembered they hadn't determined his kindred yet. Not that he had one anymore. Then again, they expected to keep him a full cycle of the moon and thought they had time.

Selene had risen high but was only a sliver of light in the night sky. The jungle air felt cool and moist, much better than the heat of the building where he'd spent the day. Jahl listened before moving far from the storehouse. Every Edenist was born with a special ability and seeing in the dark could very well be an attribute of one of the night guards, especially for those of the Kindred of Light. He rubbed the scarred birthmark on his chest absently.

Not taking any chances, he lifted a large rock with his mind and sent it to the other side of the compound, where it crashed against another building. The nearby guard on the high wall surrounding Haven immediately ran in that direction. Jahl listened as other night sentries headed away from where he stood.

Quickly, he moved to the defense wall of the compound where he'd found the hidden door they'd brought him through when he'd been captured. Silently, he lifted the bar from across it and set it against the wall. After stepping through to the outside and closing the door, he used his mind to replace the wooden barrier into its spot on the other side. The only evidence he'd left behind was the shattered vine.

Turning away from Haven, he loped into the dense jungle in the opposite direction of Loraleaf to leave a false trail. His own home was too precious for him to risk, now that he finally had one.

"Jahl."

The quiet word surprised him. He halted and waited. The bush to his right moved and Sandale emerged, naked, as was their custom, his height and blond hair easy identifiers in the moon's limited light. Behind him followed Khaos, his dark ponytail making him harder to see. Even the tanned skin of his naked body was darker, swallowing what little light there was. These brothers of his heart were welcome, but they should not have come for another thirty-seven days. "What is it?"

Sandale smiled. "It's good to see you too."

Jahl waved his hand, brushing off the sarcasm. "You weren't supposed to see me for much longer. Why did you come tonight?"

Sandale's face turned serious, his sharp jaw lowering. "It's our chosen one."

Jahl's heart skidded past a beat. "What do you mean? What's wrong with her?" He looked past Sandale and straight to Khaos. "Is she in danger?"

Khaos nodded. "We must go now."

"Open the portal." Jahl stepped back, ready to cross over to Earth.

Sandale's hand on his arm slowed his pulse. "Wait. We are too close to this compound. If Naralina discovers this hidden refuge, they will look for others and could find Loraleaf. Let us move closer to the city."

Sandale was right, as usual. They had a little time. What Khaos could sense was the future, not the immediate present. "Very well. Let's head straight toward Naralina."

Receiving a nod from both men, he set the pace of their run. He itched to open the portal to Earth. They could not lose their chosen one. They had watched her for six years now, even before they'd left the city of their birth. She was their hope for the future. She was the reason they built Loraleaf. She would be the bond that would make them whole.

"Stop." Khaos' voice sounded loud after the quiet silence. "We must go now."

Fear for Serena sliced up Jahl's spine. "Sandale."

Within seconds, Sandale stood side by side with Khaos but with a space between them two men could fit through. Each man reached beneath his other arm and pressed the chips that rested against their ribcages beneath their skin. The empty air between the two shimmered before solidifying into an opening to Earth.

Jahl's blood ran cold at the sight before him. Without hesitation, he leapt through the portal.

* * * * *

Serena Upton dared not swallow. The knife blade against her throat pressed into her skin and the slightest movement would draw blood. The question was, how much? She hoped Toni didn't do something stupid like pull one of those fight scene moves she did as a stunt woman. That would just land Toni on her back faster.

Toni had her hands on her hips with a look that had quelled many a would-be date, but it wasn't having the same effect on the four men determined to rape them. *Please Toni, just don't get them mad.*

"Listen, Dickwad. I understand you may be a little hard up, but I'm thinking, you do this and your career in acting, such as it is, will be over."

At Toni's words, Serena stifled a groan before it could move up her throat.

The leader of the four men, all of whom were nothing more than local extras on the sci-fi film she'd been working on, grinned. "I don't think so. If you happen to disappear by tomorrow, no one will know."

Serena gritted her teeth to keep them from chattering. The night air was plenty warm in the Vegas desert, but whenever she was scared, her teeth chattered and the knife seemed to press harder.

Unfortunately, with her friend, the more scared Toni was, the more aggressive she became. Serena held back a moan as Toni's head cocked to the side. Her friend was scared shitless, which meant trouble. Things would go from bad to worse fast if she didn't do something. "Pssst."

Toni's green gaze shifted to her.

"What?"

She raised her brows, the most she could do with the knife waiting to slice her throat. Her only hope, such as it was, was that the men really wanted to fuck her before they killed her. Some hope. Just the thought of never seeing her parents again had her eyes watering. Oh God, and her younger sister.

"Ah fuck." Toni's frustration mounted. "You guys must be desperate to want to do her." She pointed at Serena.

Three pairs of eyes turned in her direction. What the hell had Toni said that for? The man holding her tightened his grip as the other men gave her body a once-over. Good, maybe they would decide she wasn't worth it. With her short hair, no waist to speak of, jeans and combat boots, she looked more like a boy than a girl. Luckily, she wore her *Fantastic Four* movie t-shirt with the words "Flame on!" emblazoned across her chest. It was an old t-shirt she used when she set larger explosions since it was black and didn't show what a mess she was, or the size of her chest.

The leader strode toward her to take a better look. That's when she noticed Toni sidling toward the building they'd just left. She hoped her friend planned on getting help, and fast.

The man in front of her took some of her short black hair in his hand and ran it between his thumb and fingers. "Feels just right to me. Bet the rest is just as soft. Say Danny, why don't you use that knife for something productive? Let's see exactly what we have here."

Before Serena could tense, the knife left her throat and made a sweeping cut beneath the neckline of her t-shirt. It only sliced the collar, but the man in front of her grabbed the shirt and ripped it open. She sucked in air now that the knife was no longer against her neck, but that released her jaw and her teeth started to chatter.

The man before her didn't seem to notice as his gaze fixed on her cleavage, which was made more evident by her purple underwire bra. She crossed her arms over her chest.

The asshole laughed. "Oh yeah, we have us a winner here. Who said she wasn't worth it?" He turned around to look at the other guys, just as Toni smacked the smallest in the back of the head with a metal bar left from the last scene they'd shot. The man went down, but wasn't out. What the hell was Toni thinking? She was supposed to be calling for help.

The leader ran to aid his friend and grabbed Toni by the hair. Toni lashed out with a kick that had him throwing a fist in her direction. Toni tried to duck, but he still had her hair and the blow caught her cheek.

If only she could reach her phone in her back pocket. Serena attempted to break free, but her captor pulled her back and laid the knife against her throat again. "Where do ya think you're goin'?"

"With me." The strange voice came from behind Serena, but Toni's eyes widened in awe.

Shit, she hoped that meant Toni was impressed, because if a hero stood behind her, he'd better be big to take on these four.

"Who the fuck are you?" The man that held Toni scowled.

"I'm her agapayto, which means you are dead."

Toni's gaze moved to Serena. "Lucky you."

Lucky her what? Didn't Danny with the knife want to see too? As if he'd heard her thought, her captor swore beneath his breath and dragged her around, using her as a shield as he backed them to stand next to Toni and the leader.

Holy freak! There were three giant, heavily muscled naked men scowling at them all. She sincerely hoped they weren't in the mood for sex because if the three men before her wanted to take them, she and Toni were screwed, figuratively and literally. She glanced at the three large, but relaxed cocks and breathed a relieved sigh.

"Serena." The giant in the front with the military haircut and defined cheekbones breathed her name like a caress and her skin tingled. That was weird. It caused her frayed nerves to unravel some more. The man should be on a Marine recruitment poster with all that muscle.

One of the giants stepped around the first. He was just as built, but had longer brown hair caught back in a ponytail. "Release the women."

The hold on her tightened. Not exactly the reaction she'd hoped for. The leader, who still held Toni, did the same, wrapping his other arm around Toni's waist while he grasped her hair.

Serena was suffocating…too much restraint.

The third giant stepped forward, his blond hair down to his ears seemed normal enough, but even in the security light, his eyes shone pale. "There is no need for pain here. Let the women go and we will allow you to leave."

A growl from the first giant proved he wasn't happy with that. His hands at his sides formed fists.

If her attackers released her and Toni, she was suddenly sure they would be taken with these new men. Did she really have to choose which set of men would have the pleasure of raping her? Serena tried to take a deep breath, but the knife at her throat cut more and her fear escalated. "Scotty, beam me up. Now."

All eyes focused on her. Oh shit, she'd said that out loud. She was losing it fast. She turned her head toward Toni, ignoring the cut of the blade across her skin.

Tony scowled, her eyes blazing. "Ah fuck this."

One of the giants yelled and all hell broke loose.

The man holding her dragged her backward. She stumbled with him, grabbing his arm to keep her balance and hopefully keep the blade from cutting her throat.

Toni was down on the ground, the leader bent over at the waist, his hand still in her hair.

Two of their original attackers rushed the military man. The long-haired giant went for the leader. As the blond strode toward her, Danny pulled her back faster, out of the lit area behind the building. Where the hell did he expect to go? There was nothing but cacti and mesquite trees out here.

Just as the blond giant was about to overtake them, Danny threw her down and faced the new threat with his knife. She didn't stop to think. Crawling along the ground, she moved away from the chaos and the noise. They were too far from the security lights and there was no moon, so she felt her way in the darkness. Not the best option considering the rattlesnakes and tarantulas that lived out here.

She needed to stand up and run, but the most her brain would allow her to do was crawl. She had to get help. She had to save Toni. She had to— "Eek!"

The hand around her arm was large. "You're safe now." The soothing tone made her think of a meditation tape she'd once listened to for all of five minutes.

But this voice had her heart slowing immediately and a strange calmness settled in. She turned her head and looked at the man crouched next to her.

She couldn't see his face, as it was in shadow, but his empathy for her situation flowed through her. She would be all right. How did she know that?

"Can you stand?"

Could she? She leaned on his arm as he helped her up. "I-I g-guess I-I c-can." She snapped her mouth shut, her teeth still chattering.

His large hand cupped her jaw. "You are safe. We are here for you."

The words frightened her yet the tone relaxed her. She pulled away from him and he let her go. "What do you mean? Who are you?" There was a little more light now that she wasn't staring down at the desert floor. Quickly, she crossed her arms over her chest, to hide the fact she was half naked.

He shook his head as he smiled, his teeth standing out in the dark. "There is no need to hide your beauty." He spread his arms wide. "We don't."

She needed to get back to Toni, but she couldn't resist looking at his body again. It was far too dark to see anything below the waist. Sure, tell her to look when she couldn't see a damn thing.

"Come with me." He held out his hand. "We should go back and save those men from Jahl."

The urge to take his hand was strong, but she resisted. Okay, she'd go back, but to save Toni, not the Jahl person. She ignored his hand and started walking toward the noises.

The man's quiet chuckle as he strode next to her made her feel silly.

"I'm Sandale. I'm here with Jahl and Khaos. We are here for you."

He'd said that before and the calm part of her brain told her this was a good thing.

They walked by Danny, who lay as if sleeping, but it was too dark to tell if his chest moved. She didn't want to know. The whole night had turned into a nightmare she wouldn't forget for years and the last thing she needed was to confirm one of her attackers was dead. The question was, what should she expect from the three giants?

She had little time to ponder that. A body flew through the air and landed not five feet away from her. A grunt issued from it and she shivered. "Oh my God. He almost hit me."

"No, Jahl would never hurt you. I told you, you're safe."

Sandale's calming influence was too surreal. The fear subsided and despite the continued fighting, she felt safe. The man must be a hypnotist or something.

They had just stepped into the area lit by the building's security light when the giant with the long hair turned away from his adversary. "We must go. Now."

Yes, they should go. Then she and Toni— Where was Toni?

A car squealed into the fenced parking lot next to the building, its lights blinding them. She shielded her eyes.

Sandale's hand latched on to her arm. "We need to leave."

She pulled her arm, but this time he didn't let go and once again a feeling of calmness descended upon her. She clearly heard four car doors open, but couldn't see anything as Sandale pulled her away from the building.

"Danny! Tommy!"

The yelling didn't faze her even as her brain registered that the new male voices must be friends of her attackers. She moved her gaze to the ground in front of her, allowing her eyes to adjust to the semidarkness of the desert again.

"Oh shit!" Toni's voice came from behind a second before the first bullet whizzed by.

Men yelled at them, but Sandale propelled her along, forcing her to run as more shots rang out. She understood she was in danger. They were all in danger, but she had no fear.

The military giant, the one named Jahl according to Sandale, was gesturing for them to follow. She looked over her shoulder to see Toni being pulled along by the other giant. They were headed into the desert. Toni might be in shape for an extended run, but she would be out of breath in a few more minutes. She really should tell her giant she couldn't run that far.

Suddenly, Sandale pushed her forward and she stumbled, almost hitting Jahl in front of her. She could have managed to stay upright except Sandale's large body plowed into her and they both went down, his arm beneath her, softening her fall.

Her mind cleared from the strange calmness. Sandale's heavy weight across her lower body was too much. "Can you move? I can barely breathe."

He groaned and true fear slithered through her nerves. "Sandale? Are you okay?"

The large man managed to roll off her, but his arm still cradled her back. Carefully, she rose to her knees.

Toni dropped down next to her. "He's been shot. Those fucking assholes."

At that pronouncement, the silence surrounding them finally penetrated. "What happened to those other men?"

Toni gave her a strange look but didn't answer.

"Sandale!" Jahl knelt down opposite of her. His brow knit with worry.

The light from the moon was minimal, but even she could see the dark blood running from a wound in Sandale's gut. Without clothes, it was almost too real. Grasping for her tattered tee, she found it missing. She must have lost it. She turned to Toni. "Give me your shirt."

"What?"

She rolled her eyes, even though she was sure Toni couldn't see. "Your shirt. We need to stop the bleeding."

"Since when did you become a doctor?"

Serena waited for Toni to give up her t-shirt. Then she ripped it in half, folded it and held it against the wound.

Jahl looked at her. "You can heal him?"

She shook her head. "No. I took a first-aid class once. This is all I know. We need to get him to a doctor."

Jahl's eyes closed for a moment. "We don't have a healer at Loraleaf."

Okay, she'd never heard of Loraleaf, but she was pretty sure Centennial Hills Hospital was only about a twenty-minute drive from the set. She pulled her cell phone out of her pocket.

No service. Since when? She looked around for the light from the set building. Her heart picked up speed as she surveyed her surroundings. Even in the dark, it was clear this wasn't the Las Vegas desert.

Toni gripped her shoulder. "We're not in Kansas anymore, Toto."

She was right. Wherever they were, was jungle. Moist heat caressed her dry skin and the hard, packed dirt of the desert was now a soft cushion of plant life beneath her knees. No car with lights, no men with guns, no building set, just quiet night. She stared at her friend, her jaw tightening. "This can't be."

A hand wrapped around her wrist, slowing the rush of adrenaline before it got out of the gate. "You're safe."

Sandale's whisper had her snapping her gaze to his. He stared at her with such compassion, her eyes started to water. This big, naked man came out of nowhere and saved her. He could very well be dying and he was worried about her. She'd never met anyone like him. "Thank you."

His lips twitched up at one corner before he closed his eyes and released her.

She looked to Jahl, who watched his friend. They had to be best friends because for a military type, Jahl looked very close to tears.

The long-haired man stepped closer and stood next to Jahl. "We can't stay here. Others are coming."

Jahl nodded. "We have only one option. We must bring him to Haven."

The other man shook his head, but Jahl ignored him. "Khaos, help me lift him."

"Wait." She grabbed Jahl's wrist as he began to rise. "We need to keep something against his wound if you're going to drag him somewhere. We need rope or a belt or something. You guys didn't happen to leave a stash of clothes nearby, did you?"

Jahl looked at her as if she'd just had an alien spring from her stomach. "We do not wear clothes here. We have nothing."

She released him, feeling as if she just gave him the worst insult.

The other man, Khaos, stepped forward and looked at her for the first time. She couldn't hold his gaze. Despite the darkness, there was something unearthly about it. He sighed. "Would a strong vine work?"

If it was all they had, she could make do. "Yes, it could."

He didn't say anything. He simply disappeared into the surrounding darkness, hopefully to find a vine.

How the hell was she supposed to explain this to her family? One minute she's working on set, cleaning up after a long day of explosive work, and the next she's in a strange place, with strange men and no shirt. Her father would commit Klingon Hegh'bat if he could see her now. Despite the fact she'd just seen her family last month during Memorial Day weekend, her heart ached for them. What was new? She loved them. So what if she ran to them every time she was upset? It wasn't as if she was upset that often or anything. And truth be told, this, whatever this was, was definitely worth getting upset about.

Sandale's fingers intertwined with hers, pulling her back from the edge of hysteria once again. His large hand encapsulated hers, a solid band on his third finger pressed into her own. She held fast and looked at him. His eyes were closed but his mouth quirked up at the side again.

Her heart lurched. She wanted him to live. She wanted to learn about him. There was something between them she didn't understand and her gut told her he did.

She glanced at Jahl. He stared at her with a look of such anguish that her stomach knotted up despite the calm she felt. What was between these men? Were they brothers? Friends? Lovers?

Toni shifted closer, causing Serena to look away. She didn't even know these men but they had saved her and now one of them may be dying.

"What if we went back to the building set?" Toni addressed them all. "I'm sure those creeps have left by now and then we can get in my car and take him to the hospital."

That made a lot of sense.

"No. It is forbidden." Jahl scowled. "We must get him to Haven. They may have a healer."

Forbidden? Healer? Some of the words these guys used were typical, but others just sounded archaic. "You said 'may have'. Does that mean you aren't sure? What if they don't? At least at Centennial Hills they definitely have a doctor."

Jahl shook his head, and Sandale squeezed her fingers, gaining her attention.

"We are not from Earth. We cannot allow anyone to heal us. We are different." He paused and swallowed. "You are on Eden now. A different planet. We had hoped to woo you slowly, but Khaos sensed your danger. I'm sorry. This will be hard for you. Especially if I'm not here to help." He closed his eyes as if his words had taken too much of his energy.

Another planet? No way. Sure, she'd always dreamed of what it would be like to live on another planet with a whole different race of beings, but it was nothing but a dream. She leaned over and felt Sandale's forehead. It was very warm. He was probably as much of a science fiction addict as she was. He was just delusional from the pain. There had to be a way back to the set. In fact, they could very well be on another set. That would explain the jungle-like atmosphere. Wasn't there a couple other buildings nearby?

"I have the vine."

She started as Khaos appeared at Sandale's head.

"Good." She took the sinewy length. "Jahl, can you help me lift him?"

The big man nodded and lifted Sandale as gently as a newborn baby. She wouldn't have thought he had it in him. He just looked so tough. He must really care for his friend.

"We have to leave. Now." Khaos made his statement once again and this time she sensed the urgency.

Sandale raised his hand. "Wait. You cannot flee safely dragging me with you. You must leave me."

"No."

She and Jahl and Khaos had all answered at the same time and they stared at one other. Toni threw up her hands.

Sandale's voice turned stern. "Yes. Khaos, help me get under that Salis bush. Jahl, move the dead wood and brush around me."

Jahl stood. "We can move *you* with wood beneath you. It can go as fast as we go."

A voice in the darkness hollered to another. Whoever they were, they were close and these guys definitely didn't want to be found. Sandale squeezed her fingers. "No time." He looked to Khaos, who nodded.

Jahl shook his head, but didn't stop Khaos as he gently moved Sandale beneath what looked like a miniature Weeping Willow tree. Serena followed, folding the second half of Toni's shirt and setting it against the first half, which had soaked through.

She didn't like this. It reminded her of the Vulcan belief about the safety of many being more important than the safety of a single person. She never did like that about a logical race.

Sandale touched her face. "Go. Be safe. They need you even more now. You must be their anchor." He brushed the side of her cheek. "I am so glad I had the chance to meet you."

Serena swallowed against the constriction in her throat as tears gathered in her eyes. "Don't worry we—"

"Go. Now." Sandale's voice hardened.

She leaned forward and brushed a kiss on his cheek.

His eyes widened.

Turning to duck out, she heard him whispering to himself. "Reaching late his flower, round her chamber hums, counts his nectars—enters, and is lost in balms!"

She looked back, but his eyes had closed. Not sure she'd really heard what sounded like poetry, she scrambled out beneath the branches and wiped her eyes with the back of her hand. It was nothing. Just compassion for a wounded human being. She wasn't crying because she felt something for him. It was just, just… Oh it had to be that savior complex. She'd heard people rescued from cars or burning buildings would have that with the emergency responders. That's all it was.

Khaos turned away from her. "Jump on my back." His whisper frightened her more than if he'd shouted. She looked around for Toni and found her piggyback on Jahl.

She'd seen the muscles on these men, so she had to assume they could carry her and Toni.

Voices just yards away jerked her into motion and she jumped up on Khaos' back. He immediately set off at a run. She held on around his neck, careful to keep her arms low enough so as not to choke him. But her position kept her face against his abundant hair and though it was tied back, she couldn't help noticing how soft it was. Nor could she ignore the ginger-like scent that filled her lungs. He made her think of gingerbread men, one of her favorite cookies at Christmastime.

While Khaos jogged through the growth, she enjoyed the movement of the muscle beneath her. He carried her as if she weighed nothing, maneuvering quickly and silently. She turned her head to find Jahl and Toni, but they were nowhere in sight.

She worried about Toni, and when they didn't come to a door or anything, she had to concede they were not on a movie set. Could it be that these men had the technology to teleport to another location. She'd read of an eccentric billionaire who had been working on this. Last she'd heard he'd been successful moving from inside his house to his yard. She always kept tabs on the rich. They were the ones that would get man to another planet some day, she was sure of it.

She focused on Khaos because to think about where they were would send her over the edge into lala land and she needed her brain in working order if she planned to make it through this night.

Khaos broke into an open space in the growth. A huge stone stood in the middle of what looked to be a circle of grass. He slowed to a stop. The little bit of moonlight glanced off the stone, making it appear shiny, almost like it had a spotlight on it.

"We will wait for Jahl here." He bent his knees, which allowed her to slide off his back.

Relief flooded her. At least she had Toni. She'd been afraid she might not see her again. "Where are we?"

Khaos moved away from her. "It's a place near Haven. We will find a healer and take him to Sandale."

That sounded like a good idea to her. "Who were those people we needed to run from?" If they were the police, she planned on screaming as loud as she could.

"Lawbreakers."

"What? How do you know that? Maybe they were people from this Haven you keep talking about." She'd never heard of Haven, Nevada, but she'd just moved to the state a year ago when she'd discovered it was the perfect place for working on sci-fi films because it was an easy plane ride to Arizona and California. Plus Nevada itself was used by some lower-budget films that tended toward more fireballs, which were her specialty. Of course, it didn't hurt that Toni just happened to need a roommate.

Khaos turned and faced her. The light reflecting off the big stone illuminated his face like firelight, except there were no wavering flames. For the first time, she could really look at him.

His jaw was sculpted, more refined than Jahl's. Khaos' eyes were a lighter color too, appearing silver in the strange light, and they definitely slanted upward at the outside. He had a strong, straight nose, but his eyebrows were unique, also slanting slightly at the end.

He didn't answer her, but observed her with the same interest she viewed him, curiosity clear on his face. Self-consciously, she brushed back her bangs. Did he think she looked like a boy like her mom always teased her? Then again, as his gaze lowered to her bra-covered breasts, she had a feeling he didn't think that at all. She should probably cover herself, but the fact was, her bikini showed more of her breasts than her bra. Besides, the man was standing there completely nude.

She shouldn't look at him again, but he was naked and he must expect women to check him out if he was flaunting himself. Besides, his gaze had already moved down her clothed body and she was in the shadow.

Winning the battle over her conscience, she studied him. The light made the skin stretched taut across his smooth chest glow. She'd bet fifty Galatic Credits he was as tan as a California surfer dude at the end of August. And he was that color *all* over. Below his defined abdominal muscles that made the Terminator look like a wimp, his cock matched the skin tone of the rest of him and rested along the length of his balls.

She swallowed as that particular piece of his anatomy began to harden. She quickly moved her gaze to his thighs where his quadriceps were so well defined, the reflecting light shadowed the lines of his muscles. She couldn't see his calves as she blocked the light across his knees and feet.

"We exile our criminals."

Huh? Now what did that have to do with the— Oh right. "Where do you send them?"

"Here. To the jungle."

But that meant—she gritted her teeth hard. *Oh shit.* "You think the voices we heard were dangerous people. Hold on, does that mean you're a criminal too?" She took a step back.

A fleeting emotion passed over his face before he answered. "No, we exiled ourselves." Again, his gaze grew intense and she looked away.

As the silence stretched, she reached for something to talk about. She wished Toni were here. She'd make some smart ass-comment and things would feel normal again. "Why didn't Jahl follow us right away?"

Khaos took a couple steps back, almost as if he were afraid of her. That was just crazy, because he carried her on his back.

"He had to camouflage Sandale's hiding place."

She crossed her arms over her chest. "I would think that would take longer than making a litter for him."

Khaos shook his head. "Not with Jahl's abilities." He looked off as if thinking too himself. "They come."

Okay, that was as clear as mud. "Who?"

Khaos didn't answer. Instead he stared at the edge of the circle to her left. She listened carefully and could finally discern the swish of leaves as someone passed through.

Jahl jogged into the open area and stopped.

Toni jumped off without him bending his knees since she was almost as tall as he. "I told you I could have kept up with you. Not every female is a wimp, you know."

Serena couldn't help herself. She ran forward and gave Toni a hug.

"Hey, it's no big deal. You're good, right?"

She let go and stepped back. "Now I am." She smiled a bit, reassuring herself as much as Toni.

Jahl had moved directly to Khaos, and they conversed in low tones.

She took the opportunity to confer with Toni. "Did you see Sandale's hiding place?"

Her friend nodded. "Yeah. You wouldn't believe what the big guy can do. If I hadn't seen it with my own eyes, I'd never have believed it."

"What did he do?"

Toni gave her a shrewd look. "Let's just say that Sandale is well hidden. If he can just hold on…"

Serena crossed her arms again. "He's not going to make it without a doctor, and pretty quick."

"Yeah, about that." Toni tugged the ever-present elastic from around her wrist and pulled her hair together, flipping it through until it rested down her back in a ponytail. "Have you figured out where we are?"

She shook her head. "Have you?"

Toni glanced over at the two men. "Okay, I know you're the sci-fi geek and all, and I'm supposed to be the levelheaded one—"

"Excuse me?"

"Let me finish."

Serena pressed her lips tightly together. If Toni had figured out where they were then it was worth the sci-fi teasing Toni was so good at. Serena couldn't help that she loved sci-fi movies. She just did.

"We're on another planet."

Chapter Two

Seriously? Serena rolled her eyes. "Okay, enough teasing. Where are we?"

"I'm not teasing. Didn't you see that hole in the air we all ran through?" Toni pointed behind her as if the hole were right there a moment ago. "It was desert on one side and jungle on the other. And while you were on the ground with Sandale, Jahl and Khaos stood on either side of it and closed it before those goons could follow us. I'm telling you, it was some kind of portal and if we aren't on another planet then we are in another country at least."

She could only see half of Toni's face, but it was clear her friend was serious. She really believed they had traveled through space somehow. The idea was too thrilling to contemplate, so Serena didn't. "Okay, so what do we do now?"

"Okay? Just okay?" Toni threw her hands up. "This is huge."

She shrugged. She'd give Toni the teleport, though she herself was too busy falling on the ground to see a hole in the air, but across space? No way. Better to go along with Toni's delusion. As soon as they found a doctor, she would have him or her check out her friend and see if she'd sustained a bump on her head. It could have even been from earlier in the day. Toni had done a fight scene for the lead actress and had been thrown against a wall pretty hard to simulate a laser blast. "Of course it is. Which is why we have to figure out what to do next."

The two men approached, cutting off any further confidences.

Jahl stepped before her. "Are you well?"

Let's see, she'd been attacked after work and held at knife point, threatened with rape, had her shirt torn off, been taken to who-knows-where by three strangers through some kind of teleport transportation, and tended to a bullet wound with no real knowledge about what needed to be done. So in essence, *no*. "Yes, I'm fine."

He raised his hand and she leaned away.

Jahl scowled. "I would never hurt you, Serena. You are our chosen one. You are safe with us."

Chosen one? She didn't like the sound of that. It was as if they were in some B movie about a tribe who came upon people from the future and sacrificed them on a stone altar. She glanced at the large stone in the middle of the clearing and swallowed. "What about Toni?"

"She is safe also." He glanced at her friend, then moved his gaze back to her. "All women are precious here."

Toni snorted. "Really?"

Serena ignored Toni's doubtful response and kept her focus on Jahl. "So where is here?"

He ignored her question and raised his hand again toward her face. She grabbed it. "Whoa. What are you doing?"

"I wish to see your wound."

Her wound? Oh yeah, the knife. She let go of Jahl's large wrist to touch her neck. It was sore. The blood had dried, but there was a lot of it. "It's fine for now. You need to concentrate on Sandale."

He studied her for a moment, then turned toward Khaos. "You can take Serena to Loraleaf as you suggested."

Khaos nodded.

"Toni. We would like you to come with me to request a healer."

Serena's gut tightened. "I don't like that idea."

"Yeah." Toni moved closer to her. "I'm not exactly dressed to go visiting."

Jahl's eyes widened. "Of course not. You have clothes on. Here we do not wear clothes, but most people will understand it may take you time to adjust."

"Excuse me." Serena crossed her arms over her chest again. Not having a shirt on made it her new favorite stance. "Are you trying to tell us no one wears any clothing? Ever?"

"That's correct." Jahl seemed pleased she understood.

She didn't understand. Where the hell were they? "Are you in some kind of cult?"

Khaos interrupted. "This conversation needs to wait. Sandale could be dying and you two women are still in danger."

Jahl nodded. "He's right. Please, Serena. Climb on Khaos' back so we can move faster. Loraleaf is a long way from here. We want you to be safe."

She was such a sucker for a big, strong man asking nicely. "Okay. But will Toni come to this Loraleaf later?"

"If that's your wish."

"I wish."

"Then I will bring her once Sandale is taken care of." Jahl turned toward Toni. "We should go."

"That's fine with me, but I'm not climbing on your back. I can run on my own two feet."

"Very well. It's not far."

Toni stepped over and gave Serena a hug. "I'll see you soon. Don't let this guy push you around, okay?"

She nodded, her throat too tight at losing sight of the only person she knew in this strange place.

Toni walked over to Jahl. "Come on, big man, let's go."

Serena watched as the two ran out of the clearing. She continued to listen at the sounds they made moving through the bush until all was silent but the night creatures.

Khaos took Serena's hand, but she flinched, so he let go. He didn't want her afraid of him. If Serena ever looked at him like his mother had, he couldn't bear it. "We should leave."

"Of course." She looked back to where her friend had disappeared into the bush.

He understood Toni was the only person she trusted on his world, just as Jahl and Sandale had been the only ones in Naralina he'd trusted. If they had left the city without him, he wouldn't have survived there. "Don't worry. Jahl will bring her to Loraleaf as he said he would. You will see her soon. I promise."

She looked at him then and his heart beat just a little faster. Finally, she nodded. "Thank you for that."

"Now we should go. It's not safe outside the walls of Haven or below the barrier of Loraleaf."

She opened her mouth and he held up his hand, unable to stop grinning at her curiosity. "Please. I will answer all your questions once I know you're safe."

She stared at him for a moment before looking away. "And am I safe with you?"

He lost his smile and lifted his hand to touch her cheek, but she turned toward him and he dropped it to his side before making contact. "Yes. You will always be safe with me, Jahl, or Sandale." At the thought of his friend, his stomach tightened. Sandale *had* to live.

She continued to look worried, clasping her hands in front of her.

"Have we harmed you in any way?"

Her eyes widened as if the thought hadn't occurred to her. Good.

"No, you haven't. You've saved us from rapists and criminals. Good point. I guess I'm ready."

He turned and helped Serena settle on his back. "Hold on."

She did, her arms feeling so delicate compared to wrestling with his men. Her soft body pressed tightly against his made him thankful she still wore clothes. She smelled of smoke from the explosives she worked with but there was a hint of sweet vanilla beneath. To finally have her here with them on Eden after years of waiting, filled his body with joy.

It would be the most enjoyable run home he'd ever made, though perhaps a bit awkward. Her pheromones were enticing and causing him some discomfort, but he didn't want to block them. The men of Loraleaf understood the importance and reverence due to a chosen one. She would be respected.

When she'd looked at his body, he couldn't help studying her as well since it was the first time he wasn't seeing her through the portal. She was average height for an Earth woman, which made her much shorter than he. Khaos was anxious to see her lovely curves without clothes, but it had been her face from the first that had intrigued him.

When he and his friends first started looking for a beloved six years ago, he'd been the one to spot her in the line waiting to see a movie called *Avatar*. They'd opened the portal across the street in a closed store to remain unseen. As she came into view, he'd stopped breathing before Sandale pressed a hand on his shoulder and relaxed him. He'd pointed her out and his friends agreed. She was perfect.

She had an oval face with large, round eyes of amber that reminded him of the Savinstone, or gold as the humans called it. Beneath those beautiful eyes was a strong nose and a small mouth with full lips. That she kept her night-black hair short showed off her slender neck and perfectly shaped ears.

She had a friendly appearance when she worked or had coffee with friends, but the few times they'd seen her dressed up, they'd been taken aback. As stunning as she'd been, he much preferred her the way she was now.

He came to a small stream and easily leapt across it. He didn't mind getting his feet wet, but he didn't want to make any unnecessary noises.

She finally broke the silence. "Ah, could you give me some warning next time you're going to jump?"

He smiled, knowing she couldn't see him. "No. It's best that we stay silent."

He felt her tense against his back, and he wanted to comfort her, but now was not the time. The night was waning and they wouldn't make Loraleaf until almost dawn. She had to be tired by now.

"Khaos?" She whispered his name against his ear and a tiny shiver ran down his neck, across his chest and straight to his groin.

"Yes."

"I need to go to the bath—uh, I need to pee."

His feet slowed of their own accord at her request. When he stopped, he let her down onto a fallen tree and kept his voice low. "I will step behind that bush. Do not take long."

She nodded and he forced himself away from her side. Probably just as well as his cock was already hardening at the thought of her lowering her pants. Stepping around the giant myrtle bush, he stopped and stood with his back to her, trying to keep his mind on unrelated things. He and Sandale had left three of their best men in charge. Had all been quiet while they were gone? Though Jahl oversaw their defenses, Khaos took care of the infrastructure of the compound while Sandale was in charge of food management and mediation. Sandale was particularly good at that. With his abilities as one of the Kindred of Heart, he could turn enemies into friends in mere minutes. Khaos sighed. *Hold on, Sandale.*

"Khaos, you better get over here." Serena's whisper was full of fear and his worry for his friend switched to Serena.

Skirting the bush, he ran to her side, but perceived no threat. Had she simply become frightened without him? A warmth started in his heart. "What is it?"

"That." She pointed to a round-looking animal just three strides away. It was a welchet and it was looking at her curiously, sniffing the air, probably catching her strange smoky-vanilla scent.

He kept his voice low. "Yes, what about it?"

She wouldn't take her eyes off the little critter. "Won't it bite? Look at those fangs."

He chuckled as understanding dawned. "I never realized exactly how good this animal's defenses were until now. No, it won't bite. Those are not fangs but they are supposed to look that way. If he opens his mouth, you will see those are simply bones that grow from the front of his bottom jaw. He uses them to dig with but he can't bite with them."

She leaned closer to him, obviously not convinced. "But look at those quills all over him. Is this welchet a form of porcupine? Can't he throw those into us if he's scared?"

Khaos looked curiously at the little critter. Quills? "If you mean his fur, then no, he can't throw it at you. He may look dangerous, which I think is what his biology meant it to look like, but his best defense is that he's fast. He has six legs and can run faster than the eye can see if he's really scared."

The look she gave him had him swallowing a laugh. "Here." He took one step toward the animal and crouched down. He used two fingers to scratch at the jungle floor. The welchet couldn't resist and hesitantly moved toward his hand, its nose sniffing at the ground. Once it was close enough, he stroked the animal over its back. It immediately lost interest in grubbing and lifted its head to rub against his hand, emitting a soft, gurgling sound.

Khaos felt Serena move until she knelt on the opposite side of him from the welchet. "Can I try?"

"Of course. Stroke him along his back and he'll come to you. Just don't touch his tail. I don't know why, but they disappear faster than lightning if you do."

"It has a tail?"

"Yes." He moved his hand and the welchet leaned toward it, revealing the small nubby tail at the end of his body. "See?"

"Yes." She held her hand out like she'd seen him do and the welchet pushed against it, its sounds of pleasure growing louder.

Khaos could understand the animal's feelings. To be stroked by Serena would be paradise. "They are edible, but are tough, so that's only something to keep in mind if you are in the jungle and really hungry."

"What?" Her voice rose and the welchet scurried away. "Oh."

Her disappointment had him wanting to capture ten welchets just to make her happy, but that would have to wait. He stood. What he needed to do now was make sure she was safe. He whispered to remind her that they needed to be quiet. "We are only halfway to Loraleaf. We have to go. I'd like to get you there before Helios rises."

She lowered her voice. "You mean the sun?"

He nodded, not willing to engage in more conversation about their planet. Sandale was the one who was supposed to help her adapt to Eden, not him, and certainly not Jahl. He turned his back to her and bent his knees.

As Serena climbed on, he closed his eyes, simply enjoying the sensation of getting her settled against him. "Ready?"

"Yes."

Opening his eyes, he headed for home, anxious now to see what she would think of Loraleaf. Theron, one of the men they left in charge, would probably greet them, not willing to let anyone else find out what had happened. When Khaos and Sandale had left, they'd told Theron why they needed Jahl to escape early. It was no surprise to them to find Jahl leaving Haven. The three of them had always been in sync.

"Will there be a bed I can sleep in when we get to Loraleaf?" Serena's tired whisper interrupted his thoughts.

He should have thought of that. She hadn't slept all night and had to be tired. It would take some training to think about her, a woman, with woman's needs. There were no women at Loraleaf. He should have noticed her hold was loosening.

He slowed down to a stop and bent so she could get down.

"Why are we stopping?" She rubbed her face with both hands and blinked.

He didn't respond immediately, instinct telling him she'd argue. Instead, he swept her up into his arms, cradling her.

"What? Wait, you can't. I'm too heavy."

"You are lighter than a welchet. I'm happy to carry you."

Her eyes widened. "A welchet? You do know the way to a girl's heart."

He sincerely hoped so. "Wrap your arms around my neck. It will help our balance as I run." *And will feel very good.*

"If you insist." Though she said the words with a pout, she carefully burrowed beneath his ponytail, locking her hands over the telltale sign of his Kindred, or rather lack thereof. Just the thought of her touching that spot sent a shiver through his body that she noticed.

"Are you cold?"

"No, just anxious to get home." He started running again, just a bit slower as he had to watch that her legs and head were not whipped by sharp bushes.

It didn't take long for her to relax in his arms. His heart swelled and the need to protect her from harm or sorrow filled him with determination.

Their beloved was finally with them. Now all they needed to do was convince her to stay.

＊ ＊ ＊ ＊ ＊

Jahl closed the stone wall behind them and moved silently between the wooden buildings. He was impressed with his beloved's friend. Toni's physical abilities were well suited to life on Eden. He hoped she would find a couple of his men pleasing enough to bond with. To have two women at Loraleaf would encourage his men to find and bring their chosen ones from Earth.

Finding the building he wanted, he signaled to Toni to wait. She nodded as he climbed the outside, the wood moving to make hand and foot holes for him. Once in the upstairs window, he let his eyes adjust. Surprise was still on his side. He just hoped having Toni with him would keep Wareson from any immediate air blasts until he could make a bargain. And if he kept talking, Nassic wouldn't be able to ask a truth-baring question. Not a foolproof plan, but the best he could do in so little time.

Turning back to the window, he signaled Toni to climb up. Once she was inside, he leaned over and forced the wood to reform to its original shape.

"Uh, Jahl?" Toni grabbed his arm.

"Shhh." He turned back to her to find Nassic and Wareson standing in the room. Scrat. He nodded once. "We need to talk."

Nassic's hands formed fists. "Talking wasn't what I had in mind."

As Wareson's gaze roamed over Jahl and Toni, his hand shot out and held Nassic's arm. "Wait. He has blood on him and a woman. He's been to Earth."

Nassic spared a glance at Toni before focusing on Sandale's blood, as it had dried on Jahl's hands and calf. "Fine." He crossed his arms, probably to keep from hitting anyone.

Jahl gritted his teeth. He despised all rulers and these two had been on the Ruling Circle with his father.

Wareson used his ability to push air to brighten the lighting so they could see one other.

Toni looked from them to him and took a step forward as if she could mediate between them. "Okay, boys, I can tell you all aren't exactly on friendly terms, but since you aren't lawbreakers as Jahl calls them and he and his friends aren't lawbreakers, maybe you can set aside your differences to help a man who saved us. Sandale is hurt and dying and could, even now, be at the hands of the very criminals you fear. We need a doctor."

By the Crius, the woman had summed that up nicely. "Do you have a healer?"

The two men stared for a moment before looking at each other.

They had one! Just as he suspected.

Nassic scowled. "Why should we help you? First, you take our agapayto, then you escape our prison and now you sneak into our bedroom after having been to Earth. Did you open a portal nearby and put us all at risk?"

Jahl glared at Nassic, his control slipping. He would never put women in danger and they had a woman here. The man needed to be taught a lesson. He took a step forward.

Toni moved between them, blocking their view of each other. He pulled her back to his side.

She yanked her arm from his grasp. "Let me go. It's not like you're doing such a bang-up job here." She turned back to the two other men. "Listen, I don't know what you have against Jahl, but I can tell you the portal was opened far from here. I know that for a fact because that's where we left Sandale. He was bleeding from a gunshot wound. We didn't have time to move him to safety because the criminals were getting too close. Jahl, Khaos and Sandale saved Serena's and my ass on Earth. If these guys hadn't come along, those goons would have raped us. They can't be that bad if they saved us, right?"

This time Wareson's hands fisted. "Is this true?"

Jahl nodded. "Khaos checked on our chosen one, Serena, and discovered the women's predicament. It was not a planned crossover."

"Yeah." Toni cocked her head. "I'm not supposed to know about you all."

Nassic uncrossed his arms. "If you had a chosen one, why did you hold on to *our* beloved?"

Jahl shrugged. "I didn't have time to think about it. She ran straight into me. I caught her, sure, but the minute I saw Wareson there, I figured holding on to her was my best defense."

"Wait." Toni held up her hand. "Are you two telling me you threw this man in prison because he held on to your girlfriend too long?"

They nodded, not looking quite as sure of themselves as they had before. Jahl pressed his advantage. "We need a healer. It's Sandale's only chance."

"Please." Toni added the one word he couldn't bring himself to say.

"You must send him." A female voice came from behind the two men.

Wareson turned and brought a woman forward. She wore a long shirt that fell to mid-thigh. He put his arm around her waist. "You want us to help this man?"

Jahl remembered her. Too blonde and delicate for him. He looked her in the eye, daring her to say no.

"Yes. What he says is true. I did run into him, though I tried not to. He grabbed me, but if he hadn't, I would have gone flying. I just got scared after all your talk of criminals. As it was, I knocked him over."

Jahl didn't need to be reminded of that. "So will you send for your healer?"

Nassic moved forward. "How do we know you'll bring him back?"

Jahl forced himself not to make a hole in the floor where the other man stood and instead moved Toni out of his way so he could meet his opponent eye to eye. "Because I say I will."

Nassic snorted.

By the Crius, he hadn't come to be insulted. He lifted his hand.

Toni grabbed his arm as the other woman and Ware pulled Nassic back.

"Nase." The blonde waited until Nassic moved his gaze to her. "Why don't you go get Jerumbala? You could use a little fresh air."

"Fine, but we can't make him go. We can only ask him, right?"

"Nase." Wareson's one word used in a low tone had the other man throwing his arms up and heading for the stairs.

The woman approached and Jahl watched Wareson tense. She held out her hand to Toni. "Hi, my name is Erin, and you are?"

"I'm Toni. My roommate is Serena. She took off with Khaos. I guess we are going to someplace called—"

"Maybe we should wait outside." Jahl put his hand on Toni's shoulder. The last thing he needed was for her to tell them about Loraleaf.

Wareson wasn't fooled. "I think Toni should stay with us while you help your friend. She may not be your chosen one, but she is your chosen one's friend and you wouldn't want to return to Loraleaf without her. When you bring our healer back, then Toni can leave." He stepped behind his agapayto and rested his hand on her shoulder. "In the meantime, I'm guessing Toni wouldn't mind a little rest."

Toni addressed Erin. "I don't know. I'm a little revved up, but something to drink would be great."

Erin smiled. She was quite pretty, but she wasn't Serena. "Come then. I can get you some ice for that cheek and we can sit and chat. There are no other women here so it's great to have one, even if it is only for a short while."

They headed for the stairs as Toni responded. "No women? So nothing but naked men? You are definitely going to have to tell me all about this place. I could really like it here."

Erin's laughter could be heard before the women moved into another area of the home. Jahl just wanted to get back to Sandale.

"Would you like some ambrosia? We make it here."

Surprised by Wareson's invitation, he accepted.

The man moved to a small cold box. Jahl hadn't thought of having one in a bedroom, but it did make sense. Sex with one's agapayto was bound to make a man thirsty.

"Have a seat. I'm sure Nassic will try to talk Jerumbala out of going with you, but have no worries. The man is a healer through and through and would never leave a dying man." Wareson poured pink liquid into two glasses and handed one to Jahl.

He took it, but couldn't sit. Every minute they stayed here was more blood Sandale lost. Instead, he leaned against the wall next to the window he'd entered through. "I see your agapayto still wears clothes." He couldn't resist needling the former Naralinian leader.

Wareson took a seat, a smirk on his face. "Yes she is, even though we bonded before arriving back on Eden. If you just brought your chosen one without any preparation, I'm guessing she will have an even harder time adjusting."

Jahl took the verbal hit square on the jaw. Ithio. They had counted on Sandale to ease her transition. He took a gulp of the ambrosia to hide his worry.

"What are you going to do with Toni? I'm guessing she wasn't part of the original plan."

Jahl's confidence completely deflated. That was a problem he hadn't anticipated. Because only males were born on Eden, every Earth woman brought to Eden was required to bond with at least two men unless she decided to enter a Pleasure Temple. "I can't let her return to Earth unless she's bonded."

Wareson took another sip of his drink. "You may have a few fights on your hands back at Loraleaf. If you want, I can keep her here for you."

That was not an option. Serena would be devastated and he would never go back on his word. "No. She comes with Sandale and me when we return."

Wareson's face grew serious. "It's critical we get your man back here. If he needs time to recover, I give you my word we will make him comfortable. I don't like that there are Naralinians beyond the city walls, and with portal chips no less."

For some reason this ex-leader thought he was still in charge. There was so much he didn't know. Living high above the average city dweller, he was ignorant of its drawbacks, the fighting for position, the prejudice. There was more to life than instituting rules. Jahl sneered. "Some of us prefer it out here and came of our own accord. I'd rather take my chances with common lawbreakers than with those within the city walls."

Wareson's eyes widened. "Are there more like you, who have chosen life beyond civilization?"

Jahl clamped his jaw shut and shrugged. Wareson and Nassic had only been beyond the city walls for three years. He'd been here six. He'd learned a lot about the "society" in the jungle and was in no hurry to share. "You obviously still have your chips. Why are you out here?"

The man looked away and gazed out the glass deck doors at the darkness of the night, his countenance troubled. Finally, he turned back, staring Jahl in the eyes. "Naiveté, ignorance, lazy, call it what you will. There was more going on in the Circle of our city than we knew and we never even questioned it. We now—"

Voices on the stairs had Wareson setting down his ambrosia and standing.

Too bad. Jahl was more curious than ever about these ex-leaders of Naralina. But as Nassic and the healer came into view, all thoughts of political intrigue dissipated as hope for Sandale grew.

The healer strode by Nassic and stopped in front of Jahl. "I understand you have a man who was shot on Earth. We must get to him right away. Not only is he losing blood, but the material they fashion bullets from is toxic to us. We can talk more on the way."

The energy level and abrupt style of the young man had Jahl scanning him for his Kindred birthmark. The Kindred of Mind healers were as apt to experiment on a person as heal them because they were so fascinated with the inner workings of Edenists. Not that Jahl could be choosey. The man's birthmark sat on his breast bone between the mounds of his pectoral muscles. It was a soft-edged heart. Relief washed through Jahl. This Jerumbala was of the same Kindred as Sandale, Kindred of Heart, and they made the best healers.

Jahl opened his arm toward the stairs. "Then let us leave. Do you have everything you need?"

The healer strode back toward the stairs. "Yes."

As he'd turned around, Jahl recognized the pack on his back. "Jahl."

He turned toward Wareson, having completely forgotten him. "There is a price for our cooperation."

By the Crius, what now? "And that is?"

"You must show us how you escaped and how you were able to climb the sheer wall of our home."

Jahl nodded. "I'll be happy to." With more hope than he'd had in the last hour, he headed for the stairs. As he stepped on the first one, his arm was grabbed in a fierce grip. He halted and turned toward his adversary, ready to knock him to the ground.

Nassic scowled at him, frustration at being thwarted clear on his face. "Remember, we have your chosen one's friend."

Jahl yanked his arm away and glared. "Don't worry. I'll bring back your healer…in one piece." He continued down the stairs before Nassic could stop him. Let him wonder if his healer would be alive when he was returned. Served the man right for being such a logar's ass. No need for Nassic to know he would never harm a healer. They were far too rare and valuable. Steal one, maybe, but never harm one.

Once outside the home, he and the healer strode for the exit of the compound. Jahl filled the man in on what had happened to Sandale since they stepped back onto Eden.

After exiting the compound, Jerumbala was as anxious as he to get to Sandale and they set off at a fast pace. As they neared the place where he had portaled in, Jahl slowed, listening. The jungle was quiet except for the typical night creature sounds. An idonee bird cooed in a nearby tree and he could hear a welchet digging beneath a bush nearby.

Stealthily, he edged forward toward the Salis bush with the camouflage he'd erected to protect Sandale. He'd used natural dead items from the area, logs, dirt, rocks, and fallen leaves to barricade Sandale. Brushing back the Salis branches, he stared.

It couldn't be.

CHAPTER THREE

His camouflage was gone, whipped away like a hurricane had come through and there was no Sandale. "No!"

He strode forward and examined the ground. Footprints littered the area and a large patch of blood marked where Sandale had lain. "This can't be."

Jerumbala moved around the site, examining everything. He pulled something out of his pack and tested the blood. "This blood has low toxicity levels yet. If he or someone was able to dig the bullet out, there could be hope." The man ran his hands along the ground, feeling for the bullet.

Jahl's heart pounded. The lawbreakers. They had taken Sandale, and wounded as he was, he couldn't fight them off. He probably used his last bit of strength to render several unconscious, but he would not have had the energy to handle more. His ability to calm could slow his enemies' hearts down to a crawl or to a stop, but only if he was healthy. He may have even been unconscious when they found him.

Jahl scoured the area for clues of what happened. There were drag marks all around the Salis bush, now that he looked carefully, but it was hard to see in the limited moonlight.

"There is no bullet." The healer sighed and shook his head.

The man's words were a kick to his gut. He *had* to find Sandale. He was more than a friend. He and Khaos were to share Serena with him. They needed Sandale to be complete.

"Ah, someone has taken him. These drops of blood leave a trail. I have a shiner in my pack."

Irritation riddled Jahl. "You have a shiner? By the Crius, get it out so we can see better. We may still be able to catch up with him and get him back."

Jerumbala paused in his search through his pack. "I'm sorry. We will do everything we can to help him."

Jahl closed his eyes. It wasn't the healer's fault Sandale was gone, it was his. He should have stayed. He should have let Khaos take both women to Haven. They would have been safe and then he would have been here to protect Sandale from the lawbreakers. Why hadn't he?

"Ah, here it is." Jerumbala turned on the shiner. Its brightness lit up the area and the whole surrounding jungle.

Jahl whipped a dead section of bark from a log and slammed it over the shiner. "Careful or we'll be the next ones taken."

The healer lowered his head. "Sorry. This is only my third time out of Haven."

His mind was still on the chances of being taken by the lawbreakers to pay attention to Jerumbala. If Jahl was taken, Khaos would have to find another man to bond with Serena. Even outside the confines of Naralina, all Edenists understood the need for every woman to have at least two agapaytos.

"The trail goes this way, I think."

Jahl shook himself from his morbid thoughts and took the shiner from the healer. He studied the ground. "No, this is a decoy trail. These people know what they're doing."

He strode back to the area where the blood drops started and found the place where they, and the supposed trail, parted ways. He studied each leaf and dead branch for blood, slowly following an intricate path away from Haven and away from Naralina, into an area of the jungle he'd never been before. Many times, the lawbreakers set false trails, but he followed Sandale.

Sandale had to still be alive. He would know if… He would feel something if a brother of his heart had gone.

"What's that?" Jerumbala pointed ahead.

Jahl moved his gaze away from the ground to look. Something large and dark lay perpendicular to where they stood. Lifting the shiner higher, he allowed a little light to focus on the dark mass ahead. It appeared to be dirt.

Confused, he left the blood trail and walked forward. It *was* dirt, a mound of it. Why would someone pile— His blood ran cold. On Earth they buried their dead. On Eden they were burned. To bury an Edenist in the ground was the worst insult. This could not be Sandale. It couldn't.

He ran forward and dropped to his knees before the pile. "Nooooooo!" Pain sliced through his heart. It couldn't be. He pushed it away as he used his mind to scatter the dirt, whipping it around him, blasting everything in its path. He would prove this wasn't a grave. He would have it gone. Its very presence mocked his hope, crushed his belief. He fisted his hands as he swirled the dirt, layer by layer, sending rocks and granules into the surrounding trees, into his own skin.

"Jahl! Stop!" Jerumbala's voice was like a tiny, buzzing insect. An insect Jahl had no power over. His father had said he was useless. He couldn't control living nature like the rest of his Kindred. But he could control the dead…*the dead.* If Sandale was dead, he could control him.

Jahl pushed his fists into the ground, his mind digging deeper, throwing up small trees as he forced the dirt to reveal its secrets. *Sandale.* If he was here, Jahl would find him. His body strained as he forced the ground to move, pulling tree roots and boulders up to the surface.

A rumbling started and his body vibrated with it, welcomed it. He would find him, lift him up, carry him home. The shaking increased, until a loud crack threw him back. He landed hard.

His world went black.

"Jahl. Jahl can you hear me?" Jerumbala's worried voice pulled him back to consciousness.

He blinked, the lightening sky proving to him his eyes were open. *Sandale.* He sat up, determined to dig deeper. "I have to find him."

"Jahl. It's all gone. If Sandale's body was there, it has been ripped to pieces." The man scanned the area around them. "Like everything else."

"What?" He stood, shaking, his muscles strangely weak. He looked at where the mound had been. Before him lay a vast hole the size of a meteor crater. He shook his head. "No."

Already, ground water seeped into the bottom, filling in the space that had once been dirt and rock. He stepped to the edge and the pain returned full force. He envied the emptiness of the hole.

The devastation to his soul was too much to take. He dropped to his knees in defeat.

* * * * *

"We have arrived."

Serena scrunched her face. She didn't want to open her eyes. She hadn't been asleep, but she was so comfortable in Khaos' arms. He smelled like ginger and his warm shoulder against the side of her face made her want to snuggle.

She opened her eyes and stared at him. The sky was just starting to lighten, giving everything a pale-gray shine. Khaos' dark skin and brown hair made a stark contrast to the early day. He was comforting and relaxing.

She really needed to get out of his arms, no matter how wonderful it was. "Okay, you can put me down now."

He bent his knees, even as he lowered her legs, and she unclasped her hands from his neck. She looked around to see nothing but more jungle. They had arrived? To where?

"Come. It's this way." Khaos nodded toward the right.

She didn't see anything that way either, but who was she to argue? He obviously knew where he was and she didn't, though she would hazard a guess they were somewhere in South America simply from the humid warmth and the plant life. Then again, her world travel had only extended as far as Mexico. For all she knew, they were in California somewhere. She'd wait and ask Sandale. She was comfortable with him.

She hoped he was okay. Maybe Jahl had found a healer and was with him. She probably should be frightened to be in the hands of these three men, but as Khaos pointed out, so far they had done nothing but help her. Right now she'd be grateful to anyone just to have a bed to sleep in.

Khaos kept glancing back to be sure she followed. His attractiveness was unique and his body was to die for. She focused on his ass and the backs of his thighs, loving the play of muscle she could now see in the early-dawn hours.

He stopped and she had to catch herself from plowing into him.

"Right up here." He stepped aside and pointed to a large tree.

Huh? Beyond curious, she stepped forward to look. "Wow, how amazing is that?" There was an opening in the tree trunk and stairs had been built into it. The tree had to be dead, but it was thick. There was no handrail, but she had no problem ascending… at first. After what seemed like three stories, she was relieved to find the top. The ceiling showed a dark reflection of herself and the stairs. She touched it, feeling a square outline above her. A hatch?

Khaos came up to the step just below her. Even so, he was still a bit taller than her and his naked body radiated temptation.

Shit, she needed to stop looking at him. She must be more tired than she thought to have survived an attempted rape and then be attracted to one of her rescuers.

"Here." He reached up, his large biceps clearly defined, even in the darkness of the stairwell as the scent of ginger wafted over her before it was lifted away by the air above.

She took the next few steps and walked out onto what appeared to be a landing and stopped. "Oh my God. It's beautiful." She didn't want to move for fear the sight would disappear. Above her was a town among the trees. Treehouses filled the upper branches for as far as she could see. Rope bridges and sturdier-looking ones crisscrossed the entire area. What appeared to be open-air elevators were sporadically situated throughout the aviary-looking place.

She heard Khaos close the hatch and the whir of a machine as it locked. He stepped up next to her. "Welcome to Loraleaf."

The pride in his voice was unmistakable and she didn't blame him. She couldn't have imagined this in her wildest dreams and she had some good ones. Now that she really studied it, she could see treehouses perched on the trunks and branches at lower levels as well as above and one house that was on a nearby tree just had a few steps down to a main walkway.

How could she have not seen this from below? Even at her thought, the door to the closest house opened and a naked man stepped out. Didn't anyone wear clothes here? It solidified her guess that she was in South America. Wasn't there supposed to be some tribe that had no contact with humanity? But how would they know English? Then again, it could be a weird cult in California.

This new person had shoulder-length black hair and what looked like black eyes, but as he came closer, she could see they were simply very dark brown. He stopped in front of them and stared at her, his mouth partly open.

Khaos grabbed the man's shoulder. "Theron."

He tore his gaze away from her and looked blankly at Khaos. "Khaos." He peered past Khaos and frowned. "Where are Sandale and Jahl?"

Khaos let go of the man and stiffened. "Jahl is hopefully with Sandale. He was injured."

"Not just injured, shot saving me and Toni." She wanted this new man to understand how heroic these men had been. She had no clue if he was the chief or not, but it couldn't hurt to give credit where it was due.

Theron returned his gaze to her. "You are beautiful."

"Careful. She is chosen." Khaos' voice came out strained.

"I'm sorry." Theron turned away from her as if she was too much temptation.

She kind of liked that. On the other hand, after the night she'd had, she'd rather not be a temptation to anyone right now. "Khaos, I know you need to debrief and all, but is there a bed nearby? I just really want to sleep."

"Of course. Theron, I will return shortly."

The other man nodded before Khaos pointed. "We will take the lift."

She turned to the left and found a walkway so she headed down it, Khaos moving quietly behind her. Everyone else must still be asleep. She'd bet the place was breathtaking in the sunlight.

When they climbed into the square basket, she envisioned monkeys pulling ropes to raise them, but she actually hadn't seen that animal. She hadn't seen any animals except the welchet.

Khaos moved a lever from its bottom position to its top and the basket began to ascend. It was as if it floated on air. She looked over the side, but couldn't figure out how it worked.

"It's a combination of light and air technology." Khaos' voice held humor in it and she turned to face him. He smiled at her with pride.

"I would love to learn more. I probably have a few days because by today my employer will realize I'm not coming in and I won't have a job. Unless you could take me back by ten this morning?" It was a long shot, but she had to ask.

He frowned. "I cannot. Do you want to leave already?"

Actually, she didn't. Maybe fate had handed her the perfect vacation. She'd land another job with no problem. There weren't a ton of pyrotechnic experts hanging around Nevada willing to work on movies. Working for the casinos and special events paid a lot more, but she liked the intricacies of the movie sets, and of course, the sci-fi nature of them. "No, I don't want to leave. I was just being responsible." She'd have to return by next weekend for her family reunion, but that was still a week away.

Khaos smiled, showing beautiful white teeth and she caught her breath. He was too handsome. When he smiled like that, his eyes crinkled at their uplifted corners, softening his serious features.

"Good. We want you to stay."

His gray gaze grew intense again, almost silver, so she looked up at the platform they were coming to.

The "lift," as he called it, came to a smooth stop. They walked off and Khaos led her around the large tree the lift abutted. The walkway was made of sturdy wood about three feet wide with a railing. A person could slip through if one wanted to, but she doubted anyone just fell based on the crisscross pattern of the supports.

They then crossed a small rope bridge that brought them to a massive treehouse that looked like it wrapped all the way around a large trunk. Maybe this was the hotel. She grinned at her thought. Oh yeah, she was definitely punchy from lack of sleep.

Khaos opened the single door and let her precede him.

She stopped just inside. It was pitch black. He stepped in behind her and closed the door, making the darkness complete. His body heat warmed her back and his scent was strong. Again she had the urge to curl up against him.

His hand on her shoulder startled her. "Let me turn on the light."

He walked away and then a soft glow burned from a small lamp to her left. It looked like something she'd have in her apartment. The room came into focus and it was clear it was no more than a foyer of sorts. But off it were three doorways.

Khaos moved behind her again. "Now you will be able to see everything."

The ceiling became lighter and she watched as the branches of the tree came into view. Was it glass? "That's amazing." She stepped farther into the bare room and studied the peak. There were no panes. Wow, this cult had some incredible technology.

"Serena?" Khaos' voice had lowered and her name on his lips felt like a caress.

She turned to look at him. He gazed at her as if she were the most precious thing on Earth. Shit, a girl could get used to that. "Yes."

"This way." He held his hand out to the side again and she walked through the door.

Again she stopped. It was a large living area complete with cushioned furniture, end tables and what looked like a bar. "What is this place?"

"This is our home." He came around her. "Jahl, Sandale and I live here. Do you like it?"

She loved it! Again the ceiling appeared to be glass, giving a beautiful view of the green canopy overhead. She glanced back at Khaos. His look was uncertain now. Why would he be worried about how much she liked his home? It was like a treehouse on steroids, something she'd think of him if he didn't live in such a natural way. "I think your home is beautiful. You must love living here."

He gave her that heart-stopping smile again and she couldn't help smiling tiredly in return.

"We do. Loraleaf is special."

He could say that again. She yawned and covered her mouth. "I'm sorry. It really is lovely and I want to explore everything, but I'm not used to pulling all-nighters." Especially after being held at knife point.

Khaos shook his head. "My mistake. Come this way."

They walked through the large room and entered a hallway that curved with the trunk of the tree. She noticed what looked like a bathroom off it. A hot shower would be perfect if she could stand up that long, but she was fading fast. The next room had a large, arched opening and no doors.

Khaos stepped inside and she followed. Starting to understand the configuration of the house, she looked up at the clear ceiling. Then she took in the interior with its rounded walls, curved windows and three large beds, one a lot larger than the other two. "You all sleep in here?"

"Yes. Sleep in whichever bed you like. Make use of anything here. The meal room is on the other side of what I believe you call a living room. Your eyes are closing, so I will leave you to your rest."

"Thank you." She walked toward him and took his hand. "Thank you for all you have done for me and Toni." She lifted up on her tiptoes and kissed him on the cheek.

His hand squeezed hers back and when she lowered herself to her heels, his eyes were intense once again. "I'm glad you're here." He turned away before she did and let go of her hand. "I will darken the room so you can rest. Have a good sleep."

Distracted by the darkening of the room, she missed his exit. She sighed. The man was simply beautifully made, but his eyes unnerved her. She turned and walked to the closest bed. Sitting on it, she unlaced her black combat-style boots and toed them off. The softness of the bed called to her, but she didn't want to sleep in her filthy clothes, or what was left of them.

She made herself stand again and look for a robe or t-shirt or anything, but there wasn't even a top sheet or blanket. Then she spotted what appeared to be clean towels and took one down. When she returned to the bed, she quickly stripped, leaving her clothes on the floor and climbed into it, covering herself with the huge, soft material.

She sighed as her body relaxed and the spicy scent of ginger sent her off to sleep.

* * * * *

Jahl stared at the ceiling above him. He should be home in Loraleaf, not in a room owned by people he didn't trust. He would have to tell Khaos that… He would have to tell Khaos about Sandale when he returned home. He had his chosen one waiting to be wooed. How in the Crius name was he supposed to do that? The plan had been for Sandale to help her adjust. Jahl didn't know a damn thing about courting a woman.

Khaos wasn't much better. He'd never been good around females. Even at the Pleasure Temples, he hardly said a word, letting them do whatever they wished. A woman wanted a man to lead, show her what he wanted from her.

Jahl ground his teeth and rolled onto his side. He should rest. That's why he was still at Haven. His beloved's friend, Toni, had just fallen asleep when he'd arrived back with Jerumbala. The healer had offered to numb his pain and he'd been tempted, but it felt disrespectful to Sandale. The pain made him feel as if he were still connected somehow.

As soon as Toni woke, he would go home—to Khaos, to Serena—and mourn.

A knock at his door gave him a welcome distraction. He threw his legs over the side of the bed and sat up. "Come."

The door opened and Wareson stepped in carrying towels. "Was wondering if you were up for a swim."

Jahl relaxed at the request. "Now that sounds good. You have a waterhole near here?"

Wareson nodded. "We do, just outside the sunset side of the compound."

Jahl stood and rolled his shoulders. A little exercise never hurt, maybe even a competition. He sized up Wareson. The man was just a bit taller than he, but Wareson's long hair was bound to get in the way of a stroke. He ran his hand over his very short hair.

"If you want to talk…" Wareson hesitated.

He tensed. "Huh-uh. I only go if we promise *not* to talk about Sandale."

"But your loss—"

"If Nassic drowned this afternoon, would you want to 'talk'? Because if you want to know what it feels like, I'd be happy to make that happen."

The man went rigid and anger poured from him in waves, the air actually moving outward from his body.

Jahl didn't even have to brace himself. The push of air was nothing like what he'd withstood when he was their "prisoner."

The breeze died down quickly. Wareson looked at him and simply nodded. "This way."

If there was one thing he liked about Wareson, it was he never used any more words than necessary.

He followed the man out into the daylight. Something about the brightness insulted Jahl. It should be gloomy, saddened by the loss of one of its creatures. Sandale had been the best of the three of them, always calm, supportive, diplomatic and a great mediator, even between himself and Khaos. A being of such brilliance and warmth should be mourned, recognized. They hadn't even been able to burn him on a burial pyre as befitted him.

Jahl batted away the bushes as he followed along a well-worn path. He wanted to hit something, anything. He looked at the man in front of him. What would it take to make him angry enough to throw another air blast? Threaten Nassic again?

Wareson stopped. "Maybe this will help."

"By the Crius, is this natural?" Jahl stared at the oblong pond that had to be the length of his parents' home in the city but half the width. A waterfall filled it at one end and a small stream emptied at the other. Except for a few boulders here and there, which he could easily remove, the water was clear. He could see the muddy bottom and even a couple nerie fish resting in the reeds on one side.

Wareson stepped in. "Partly, but one of my men is Kindred of Water and he made some improvements. We wanted to move those three boulders to the center to form an island, but other projects took precedence once we discovered Erin would be on a nude cruise. Now that she is here, it paves the way for others to bring their chosen ones."

Jahl walked past Wareson, barely listening, anxious to stretch out across the water's surface. He set out, kicking his feet angrily even as his arms pummeled the water on every down stroke. Once at the end, he turned and headed back, ignoring the man still standing in the shallows. Back and forth he shot across the water, beating it down, pushing his muscles harder and harder.

By the time he'd started to slow, Wareson was exiting the pond and grabbing one of the towels he'd brought. Jahl had passed him many times, but it was obvious the man was simply relaxing. He had muscles equal to his own and probably could have kept pace. Then again, maybe not. Jahl came to a stop in the shallows and let his feet drift to the bottom, leaving him in a crouch. He stared at the reflection of sunlight on the water, sparkling happily, and frowned at it.

"Your chosen one will not be impressed with that face."

Jahl looked at Wareson sitting on a log along the side of the pool. "Serena?"

Wareson nodded. "It will be a difficult adjustment for her. Do you have any other women at Loraleaf?"

Ah, the man was fishing for information. "Do you have any other women besides Erin here at Haven?"

Wareson's smile acknowledged he'd been caught. "No, we do not. As I said, now that Erin is here, it will make it easier for others who follow."

Jahl ground his hands into the muddy bottom of the pond. "We do not have any other women yet. It's one reason I wasn't opposed to bringing Serena's friend with us. Not only was she in danger as well, but having her will help Serena adjust."

"I think it will help even more now that Erin and Toni have talked, although it wasn't for long. If you want us to visit Loraleaf with Erin, I know she would be happy to help your agapayto."

In other words, for Wareson to allow Erin at Loraleaf, Khaos and he had to first bond with Serena. It seemed to him that was the hardest part. But he also wasn't fooled. Wareson would love to know where Loraleaf was. Of course, all he needed to do was have Nassic ask. Jahl would not be able to refrain from telling the truth. "I think we will manage without your mate's help. We hadn't planned on another woman anyway." No, they had planned on Sandale. It always came back to Sandale. He was their pivot point. They were rudderless without him, like bees without a queen... except they now had a queen. Jahl's heart lightened at that thought.

Wareson studied him. Opened his mouth and then closed it again.

Good, the man could keep his word. Jahl sensed he wanted to bring up Sandale.

"You promised you would show us how you escaped if we let you take our healer. I know our healer was of little help. So perhaps you could tell us your Kindred."

Jahl snorted. "I told you before, I have no Kindred. It was burned from me long ago by my father." He stood, pointing to the scarred birthmark on the far left side of his chest. His brothers had held him down while his father erased any relationship to him.

Wareson didn't say a word. The man was smart. There was nothing to say about a father who denied his own son, about a father who thought his son's ability worthless and a disgrace.

Strangely curious what this former Naralinian leader would think of his ability, Jahl turned and faced the three boulders. At once, he levitated them out of the ground and the water and slowly brought them together, then lowered them into the pond. He turned back to Wareson. "That is how I escaped. I can move that from Eden which is dead."

"I have never seen anything like it. That is a unique gift. Thank you."

The man did not mock him as he expected. "That's easy."

"I imagine your ability came in handy in the building of Loraleaf. I know we could have used you when we added the cyndistone to our walls. It took us months."

Jahl kept his smile to himself. He wouldn't tell Wareson his abilities had not come into play in the defense of his compound, only in the building of it. "I could have had your walls up in a day."

Wareson groaned. "I wish I didn't know that."

He shrugged. "That's why it was so easy for me to leave when I wanted to."

"You simply moved wood or stone out of your way and then you put them back so we wouldn't know."

Jahl nodded.

"I think our city fathers would have loved to have had you around when they built Naralina."

"Some fathers don't deserve this 'gift', as you call it."

Wareson studied him for a moment. "I think you and Nase have more in common than you think."

He grunted. Not likely.

"I wanted to thank you for not opening a portal near Haven. When we left the city, they were working on the technology to track portal openings beyond the city walls."

"Still?" Jahl frowned. "They were working on that six years ago. They should have figured that out by now."

"They were?" Wareson looked toward where the city would be if there weren't decods of trees between it and them. "I wish… Do you have anyone inside the city walls you communicate with?"

Ah, he saw what Wareson was thinking. "No. You don't either, do you?"

The man shook his head. "I want to. That and more women are my priority."

Of course, Wareson, Kindred of Air, one of the five leaders of Naralina, would still want to be involved in the happenings of the city. "My first priority is getting back to my chosen one and making her our agapayto as soon as possible."

"Then maybe we should head back and see if Toni is awake."

Jahl nodded. If she wasn't awake, her bed may just shake until she was. She could sleep once they returned home.

Wareson waited for him to walk out of the water and handed him a towel. "I have to ask. If you had your chosen one on Earth, why did you want Erin when you ran into us in the jungle?"

"Khaos thought she would make a good bargaining chip to find out where you had settled. As it was, you led us straight here."

Wareson shook his head. "Not very smart of us, but we had not expected you."

Khaos had expected *them*, at least near Haven, though he hadn't known the compound existed at the time. He had simply sensed the direction they were headed, but Wareson didn't need to know about Khaos' ability. Jahl still had to make his mind up about these former Naralina leaders. They *had* imprisoned him. Then again, it had given him an opportunity to investigate their compound and learn enough to know they weren't lawbreakers. "I have a question for you."

Wareson threw his own towel over his shoulder. "Yes."

"As rulers, you were exempt from the law requiring every woman to have at least two agapaytos. Why did you and Nassic choose to share one woman?"

"We didn't think that exception was fair." Wareson grinned. "Besides, Nase and I had been friends for so long, we preferred to have one beloved. We knew it would bind us together."

Jahl nodded. His own father had taken advantage of that particular law. Jahl often wondered what it would have been like growing up if he'd had two or more fathers. Reflexively, he rubbed his chest.

"If you want to bring Serena here to talk with Erin at any time, you are welcome to do so." Wareson put his hand on Jahl's shoulder, a sign of friendship.

He could do no less. He placed his hand on Wareson's shoulder, accepting the friendship offered, but only with Wareson. He still had strong reservations about Nassic.

* * * * *

Serena lay with her head on Khaos' naked thigh as he popped grapes into her mouth. Above her the trees swayed and sunlight splashed against her naked skin. She loved this. He held her chin, occasionally stroking her bottom lip with his thumb. She nipped at it and he chuckled, his eyes crinkling in the corners.

A man's hands smoothed their way up her legs. She tried to look down, but Khaos held her chin firmly and shook his head. His lips turned up into a sensuous grin and he winked before popping another grape into her mouth.

Reaching late his flower. A voice drifted through her mind as hands caressed the insides of her thighs and moved toward her heat. That voice was somehow familiar, but Khaos distracted her by stroking her bottom lip. She licked his thumb and watched as his eyes darkened from a light gray to a steely smoke.

The other man's fingers lightly touched her pussy, gently discovering her, coaxing her to open her legs to allow further exploration. Her insides tightened at the erotic sensations curling in her belly and she gave in to the urge to spread her legs, moisture gathering among her folds.

Khaos slid his hand into her hair, running his fingers over her scalp, the grapes forgotten. The other man blew across her opening and she tensed, but Khaos' hand ran down her neck, past his other that held her in place, and along her collarbone. His touch was light, leaving sensual tingles in its wake. *Round her chamber hums.* Again the voice pulled at her focus, like a bee buzzing nearby.

And then there was a lick against her opening. Fire at the spot ignited a distinct trail into her core. Instinct had her arching upward, her head pushing back against the muscular thigh beneath her, her nipples hardening. Khaos didn't ignore her invitation. His hand swept downward to her breast, palming the whole globe and lightly squeezing.

Counts his nectars—enters. The tongue at her opening began to lap and explore her, sometimes thrusting inside and other times barely touching her clit, teasing her with where it might go next. She felt as if her body was kindling and a master fire-starter had lit strategic places to produce a slow burn.

Khaos moved his hand to her other breast and circled the areola before stroking his fingers lightly over her nipple. Heat sped from that spot to meet the fire burning in her core, her tension rising. Fingers now held back her folds as the tongue lapped upward onto her clit and back to her opening, thrusting inside before repeating its path.

She bent her knees, unable to keep from pushing her hips against the talented mouth between her thighs. A low chuckle vibrated her clit. Khaos' hand began to roam from one nipple to the other, along her neck then down beneath a breast, soothing while stimulating, fanning her flaming need as the other man continued his revolutions, lapping upward, circling her clit, licking downward with a thrust inside.

Khaos' hand slowed and came to rest on her right breast, two fingers against her nipple like an old-fashioned clothespin. He smirked, too smug in his ability to please her. "Are you ready, my love?"

She forced her mouth to form the word so wanted. "Always."

His eyes darkened again and her heart skipped.

"It is time." His low tone raced across her skin a second before the man between her legs licked up to her clit and began to suck. *And is lost in balms!* She moaned in pleasure and Khaos closed his fingers against her nipple, rolling it, sending fire like a torch thrower straight to the blaze already burning in her pussy.

She closed her eyes and grasped the head between her thighs, the inch-long hair giving away her seducer.

Jahl took her hands from him and held her wrists as he plundered her clit with his expert tongue, sending more fire to her center. Khaos let go of her chin and gave the same attention to her other nipple, completing a circuit that threw her straining body into the flames of orgasm. She yelled as she burned up in the conflagration.

The lips on her own devoured her sounds and her passion, while the mouth between her legs slowed, no longer feeding the fire but banking it until next time. She opened her eyes, the light blinding her. Shading her eyes, she focused on the sun shining into the bedroom.

A dream. She sighed. A very wet dream.

CHAPTER FOUR

She looked down at herself to find the towel thrown off and her legs spread. Touching her pussy, she quickly pulled back, its sensitivity sending a burst of fire along her limbs. Holy hell, what was that? She sat up and pulled the towel toward her. It hadn't been *that* long since she'd last had sex. Her ex was only an ex by a couple weeks. The sex in the dream had seemed so real she'd actually climaxed without even touching herself. She didn't remember that happening, ever. She didn't blame her brain for conjuring Khaos and Jahl for her partners though. Those two were hunks with a capital H. She must need a vacation more than she realized.

She stood and strolled to the large square window. No glass covered it, just a fine mesh allowing the outside air and sounds into the room. She stared in wonder at the now bustling tree-town. Naked men were everywhere and they were all drool-worthy. Didn't that tribe in South America wear something to cover their male parts? She shook her head. She was never good at keeping up with current events.

She couldn't help watching them move, their nudity revealing their toned muscles. Though they all were tan, which made sense, they were different heights and shapes and hair color from shiny black like hers to bright blond like Sandale's.

Her mood saddened. Was he all right? He'd saved her from being raped and very possibly killed. Actually, all three of them had, but he'd helped her, calmed her. She owed him more than a thank-you. Maybe she could have something published in the paper about her three heroes. That would have to wait until she returned home though. She doubted they had a paper in the jungle, but then again, they had an elevator. A cult in California seemed more plausible now that she thought about it.

The place was a mystery. Completely hidden from view and yet built on trees. A clear ceiling in the house that could be made dark but no television that she'd noticed. It did, however, have a bathroom and she was in dire need of a shower. Even the towel she'd wrapped around her had explosive smudges from her work on the movie.

Turning from the window, she moved through the archway of the bedroom. Weird that there was no door, but if everyone was naked, why would they need one? But what if they had a woman in the room? She halted mid-step. All three beds were in the same room with that really big one in the middle. Did one man have sex with the other two watching?

The sinfully wicked grin on Khaos' face from her dream reemerged. Did all three participate at the same time? An erotic shiver passed through her. Just because she dreamed it, didn't mean it was the reality, just wishful thinking on her part. From what she saw of Jahl, he was as hard as a rock, almost bullish in his actions…except when Sandale was hurt. His emotions had been clearer than day even in the dark of night. He was scared he'd lose his friend.

Continuing down the hall, she pushed aside her thoughts. It was none of her business how these men lived. They obviously weren't gay because then there would only be the one giant bed. So they probably had girlfriends. She opened the door to the bathroom and walked in. It was nicer than hers. A toilet much like she had at home was located in one corner, a huge sink that three giant men could all use at the same time was next.

She turned to her right. "Oh wow." The shower was entirely glass and the whole top part had a stone ceiling with hundreds of tiny holes. Taking a shower in there would be like standing outside in the rain because the outer walls of the shower were also clear and the outside tree branches were the décor. They were probably so high up, they didn't worry about anyone seeing them. She could just imagine looking up and seeing those three brawny men showering. What woman wouldn't fall right off one of those bridges?

There was no tub and she would have liked a soak, but she couldn't wait to try the shower. She looked around for another clean towel but didn't find any, so she ran to the bedroom and grabbed one. Before ducking back into the bathroom, she peeked in the living room, just to make sure Khaos hadn't come back yet.

Satisfied the treehouse was empty, she returned to the bathroom. Dropping her towel, she opened the shower door and stepped inside. So how did it work? Actually, that there was even a bathroom this high in the trees boggled her mind. She walked around the whole shower, but couldn't find any controls. They wouldn't be on the outside would they?

She peered through the glass but didn't see anything that resembled controls. Okay, she needed to think like a six-foot-six giant who showered with his friends. Would there be three controls? She looked up at the ceiling of the shower and sure enough saw three sets of buttons. Duh, of course these guys would reach above them. At a mere five foot nine, this was going to be a challenge.

She really hoped the square button turned it on. She jumped and missed. Ugh. She tried again, just brushing the button, but didn't get it depressed. A third time was a charm and she pressed it hard. Nothing. Now she'd worked up a sweat and really wanted warm water.

Time to try the round button. Thrusting herself upward, she nabbed it on the first try. A quiet whirring sounded and she waited. Water started flowing from above like a gentle rain. She would prefer a hard blast like a thunderstorm, but she'd take what she could get. At least it was warm. She had no soap and didn't see a soap dish. Great, probably one of those buttons. She ran her fingers though her short hair to get it thoroughly wet. As she did that, it started sudsing. Huh!

Serena tasted the water. *Blech.* It had soap in it. She used it to her advantage and quickly lathered her hair and her body. So how was she supposed to rinse out the soap? She looked at the large sink on the other wall. What if it had soapy water too?

Her suds started to run down her body and onto the floor to a drain at the corner. Tasting the water again, she found it clear of soap. Oh, how cool. A programmed shower, and from the timeframe, she'd say she was in Jahl's because the other two had longer hair and would need more shampoo time. After rinsing her body, she just stood with her eyes closed, the warm rain falling on her. She needed one of these.

The water started to cool. That must be to leave Jahl refreshed in the humid weather. She opened her eyes in preparation to leave when two men outside caught her attention. They stood well below the house looking up, but even from where she was, she could clearly make out Khaos' features. She couldn't see the color of his eyes from this distance but instinct told her that at the moment, they were the dark gray she liked. The man next to him was Theron who she'd met earlier. Neither of them moved.

Oh shit! They could see her! She pulled open the shower door and grabbed the towel she'd left on the sink. The water in the shower stopped on its own.

What an idiot she was.

Running out of the room, she sped back to the bedroom to dry off. At least that room didn't have floor-to-ceiling windows. She had just started to pat herself down when the outside door slammed open. Quickly, she wrapped the damp towel around her.

Khaos ran into the room, stopping when he saw her.

"Hi." She smiled crookedly, not quite sure why he was in a hurry.

He strode toward her. His hands cupped her face and she looked at him, her eyebrows raised.

"You're beautiful." The simple way he said it made her warm all over. Then he lowered his face and gave her a gentle kiss. She'd never felt so precious in all her life.

When he pulled away, his eyes were a deep-gray color. She liked that color.

"Thank you." He gazed at her as if he wanted to see into her soul.

She wasn't sure there was much to see there, but looking at his finely sculpted face was rather enjoyable.

"Why do you cover yourself?"

"Excuse me?"

He let go of her and touched the towel. "Why do you hide your beautiful body beneath this?"

She opened her mouth to say it wasn't right to be naked then remembered where she was and let her gaze roam down his chest and abdominals. She didn't look farther, though she had to admit, she liked that she could. They were obviously from different cultures. "Where I come from, we remain clothed. Surely your women don't walk around nude."

He cocked his head, never taking his eyes from her face. "We have no women. You are the first."

Conflicting emotions crashed inside her at that pronouncement. Disbelief, pride, fear collided, making her grasp the towel even tighter. "Why?"

His gaze softened. "No females are ever born here. We have to go elsewhere to find our beloved. We were waiting for you."

She backed up a step. "For me? That can't be. You didn't even meet me until last night." She calmed as she remembered how they met. "You saved me, remember?"

Khaos shook his head. "No, we found you six years ago. We were waiting until… Until Loraleaf was ready for you." He gestured to the room. "We have been watching and waiting. But when you were in trouble last night, we had to come."

His face had grown hard again at the mention of last night, his eyes taking on the intense silver she didn't like. Were they stalkers? She tensed. "Exactly how did you know I was in trouble?"

Khaos' intensity disappeared in an instant, and she almost thought she'd imagined it. He moved his gaze from her face, as if embarrassed. "I sensed you were in trouble."

She looked askance at him. "Sensed? As in, psychically?"

He nodded.

She turned away from him and strode to the window. She used her hand to count off the pros and cons of her situation, a habit her family rolled their eyes at but it helped her to think. On one hand, she had three stalkers who had seen her six years ago and only made themselves known when she was in serious danger. That was creepy and a solid con.

Secondly, one of them was "psychic," one of them some kind of military and the third a hypnotist. Hmm, she wasn't sure if those were pros or cons.

They saved her, definitely a pro, brought her to this Loraleaf, again another pro, and made her feel like the most important person on Earth. Definitely a pro. Oh, and they were all drop-dead gorgeous hunks who had been perfect gentleman, except for maybe that kiss, but she wasn't complaining. In fact, she couldn't wait to tell her sister about this particular adventure. Jaelene would think she made the whole thing up. Satisfied she was in a good place, she turned back to Khaos, but he was gone.

"Khaos?" She walked down the hall until she came to the living room.

He sat in a large, cushy chair, a drink in his hand that was clear but had an orangey-pink tinge. He stared at it as if it held the answers to the mysteries of the universe.

"Is something wrong?"

He looked up at her with such hurt in his eyes, a lump formed in her throat.

"No, I was just thinking about what to make you for food." He looked away. "We don't have a lot of what you might be used to."

Bullshit. Food didn't cause anguish. But really, who was she to question him? As much as she wanted to make him feel better, she didn't even know him. Instinct told her he needed to know he was special. Hell, even if she was wrong, it never hurt a person to hear they were valued. "You are so thoughtful. I really appreciate everything you have done for me, for us. I'm pretty sure I wouldn't be alive right now if you three hadn't come when you did. I will always be grateful for that."

He stood swiftly. "We will always protect you." His gaze was fierce but at least he no longer looked pained.

"What are you drinking?"

His face lightened more. "It's ambrosia. Would you like to try it?"

She nodded, awareness of being hungry suddenly flooding her.

Instead of getting her another glass or letting her have his, he brought his glass to her lips. She opened her mouth and let the liquid flow over her tongue. It had a semisweet flavor with a mango, coconut taste. After she swallowed, a trace of spice tickled the inside of her mouth. "That's delicious."

"Come with me, I will make you something to eat." He made to grab her hand, but just brushed it at the last second. "This way."

"Wait, I need to get dress."

"No, you don't."

She put one hand on her hip. "Oh yes, I do. You go ahead. I'll be right there."

He shrugged as if she were crazy but he'd let it go. "Very well." He strode toward the opening on the other side of the living room. She watched his powerful back muscles and ass as he left the room and sighed. She was going to miss that when she left.

Shaking her head at herself, she returned to the bedroom. She looked at her clothes lying on the floor. "Not a chance." No way would she put those back on.

Scooping them up, she ran back to the bathroom and pushed the round button on one of the sinks after dumping all her clothes into it. Sure enough, clear water came out, then soapy water poured onto them and she hand-washed them. She had to press the button three more times because it wasn't long enough.

Glancing in the mirror, she froze. On her neck were two long cuts, each running into the other. She touched them with her finger and came away with spots of blood. Taking her towel, she dabbed at the wounds. How could Khaos tell her she's beautiful when she had these across her neck? She shivered. If they had gone much deeper, she wouldn't even be here. Another good reason for her to be grateful to her rescuers.

Carefully, she hung her wet jeans, underwear, socks and bra back in the bedroom on the towel racks in there and put the towel she'd used as a blanket on the floor to catch any drips.

"Great, now I have clothes for tomorrow, but what about now?" She looked around the bedroom. There wasn't even a dresser, never mind a closet. How weird to live without clothing. She moved back to the towel racks and rifled through the materials on the shelf above them. She found a thinner material that looked like aqua silk but was softer. It was bigger than the other, thicker towels, could even be a sheet.

She took it out and unfolded it. Oh, it was perfect, much smaller than a sheet. Taking two corners, she wrapped it around her back and pulled it up beneath her arms. Then she crossed the sides over her chest above her breasts and tied the ends behind her neck. It looked like a wrap she might wear over her bathing suit, only in this case it would cover her birthday suit. She grinned.

Pleased with her own creativity, she strode to the kitchen, the smells coming from there telling her food was almost ready. She inhaled and her stomach grumbled. She'd bet on some kind of chicken dish with local spices.

She paused at the kitchen archway. Khaos' back was to her and he used a utensil of some sort to put a steaming pastry onto a plate. It looked like a calzone, but much lighter. His long hair, tied back in the ponytail that fell to his shoulder blades was dark against his deeply tanned skin and his biceps flexed and contracted as his arm moved. Seriously, with this kind of scenery, who needed to eat?

Her stomach grumbled as if it thought she would ignore it, and Khaos turned around at the sound. His gaze swept her clothing and he frowned. Pride in her creativity dissipated. She really needed to talk to a woman. Shit, that's right, there were none.

Khaos put the plate down on a wooden table that looked like it was made of logs. She sat on what appeared to be a stump but with a very soft cushion on it. She inhaled the scents of the plate in front of her. "Hmmm, this smells wonderful."

He didn't say anything, just leaned back against the log counter and folded his arms.

She picked up a utensil similar to a fork, but that had more than double the tines and cut into the light pastry. Her stomach growled again as if it couldn't wait another second, but the steam wafting above the dish warned her it was hot. Scooping a bit onto the fork, she blew on it to cool it off, then popped it into her mouth.

Multiple flavors vied for attention. There was definitely something like chicken with chickpea, a mild curry, garlic, tarragon maybe, a strong-flavored potato with a tinge of hotness, maybe a tiny amount of red pepper? "Khaos, this is amazing. What is it called?"

"Rhoade."

Roady? It needed a more sophisticated name. Whatever its name, it was good. She blew on another forkful and stuffed it in her mouth. This time she focused on the pastry, which contained another spice she couldn't name, but it was almost like a cinnamon, which complemented the inside. When she swallowed, she looked up at him. "I love this."

"It was Sandale's favorite." Worry filled his features. "Jahl should have returned by now."

Serena put down her fork, giving him her full attention. "But Sandale lost a lot of blood. Even if the doctor could retrieve the bullet and stitch him up inside and out, he could not be moved quickly."

Khaos shook his head. "Jahl could make a litter. No, either Haven didn't have a healer or they refused to release one to Jahl."

She rose, her roady no longer holding her interest. Taking Khaos' hand, she squeezed. "Listen to me. We can sit here and come up with a dozen reasons why Jahl has not returned, but that won't make him get here any faster. What *would* be productive would be to prepare for his, Sandale's and Toni's arrival."

He held her hand like it was a lifeline. If she was the lifeline in the room, they were in trouble. With her other hand, she ticked off her ideas with her fingers one by one.

"For example." She lifted a finger. "If Sandale is on a litter, how are you going to move him up here, or can you make arrangements for him to stay below? Because I'm sure just bringing him up those stairs in the tree trunk will be difficult. Then there's Toni." She lifted another finger. "She and I are going to need a place to stay. While I do appreciate you allowing me the use of your bed, I can't sleep there when you're there and Toni certainly can't sleep there as well."

She paused as she remembered her dream and flushed. Being in the same bed with Khaos wouldn't be so bad, but that wasn't the point.

He took her hand with two fingers up and brought it within an inch of his lips. "You are right. Thank you." He kissed her hand and rubbed it against two days' growth of beard. Its roughness was stimulating and she held her breath to see what he'd do next. But he let that hand go.

Disappointed, she squeezed his other one. "And lastly, I'm going to need to contact my family and let them know where I am." She grinned.

He stiffened. "Your family?"

"Yeah, you know, my mom, the one who birthed me. My dad, who kind of helped create me." She winked to assure him she was just giving him a hard time. "And my sister."

"You have a sister?" His eyes had widened as if he'd never considered such a thing.

She rolled her eyes. "Yes, I do. She's younger than me by a couple years. Her name is Jaelene and I can tell you she is going to be so jealous when I get home and tell her about this place."

His grip on her hand tightened. "You speak with your family, have a good rapport with them?"

She crinkled her forehead. "Of course. Don't you?"

He moved his gaze to look past her shoulder. "No."

"Why?"

Khaos dropped Serena's hand, the emotions roiling through him difficult to contain. No one ever asked about his family. He moved away from her, unseeing. The pain he kept buried daily rose up and closed his throat. Family was not a comfort to him but a source of anguish. The image of his mother's gaze as she looked at him with disgust and fear flashed through his mind and he balled his fists.

Desperately, he forced himself to swallow. *Don't let her see your shame.*

"Khaos?" The touch of her hand on his shoulder sent a shudder through him. She was happiness and love. Everything he craved to give her. He couldn't let her see he wasn't worth hers in return.

He should turn around. Smile at her. *Not yet. She'll see it in your eyes.* He forced his fingers to relax and crossed his hand over his chest to grasp hers. Soft. Delicate. Some of his stiffness eased. "I didn't know you were close to your family. Do you miss them?"

Her other hand rested on his arm. "Sometimes. Well, mostly when I'm afraid or unsure. They're like a comfy blanket. You know, a safe place."

He closed his eyes as he envisioned what that might be like. Serena wrapping him in her arms was the image he envisioned. His lips twitched and he turned toward her. "I hope you consider being with us a safe place too."

"I do now. At first I wasn't so sure. I mean, you came out of nowhere. But you saved me and you've welcomed me into your home. I'm very grateful."

He stared into her round amber eyes, so large for her delicate face and so honest. He wanted more than her appreciation. He touched her cheek hesitantly, watching for any sign of withdrawal.

She turned her face into his palm and his heart skidded in response. To love her, touch her everywhere, would be paradise. He wanted her to look at him with need.

She broke away. "I think we should get to work, don't you? We have a few items on our to-do list and Jahl, Toni and Sandale could arrive at any moment. We don't want to be caught with our pants down."

"What?"

She looked at him, her gaze wandering down the length of his body, causing a rush of blood to flow to his groin. Her gaze stopped on his stiffening cock.

She swiftly raised her eyes to his face. "Never mind. Let's just try to focus on what we need to do."

He allowed himself a crooked smile. That he distracted her sent a warmth around his heart. Maybe Sandale was right. Maybe he could be worthy of her.

"First, I need to finish this delicious meal." She moved back to her seat and took another bite of rhoade. Her face scrunched adorably. "Darn, it's cold. You don't happen to have a microwave?"

He hadn't been as studious as Jahl and Sandale when it came to learning all of Earth's quirks, so he ignored the question. "I can warm it for you."

She smiled. "That would be great because this is really wonderful."

Knocking down the feeling of pride over such a small thing as making her a meal, he picked up her plate and placed it in the inducer. After a few seconds, he took it out and put it before her. "Try this."

She cut into the steaming rhoade and popped it into her mouth. "Ouch." She covered her mouth with her hand and blew out. "Yup, that'll do it."

He chuckled. Introducing her to the wonders of Loraleaf would be a pleasure in so many ways.

After chewing a mouthful and taking a sip of ambrosia, she smiled at him. "I could eat this every day. Really. So how are we going to get Sandale up the stairs and into this house or another one?"

He loved that she was so practical. It would benefit her in adjusting to life in Loraleaf. "I can speak with Theron about modifying the entrance and making the lift longer in case Sandale needs to remain horizontal."

"How long would that take?"

He shrugged. "Without Jahl? Maybe an hour."

"Oh good." She took another bite.

He watched as her lips covered the mouthful. She had soft, pink lips that would feel so good around his—

"So what about sleeping arrangements? I will need a place to stay."

"You stay here." That was the whole reason for bringing her to Loraleaf. The attack had simply caused it to occur before they could woo her. But now that she was here, she would stay.

She smiled apologetically around her food. When she finished chewing, she wiped her mouth with the napkin he'd provided. "That's very kind, but as I said, I can't very well share a bedroom with three men."

"Why not?"

Her eyes widened. "Because… Because, well, it would be different if we had a relationship. Maybe you have a guest room?" Her voice rose in hope.

She *did* want to stay. She just didn't want to stay in the same room, but soon she'd learn it would be the same bed. There was a reason one of the beds was so much larger than the others. They had built it big enough for the four of them. "You will stay in our bedroom."

She looked down at her food, obviously trying to come up with another argument to throw at him.

He needed Sandale to help her ease into this. "It's your choice where Toni stays. She is welcome to stay here as well. But if you prefer, I'm sure Theron or one of the other men would be happy to have her. She may even find a particular group of men to her liking."

Serena coughed into her ambrosia before wiping her mouth. "Group of men?"

"Yes. All of us live with at least two men to a home. Our largest filoz is five, but they are at the far end of Loraleaf as they needed a particularly big tree."

Her eyes widened. "So you all get along?"

He grinned. "Mostly. We argue sometimes and there are occasional fights between filoz, but since we all came here of our own accord, we are content."

"Except you have no women."

He gazed at her and smiled in appreciation. "We do now. And more will come. Other filoz are already making contact. Once they heard you had arrived, they couldn't wait. Our hope is that soon we will have many women here. I think you will like having other women around, right?"

She took her last bite and chewed on it, obviously thinking about what he said. Good. He wanted her to become used to the idea of staying.

"It would make me feel more comfortable. I mean, is it okay to leave the house with so many men? I won't be attacked or anything, will I?" She shivered slightly.

By the Crius! They had so much to teach her. Where were Jahl and Sandale? He needed help. Too much information and she'd want to leave. Too little and she'd be in danger. "You will never be in danger of attack as long as you remain within Loraleaf. I promise you, nothing like what you experienced last night will ever happen here. Women are very precious to us as we have so few."

"But what about getting hit on?"

He stiffened. "No one would ever hit a woman here."

"No, not hit." She shook her head. "I mean, will other men be interested in taking me home with them."

He crossed his arms. "They may be, but they know you are our chosen one and so will not make you uncomfortable in any way."

"Jahl used that term last night. What does it mean?"

"It means Sandale, Jahl and I have chosen you for our agapayto." At her wrinkled brow, he continued. "It means our beloved. I believe the term your people use is 'wife' but ours means more than that."

"Wife?" She swallowed hard, her body tensing. "Okay, I think I need to call my family sooner rather than later."

Scrat, he'd scared her. He couldn't ease her into life here by himself. He definitely needed help. "You'll have to wait until Jahl and Sandale return."

Her eyes widened in disbelief. "Really? Why?"

Because he didn't know what to do. He couldn't even open a portal so she could talk to her family without—ah. "Because I cannot open a portal without one of them. It takes two men to open the pathway to Earth." He grinned, pleased he had a legitimate reason to deny her request.

"Earth? Um, aren't we on Earth? I mean California was still on Earth last I checked." Her voice quavered and he didn't need to be Sandale to see she had begun to panic.

He approached her like the skittish welchet and knelt on one knee next to her seat. "No, you aren't." He laid his hand on her lap, wishing he could calm people like Sandale could. "When we saved you, we opened a portal to Eden, the planet we live on."

She frowned. "How can that be? How can another race of humans live on another planet, live in a jungle and have the kind of technology you claim." She shook her head. "No. I don't believe it."

Damn, what should he do? Let her believe what she wanted until his friends returned or force her to face the truth now? His gut told him to let her come to the truth slowly, in her own time. It was that or the cowardly side of his brain talking. He smiled kindly, as if he were speaking to a young child. "Okay, you don't have to."

She squinted one eye at him. "Aren't you going to try and convince me?"

He held back his grin. "No. As you said, we have a lot to do with three people coming home." He rose, intending to escape the conversation. He made it to the opening of the living area before she stopped him.

"Wait." She turned around on her seat to face him. "Promise me that wherever I am, I can return to my family when I want."

He tensed. Just the thought of losing her had his stomach tightening, but at the fear in her eyes he couldn't help reassuring her. He forced a chuckle. "As long as there are two men with chips, you can always go home, but I hope you will stay. All three of us have wanted to learn more about you for a very long time. Certainly, you can stay to satisfy our curiosity." He moved his mouth into a seductive grin and gazed at her body from her pixie-like face to her pale bare feet.

Her eyes widened and she caught her breath.

Her reaction to his look had his heart slowing. He turned and left before she could ask anything more, his step a bit lighter. It had been the act of a desperate man to try seduction as a distraction, but to see how well it worked, it may just be the route to her heart.

Seduction, he could do.

* * * * *

Almost home. Jahl's anticipation warred with his dread. How could he tell them they had lost Sandale? Nothing could soften the loss. He'd just say it. Then would come the endless questions. For the first time since escaping Naralina and building Loraleaf, he didn't want to be its leader. He didn't want to answer the questions about the death of a man who meant more to him than himself.

He would refuse. He would simply tell them and put off questions for another time. Yes, he could do that.

"Hey, I thought you wanted to be home. You're moving slower than a cactus grows in a drought."

He'd forgotten about Toni. What was he going to tell the men about her? He halted. "You need to know something before we get there."

She stopped when he did, pulling the hair tie from her hair and retying it. "Shoot. I mean, go ahead. Tell me."

Toni's cheek had already started to turn blue. He fisted his hands over the fact he'd let the human live who had dared hit a her. Women were meant to be protected by men, not hurt by them. Not even the sassy one before him.

"Hey, Jahl. You're scowling at me. What did I do now?"

He shook his head and forced his hands to relax. "You didn't do anything wrong. Does your cheek hurt?"

She lifted her hand to her face and pulled it back quickly. "It does when I touch it." She smirked.

"I'm sorry you were hurt. I promise you will be safe from harm while under my care. Here, every woman on Eden is expected to take more than one mate. This guarantees their safety."

She waved her hand. "Yeah, Erin told me. And you three had decided on Serena."

He felt one responsibility lift from his shoulders. He should have known the two women would talk about the important things. Maybe Toni could help Serena adjust. "Did she also tell you an unattached woman has two choices?"

Toni cocked her head. "No. I didn't know there was any other choice beyond taking on a couple aga—whatevers, and that the men are already paired up or in threesomes or more. Sounds pretty sweet for a woman." She wiggled her brows.

"So you won't mind picking from the filoz at Loraleaf?"

"Whoa." Toni thrust both her hands out in front of her. "I never said I was ready to settle down."

"So you would prefer to go into a Pleasure Temple?"

"What's that?" Her head pulled back as if he smelled like the dung of the feroon.

"It's where men learn to pleasure women. That is the only choice besides bonding. Otherwise, we would have men killing each other over women." He hoped this woman chose bonding. She would be an asset to Loraleaf. Her physical condition was stronger than any he'd ever seen in a woman, not that he'd seen many.

"What about me going back to Earth?"

"That can be arranged but only after you have chosen one or the other."

"Really? That doesn't make sense." She looked askance at him. "There's something you're not telling me."

He nodded. "True."

"Care to elaborate?"

"No."

She put her hands on her hips. "And exactly how long do I have to make this choice."

That was a good question. He had no idea. "Until it becomes inconvenient to not choose."

"Inconvenient for whom? Me?"

He turned around, done with the conversation. "No, me. Now we need to go. We're almost there."

He heard her arms slap down to her sides before her footsteps on the jungle floor made it clear she followed. He allowed himself a small smile. Though he brought sad news, maybe Toni could be a welcome distraction for the men, allowing him and Khaos to mourn in peace.

Khaos, him and Serena. Would Serena be saddened by Sandale's loss? Would she understand? How were they supposed to convince her to be their agapayto without Sandale's ability to calm?

He needed her. Even more now since losing Sandale. The void in his heart ached and his gut clenched. But would she fill it? Could she accept him and Khaos as her beloved without Sandale?

His uncertainty felt odd, like he had donned clothing. He didn't like feeling this way. He needed to take charge. He needed to face a life without Sandale. Too many people depended on him. Serena could help them adjust as they would help her. Yes, supporting each other would work well.

Relieved he had a plan of action, he picked up the pace, looking back now and again to be sure Toni was keeping up.

Finally, he slowed to a stop. "We are here."

She ran up to him and stopped, her breathing heavy. "Where?"

"You should have told me you were tired. We could have rested."

She gave him a cold look. "And have you complaining it took longer than it needed to because I insisted on running on my own two feet? I don't think so."

He shook his head, glad Serena was not like Toni. Serena would not attempt to run like the men. She'd let them carry her. Thinking of her had him anxious to see her again.

Toni took a deep breath. "Okay, I'm ready."

"This way." He started forward.

"I don't see anything here."

"You're not supposed to." He sighed. "It's hidden."

"Oh, like a hidden passageway. I like it."

Jahl continued to the main entrance.

"Oh wow, now this is unique." Toni stood at the bottom of the stairs. "What if someone finds this?"

"They won't." He moved his hand and the trunk closed behind her.

"Right. Forgot you could do that. Shit, now I can't see a thing." She started up the stairs behind him anyway.

He had to give her credit. She wasn't fearful and had embraced Eden quickly. He could think of a few filoz who would be interested in her. As he pushed open the hatch, light flooded the stairway.

"That's very helpful. Thank you." She came up the stairs much faster and stopped below him. "Are we at the top?"

He nodded and stepped out onto the main level of Loraleaf.

"Holy shit! This is amazing." Toni turned in a circle, taking everything in. She stopped with her back to him. "And so are you."

He turned to see who she spoke to and found Theron. And now it would begin. He quickly spoke first. "Theron, this is Toni. She came with us when we brought Serena."

Theron looked the woman over with appreciation, but little interest. "Yes, Khaos told us to expect her. Welcome to Loraleaf."

"Thank you."

"Where's Sandale?" Theron looked past Toni.

CHAPTER FIVE

Jahl took a deep breath. Having to say the words out loud seemed to make it too final.

Toni answered, "I'm afraid he didn't make it. He was shot rescuing us. He was a hero."

"Huh?" Theron looked to Jahl for confirmation.

He nodded. "It's true."

Theron's mouth opened but no sound emerged. Jahl understood, but had nothing to offer. He started for the lift.

"I know this must be a shock, Theron." Toni's voice halted him in his tracks. "I think Jahl and Khaos will need some time to deal with this. Maybe you could let the others know. I'm sure the guys will eventually explain, but right now they need some time alone."

"I understand."

"Thanks."

When Jahl heard her footsteps behind him, he continued to the lift. Once she joined him, he threw the lever. As they floated upward, he turned to her. "Thank you."

"No problem. I worked at a mortuary for a while. I get it."

He wasn't sure what a mortuary was, but he was grateful anyway. Now he could avoid his men for a time. But he couldn't avoid Khaos and Serena.

When the lift stopped, he motioned Toni to go ahead of him. She may not be his chosen one, but she was a woman and very important on Eden. When he opened the door to his home, he heard footsteps.

"Khaos?" The feminine voice in his house was such a different, welcome sound.

He prepared himself as best he could. "No, Jahl."

Serena came into view and his heart swelled, forgetting his pain for a moment. The blue table cover she wore clashed with her eyes but she was beautiful to him.

"Jahl."

"I brought Toni back as promised." He stepped to the side and watched as Serena's face lit with joy.

"Toni!" She ran into her friend's arms as if they hadn't seen each other in years. He could tell they were close. Still, he wished she'd run to him like that.

Serena wiped a tear of happiness from her face and turned back to him. She placed her hand on his arm. "Thank you." Her sweet smile begged to be kissed, but he held back. Soon.

Serena looked behind him. "Where's Sandale? Did you run into Khaos? He had arranged a way to bring Sandale up here. Did you see him?"

He looked at Toni and she nodded.

"What?" Serena's smile disappeared. "What's wrong?"

Toni grabbed Serena's shoulders. "Sandale didn't make it."

"What?" Serena backed away, shaking her head. "No. That can't be. He saved me."

Jahl clenched his jaw at the tears in her eyes. She looked at him for confirmation. All he could do was nod, his own eyes watering. He had to be strong for her. For everyone.

She sniffed as a tear ran down her face. "Oh Jahl, I'm so sorry." She ran to him and wrapped her arms around his waist. Her sympathy almost unmanned him. His whole body tensed against the tears that threatened.

Toni punched him in the shoulder and he snapped his head to look at her. She made a circle with her arms.

He looked down at Serena, her face buried against his chest and gave in to his own need. Gently, he wrapped her in his arms and closed his eyes against the pain as silent tears tracked down his cheeks. Thank the Crius he had her to hold on to. If only Sandale could have had her in his life before…

He opened his eyes, unwilling to think the thought. Sandale would always be alive in their hearts. He refused to let him go. Lifting his head, he found himself alone with Serena, Toni having left.

At the sniffle against his chest, he leaned back and lifted Serena's chin so he could look at her. "He will always be with us. We have each other and we will continue on together. Don't cry. His greatest wish was to meet you in person and he did."

She pulled out of his arms. "I'm not that special. But I am pleased he had his wish fulfilled."

"You're wrong. You're very special to us." Jahl wanted to make her understand she was their chosen, but he didn't know what to say.

"What's wrong?" Khaos walked in and made straight for Serena. "Are you okay?"

She looked to Jahl.

Khaos followed her look. "No."

Jahl's throat tightened, making his voice scratchy. "Yes."

"No. Not Sandale." Khaos shook his head. "No." He spun and ran out the door.

Serena ran after him. "Khaos!"

Jahl grabbed her. "Let him be. He needs to come to terms with this on his own. Trust me, I know this."

She looked up at him with anguish-filled eyes. "It's all my fault."

What? He started to ask but she turned away and fled toward the bedroom. Jahl rubbed his hands down his face. Now what was he supposed to do? *Damn it, Sandale, we need you.*

Toni strolled into the foyer. "Hey, Jahl, do you guys have any peanut butter?"

Serena sat at the head of Khaos' bed, her legs crossed under her. She was the reason Sandale died. He'd pushed her on purpose. It all made sense. He had been getting her out of the line of fire and when he took the bullet destined for her, he'd slammed into her. If not for him, she'd be the one gone from this world. This world?

Sandale's words came back to haunt her. *You are on Eden now. A different planet.* She'd brushed it off, thinking him delirious. She raised one finger. Then Toni told her they were on another planet, that they'd walked through an air hole. She raised another finger. She'd chalked that up to a bump on the head or because Toni always made fun of her love for sci-fi movies no matter how good they were. Serena just loved the idea that maybe, just maybe, the people on Earth were not alone in the universe.

And Khaos. He mentioned it as if it was a given. *It takes two men to open the pathway to Earth.* She raised another finger. Three people, one who saved her life, sacrificing his own, one she trusted, and one who safely brought her here, had all told her the same thing. She stared at her three fingers, then looked outside at the tree branches full of bright green leaves, then back at her fingers. Wasn't it Mr. Spock who said something about if a person eliminated the impossible than the improbable must be the truth, or something like that?

Her mind skidded backward. The swift change from desert to jungle. She hadn't seen how that happened.

The naked men. Unless she was in a large nudist colony, it was very weird.

The strange animal. Granted, she was no expert, but something like that would have hit the news.

The hidden tree-town. She'd heard of resorts like this but not places that people lived in, or where only men lived.

The elevator without electricity. That was beyond comprehension.

The pre-programmed shower. Could be the latest fad of the rich and famous, but these men were neither.

The strange vocabulary words. Present and past English words with others that were completely unknown.

It all fit together like a puzzle and presented a clear picture.

She was on another planet.

Even as her brain processed that information, her heart started pumping harder. She was on another planet, on Eden. *Oh my God.* It was a dream she never thought real. Now it was.

She lifted her gaze from her hand. No one would believe her. She glanced at her cell phone on the chair in the corner of the room. She could take pictures, but they still wouldn't believe her. Might as well turn that useless piece of technology off.

What if she couldn't go home? A pain rifled through her chest at the thought of never seeing her family again. She couldn't even contemplate that. If Khaos and Jahl were able to bring her to Eden, they could bring her home. She just had to make sure she didn't piss anyone off.

She jumped off the bed. She was on another planet! She needed to explore. She needed to— What she needed to do is find some way to help Jahl and Khaos cope with losing Sandale. The man had died bringing her here, saving her from rape and even death. She owed them.

Movement by the archway caught her attention. "Oh hi."

Toni leaned against the side of the opening, eating some kind of fruit. "Hi. Are you okay?"

The bruise on Toni's cheek had turned darker. "Are you okay? You're the one with the black and blue face."

"Yeah, I'm fine. It's going to look a lot worse in a day or two. I've had them before."

As a stunt woman, Toni was used to getting banged up. Serena always felt like a wimp next to her.

"You didn't answer my question. How are you?"

She shrugged. "I don't know. I mean, I'm on another planet with all men and one of them died saving me. I feel like I'm all over the place."

Toni arched an eyebrow as she took another bite of the yellow-colored fruit.

Serena tried to explain. "I mean emotionally. I'm excited to be here and grateful to have been saved. And though I didn't even know Sandale, it hurts that he's gone. I feel this incredible guilt."

"For what? What did you do?"

She padded over to the end of the bed and sat facing her friend. "It's not what I did. It's just that he died saving *my* life."

"I get that." Toni nodded.

"I wish there was something I could do for Jahl and Khaos. I mean, their best friend died saving me. Speaking of, where is Jahl?"

Toni jerked her head toward the hallway. "He left. Mumbled something about finding Khaos and practically ran out of here."

Serena slumped.

"You could always become their wife. From what I understand that was their intention in bringing you here."

Her heart skipped a beat. "What? Are you crazy? I don't even know them. And which one am I supposed to marry?" She shook her head. "I don't think that would help their relationship at all."

Toni moved away from the archway and sat down on the bed next to her. "You wouldn't have to choose. They want it to be a three-way marriage."

"Huh? How do you know?" Maybe her friend did bump her head. She leaned back a little to see if there was any disturbance in Toni's ponytail.

"Look at me, Serena."

She did. Toni rarely used that tone and it reminded her so much of her mom. "Okay, okay, I'm looking."

"Listen. When I went to Haven, the woman there—"

"Khaos told me I was the first woman."

Toni sighed. "Can you focus here?"

She nodded, though her mind was anything but focused at the moment.

"You are probably the first woman in Loraleaf. The woman at Haven—her name is Erin—is the wife of these two hunks, Ware and Nase. It's a threesome forever thing and she said there is even more to the bonding than a marriage like we think of it. The woman actually becomes connected to the two men in some way. She said it has to do with the bonding act, which is when they have sex with you, one right after the other combined with being on the planet."

"Bonding?"

Toni nodded. "Yeah. Erin said when she bonded with Nase and Ware, they were still on Earth, but once they arrived on the planet she developed an unexplainable connection. With Ware she can now sense his emotions, which she loves because he is a very quiet person, but he can sense hers as well so she can't hide how she's feeling. With Nase, it's harder to explain. She says it's an energy thing where they sense and influence each other's energy."

Serena stared at Toni, open-mouthed.

Toni raised her hands. "Hey, I know. I don't get it either. I'm just telling you what she said the bonding was like."

"Okay, but it's not like I'm going to do this. I told you, I don't know them."

"But they know you."

It was her turn to raise a brow. "Really?"

Toni stood and faced her, one hand on her hip. "It's your life, you decide what you want to do. But Erin said the men choose a woman based on her interest in other worlds, then they watch her for years to see if she's right for Eden."

Khaos' comment floated through her mind. *We have been watching and waiting.*

Toni looked away. "There are only two choices for women on Eden, either be a wife or join a Pleasure Temple. I'm guessing women's liberation hasn't hit this planet yet. From what I've gathered, that's because there's only about one woman to every hundred men. It might even be more. Erin wasn't sure. She only arrived a few days before we did."

"One woman to every hundred men?" That was better odds than even Alaska.

Toni grinned. "Yeah, so many giant men, so little time."

She smiled. Toni liked men, but found few who were taller than she was. At six feet two inches, she was the perfect height as a stand-in for kick-butt action heroines in the movies, but for dating, her height and muscle mass tended to be a liability. Here, the men even made *her* look small.

"Speaking of time." Toni winked. "What do you say we do some exploring? This Loraleaf looks fascinating."

"I don't know. I feel bad enjoying myself after all Sandale sacrificed for me."

"So what are you going to do? Sit here and mope? Bake them a cake? You know the only thing that will make his sacrifice worthwhile is to marry these two, and you don't want to do that, though I have to say, I know you won't do better on Earth."

The conversation had turned surreal. Better to go with Toni than think too much. Besides, she was right. What could she do? On Earth people made food, sent flowers, attended the wake. She had no clue what they did here. Maybe she could find out. "You're right. I need to learn more about this place if I'm to help those men before I go home. I have less than a week before my family reunion, so I need to figure out what I can do."

Toni gave her a strange look, then shrugged. "You do know you can have sex with them and not worry about STDs."

"I can?"

"Yup. Erin told me there are none on this whole planet. Can you imagine? And I just got my etonogestrel implant a month ago, so I'm good for almost three years. I can have unprotected sex with these naked muscle men with no chance of pregnancy. Seriously, I can't wait to get out there. Let's go."

"Hold on. Are you going out there in just your bra and jeans?"

"Sure. It's either that or strip and something tells me that wouldn't be wise. Erin had my clothes cleaned for me and Ware dried them just by looking at them. That was really cool." Toni started out of the room.

Ware dried them by looking at them? Serena shook her head. "Toni, wait."

She caught up with her friend as she was about to leave the house. "Just give me a second, I need to put something on my feet. My socks are still wet so I'll throw on my combat boots without them."

She ran back to the bedroom and pulled on her shoes, glad there was no mirror in the bedroom to see how ridiculous she looked in combat boots and a pareo, but they were excellent for wearing when working with the explosives she set when filming. Once she had them tied up, she ran back to the Toni. "Okay, let's check this place out. Maybe I can learn something."

They had the lift to themselves, but when they stopped at the bottom, which appeared to be the public areas, there were naked men everywhere. They passed two as they walked across the bridge to the entry platform. Both men nodded.

Serena did the same, but it was hard not to look down at their bodies. She'd never seen so much unadorned muscle in her life. As they reached the platform, she recognized Theron.

He must have seen them coming down the lift. He waited for them. "Good afternoon, ladies. Jahl asked me to watch over you and help in any way I can."

In the bright daylight, and now wide awake instead of asleep on her feet, Serena studied Theron. He wore his shoulder-length black hair loose. His cheekbones were more prominent than Khaos' and his lips fuller. His straight nose had a slight bump halfway down it. Maybe he'd hurt it when he was younger.

Toni pointed. "We thought we would explore Loraleaf."

He nodded at her then brought his gaze to Serena. His eyes turned that almost black color she remembered from when she arrived. "I will be happy to be your guide."

"I don't want to take you away from your work." She looked back toward the treehouse she'd seen him come out of when she first met him.

He shook his head. "There isn't much work being done anymore today." He looked away, the sadness in his face clearly visible. "We are all trying to accept that we have lost one of our own."

She rested her hand on his arm. "I'm so sorry. If he hadn't come for me, he would still be alive."

His gaze snapped back to her. "No. Don't think that. Sandale wouldn't want it any other way."

"That's what I tried to tell her."

Serena looked at Toni, her mouth open in disbelief. Toni hadn't said that.

"I think having a guided tour would be perfect, don't you think, Serena? Maybe then we can understand more about this place." Toni's none-too-subtle elbow to the ribs prompted Serena to answer as she wished.

"Yes. That would be helpful."

Theron bowed slightly and opened his arm for her to move forward. His gesture reminded her of Khaos. Was he okay? Did Jahl find him?

Theron pointed to a good-sized house just off the walkway. "Here we have our bakery. If you inhale you may smell vestiges of today's treats."

She breathed in and did notice a spicy scent in the air, but she had no idea what it was. "Do all men know how to cook?"

"Of course, but those who are very good at certain types of cooking or baking may hone their skills and do so for others. It is much like this in Naralina."

"I've heard of this Naralina." Toni tapped her shoulder and Serena turned around.

"What did you hear?"

"Erin said she saw it from afar and it was a large, white city with gold accents. She said it rose high as if it was built on a mountain, and it is completely walled in."

"Oh yes. Khaos said they exile their criminals." Serena turned back to Theron. "But the men here aren't criminals, are they?"

"No." He hesitated, obviously choosing his words carefully. "I'm not sure how to explain it in a way you would understand. We were all unhappy there for one reason or another and chose to leave, but leaving the city is considered against the law, so technically we are lawbreakers. But we aren't 'criminals' as you call them. What Jahl, Khaos and Sandale have built here is all that is good about Naralina, and they are far better leaders than what he had back in the city."

She wanted to ask more questions about the city, but learning about Loraleaf was the priority. "And how does Loraleaf work? Do people buy things from each other and work for each other?"

Theron pointed forward and they continued their stroll, stepping aside when men walked by. "No. Our society isn't based on remuneration. We all work for the common good, each having something he can contribute. Some grow food, others raise animals for food, some build furniture while others build homes."

Serena couldn't resist asking. "What do you do?"

He smiled, his teeth gleaming. It reminded her of Khaos' smile. She glanced above at the tree canopy as if she could find him there.

"I create reflections."

"Reflections?"

He nodded and brought them to a bridge off the main walkways. "Reach your hand over this railing."

Hesitantly, she did as he suggested only she couldn't go far. She hit what felt like a wall, an invisible wall. "Oh wow, what is that?"

Toni stepped up and tried as well. "It's the edge of the town, right?"

"Exactly." Theron's eyes gleamed with energy. "I use my reflection abilities and combine them with another man's air abilities and we fuel them with eyllen to create thick walls to protect our home. It took us a couple years to perfect it, but now Loraleaf is impenetrable, if anyone can even find it."

She and Khaos had arrived in the early morning and she had seen nothing. "Oh, I get it. You reflect the light to make it appear as if there is nothing here, when there really is. So your enemies would first have to find you to know where to attack."

"Exactly."

"That's amazing. So how can you reflect light?"

Toni grinned. "The Kindred, right?"

Theron seemed to force himself to look at Toni. "Yes. I am Kindred of Light."

Toni caught the excitement. "And Jahl is Kindred of Eden." She looked at Serena. "He can move natural things like rock and dirt."

She couldn't resist asking. "What kindred was Sandale?"

Theron's smile disappeared. "He was Kindred of Heart. He was especially good at calming people and was an excellent mediator when we needed one."

Serena's heart constricted. If it hadn't been for her, they would all still have Sandale… Including her. She stilled. Where had that thought come from?

"I bet he was needed with so much testosterone around here." Toni smiled, her attempt at levity forcing a crooked smile from Theron.

Sandale's touch now made sense. He *did* calm her. Serena still wasn't sure how it all worked, but she had been on the receiving end of his ability. "What about Khaos?"

Theron sighed. "I'm afraid only Khaos can answer you. I do not know, nor does anyone else here. He hasn't revealed that and I have never noticed a birthmark. There was rumor he may not have a kindred and that is why he left the city."

Serena keyed into Theron's remark. If Khaos didn't have a kindred, then that could explain some of his hesitancy around her. Maybe he felt he was odd compared to the rest of his race.

Toni watched two men walk by with drinks in their hands then focused on Theron. "Where did they get those?"

"From Libations. Would you like to go there?"

Serena shrugged. "Sure, what is it?"

"It's a place to have a drink or two or three, depending on your interest in drinking either to relax or become energized. Everyone has their favorites."

"Oh, a bar." Toni licked her lips. "I, for one, am parched and think we should raise a toast to Sandale."

"That would be nice." Theron sighed. "We usually have a burning ceremony but since Jahl didn't bring back his body, there's nothing we can do."

His comment caught Serena's interest. "Don't you have memorials?"

"What is that?"

"That's when family and friends come together and talk about the person who has passed away. We usually have a picture of the person and people take turns speaking. Some of these can be very somber while others prefer to celebrate the person who has gone."

Theron's eyes grew round. "That is an excellent idea. With our burning ceremony, we celebrate a person's life with everything the deceased liked from food to songs to favorite free time activities. Then we light the fire. People take turns watching the fire so the man is never alone as his spirit rejoins Eden. We could do something similar with a statue."

Toni cocked her head. "A statue? Wouldn't a picture be easier?"

"No, we do not have pictures, or even a painter but we do have a sculptor in Loraleaf."

Serena laid her hand on Theron's arm. "I think that would be a wonderful tribute to Sandale. Maybe we could even have a big fire, too."

Theron didn't look at her face. Instead, he focused on where her hand touched his forearm. Gently, he lifted her hand from his arm, squeezing it before letting go. "This 'memorial' feels right. I will talk to Jahl and Khaos about it."

Serena clasped her hands in front of her. She had the distinct feeling she'd done something wrong by touching him.

"So, how about that drink?" Toni interrupted the awkward silence.

"Yes, of course. This way." Theron started forward and Serena fell into step with Toni behind him.

She cocked her head at her friend and pointed at Theron. Toni rolled her eyes, obviously not thinking the breach was too horrendous, whatever it was.

They followed Theron across two sturdy bridges then up a lift, across a rope bridge and finally along a wooden walkway connecting two trees. Around the side of the trunk of the second tree was a large treehouse.

Serena loved the bridges because the views of Loraleaf from higher up were spectacular. Toni, however seemed more interested in viewing the men. Serena was also impressed with the Edenists, but Sandale's death had her nervous about meeting more of them. They could very well blame her for their leader's death.

At the door of the bar, Theron stopped, looking uncertain. "There are a lot of men inside, are you sure you want to go in?"

Toni peeked around his shoulder. "Hell, yeah."

"Serena?"

"Is there anything we should be worried about?"

He hesitated, but then shook his head. "No, you are with me and everyone knows you are Jahl's, Khaos' and San—ah, chosen one. It's just that… They will look. They have not seen a woman, even their mothers, in over five years. I could block your pheromones so they won't be as attracted to you if you want."

Block their pheromones? "You can do that?"

"Yes. All Edenists can do that. It helps the women of the Pleasure Temples walk through the city without too much hassle. Only the man who does the blocking—"

A sudden burst of boisterous laughter drowned out the rest of what Theron said.

Toni stepped forward, obviously anxious to check it out. "Shit no. I'm hoping a few *will* be attracted to me."

Serena swallowed. She wanted to turn around, but Toni was so excited, she didn't have the heart to deny her. "Then let's go inside."

The noise they could hear outside ceased the second they entered the establishment. It wasn't dark inside at all, which was strange. Instead, it had open panels on the ceiling, letting in the warm jungle air while dark squares in the walls blew the air around. She'd bet there were some kind of fans at work.

Toni waved. "Hi, everyone. I'm Toni and this is Serena."

A few of the men nodded, but many wore a look of pure fascination.

Theron motioned to a few men sitting in chairs with a small table between them. The men immediately stood and gave up their seats, smiling as they walked away. Serena and Toni sat.

Theron remained standing. "I will bring you a drink. Is there anything you particularly like?"

Serena was about to ask for ambrosia, but Toni spoke up. "How about we try a couple of each, so we can get a feel for what we like."

Theron nodded. "I can do that."

"I'll take care of that for you, Theron." The man who patted Theron on the shoulder was of the same height, but he sported a nicely trimmed beard and bright-green eyes. His light-brown hair was cut to just above his ears and he had a birthmark on his forearm just like Sandale's.

"Thanks, Rekah. Ladies, this is Rekah. He is part of my filoz."

Serena smiled. "It's nice to meet you."

Toni practically purred. "The pleasure is all mine."

Rekah nodded slightly at Toni and quickly turned to converse with Theron.

"Down, girl. You'll scare them away." Serena couldn't help chuckling. This place had to be heaven to Toni. It should be for her as well, but with Jahl and Khaos saying she was their chosen one, she needed to be mindful of that, even if she wasn't ready to marry two aliens.

"Hey, if they scare that easy, I'm not interested."

Serena cast a glance to see what Theron thought of Toni's attitude, but he wasn't paying attention. She followed his line of sight and noticed a group of four men huddled together. They obviously concerned Theron for some reason because he didn't stop looking their way as he took a seat.

She turned to ask Toni what she thought, but Toni was winking at a couple of men at a table nearby. She swatted her friend's arm. "What are you doing?"

Toni wiggled her brows. "I'm making first contact."

"Seriously?"

"What? You may be spoken for, but I'm a free agent. I need to check out all the teams, if you know what I mean." Toni waved to three men at another table.

Serena grabbed her hand as she scanned the crowd. There had to be over thirty men in the bar and they all smelled female. "Careful, someone could get hurt."

Toni pulled her hand away. "Don't worry. These guys aren't like those idiots at the film set. According to Erin, these men are raised to put women on a pedestal and to give them as much pleasure in bed as possible. There's nothing to worry about."

Serena glanced again at Theron and his frown had deepened as he continued to stare at the men at the far end of the bar.

"Toni, I'm not worried about you or me. Theron said these men haven't seen a woman in six years. That's a long time. What if more than one group is interested in you? That might start a fight."

Her friend tore her gaze away from the men for a moment and looked at her. "Do you really think they would fight over me? Oh wow, that is so barbaric." Toni looked anything but disgusted.

Serena gave up being the voice of caution and smiled as Rekah brought a number of drinks on a tray.

"Here you are. These on this side will relax you and these on this side will energize you. But don't drink too much of one kind as they can cause severe headaches when you get back to normal."

"Ah, a hangover." Serena picked up a relaxing drink and held it up to Rekah. "That's what we call it when we drink too many drinks and wake up the next morning either with a splitting headache or vomiting the contents of our stomach."

"Yes, that is exactly the effect these can have." Rekah sat across from her, on the other side of Toni.

Toni grabbed one of the energizing drinks and threw it back. Great. Did she plan to get drunk? Serena took a sip of hers. The creamy cinnamon flavor was delightful. They must have quite a bit of spices in Loraleaf.

"Hey, Serena, will you look at the size of that guy's cock?"

Serena wanted to crawl under the table. She'd never known Toni to be so crass. Quickly, she placed one of the relaxing drinks near her friend's hand then moved the energy drinks away. Sure enough, her attention taken by the hunks in the room, Toni threw back the blue-colored drink.

"Rekah." Theron's tone was hard.

His friend also stared at the group of four men. "They are escalating."

"That's what I feared. Find Jahl."

Serena looked from Theron to Rekah, but Rekah turned and strode out the door. She leaned toward Theron, not wanting to distract him too much, and kept her voice low. "What did Rekah mean?"

Theron inhaled deeply, but didn't take his eyes from the rest of the room. "Rekah is Kindred of Heart. He can sense people's emotions. He referred to the four men standing over there. They are ready to take down any man who approaches this table."

Oh wow, that was like a Betazoid from Star Trek. Wouldn't the writers just love to know they got that right? Toni reached for another drink and had to tear her gaze away from the men to find one. "Hey, why did you hog all the drinks?"

"Because we need to stay sober. See those four men over there?"

"Honey, I saw them the minute I walked in here. They are the biggest in the room. I actually feel petite looking at them."

Serena took another sip of her drink, hoping it could relax her enough to keep her teeth from chattering. "Well, if any other men approach this table, all hell will break loose in here."

"Oh shit." Toni looked at the men in question. "Would it help if I went over to speak to them? Maybe that would calm down their competitiveness."

"No." Theron's voice sliced through the noise easily. He lowered it. "They have been in here since this morning. They have had too much to drink and if you approach them it will make matters worse."

Serena's jaw tensed more. She forced it to form words. "Maybe we should leave."

Theron shook his head. "At this point, if we left we'd be followed by far too many men. A fight in here is one thing, but a fight on the bridges could mean bad injuries and we have no healer. No, we wait for Jahl."

"But how will Rekah find Jahl?" She glanced at the four men again before returning her gaze to Theron. "He left to find Khaos."

"Rekah will focus on the man feeling the most grief. That will lead him to either one of them. But I doubt it will be Khaos. If he doesn't want to be found, he won't be. He is different from most of us. Rekah may not be able to feel his emotions. I'm not sure. He's never tried before."

Her attention was caught by a man who rose at one of the tables Toni had been flirting with. Oh no. He didn't approach, just stood there talking to his friends. Her teeth started chattering so she took another sip of the relaxing drink. "Does Rekah always sense people's emotions? I mean, does he just walk around reading that? Or is he inundated with them?" She was babbling a bit, but anything to keep her mind off the fact there were thirty men in the room all poised to prove who was best in front of Toni and her.

Theron removed his hand from his drink, obviously aware of the man who'd stood. "No, our abilities aren't like that. We have to focus to use them, much like you might focus to sing or dance."

"Oh, I see." But her mind wasn't really on the conversation. The man who had risen walked toward them and then moved to the bar. She let out a breath. "That was close."

Toni remained turned toward her, her back to the men she'd flirted with. "Sorry, I didn't realize how on edge these men were. I'm not going to look at any of them."

Serena shook her head. "It's not your fault. We're just in a new situation and we don't know how to act here." She turned toward Theron and whispered in his ear. "What will Jahl do when he gets here?"

A shiver raced across Theron's skin and she looked out at the crowd to see if something there had caused it, but she wasn't as good an observer as he was and didn't see anything. He turned his head slightly toward them, though his gaze never left the main group of four. "Jahl's one of our leaders. My hope is that these men are not too far gone and will listen to him."

"Oh no." Serena watched as the man who had gone to the bar approached their table.

Theron spun around and stood in one fluid motion, stepping between their table and the good-looking hunk who would definitely interest Toni. Too bad ninety percent of the men in the bar did as well. She glanced to her right to see what kind of impact Theron's intervention had on the group of four. She groaned.

Chapter Six

"Oh, shit." Toni stiffened and Serena agreed with her sentiment.

The four giants in the back strode through the bar, directly toward Theron. She stared anxiously at Toni. "What should we do?"

"I think it's time to run some interference. We have no idea when Jahl will get here."

Before she could ask what Toni meant, she was pulled up with her friend to stand between Theron and the four men. Serena's back was to Theron as she looked up at them. A half smile was the best she could do.

Toni's was wide and completely faked. "Hello, gentleman. I was wondering when you would come to chat."

The man in front of Theron yelled over. "Hey, I was just coming over."

"Yes." Another man spoke from behind them. "He was going to invite them to our table."

Serena gave up on her smile and clamped her jaw tight. She'd swear she could smell the testosterone around her.

One of the four giants pointed his hand at those behind her. "Too late. They're with us now."

Okay, this wasn't happening. Before she could form another thought, Theron pulled her and Toni by the hand and barricaded them behind their table and chairs.

"I was afraid of this." Theron stood in front of them, shielding them with his large body.

Unfortunately, with them out of the way, the men had a clear shot at each other and they took it. Fists started flying. At first it was like any bar brawl. Serena watched from the relative safety of their sideline barricade and jerked at a particularly severe hit. "Oh that had to hurt."

More and more men pounced on each other. Did they even know why they were fighting? One man thought he was clever and tried to sneak around Theron to grab Toni, but he now lay sprawled out on the floor.

And then it escalated.

She watched as chairs sailed through the air, crashing down on unsuspecting men, though no one had thrown them. Bursts of blinding light went off, causing her to shade her eyes. Vines came down through the open ceiling, wrapped around one man's leg and hoisted him outside. That sight in particular had her clamping her jaw. She grabbed Theron's arm. "What's happening?"

"They're using their Kindred abilities."

She stared in shock as water appeared to leap from the faucet and dump onto a man about to throw a punch, causing him to sputter instead. This was too weird.

* * * * *

Jahl entered the bar and stopped. It was wall-to-wall men attacking one another. Sandale could stop this in an instant, but Sandale wasn't here and he had only one goal. "Serena!"

"Jahl, over here."

He heard her voice, but couldn't see her in the mayhem. Concern wormed its way into his gut. He shoved the man in front of him out of the way and gave the next one a punch to the jaw that laid him out cold. No one would stand between him and his chosen one, not even his own men.

A chair flew through the air at his head and he sent it back from where it came, not caring if it hit anyone along the way. He stepped over two men grappling on the floor and hurled the table headed in his direction out the open roof.

Another couple punches and one kick to a stomach brought him to the middle of the bar.

"Jahl." At Theron's voice, he halted.

Jahl looked to his right to catch Serena's relieved look at seeing him. That was all he needed. Slamming two heads together in front of him, he jumped over the crumpling men and landed in front of Theron.

Theron nodded toward the room. "I sent for you when things were much calmer. My hope was you could talk to them, but I don't think that would be a good idea now."

Jahl stared at Theron as if he was a Crius that just came back to Eden. "No?" He stepped around the man and put his hands on Serena's shoulders, examining her from her face to her boots. "Are you unhurt?"

She nodded. "I'm fine, thanks to Theron."

He glanced at Toni and received another nod. He needed to get them out of here. "Theron, give us three reflections. Two of us in other parts of the room, and one of men fighting right here."

"Done."

"Good. Everyone hold on." The floor beneath their feet moved and they started sinking.

Serena grabbed on to him. He held her steady, his arm around her waist, anchoring her to his side. She felt good there. Within seconds, the circle of floor they stood on separated from the rest of the building and slowly descended toward a platform next to the bridge below.

Once they landed and all stepped off, he sent the piece of floor back to the bar. No need to have anyone fall through the hole.

"How did you do that?" Serena still watched the floor as it slipped into its original spot.

He stiffened. "I can control any natural thing…that is dead."

"So that's what Toni meant. I didn't really understand what 'control' meant until now. That was incredible." She smiled at him. "I've never seen anything like it."

His body relaxed at her open admiration. He turned toward Toni and Theron, his hand still on Serena's back, not in any hurry to let her go. "What happened? Why was my chosen one exposed to that brawl?"

Toni raised her hand. "That was my fault. I flirted with a few of them and they went nuts."

Serena grabbed his arm before he could speak. "It's not her fault. We just don't know what to do and what not to do here."

He covered her hand with his. "I know. But you will learn." He looked at Toni. "First rule you need to learn is you cannot go into public places. If you wish to meet the many filoz in Loraleaf, I will have Rekah arrange for you to meet them privately."

Toni gave him a seductive smile. "I like the sound of that. Exactly how private could these meetings be?"

He scowled. This woman could cause serious trouble. "You do realize if you have sex with multiple men in a row you will be mated to them spiritually and physically?"

She took a step backward. "I forgot. Okay, so maybe just one at a time."

He stared at her. It might be that a Pleasure Temple was the best place for Toni, but he'd hate for Loraleaf to lose her.

He turned to deal with Theron, but before he could voice his displeasure, the man spoke.

"I will be sure this doesn't happen again. I thought our citizens better behaved."

So did he. Damn pheromones. "But to take them into Libations. What was the purpose of that?"

"You're right. I should not have mentioned it." Theron's acceptance of the blame eased Jahl's tension, but he was still surprised by the man's unusual lack of judgement. Jahl glanced at Toni. Could Theron have wanted to please a woman too much?

Serena interjected, "We wanted to go, so we could learn more about Loraleaf."

He was pleased she had an interest in their home, but the fact remained, Theron had erred. He turned to her. "I think it would be best to return to the house for the rest of the day until I can speak to my men. I should have done so as soon as I returned."

She shook her head. "No, you had personal matters to deal with. Family should always come first."

"I have no family." He spit his final word as his gut tensed. Would he ever be able to mention that word without anger?

"I meant your fi-filoz. That should come before your public duties, always."

"That isn't possible sometimes." He looked away, remembering other times when he should have let his leadership duties go.

"Did you find Khaos?" Serena's concern brought his attention back to her.

He shook his head.

"Has he disappeared before?"

"Once, but that was while we were still in Naralina." Khaos had been banned from school after he was caught fighting those who would tease him. It had taken Sandale's abilities with the teachers and Jahl's expert tracking to get him back into school. Even still, it was a two-day process. He didn't have two days now. If he left, Theron would be in charge and he was having doubts about Theron. He didn't seem focused.

All he could do is hope Khaos returned. For all his physical strength and honor, he was as bruised inside as Jahl. Too many times he'd been told he was an aberration.

Jahl turned back to Theron. "You better locate Konala and see what he can do to take care of the injured. Perhaps you can find a Water Kindred too and deluge them to stop the fight."

Theron nodded and strode away.

Jahl took Serena's hand. "Come." He started toward the closest lift. He liked the feel of her hand in his. It seemed natural. "I want you women inside before any more of my men get it into their heads that it would be a good idea to fight over Toni."

They continued to the treehouse in silence. He was not in the mood for chitchat. Serena's point had him feeling guilty about not sending men out to try to find Khaos. Even if it was fruitless, he needed to try. Loraleaf was governed by his filoz and with Sandale gone and Khaos missing, he could be forced to step down.

Once he had Serena and Toni safely inside, he stopped. "I have a matter to attend to. I will return later." Letting go of her hand was far harder than he'd expected and he hesitated.

She gazed at him in confusion. "Jahl?"

Finally, he squeezed her hand and let go. Once again matters of the community came before his filoz. He turned quickly and left.

He strode toward the lift. Unlike Naralina, which had a five-kindred oligarchy, each person from a different kindred, in Loraleaf, he, Sandale and Khaos had taken command with just the three of them. They had led the men out of Naralina to this place to build their own community. Like Nassic and Wareson, his filoz had also decided to ignore the Naralinian rule for leaders, which allowed each to take his own agapayto, and chose instead to follow the rule for the general populace, which required every woman to have at least *two* beloved. Until today, Jahl had believed they'd made the right decision, but now…

If Khaos didn't return, Jahl would either be forced to bring another man into his filoz or give up Serena. He couldn't find it in his heart to do the first and the second was not an option. He rubbed his hands over his face just as the lift came to a stop. Even if he wanted to bring another man into his home, there weren't any single men in Loraleaf. It had been a stipulation he made of those following him before they escaped the city.

He strode across the bridge. He needed to check on—

"Jahl." Rekah emerged from the entrance to Loraleaf. After he'd found Jahl and told him about the tension in the bar, Jahl had sent him out to meet the incoming night patrol.

He tensed. "Did they find something?"

The man's scowl revealed much. "It isn't good."

He couldn't resist looking up at his home. She was safe, for now. Turning his attention back to Rekah, he spoke, careful to keep his concern from his voice. "Show me."

Rekah led the way back outside to the jungle of Eden. "According to the men, it's about half a day's run to the spot. We won't be back until long after dark."

"Then let's get started." They both broke into a run, Jahl following closely behind Rekah. The man's ability to sense emotions made Jahl uncomfortable, so he shut off any thoughts of Serena and focused on the ground they traversed, watching for any sign of lawbreakers or Khaos.

Once again, Jahl wished he could be certain about the Naralina discoverists having figured out how to track portals outside the city walls. He'd been surprised they were still working on it when Nassic and Wareson left. If that technology had not advanced then he could be using one right now and be back to the house by dinner. They needed to find a way to obtain information from the city. Sneaking a man inside would be almost impossible with the portal tracking the city used inside its walls, but if they could identify someone already there that they could trust, it could add another layer of security for them all.

When Rekah finally slowed a few hours later, Jahl's concern grew. This was much closer to Loraleaf than he was comfortable with.

Rekah walked around a large boulder and pointed.

In the fading daylight he clearly made out the large, wasted animal carcass, the blood on the trees and the disturbed ground, his worry sure to be read by Rekah. "Do you feel anyone nearby?"

Rekah looked off into the trees. "No, no one."

This was too close. Halfway between Haven and Loraleaf. The lawbreakers were exploring farther. Jahl stared at the blood on the tree. At the other sites they'd found far from home, he'd thought it no more than some ritualistic painting, but this one was a distinct sign. It appeared to be a circle with two lines crossed over it. Either that or the bark of the tree caused the blood to gather in that shape.

Rekah interrupted his thoughts. "Should we let Haven know?"

Jahl ground his teeth. He had enough to worry about with Loraleaf, Serena, her friend, and Khaos being gone. He didn't need this now. He didn't want to send a man to Haven, but he had no choice. Haven was simply a settlement of Naralinians, not a group of uncivilized lawbreakers as he'd discovered while detained there. The fact was, the two communities might need each other one day. He just hoped that day wasn't soon. "Yes. These are getting too close."

"I can go." Rekah's willingness soothed his irritation.

"Bring Konala or Theron with you, both if they want to go. It's not safe for us to travel alone anymore. But remember, the location of Loraleaf must remain a secret and they have a truth-reader there." Nassic, one of the two leaders is Kindred of Mind."

"Nassic? Wasn't he part of the Ruling Circle of Naralina?"

Jahl nodded. "Yes, and so was Wareson. I attempted to find out why they no longer rule, but…" Sandale had been his priority. "But we were interrupted."

Rekah looked at him and nodded, probably feeling his grief.

Fine. There wasn't much he could do about that and he certainly wouldn't try to hide it. However, the dead animal needed to be buried. Using his mind, he opened up a hole in the ground and moved the feroon into it. Then he pushed the ground back, a small hump all that showed Eden had reclaimed one of its own.

"Let's go back. I want regular high patrols of two or three each. We need to be ready to be discovered."

They both turned and headed for Loraleaf. Jahl couldn't help scanning the ground as he made his way home, looking for any sign of Khaos. They needed to share in their grief, not hold it separately. He couldn't stand how alone he felt. It was only a day since losing a brother of his heart and only half a day since Khaos left but for a man used to always having two companions, it felt like a turn of Selene had gone by.

Khaos was strong and smart. Jahl would know if something had happened to him. Then again, he hadn't known about Sandale. For all he knew, Khaos could be dead too. His heart lurched at the thought and he smashed it. It wasn't true.

"Jahl, did Theron tell you Serena's idea of a memorial for Sandale?"

It took him a moment to refocus his thoughts. Luckily, Rekah was a patient man. "No, I haven't seen him since we left the brawl." He couldn't help shaking his head at his men's behavior. Just one more reason to bring more women to Loraleaf.

"It is much like our burning ceremony, except instead of a body, we would have a statue. I think it would be good for the men. Even those who didn't know Sandale well seem lost without the usual farewell. I think this memorial thing would give them a sense of normalcy. It would validate that we are still civilized and we will remember our brethren after they are gone, even though we no longer reside within the city."

Jahl hadn't thought about that. He was too close to Sandale to recognize grief in others. "Then we should do it. I will check with Theron and see what needs to be prepared. Thank you for bringing this to my attention."

The rest of the run home was accomplished in silence. Rekah was the closet person they had to Sandale as far as emotions were concerned. But while Sandale could calm, Rekah could merely report on what someone was feeling. Jahl wanted to have Rekah tell him what Serena felt but he was afraid of the truth. He needed more time. *They* needed more time. *Damn it, Khaos. I need you back here.*

* * * * *

Serena relaxed in a large stuffed chair and watched Toni as she stared out the window. It was dark now and the view was bound to be less enjoyable for her. She'd spent all afternoon observing the men below and had let out a sigh every once in a while.

Now that they had eaten, her friend was back at the window.

"Toni, it's been dark for hours. Can you really see anything out there?"

Toni turned to face her. "Not really. The moon is just rising."

"I imagine most of the men are home at night. Tomorrow will be another chance for you to meet them. Jahl said he'd have Rekah make the arrangements."

"I know." Toni walked over and flopped onto a large couch. "I feel like a kid in a candy store and my guess is that if given my way, I'd probably enjoy my eye candy until I couldn't see."

Serena smiled. "So instead of a stomach ache you'd have an eye ache?"

Toni raised one eyebrow. "Yeah, something like that."

Hearing a noise, Serena glanced toward the entryway, but the door didn't open. Disappointed, she turned back to her friend. She'd just met Jahl and Khaos and yet she wanted them to come back. Beyond them being her own personal eye candy, she found them "fascinating" as Mr. Spock would say. She wanted to know more about each of them, and to be truthful, she was worried about Khaos.

"That was weird this afternoon." Toni waved toward the entryway. "Our hosts, for wanting us around so much, certainly are scarce."

"I know. One minute I feel like I'm the most important thing in the world to Jahl and the next I feel like I'm an inconvenience."

Toni smirked. "I know I'm an inconvenience. I wasn't supposed to be here."

"Do you want to leave?" If Toni left, she would go, too.

Her friend seemed to ponder that a minute. "You know what? I don't think I ever want to leave."

"What?" She couldn't be serious. Any second she would break into a laugh.

Toni didn't laugh. "Think about it. What do I have to go back for? It's not like I have any family waiting for me like you do and I haven't had a boyfriend in over a year. Sure, a few good one-nighters, but nothing worth sticking around for. Here, there are so many men to sample, I'm not considered an Amazon, and women are treated like queens. Tell me, how can Earth compete with that?"

"I don't know. I just figured you'd want to go back. I mean, really, you would want to live on this planet?"

Toni shrugged. "Hadn't really thought about it until now. But I'm seriously thinking about it. Eden has a lot going for it."

Serena took a deep breath to settle her nerves at Toni's revelation, inhaling the faint scent of spruce from her chair. Jahl's chair. Funny how she could tell the men by their scent. They must wear an all-over body spray or something. "I thought I was the sci-fi geek who wanted to know there was life on other planets."

Toni repositioned herself to lie across the whole couch, something her tall frame could actually do comfortably. "You were and still are a certified geek. And look, you got your wish."

"Yes, but at what a cost? I'd rather have never known there was an Eden and have Sandale still alive than be here now."

"I know."

They sat in silence for a bit. She kept thinking of Sandale. His last words to her floating across her mind. *Go. Be safe. They need you even more now. You must be their anchor. I'm so glad I had the chance to meet you.* He knew he would never see her again. He *knew.* She tugged the pillow out from behind her and hugged it to her. She needed to get a hold of herself. She'd barely met the man. But she'd had a connection with him, just like she felt with Khaos and even Jahl. Maybe it was the planet.

"Okay, enough moping." Toni stood. "If we are going to be staying here for a while, then let's get settled in. This place is obviously a bachelor pad." Toni headed for the hallway.

Uh-oh. She didn't like the sound of that. "Hold on." She jumped out of the chair and tromped off after Toni. She found her inspecting the bedroom.

"There's only three beds and four of us. Maybe you and I should take the middle bed. It's plenty big enough. Heck, we could put three rows of pillows between us and still have enough room." Toni kicked off her sneakers and lay down.

Serena untied her boots before taking them off and putting them against a wall. Padding over to the bed, she looked at Toni sprawled on one side. She was right, this bed was plenty big enough. Hesitantly, she sat on the edge before swinging her legs up and lying down.

Orchards. A distant memory of her family going apple picking in New England one fall when she was growing up hit her full force. She sat up. Sandale smelled like apples. She shot off the bed. "I don't like this one."

Toni peered at her through one open eye. "Really? What's wrong? Is it too hard?"

She nodded. She just couldn't impose on Sandale's bed without it being offered. It was wrong. It was his. She wasn't there to replace him. She was just a visitor.

Toni rose and moved to the next bed, the one Serena had slept on earlier in the day.

"Okay, how about this one?" Toni lay on it and closed her eyes.

Serena plopped down next to her. There was still plenty of room. It had to be a king, if they had those type of sizes in Loraleaf. "I like this one." The scent of ginger wafted over her. It was a comforting scent.

Toni sat up and looked across the room at the bed on the far side. "You do know if we are going to play Goldilocks, we really need to test them all."

At that Serena laughed. "You're right." It really did kind of feel like they were in the house of the three bears. The difference being the bears were all big and there was no little bear.

She jumped out of the bed and ran to the one on the far end of the room, expecting to smell spruce as she lay down. She wasn't disappointed. There was something Christmas-like about the scents these men used and it made the place homey.

Toni lay down next to her. "This one is definitely the hardest. I think according to Goldilocks, that means we have to take the middle bed."

"Nope." Serena sat up. "We will have more privacy with the first one."

Toni cocked her head on the pillow. "I don't see any privacy in this room at all."

"That's because you can't see the future like Khaos and me. I see a rope going across the ceiling and hanging from it are many long sheets."

Toni chuckled as she rose. "And I'm guessing in this future, you and I put that privacy barrier up."

Serena smiled.

* * * * *

Jahl pushed Khaos away. "Go. Take the women. I'll bring Sandale."

"That won't work."

"By the Crius! Go!"

Khaos looked toward Sandale.

Jahl followed his line of sight. Blood flowed from Sandale to his feet, making the ground muddy. He had to save him. Couldn't Khaos understand that? He looked back at Khaos. "Please. Go."

Khaos shook his head before hoisting Serena up on his back and starting to run, her friend right behind him.

Jahl turned back to Sandale but his eyes were closed. "I will not let you die." He pulled every dead item within his vision to one place and quickly meshed them together. Setting the small platform next to Sandale, he bent to pull his friend onto it but Sandale slipped from his arms, the blood making it impossible to get a good grip. Desperation set in.

People yelled behind him, making him rush. "Sandale, help me."

He finally had a good grip on his friend's hands and pulled him over the platform. The noise of people as they ran through the bush told him they were almost upon him. He lifted the platform with his mind and made it move forward but a strong wind pushed back, tipping the platform, rolling Sandale off, his body hitting the ground with a thump.

"No!" He lowered the platform to roll Sandale back on it, but the platform whipped up and flew at him. He stopped it with his mind, but he couldn't stop everything. A wind tunnel centered around him and Sandale. As rocks came at them, he sent them upward, outside the spiral of air. He wouldn't let them kill Sandale. He'd die first.

Branches started to spear through and he fought them back as the wind picked up speed. A boulder came at him. Jahl pushed it back just in time and then the wind tunnel disappeared, stopping faster than it started. All the debris dropped where it was, forming a circle around him and Sandale. Relieved and not about to question why, he turned his attention to Sandale.

A branch half the length of Sandale's body protruded from his stomach. Blood poured onto the ground. Jahl fell to his knees, the pain in his chest twisting through him. "No. No. No. No. N—"

"Jahl, wake up. It's okay. Everything's okay." Serena's soft whisper penetrated his dream, pulling him from the horror of losing his friend again.

He opened his eyes to find her kneeling next to his waist, her hands on his shoulders as she bent to whisper him awake.

He turned his head to look at Sandale's empty bed and closed his eyes against the loss. He'd hoped, just for a second, Sandale's death had been a dream as well. Opening his eyes again, he looked into Serena's concerned gaze. "I'm sorry I woke you."

She shook her head before giving him a stern look. "You were thrashing and yelling. You were dreaming about Sandale."

She wasn't asking him a question, so he had no need to answer.

"Do you want to tell me about it?"

"No." He grabbed her shoulders and pulled her down to him, her body stretching out on top of his. The thin pareo she wore didn't disguise a single curve on her body. In fact, the silky feel of the material between them aroused him.

"Then I guess I should go back—"

He rolled her over, well aware Toni slept on Khaos' bed behind the makeshift curtain. Where the hell was he? Jahl kept his voice to a whisper. "No."

She felt too good beneath him. He wanted to lose himself in her body, escape from the torture of his loss for just a little while. To reach orgasm with her would be sweet relief from reality.

"Jahl." Her whisper was worried. "You're going to wake Toni."

He smirked inside at that. "If I didn't wake her with my nightmare, I doubt very much I'll wake her by pleasuring you."

She swallowed hard at his statement and he couldn't resist the call of her neck. Bending his head, he licked above her wound, careful not to touch the healing skin. Then he moved to the side and sucked on the pulse that beat faster against his tongue. Her response pleased him. He released her skin and trailed kisses down to the silky fabric covering her, wetting it as he went.

"Um, Jahl, I'm not sure this is a good—oh."

He'd discovered the hard tip of her nipple and latched on to it with his teeth. He gently held it and tugged.

Serena's heartbeat beneath him increased. Lightly, he rolled the tight nub beneath the wet fabric. Her gasp made him bold. Widening his jaw, he released her nipple, and with his teeth, tugged the silky material down to expose her flesh.

Without preamble, he covered her breast with his mouth and sucked.

Serena's hands grasped his head, but didn't attempt to move him away.

Good. This was the response he wanted from her. Slowly, he released his suction to nibble at her perfect nipple. His cock was harder than any rock he'd ever moved, but tonight was not about him. It was about her.

With his fingers, he pulled the pareo beneath her breast completely, wishing now he hadn't darkened the ceiling. He wanted to see the moonlight on her flesh. Some light filtered through the window, and though meager, it was enough for him to enjoy the sight of his beloved, her breast a light globe against the darkness of the cloth. He couldn't resist and licked at the hard nub straining for more attention.

As he moved to find her other nipple, she let go of his head, but arched her chest closer to his mouth. Ah, she liked his attention. Validation coursed through his veins. The years of training in the

Pleasure Temples were worth this. He would make his teachers proud this night, holding back his strength and his need.

He pulled the material to the side and lapped at the areola of her right breast. The skin was bumpy in its excited state. Laving his tongue across the hard nub caused a soft hiss on Serena's part. He cupped the whole breast in his hand, pushing the nipple into his mouth so he could scrape his teeth across it.

She moaned quietly.

The sound made him want to feel how wet she was, but he refrained. Instead, he moved his body upward against her hard nipples and licked at her lips. Hesitantly, she darted her tongue out to connect with his. He took the opportunity to breach her mouth and swept inside to taste her.

Her sweetness surprised him. Never would he have expected her to taste like the most precious of all flavors. One of her hands grasped the back of his neck as if she needed his assault on her senses. He wanted to plunder her mouth and her pussy, but he held himself back, lightly sweeping her tongue with his.

Serena's other hand wrapped around his back and her hips rose, pushing against his erection. He broke the kiss to fill his lungs with air. Slow. He must move slowly. He forced his own need down. Pulling back, he knelt between her shapely legs and painstakingly parted the pareo, letting his fingertips brush against her skin as he swept the material aside, revealing her bare waist, hips and thighs, her entire nakedness. She was far silkier than any clothing could be.

He lowered his mouth to her belly and kissed it. In response, her knees rose on either side of him. He brought his hands down her ribcage, over her hips until he reached her thighs, careful to keep his touch light. As he moved his hands over her legs to the insides of her knees, he marveled at the contrast between his dark, blunt fingers and her pale, delicate body. It would be too easy for her to get hurt. She was so small.

A surge of protectiveness pounded through his blood and had his back muscles bunching, but he kept his hands gentle. He'd never let anyone hurt her. She was too special. Unique. Jahl stroked his fingers closer to her folds, anxious to feel their moisture. He focused on Serena's breathing, taking his cues from the small noises she made as she exhaled. As he spread her to bare her opening beneath a trimmed mons, her breath hitched and held.

He lowered his head and licked, fully tasting the wetness that was her. It was an aphrodisiac he couldn't resist and his tongue plunged inside for more, his cock jerking in response. Serena moaned and her hand came down upon his head, holding him there.

Yes, he was here to please her, to bring her to fulfillment. The need to see her reach orgasm flooded him. His tongue began to stroke like his cock wanted to and Serena's hips pressed higher, and her small hand held his head between her legs.

He grasped her ass with both hands and held her to her pleasure. Her hands moved to anchor onto his shoulders. He thrust his tongue deep, loving her flavor as his need for her escalated. He couldn't get enough of her and started to alternate his thrusts with wide licks over her clit. Back and forth he went, his mouth craving her even as her nails dug into his shoulders.

Squeezing her ass, he lapped up to her clit and circled it again and again. Serena's moans grew louder, heightening his frenzy, pushing him to excite her more. He held her clit against his teeth and flicked his tongue. She arched back, stiffened and a pleasure-filled cry filled the room. At her release, he thrust his tongue inside her opening, mimicking what he would do soon to make her his bonded one. Her fingers let go of his shoulders, then latched on again and he continued to thrust.

When her hand returned to the back of his head and pulled at his short hair while her hips pressed down against his hands, he reluctantly closed his mouth and lifted his face to gaze at her. Her head was to the side, one hand resting on her stomach, the other fallen to the bed when she released him. She looked satisfied.

He wanted to take her, his cock aching, but a stanza from Sandale's favorite poem haunted him.

Come slowly, Eden!

Lips unused to thee,

Bashful, sip thy jasmines,

As the fainting bee,

Those words were Sandale's and yet not. They were from the original High Poetess of Eden, Emily Dickinson. But Sandale repeated them over and over and told Jahl he must remember them when they finally brought Serena home.

Now he understood. Serena had to be wooed into Loraleaf, not pushed into it and yet that was exactly what he'd almost done.

Carefully, he pulled his large body from her and moved to her side, lying on his back. He wanted to hold her close, but resisted the urge. Yet the need to have her body curled up against him was too strong. He didn't have the willpower to let her choose that. "Come."

She opened one eye and shyly smiled. "I think I just did."

His lips quirked at her remark and warmth flooded his chest. "Yes, you did." He resisted the urge to ask if she enjoyed his mouth on her pussy. She'd obviously found her pleasure. "And I think I'm addicted to your taste."

He couldn't tell in the darkness, but he would swear she blushed. He waited. Wanting her to move against him, trying to will her to do so.

"Why did you do that?" Her voice, so soft in the quiet room, flowed over him like a soft breeze.

He could tell her it was because she deserved that and so much more. But Sandale's words about moving slow echoed in his head. He didn't want to scare her with the strong feelings he had. "You felt so good against me, I couldn't resist."

"Really?"

He sighed. He almost wanted to tell her he was lying just to prove how silly her question was. Once again, he tamped down his inclination. "Yes. I like how you feel against me. If you would like to move over here, I promise I will allow you to sleep." Ugh, now why did he say that?

"Okay." Her shy assent rewarded him and she wrapped her pareo about her and rolled against him, hesitantly putting her head on his shoulder.

A feeling of completeness took him by surprise as he wrapped his arm around her. It wasn't as if he wasn't whole to begin with. How odd.

Her hand settled on his chest and his heart melted. Maybe having her here would keep away the nightmare. His cock jumped at the thought. Either that or her soft body melded to his with just the light material between them would keep him up all night. Either way, he was in a better position than earlier.

Preparing for a night of wakefulness, Jahl stared at the dark ceiling and began a list in his head of all he needed to do in the morning since it was only him. Tasks he felt more than ready to tackle now that he had Serena by his side.

CHAPTER SEVEN

"Hey, don't you think you should get up? The morning is half gone and I'm starving."

Serena opened her eyes to find Toni staring down at her, one eyebrow raised, the bruise on her cheek already turning green on the edges. "What time is it?"

"Who the hell knows? I can't find a clock in here anywhere, but since the ceiling is see-through now and the sun almost overhead, I figure it's maybe ten thirty."

She sat up and rubbed sleep out of her eyes. Boy, did she need a cup of coffee.

"I get that you're tired from your romp in Jahl's bed, but didn't that make you hungry? That man is all muscle. I bet he was a hard ride." She smirked, showing just a little bit of jealousy.

Jahl's bed? She looked at the room. She *was* in Jahl's bed. "Oh God." She fell back and put a hand over her eyes as if she could hide from the fact she'd not only let Jahl bring her to orgasm last night, but had enjoyed it thoroughly. She wanted it to be another dream, but the reality had been so much more pleasurable, she couldn't deny it. He'd been so gentle. That was a surprise because he didn't appear gentle during the day between his hard body and sharp military-like movements.

"Uh-huh, no hiding in bed all day." Toni tugged on her arm. "We need to eat and since Jahl isn't here, we have to figure out breakfast for ourselves."

Serena pulled her arm back and rolled over. How could she face Jahl? And what if Khaos came back? What would he think of that?

"I was able to make what looks like coffee."

Serena snapped her head around. "Did you say coffee?"

Toni nodded, the knowing look on her face could mean she was telling the truth or lying to get Serena up. She sniffed the air but could only smell Jahl's spruce scent, probably because it was all over her pareo. Even if Toni was just trying to get her out of bed, it wasn't like she could hide from her actions. She'd spent the night with Jahl. "Okay, I'm getting up." She sat and gave Toni a pout.

"Good. Because though I know you doubt me, I really did make a coffee drink and there's plenty if you want it."

"Thank you." She smiled and finally rose from the bed, fixing her current clothing to be sure it covered all her assets. She finally really looked at Toni and froze. "Where did you get that?"

Her friend wore a green cloth with arm holes and a rope around the middle. It looked like something from *Robin Hood*, but Toni had no leggings. In fact her long, toned legs were bare up to mid-thigh.

Toni pointed over her shoulder. "Over there where the towels are kept. This one was the only one long enough to cover my butt that wasn't thick like those other ones or thin like yours."

"But you cut a hole in it."

Toni grinned. "Yeah. I made it a v-neck but not too low. We already discovered how horny these guys are."

Serena swallowed her rebuke. She had been about to argue the cutting of the material, but Toni was right, she needed to cover up, and wearing her jeans and bra everyday wouldn't be fun. "I'm not sure they are horny. I think they just crave female attention." At Toni's shrug, she shook her head. "Let's get some caffeine."

"Sounds good to me." Toni strode out.

If Toni didn't think she looked like an Amazon, she was out to lunch. Serena looked down at her wrinkled pareo. Time for a new outfit. Walking over to Khaos' bed where Toni had slept, she changed into her jeans and bra and headed for the kitchen, stopping first in the bathroom to let the pareo soak in soapy water.

It didn't take her and Toni long to find eggs and baked goods from the bakery. The only strange part about the meal was the lack of sweetness. She did find a very small jar of honey but didn't dare use it. She looked for sugar for her coffee, but had to drink it black, not something she preferred, but her need for caffeine made it doable. Besides, she wasn't putting honey in coffee.

They had just finished washing the dishes, not sure if the machine that looked like a dishwasher was indeed for that purpose, and were toweling them dry, when someone knocked on the front door. They looked at each other.

Toni shook her head. "I'm not going to check. I've learned my lesson. You're the one who's already 'chosen.'"

Serena squirmed at that word, but since it was what the men of Loraleaf understood, she supposed it would keep her safe. Barefoot, she padded over to the front door and opened it a crack.

"Serena?"

"Oh Theron, come in." She opened the door wide to find Theron was not alone. Another man with unruly blond hair and light-blue eyes stared curiously at her.

He hesitated. "Are you alone?"

She smiled. "No, Toni is here."

Appearing relieved, he and the stranger walked in. "Serena, I'd like you to meet the other man in my filoz, Konala."

Ah, so this is who Jahl had referred to yesterday. "It's nice to meet you. I understand you know something about healing?"

Konala shook his head. "Not really. I can make a difference with animals, but people are a bit of a challenge for me."

"Why? I would think many of the same principles apply."

Konala gave her a self-deprecating smirk. "They would if I was Kindred of Heart or Mind, but I'm Kindred of Eden. I can sense how animals feel and influence their actions, but with humans I'm lost. That's where Rekah is helpful."

The kindred thing was a bit confusing, but she got the gist of how it worked, even if she couldn't keep track of who was what. "Since I'm from Earth..." Boy, that sounded weird. "I'm pretty impressed with these special abilities you all have."

Konala tilted his head. "But we are from Earth, too."

"You are?" Did people on Earth hide their abilities? Was she the only one who didn't know Eden existed?

Theron interrupted her thoughts. "What he means is we *were* from Earth. Our ancestors were brought here centuries ago. As we settled on Eden, we developed these abilities in order to survive here or at least that was what we were taught in school."

"Oh my God, ancient aliens."

Theron looked at her as if she'd turned into a sandworm before his eyes.

"It's the ancient alien theory. It's right. Wow." That was a huge surprise because of all the theories regarding life on other planets, that had been the one she'd discounted immediately. Showed how little she knew.

Theron shook his head. "I'm not familiar with that. It was the Crius who brought us here."

Her mind whirled, putting the pieces together. Everything she'd expected such as spaceships, robots and scary creatures from the sci-fi movies she so loved was the opposite of what she found here.

"Who are the Crius?"

Konala answered. "They were the aliens who transported our ancestors from Earth to Eden. They wanted to colonize this planet with a life form. There are a few remnants they left behind, but they have not returned in centuries."

"We don't even know if they still exist." Theron shrugged, these aliens of far less importance to him than to her.

"Hey, who was it?" Toni walked in from the living room. "Oh, hi."

Toni's entrance gave Serena a minute to shove aside her excitement and focus on her new reality. "Konala, this is Toni, a very good friend of mine. Konala is part of Theron's filoz."

"It's nice to meet you. So what brings you two here?"

Konala opened his mouth, but Theron spoke first. "Jahl asked us to show you what we are working on to give you a little time outside of the house. He doesn't want you in public places, but thought you should learn a bit about Loraleaf."

Serena gave a sigh. She hadn't expected such thoughtfulness from Jahl after his reaction to yesterday's debacle. He continued to surprise her. "I would love that."

"Me too." Toni gave an embarrassed smile. "And I promise to behave."

Serena put her hand on Toni's arm. "Hey, we all make mistakes."

Toni nodded. "Yeah, some of us more than others."

"Excuse me?" She gave her friend a look of incredulity, but it was common banter between them. "Need I remind you about the Luxor incident?"

Toni waved her hands. "No, please."

"I didn't think so." She winked at the men who stood there watching them. They probably hadn't seen many women interact. "Let me put on my shoes and we can go."

She left the three of them and returned to the room. As she sat on Khaos' bed to put on her socks and boots, his ginger scent floated around her like a tease. "Please come back." She hoped somewhere in the universe her message would be heard.

After tying her combat boots, which looked much better with her jeans than her makeshift pareo, she left the room.

As she walked into the foyer, Toni was nodding. "Sounds good."

"What sounds good?"

"You're going to go with Theron to check out what he's doing with some kind of energy rock, while I hang out with Konala and the domesticated animals they use for eggs and milk and stuff."

She smiled wistfully. "That's a good idea. If I go home and tell Jaelene I was around animals on another planet while she was back home, she'd have my head. My sister, Jaelene, loves animals. She was always bringing home strays and saving the weirdest little critters. She even brought home a baby possum once."

Toni chuckled, and the two men nodded as if they could understand her sister. She liked that.

The four of them took the lift down, but then Toni and Konala headed in the same direction as the day before, while Theron brought her to another area of Loraleaf, which once again required bridges, though no lift rides. On their way, she saw two men use vines—one to lower himself to another level and another to swing from one bridge to another. It reminded her of Tarzan except they didn't yell or anything.

She pointed out the second man to Theron. "Are those vines safe to swing on?"

He smiled. "Yes. That's the infragilis vine. Once it's cut from the tree, it never breaks. If you look closely, those vines have been mounted to strategic branches. Using them helps us keep our bodies strong during day-to-day activities."

She peered up to find the knot on the vine, but it was too high. "What if the knot comes undone?"

Theron chuckled and she brought her gaze down to find out what was so funny.

"They aren't knotted. Jahl fuses them. They cannot come off unless Jahl forces them to."

"Oh." The Kindred abilities came in handy in lots of ways. It was so interesting. She examined the ropes on the next bridge and found them to be made of the same vine and as Theron had said, there were no knots. All of it was fused together. She stopped and looked back the way they had come. There were bridges and ropes everywhere.

"What is it?" Theron stepped closer to find out what delayed her.

She turned her head to find him at her shoulder. "I was just thinking, Jahl did *a lot* of work here."

Theron stared at her, or rather at her eyes. His usual brown eyes had grown dark, like the first time she'd met him.

"Theron?"

He blinked and quickly stepped away. "Yes, it was, but Jahl was determined to make Loraleaf as safe as possible. I will show you some of the work we are doing now." He turned and strode along the walkway.

Shaking her head at his odd behavior, she ran to catch up. This area of Loraleaf was quieter with few men walking or swinging from one place to another.

"Here we are." Theron stopped in front of what looked like a stone house built around the tree. But it was three stories above the earth, or did they refer to it as above the eden?

"Why is this place stone and the rest wood?"

"Because in here we work with eyllen and it is very volatile. Toni said you work with volatile explosives and you would find this interesting. His worried look had her quickly reassuring him.

"She's right. I do and I am. Please, I'd love to learn about this eyllen."

Theron pulled a lever, the door opened and they proceeded inside. Though the outside was all stone, the inside looked like a science lab with bright white lights and shelves and shelves of vials, jars and equipment. He walked her through the first lab, by the men working there and then down a stone hall that had a couple other labs off it before he opened the last door and stepped aside. "This is where we are working to create controlled explosions."

"Explosions?" How could such an advanced civilization not have explosions yet? She stepped inside to find it much darker than the other rooms and much smaller. No one else was in the lab and it wasn't filled with the usual equipment. Just a few stone boxes sat on a shelf along with various combustible materials, some of which she recognized and some she didn't.

Theron moved to a table where a very small amount of material was on what looked like a fire-retardant pad of some sort. "This is what I have been working on. A small controlled explosion. What I can't figure out yet is the right ratio of eyllen to burn material. Unlike Earth, we do not have gunpowder, bullets, guns, or even gasoline as those are made of material not found on Eden."

She walked around to the other side of the table. "But you can make gunpowder. All you need is charcoal, sulfur and saltpeter. Do you have those?"

Theron shook his head. "We don't have sulfur on Eden."

"Oh." That was the only way to make gunpowder. "Why do you want to create a controlled explosion?"

Theron's eyes lit with excitement. "Jahl believes we have done well to hide and protect ourselves within Loraleaf, but he has concerns if we are attacked. He would like to have a way to defend a perimeter." Theron's demeanor cooled. "Unfortunately, we have one serious weakness. We could not find a way to enclose the base of the trees without killing them."

"And the people you think might attack are the criminals?"

Theron looked away. "Yes. But there could be others. We don't know for sure."

Serena could tell he was hiding something. What other people would attack them? People from Haven? People from the city?

"Eyllen is what we use to ignite the combustible material. It is the energy source for everything on Eden, but it is only stable when beneath the ground. That is why Jahl built this lab out of stone, so we could bring some up and work on it. It reacts to sunlight as far as we can tell." He moved to what looked like a stone safe, only there was a window in it made of some type of reflective glass. "This container is dark inside."

Curious at such a strange element, Serena peered at the rock the size of her fist. It looked like a hard blob of mud that had dried, somewhat anticlimactic for an energy source. "It seems you would need a lot of this. How much does it take to provide power to a house?"

Theron looked at her. "That sample you see there could power all of Loraleaf."

"What? That can't be."

He nodded, a grin forming. "Yes. Here, let me show you. This box allows us to control the ultraviolet rays going into it. Move that slide just a bit to allow some ultraviolet light from this lamp into it and watch what happens."

She took the lever between her fingers. She'd been around explosives most of her adult life and didn't take Theron's words lightly. Carefully, she moved the lever a tiny bit and then moved it back. When she looked in the window, not only was the rock glowing, but it had turned a bright orange and seemed to pulse. "It has changed color and seems to be throwing off light."

"Exactly. Now feel the box."

She tapped the outside before placing her whole hand against the side. It was hot, but not quite burning. "I barely allowed any light in there. How long will this last?"

He shrugged. "It's hard to say. Some eyllen is stronger than others. This is a particularly pure piece so it could burn for days."

"Oh no. I hope I didn't delay any of your experiments." Though she was thrilled to have seen with her own eyes what the eyllen could do.

"No, I'm not working with that right now. But you can see how using the eyllen for explosions can be dangerous."

Serena nodded. That was an understatement. "Wouldn't it be better to use something else?"

Theron nodded. "Yes, it would, if I could figure out what."

Her immediate thought was a spark, which could be created in many ways, but that would need to touch off gunpowder and that wasn't in existence. "I see your quandary now."

Theron picked up what looked like coal. "I was thinking if I used—"

A knock on the door interrupted him and he put down the black chunk to answer it.

"I've come for Serena."

At the sound of Jahl's voice, she moved around the table in the lab to see him. His gaze immediately shifted to her and became possessive. Memories of him looking at her in the dark, his head between her legs, filled her vision. She flushed as titillating heat flowed over her skin.

"Of course." Theron's voice brought her back to reality.

"Come." Jahl used the same tone he had in bed. It was authoritative, a command, a tone she usually rebelled at, but underneath she caught the hint of a need so deep, she couldn't even guess at what it was like. Despite what it might look like to Theron, she took Jahl's hand and looked back at him. "Thank you for showing me your work. I will think about the ignition issue. There must be a way."

Theron didn't meet her gaze. "I appreciate that."

Jahl pulled her from the room and as soon as the door closed, brought her into his arms and kissed her. This wasn't the tender exploratory kiss from last night. It was purely possessive as if just seeing her in a room with another man had him marking his territory.

As his tongue thrust into her mouth, she tried to remember why she should be affronted, but excitement spiraling down to her core had her wrapping her arms around his neck instead.

At her movement, he released a low groan and pressed her against the wall, his hard body fitting her in all the right places. Instinctually, she titled her pelvis forward, pressing into the ridge of his erection.

A door opened down the hall.

Jahl pulled away. "I apologize. I should not have lost control like that."

She stayed against the wall, trying to catch her breath. He ignited her desire so quickly, it scared her. She should be upset with him, but his confession wriggled itself into her heart. She'd never had a man admit he couldn't resist her.

He didn't look at her as if he expected to be chastised. This man who appeared so hard core on the outside had some interesting weaknesses. That she was one of them had her falling for him. Falling for him? She shook her head. That couldn't be. She'd just met him. It must be this vacation mindset she was in. "Did you want me for something?"

His gaze snapped back to hers and she swallowed. Raw desire filled his eyes.

"You had come looking for me?"

He blinked before grabbing her hand again. "Yes, I want to show you something." He started walking through the hallway before she could respond. Unlike when she entered with Theron and all the men focused on their work, as Jahl pulled her out, everyone stopped and grinned.

She glanced down at Jahl's package. He sported an impressive hard-on. She was rather proud that she'd caused it and that his anatomy had graced him with such a large cock.

They exited the building, Jahl walking quickly. The man had long strides and she had to take two steps to his one. Out of breath, she finally pulled hard on his hand.

He stopped immediately, concern in his eyes as he turned. "What is it?"

She took a moment to fill her lungs with air. "You're walking too fast. My stride is half yours. What's the rush?"

A distinct flush came to his cheeks. "I'm too used to men. You're right. I need to remember how delicate you are."

She put her free hand on her hip. "I wouldn't say I'm delicate. I may not be as big as Toni, but I'm no petite wuss."

His lips quirked up just a bit on one side and it occurred to her she had yet to see the man smile.

He squeezed her hand, still within his massive one. "No, you aren't, but compared to Khaos, you are like the sherry flower, so delicate a breeze could knock you over."

A breeze? Seriously? She opened her mouth to argue when he pulled her into his arms again.

"See. I but give a little tug and you're in my arms."

She rolled her eyes. So not fair. She was pressed against overly large pectoral muscles that made almost anyone, even in Eden, look wimpy. She'd concede his point to herself, but not to him. "Maybe it's not that I'm delicate but that you're so full of brute strength."

His face grew serious. "I'll always be careful with you."

"I appreciate that. I do admit I'm smaller than you are." She held up her hand to keep him from interrupting. "But I'm not petite."

He looked like he was about to smile. Instead, he simply nodded and released her from his embrace, but not his hand. They started walking again, once more in silence but true to his word, he slowed his pace so she didn't have to run.

Jahl obviously enjoyed holding her hand, which she found endearing. The men she'd dated hadn't been so keen on that. For Jahl, it was as if he always wanted to have a connection with her, like last night. He'd wanted her to sleep on his shoulder. She hadn't let on how much she loved that. His chest was hard with a light coat of hair that was soft against her hand as she had placed it over his strong heart. She felt protected with him. But Khaos had been hesitant to touch her, which just made her want him to even more. Again she gave in to the urge to look up into the trees as if he would be there, somewhere. But all there was were the men of Loraleaf going about their daily routines. Not that she minded the view, but the one man she was most concerned about wasn't among them.

Jahl brought her to the lift near the house, a good indication that what he had to show her was in his treehouse. Once inside, he brought her straight through the living room to the hallway. Did he think to finish what they started in the lab? A tingle of excitement raced across her nerves and she tamped it down.

He stopped in front of a closed door next to the bathroom. She didn't remember there being a door here.

"This is for your friend." With that pronouncement, he opened it and let her precede him.

He'd built a room. Or rather divided Khaos' bed off from the bigger bedroom. What had been a makeshift divider of cloth was now a solid wall of wood. "You created this with your Kindred ability?"

"Yes." He looked pretty proud of himself and he had a right to be.

That he could construct a separate room in so little time was astounding. That he did it for her friend, a woman he owed nothing to, was so generous. This hard man hid some soft feelings and her heart beat a little harder for him. If she wasn't careful…

He walked to the side of the room that abutted the bathroom. A door stood, not to the bathroom but to the outside. He opened it. "Here is a separate entrance for her as well."

Serena moved closer. A new walkway was built alongside the clear glass that served as the shower's walls and continued around to the front. "Wow, this is amazing. She's going to love it."

"There's more."

She followed him back inside.

He pointed to the wall between the bedrooms. "I have added a sound barrier in this wall so we don't have to hear what goes on in here and you don't have to worry about being quiet."

She flushed at the reminder of last night. He obviously wanted her again. No one she'd ever dated had gone so far to accommodate her because they planned to have sex with her. Jahl was definitely special.

He walked to another spot in the room and she gazed at the mounds of muscle moving in his back. Just knowing he wanted her that much had her knees feeling weak.

"And I was able to move a small cold box in here."

"Oh, Toni is going to love this." She smiled at him. That he had gone to such lengths for her friend, warmed her heart.

He looked a little uncomfortable with her praise. Didn't he do it for her, for her friend?

"There's more." He walked out and she followed, too curious not to.

He stopped before a much smaller archway with double doors. "This is our room."

Not sure if he meant his and Khaos' room or the room for all three of them, she ignored his statement and touched the wood on the doors. "This is beautiful." The wood itself curved to accommodate the arch at the top and was all one piece. "I've never seen anything like this."

He did stand a bit taller at that before he threw the doors open.

Her gaze went straight to the one huge bed that had been Sandale's. No other bed graced the room. Only one bed?

Jahl moved inside, obviously excited to show her the improvements he'd made, which included a balcony, a small dresser, and a new door that led directly to the kitchen. It was all beautifully done, but she couldn't stop looking back at the one bed.

She finally couldn't keep silent any longer. "Where do I sleep?"

They stood in front of the finely wrought dresser he'd made. He frowned down at her. "Here." He pointed to the large bed with the log headboard.

She opened her mouth to ask the inevitable question of where he and Khaos would sleep, but he guessed her intention.

"With us. When Khaos returns."

She hoped he did. When she finally returned home to her apartment, Jahl would be alone and something told her Jahl didn't do well alone.

She swallowed. The idea of sleeping in that big bed with Jahl and Khaos had her sex drive revving. She'd never even contemplated sex with two men. The guys she had dated were far too macho to share. At first glance, she had thought Jahl the same way, but it was clear his bond with Sandale and Khaos was far stronger than anything she'd witnessed between men on Earth. She didn't know how to have sex with two men, never mind two men she cared about. Anyway, she was just on vacation but this room screamed long-term relationship with two men.

The situation was too serious for her, so she fell back on sarcasm. "Do you really think if we all got into that bed together we would get any sleep?"

Jahl shrugged. "Some."

Oh God. Her toes curled inside her boots at the zing of anticipation that sped through her body and straight to her core.

Okay, next tactic. Avoidance. "I just can't believe you made all these structural changes for me when I'm not going to be here that long."

He scowled at her and if he'd done that when she'd first met him, she would have run far away, but she'd begun to understand him. Still, she had to keep herself from taking a step back.

"We want you to stay…forever."

She did back up a step then. "Ah, I think somewhere our communication lines crossed. I mean, I'm very grateful to you for saving me and for bringing me here for some much-needed rest and relaxation. But I need to go home."

"Why?" He was completely perplexed.

"Why? Because it's my home. Because we have a family reunion this weekend and they expect me. It's where I belong. On Earth." She added the last part to stress that they were literally from different worlds.

"But this can be your home. We can be your…family." He lifted his chin like he'd just solved a very important problem.

"Yes, you could. But I *love* my family. I'm in no hurry to trade them in." How could she make him understand?

He went back to scowling. "This is why we needed Sandale."

"Jahl, Sandale wouldn't have made a difference. My family is important to me like Khaos is to you. You said you have no family, but what about your mother and your father?"

His look turned darker. Maybe that hadn't been the wisest subject to broach.

"My father wanted nothing to do with me and my mother and brothers were happy to follow his lead. But I was the oldest and I should have been—" He clamped his mouth shut.

She couldn't leave it alone. "Are you sure? Maybe you just interpreted what he said to you the wrong way. My family and I have many misunderstandings." Especially about her interest in sci-fi movies. Go figure.

Jahl pointed to the burn scars on the far side of his left pectoral muscle. "There was no misunderstanding when my father erased the birthmark from my chest by burning it off while my brothers held me down. There was no misunderstanding when he refused to acknowledge me as his son since I could only control dead nature instead of living nature. There was no misunderstanding when he banned me from the house they all lived in to make my own way when I was but ten years old."

Oh my God. She couldn't begin to imagine. How could they? How could they treat such a warmhearted man like Jahl that way? She could almost picture them shooing him out the door, his heart breaking but lifting his chin as if to say, "Screw them." If only he could have known the type of love she had. Her family was everything to her, if they turned their backs on her…

Jahl stood there, his face and body hard but his heart a scarred mess. She wanted to comfort him, tell him he was worth so much more, but his pain was so old. What made her think she could make a difference? "I don't know what to say."

"There's nothing to say. It's history. You are the future."

"Me? Why me?" She backed up another step, Jahl's gaze too focused on her.

He moved, covering the space between them in two strides. His hands grasped her shoulders, but not roughly. "Because you are our chosen one. We want you for our beloved."

It was too much, too fast. "But why me? Why am I your chosen one? Why not another woman, why not Toni for example?"

He tilted his head in confusion. "You are not Toni. You are Serena, caring, curious, helpful, interested in other planetary life. We have watched you and waited until we could make Loraleaf safe for you and others who would follow you."

"Others?" She started to feel like she was in a sci-fi horror movie. Would cloning be next? Is that why all these men had such amazing physiques and got along so well? Suddenly, she wished Sandale *was* here to help her calm down.

Jahl's face softened as if he sensed her rising panic. "Yes, other women. Many filoz have been waiting to woo their woman to Eden. Some have already begun. They waited for us to bring you, so you could help others understand, transition to our life here at Loraleaf."

Her heart went out to him. She understood what he wanted for his people. But being sympathetic toward his cause did not convince her to give up her own life. She stared into his dark blue eyes. They begged her to stay though the word "please" had yet to cross his lips. She didn't want to hear that word from him…ever.

She lifted her hand to his face. Unlike Khaos, he didn't hesitate. He grasped it in his own and kissed her palm. She couldn't destroy his hope in one single conversation.

"I think I need to learn more about Eden and Loraleaf."

He nodded. "You will."

"You have had six years to learn about me, but I just met you a couple nights ago. I need to get to know you as well."

His gaze left hers. The silence was a sign he would refuse to share himself. But he finally focused on her again. "If that is important to you, I will tell you what you wish to know."

Her heartbeat sped at his concession.

"But make sure it's necessary because some parts of my life aren't pretty."

She swallowed. "I understand."

"Good. Now I must go and attend to other concerns. Do not leave the house until I return." He leaned down and gave her a kiss. It started as a quick goodbye kiss, but after he'd brushed her lips, his arms wrapped around her and he pulled her close. "Serena." He breathed her name before his tongue invaded her mouth and the kiss turned erotic.

Heat flared in her belly and she welcomed his taste. His hand tilted her head to better his access to her mouth, and she held on to his shoulders as her world tipped.

He pulled away, looking bemused by his own actions. Without a word, he turned on his heel and strode out of the room.

She sank to the floor, her knees too weak to support her, her mind too jumbled to think and her heart torn in a million directions. What the hell was she doing? She needed to go home, regroup. Talk with her family. Could she tell them about Eden?

Stunned, she stared at the wooden planks of the floor. She couldn't. They wouldn't believe her. She would have to keep all of this to herself. She'd never kept anything from them. Okay, maybe the candy bar she stole from the grocery store when she was eight, but other than that… There was that spring break in college. She didn't tell them about the skinny dipping episode. So she did have a few small secrets but this… She looked around her at the treehouse, the furniture, the clear ceiling. So much that was familiar and yet different. Two civilizations of humans on two different worlds. It would all fascinate her if not for her feelings for Jahl.

And her feelings for Khaos? She missed him. He'd been gone for the same amount of time as she'd known him and yet there was something about him that called to her. She shook her head and rose from the floor to sit on Sandale's bed, the scent of apples filling her nostrils. And he was another man, another Edenist, who called to her but was gone. What if Khaos or Jahl died as well? A shiver ran through her at the thought and her heart froze.

She couldn't have feelings for these men. She didn't know them yet. But her conscience told her she did. They did not hide behind lies and stories. Her instinct said she could trust them, but could she trust her own heart?

"Serena?" Toni's voice came from the entryway and she made herself stand and leave the room.

She met her friend in the living room and pretended her world hadn't just flipped itself upside down. "Hey, how were the animals?"

Toni pointed to the kitchen. "Cool. Let's talk in there because I'm hungry. I seem to have a much bigger appetite here."

She followed Toni into the kitchen and poured herself some ambrosia. As she sipped, she still couldn't believe how good it was. There was so much that *was* good in Eden.

Toni pulled out their leftovers from last night's dinner and took down some plates. "They really know what they're doing here." She plunked it on the log countertop. "The whole place works like a giant commune and there is very little waste. I hate to admit it, but putting the rustic appearance aside, these people are more advanced than we are."

Serena nodded, though Toni had her back to her. "I agree. It's strange that they wear no clothes and live in the jungle, yet they have an unending energy source and are so attuned to their environment. I think some of the advancement is because of their abilities."

"Definitely." Toni popped two plates of food into what ran like a microwave and turned to face her. "Yet they have no women born on this planet."

"And they have no explosives or bullets either."

Toni shrugged and turned to take the plates from the microwave. "I guess that's what happens when you have the same race populating two different worlds." She set the plates on the table and sat. "They each evolve differently."

Serena wasn't hungry but to be polite she picked at the food. She was so confused about her feelings for Jahl and Khaos. She could easily fall for them, but then what would she do? Maybe she should leave before that happened.

Toni set her fork down hard. "I've made a decision."

Serena widened her eyes. "About what?"

"I'm not going back to Earth."

CHAPTER EIGHT

Oh no. "Really?"

Toni nodded. "I wanted to tell you first. I love it here. I fit in here. It's like," Toni looked away, "I belong here."

Her heart squeezed at Toni's admission. As an orphan with too many foster homes to count, Toni had never felt like she belonged. "I'm happy for you."

Toni's gazed returned to her. "You are? I thought you'd be mad."

She truly was happy for Toni and focused on that instead of on the heartbreak she'd endure when she returned home and left her best friend behind. "No. I want you to be happy and if this place feels like home to you, then I want you to stay. You deserve a home."

Toni's eyes appeared to water, but that couldn't be. The woman never cried. She gave a quick nod and looked at her food. "Thanks."

Serena stared at her friend as she shoveled in another forkful. Everything was changing and for Toni, it was all for the better. The question she had was what changes were in store for her? When she returned home, she'd have to find a new apartment she could afford on her own and find a new job to pay for it. Maybe she'd move closer to her family. Iowa wasn't exactly a hot bed for sci-fi film makers, but she could fly to jobs.

Could she keep her mouth shut about the realities of other planets now that she'd been on Eden? Shit, things were getting complicated. It was as if she knew too much now and with her friend here, it would never be the same.

Wistfully, she wished she could go home, but now she was concerned about how she would fit back into her "normal" life.

"Have you thought any more about bonding with Jahl and Khaos?"

"Huh?" Toni's question caught her by surprise. "Not much. That whole idea is a bit hard to grasp, especially when Jahl is the only one here. What about you? If you stay, will you bond with a filoz?"

Toni sat back and wiped her mouth. "I don't think that will be my first choice."

"What was your other choice again?"

Toni grinned. "A Pleasure Temple where I would teach these men how to pleasure women."

"Are you kidding?"

"Nope. But I admit, I need to learn more about that option. I want to make sure I can choose who I teach on the slim chance one of these Edenists is born ugly." She held up her hand. "I know, I know, they're all gorgeous, but I heard Khaos might not have a birthmark, yet everyone else does. If that's the case then there's a slim chance another man may be born less than handsome."

"But…" Serena paused, not sure what to say. "But you would have sex with many different men? Are you sure it's what you want?"

Toni frowned. "No, I'm not sure. I just want to learn more about that option. I like the idea of testing the waters, so to speak, before I commit to bonding with four or five men."

"Not two or three?" Serena smirked.

"No way. I would want some variety. Besides, can you imagine how high my pedestal would be if I bonded with five men?"

Serena laughed. Toni was great at keeping the mood light, despite her troubled past. She would miss her friend when she returned to Earth.

"Speaking of pedestals, I ran into Jahl on my way back here and he said he didn't think he'd be back tonight, but if we needed anything, we should contact Theron."

"Why won't he be back tonight?"

Toni shrugged. "No idea. He just said the usual." Toni lowered her voice in an attempt to copy Jahl's. "I have other matters to attend to."

She laughed, Toni's voice not even remotely close, but she did Jahl's facial expression perfectly. Guess she would be in that big bed by herself tonight, but what about tomorrow? "Oh, I almost forgot. Jahl has a present for you. Come on, I'll show you." Serena stood, excited to show Toni her new room.

"For me? Why?"

Serena smirked. "You'll see."

Toni rose reluctantly. "This better not be a gag gift or a trick to get me to bond."

"Oh, please. Come on 'fraidy cat." Serena walked out of the kitchen, her heart warming just thinking about Toni's reaction.

"Hold up, where are we—"

"Ta-dah." Serena held open the door to Toni's room. "It's all yours."

Toni stood in the doorway, stunned.

"Go ahead." She nudged her friend in the ribs. "Check it out."

Toni walked in and looked around. "Wow." She turned to look at Serena. "Honey, that Jahl is a keeper."

As Toni inspected the outside entrance, Serena froze. Jahl was a keeper? Shit.

* * * * *

Khaos sat on the tree branch, staring at his home in Selene's feeble light. Footsteps below caught his attention. He watched the guard walk his path along the bridges. There would be no problems tonight. All would remain quiet and safe.

He had tried to stay away. He didn't deserve to be a part of his filoz anymore. He'd failed Sandale. He should have seen what would happen. He'd lost his concentration in his anger over the attack on Serena and missed the warning that could have saved his true brother.

Serena. Even her name was like a soft song on the wind. It was she who drew him home, forced his limbs to move when his mind no longer wanted him to.

He couldn't resist the pull on his broken heart. Jumping from the branch, he used a vine and swung onto the landing. Silently, he let himself in.

Jahl had set the ceiling to darkness, making the walk to the bedroom difficult. When Khaos reached the room, he changed the setting, letting the stars that wished to sparkle between the trees shine in. The moonlight also filtered through showing him a new wall, and only Sandale's bed was present.

Stepping to the side of the bed, he stopped. Jahl was not there but Serena lay on her side, her breathing even. In her sleep, she couldn't reject him or know of his failure.

He joined her on the bed, his body cupping around hers of its own volition. The scent of apples filled his nostrils and tears came to his eyes. The pain in his heart threatened to overwhelm him and he wrapped an arm around Serena.

In her sleep, she grasped on to him, holding him steady in the sea of his sorrow. He buried his face in her hair, inhaling her warm scent. *Home.* The thought flew through his mind to bury itself deep in his chest. A yearning for that which he'd never had rose up to close off his throat. He needed her in so many ways.

The hand on his arm squeezed. "Khaos?" Her whisper was so light, it seemed to brush across his skin on its way to dissipation.

He sniffed as he tried to open his throat.

"Oh Khaos." She turned in his arms and hugged him to her. Her womanly comfort broke down his tenuous control. He grasped her to him as he silently cried against her hair. Too much hurt, too much sorrow buried inside him forced its way to the surface and released itself into her willing arms.

She stroked his back, soothing his pain. Her body, clothed in her silky wrap, pressed against his as if she would take his sorrow into herself. Wetness on his shoulder pulled him from his pain as concern for her pushed into his mind.

He pulled away to gaze into her face. Tear tracks ran down her cheek. He cupped her chin and swallowed to force his voice to a whisper. "Why do you cry?"

She smiled compassionately. "Because I feel bad you are so sad. Does that make any sense?"

He nodded, unable to say anything else as her sweet confession constricted his chest. In the moonlight, her eyes sparkled, their wet sheen catching the silver light. She was too tempting—like a siren calling to him. He risked everything, unable to resist, and lowered his lips to hers.

Her warm breath melded with his as he tasted her. Her tongue begged entrance to his mouth and he willingly opened to her, allowing her to explore. Her sweetness was intoxicating. He never wanted the kiss to end.

He moved his hand to the back of her head, cradling her. Tentatively, he slid his tongue inside her mouth, fully tasting her sweetness. She groaned as he explored her, indulging his need for her. But he wanted more, to sample every part of her.

Pulling back, he nibbled at her lips before tasting her jaw, her neck, the top of her shoulder. It wasn't enough. He deftly untied the material behind her neck, letting it fall to the side as he rolled her to her back.

The moonlight shone down upon them. As he lifted himself away, her beauty was displayed before him. He stared, unable to tear his gaze from his chosen one. Her belly rose and fell in rhythm with her heated breathing, her hip bones just making themselves known as she exhaled.

"Khaos?"

He moved his gaze to her face. "Yes."

"Are you okay?"

He smiled, the movement filling him with joy. "More than okay. I'm in love."

Her forehead crinkled. "But how—"

He pressed his finger against her lips. "No. Don't say anything. Just feel." He lowered his mouth to her breast and licked across her hard nipple. She sucked in her breath beneath his finger.

Happy to please her, he brought his mouth down and nibbled.

Her mouth opened and she sucked hard on his finger, causing his balls to tighten. He glanced up to see a cocky grin on her face. He smirked. If she wanted to play, he was more than willing. Lowering his head again, he sucked on her other nipple, tonguing it inside his mouth.

She hissed around his finger then scraped her teeth along its length.

His cock jerked in jealousy. He was harder than a feroon's tusk and he wanted to drive it home inside her. He smirked at her before backing up and lowering his head over her mons.

Her eyes widened and her breathing increased with her anticipation. He winked then lowered his lips to her clit. He kept them there, unmoving, teasing both of them and heightening their pleasure.

Serena bit down hard on his finger and it took all his willpower not to pull away from her mouth or her clit, but he laughed inside at her message. Lightly, he started to suck her sweet nub.

Serena's moan traveled straight to his groin. He had to have her. When her mouth opened, he retrieved his finger and found her nether lips with it, stroking the moisture that proved her ready. At her opening, he slowly inserted his finger, while keeping her clit inside his mouth.

"Oh God, Khaos, please."

He released her clit. "Please what?"

She stared at him. "I need you inside me."

His crooked world righted itself at her words. "Are you sure? I can pleasure you in other ways if you like."

Her brows lowered. "Damn it. Jahl already did that. It's not enough."

He grinned, relieved to know Jahl had made progress with her. A new confidence in their ability to bond with Serena had him pulling himself over her. "You want me?"

She rolled her eyes at him and he stifled the laugh that threatened to burst free. By the Poetess, he loved this woman.

"Yes, I want you. Can't you tell?"

He couldn't help it. The joy inside him grew. "I'm not sure. Can you show me?"

Her amber eyes widened before a smirk turned her mouth up. "Of course." Grasping his head in both hands, she pulled him down for a kiss and swept her tongue inside his mouth, even as her hips raised and ground against his erection.

Holy Bendis. He pulled his pelvis back and touched her opening with his cock, and he pushed his tongue deep inside her mouth.

She didn't wait for him. Lifting her hips, she pressed herself against him and he could resist no longer.

He plunged inside her sweet body, her sheath enveloping him.

Her mouth opened and her head dropped back to the pillow. "Don't move."

"I hadn't planned to yet. Are you all right?"

She nodded and her tongue came out to lick her swollen lips. "Yes. It just feels so good. So full."

He couldn't help the pride filling his soul. "Let me know when you want me to move. I don't want to pump into you, bringing us both to the height of ecstasy until you're ready."

She moaned, closing her eyes for a moment. When she opened them, she looked askance at him. "That was more of your teasing, wasn't it?"

It was his turn to smirk. "Maybe."

She squinted at him just before her sheath tightened around him, sending hot need through his cock.

"Uh." He closed his eyes to regain control, forcing his hips not to move. He opened his eyes to find her smiling innocently at him. "Touché." He lowered his head and kissed her lightly on the lips. When he lifted his head, her grin was gone.

"Now, Khaos. I want you, now."

He shuddered as her words released him from his torture and he pulled his hips back, moaning at the loss of her warmth. He pushed himself back in as deep as he could go, watching her breasts bounce with his movement. Pleasure wrapped around his cock when he entered and then again as he exited, starting a rhythm she would enjoy.

But though he wanted to keep it slow and long, Serena grasped his shoulders, lifting her hips with every thrust he made, burying him deep within her. When her legs wrapped around his ass and pulled him forward faster, he needed no other urging.

Pumping into her now at her command, he felt her sheath tightening, squeezing him as she began to come. It blew what little control he had left and he grasped her to him, his mouth on hers as her scream filled him and he filled her.

* * * * *

Serena purposely kept her eyes closed. Her body was sated but her heart was confused. Her feelings for Khaos were much stronger than she'd guessed. She didn't want him to ever leave her side. There was something between them, just as there was something between her and Jahl. But she had to go home.

"Serena?"

"Hmm."

Khaos kissed her temple before pulling her body against him, her back to his front. He wrapped his arm around her waist and maneuvered his leg between hers. "Sleep well."

She held on to his arm, not wanting to leave him, but what if he left again? She tensed. "Khaos, now that you're home, will you stay?"

He rested his forehead against her hair. "Yes. I will, for you."

"Promise?"

"Yes, I promise." His smile was in his tone.

He thought she was silly. So did she, but until she figured out how she felt about him and Jahl and Eden, she wanted him near. "Thank you."

He squeezed her in response as if he'd never let her go.

He and Jahl were such opposites and yet not. Jahl was forceful yet gentle. Khaos was hesitant yet assertive. And Eden? Eden was beautiful, fascinating and dangerous. Shit, her heart was going in every direction.

Holding tight to Khaos, she used her free hand to count her thoughts. First, she really liked both these men who wanted her so much. Second, she loved Eden and wanted to learn all she could about it. And now third, her very best friend in the whole world, or rather worlds, would be staying in Eden. She made a fist, clearing her count.

But she loved her family so much. She could never give up her father's bear hugs or overbearing protection. She opened one finger. She needed her mom's wisdom and heartfelt understanding. Another finger rose. She just plain enjoyed her younger sister, who forever took on a new mistreated or abandoned animal. She uncurled a third finger.

Three for three. She sighed. She still had a few days before she needed to make a decision. She couldn't stay longer than a week because of the family reunion, plus it could take weeks to find another job and she did have bills to pay.

Khaos murmured in his sleep, the vibration sending a pleasurable shiver through her body. His arm tightened at her response to him. She smiled. She lay in the arms of a wonderful man with a heart of gold and a body to die for. She really needed to just enjoy her vacation and let the future take care of itself.

* * * * *

Jahl waited while Konala and Rekah climbed the stairwell to Loraleaf. Once they opened the hatch, he closed the tree trunk. All his men were back in Loraleaf, at least until tomorrow. Daily patrols would now require three men.

Slowly, he climbed the stairway, his mind troubled by the news from Haven. They too had found sites with similar blood markings and he'd gone with his men to see one himself. The round circle with the X across it was very clear on that site. It meant the lawbreakers were organized in some way which made them more dangerous. Though they hadn't discovered Haven or Loraleaf yet, his gut told him it was just a matter of time.

As he emerged into Loraleaf and closed the hatch, his thoughts swung to Serena. Though he had other men he needed to talk to, he found his feet carrying him back to his house. She was all he had left and even she didn't want to stay. That she could have left the planet while he was handling his duties as leader of Loraleaf had panic rising in him. Damn, he needed Sandale and where on Eden was Khaos? He couldn't handle this alone.

His brain told him to calm down, but his heart wasn't listening. Serena couldn't leave without two men opening a portal and no one in Loraleaf would dare do that without his knowledge.

Striding across the bridge to his house, he attempted to envision her at the kitchen table. Visioning was what Sandale told him to do when anxious, but he couldn't see her there. He threw the door open and bellowed. "Serena!"

A door slammed in the house and he headed for the noise.

"Shit, it's you." Toni stood wrapped in a table covering.

Why did these women like table coverings so much?

"Do you have to be so loud? I was kind of busy."

He took in her disheveled hair and the redness of her lips and flushed. Scrat, he must be losing his mind. It was just another afternoon to everyone else. Hopefully, he didn't interrupt a bonding. "Where's Serena?"

Toni shrugged. "Last I knew she went to Theron's lab to work on some experiment."

Of course. Theron had said she'd been very helpful, coming up with ideas he hadn't thought of. Jahl nodded once at Toni and walked away, his total focus on Serena.

Unfortunately, no one else was focused on Serena. As he came out of the lift, he found the sculptor who wanted his opinion on the statue of Sandale. Once he made a few suggestions, Jahl headed for the lab, but then the man he'd put in charge of games at the memorial stopped him and asked more questions. Didn't they see he was in a hurry?

He hadn't seen Serena since he left yesterday. He was losing her. Without Sandale or at least Khaos, she would return to Earth and he'd have no reason to go on. He halted at that thought. A man behind him plowed into him at his sudden lack of movement.

"Oh sorry."

Jahl stared at him, unseeing. What if Serena returned home and Khaos never came back? The only thing he'd have left was Loraleaf, but could he stay while others brought their chosen ones, made them agapaytos and had sons? His gut twisted.

No. He wouldn't allow his life to go that way. He would send out more patrols, not just to watch for lawbreakers but to look for Khaos. The man needed to come home.

With determination in his stride, he opened the door to the lab. His men glanced his way before returning to their work. When he came to the end of the hall, he heard Serena's laughter. The sound filled some of the holes in his soul. He wanted to hear that more often. He opened the door, anxious to see her and froze.

Serena was focused on a small pile of debris, poking it with a knife, but Theron's hand rested next to her other one that grasped the table and Theron's gaze was not on the experiment. His eyes had turned dark brown as he gazed at Serena's face, his feelings far more involved than they should be.

Jahl fisted his hands to keep from killing a very important member of his community. "Serena."

She looked up at his harsh tone, her eyes wide in surprise. Theron flushed and stepped away from her abruptly. It was all Jahl needed to see. Theron had feelings for his chosen one. How could he have been so blind?

"Jahl, I'm so glad you came." She smiled excitedly, glancing down at the table before meeting his gaze again. "I think I may have found a way—"

"Come." He extended his hand.

"But…" She frowned.

"Now." His chest tightened at the scowl she gave him.

"Excuse me, but I'm a little busy here."

Theron cleared his throat. "Go ahead. I can finish the experiment from this point."

She turned that scowl on Theron before dropping her instrument on the table and walking to stand before Jahl. "We need to talk."

The fire in her eyes told him he wouldn't like what she had to say, but as long as she focused on him, he could handle it. He held out his hand again.

She ignored him and swept through the door. He glanced toward Theron, but the man wouldn't hold his gaze. Forcing himself not to cross the room and strangle him took all his willpower. He turned and slammed the door shut behind him so hard it cracked.

He caught up with Serena outside the lab and took her hand. She tried to pull hers back but he wouldn't let go. She was his. He strode down the first bridge, his focus on bringing her home. He scowled at every man they passed, forcing them to look away.

"Jahl, stop."

Her voice penetrated his red haze and he halted. "What is it?"

"Let go of my hand."

Reluctantly, he released her.

"Thank you." She put both her hands on her hips. "We need to talk about your behavior in there."

"When we get home." He started to turn to continue on their way.

"No, now."

He stopped. One of his men walked between them and Jahl scowled. "Fine. What do you want to say?"

Her eyes widened at his acquiescence before she lifted her right hand and held up one finger. "First, you can't expect me to drop whatever I am dong simply because you need me for something."

"Even if I need to make love to you?"

She blushed. The red filling her cheeks had his cock taking notice. At least she was attracted to him.

Serena held up another finger. "Second, you can't treat me like I'm some unruly child. I'm a grown woman who can make her own decisions and can walk on her own two feet."

He let his gaze move from the tops of her feet, over her jean-clad legs, across her purple-covered breasts and to her slightly open mouth. "I like the feel of your hand in mine."

She swallowed before licking her lips and holding up another finger. "Third, you were rude to Theron. He didn't deserve that."

Jahl's blood cooled. "He did. You can't help him anymore."

"What?" Her hands returned to her hips. "You can't tell me what to do."

Jahl rubbed his hands over his face. By the Crius, this was not going well. What would Sandale do? He'd touch her, and that would calm her. Jahl was no good at that. "Actually, I can." He raised his hand as she opened her mouth to interrupt. "As the leader of Loraleaf, I can tell you what to do, but I think you will agree with me it is best not to spend any more time with Theron."

"Why? He's done nothing wrong."

"He's fallen in love with you." Just saying those words had his chest constricting.

"What?" Serena shook her head.

Even though he was afraid of the answer, he had to ask. He tensed, ready to protect his heart. "Are you in love with him?"

"No. He's just a new friend. We have an interest in common, that's all."

His gut loosened at her answer. "It's more than that for him."

She looked at him shrewdly. "And how do you know?"

"I saw him gazing at you when you weren't looking. He cares for you in that way."

"And how do you know what a look of love would look like?"

He had nothing to lose by telling her, and yet he found his hands forming fists as if he could protect himself from her reaction. "Because I love you and I know how that feels."

Serena's mouth opened but nothing came out.

He held his breath, unable to look away from her face. Myriad emotions passed over it. He didn't expect she returned his feelings. It was rejection he feared.

Her face softened. "Jahl, I care for you, but I don't truly know you. But because I do care about your feelings and about Theron's, I won't work with him anymore."

That she had grouped him and Theron together concerned him, but if she had no more contact with the other man, then hopefully she wouldn't grow more fond of him. "Can we go home now?"

She nodded and when he held out his hand, she grasped his. Hope blossomed anew and he kept his stride manageable for her. He glanced at her profile as they walked in silence. He could almost see her thinking. Now if he could just have some help from Khaos, maybe she would agree to stay.

They entered the house and he stopped midstride. "Khaos?" The brother of his heart stood at the bar pouring himself ambrosia. Happiness and relief filled his heart.

Khaos grinned. "I couldn't resist Serena." He motioned toward her with his glass.

Unreasonable irritation burned through him at the remark. "And what about Loraleaf? Did it occur to you that without you the leadership of our community would have to go to another filoz? How about the fact I would have to take another man into our home in order to keep Serena? Or worse, she would have to return to Earth?"

Khaos' eyes widened. "I didn't think of that. No."

Jahl took two steps forward, his hands forming fists, unable to stop from pouring out his anger. "And while you were conveniently gone, we found another lawbreaker site halfway between here and Haven, a brawl broke out in Libations over Toni and Theron fell in love with our chosen one. Exactly how much more were you going to expect me to handle without you?"

"I didn't know." Khaos stiffened. "If I had, I would have come back sooner."

Jahl started for Khaos, anger wiping away all logical thought, but Serena grabbed his hand.

"Jahl, what are you doing?"

He didn't look at her, his focus strictly on Khaos. "How could you know? You were too selfish. Don't you think we needed you to mourn together?"

Khaos scowled as he stepped around the bar. "You had time to accept Sandale's death. I didn't. I didn't even see him. I needed time, just like you had."

"Time?" Jahl laughed caustically. "You mean while I waited for our chosen one's friend to sleep and kept Nassic at bay so he wouldn't discover the whereabouts of Loraleaf? No, I didn't have time to accept Sandale's death. By the Crius, I don't accept it!"

"Neither do I!"

"Stop!" Serena stood between him and Khaos. "Why are you fighting?" She looked at him. "Jahl, you have wanted Khaos to come back and now that he's here you sound like you wish he weren't." She turned away to look at Khaos. "We are all hurting. There is no corner on the market on the pain of Sandale's death. You two need each other."

Khaos looked away, his voice low. "But if I had been focused, I would have seen the danger to him and warned him. I failed him."

"No, I failed him." Jahl brought his fist to his chest. "I should have stayed with him while you took the women to Haven."

Serena threw her hands up. "You two need to get a grip." She spun on her heel and stalked off toward the bedrooms.

Jahl stared at Khaos. Anger, guilt, sorrow and love grappled within his heart. He should welcome Khaos home and offer him forgiveness, but his own heart was too wrecked to offer anything. Unable to breach the gap between them, he turned away and left, leaving more than half his heart at home.

CHAPTER NINE

Serena sat in the living area of the treehouse alone, sipping on the ale she found in the refrigerator, or cold box, as they called it. Khaos and Jahl's argument left her feeling depressed, and she admitted to wanting time alone. It didn't help that clouds had moved in and with the clear ceiling, the gray outside permeated the house. Even the tree leaves appeared duller.

Something about the men's argument bothered her but she couldn't quite put her finger on it. It niggled at the back of her brain. Yes, she was uncomfortable having two friends who admitted loving her, fighting each other. That entire scenario made her question her own beliefs as it was.

She's always figured someday she'd walk down the aisle, her dad giving her away to a man she loved. Just the idea of him giving her away to two men had her smirking. Her bear of a father would be in shock. But if she insisted, he'd look sternly at them and demand they both love and protect her, meaning put her on a pedestal. Then he'd grab a scotch and throw it back. He'd do anything for his daughters.

She sighed and took another sip of ale. She missed not being able to call her mom or dad if she wanted to, but she'd only been gone four days. It was her pathetic need to have them close when she was conflicted. And she was very conflicted. To have two men loving her when she didn't even know them was strange. Though to be truthful, she already had feelings for both. That was something she simply couldn't understand. She must be missing something.

The door to the treehouse opened and she tensed.

"Hey, why's it so gloomy in here?" Toni strode in with her Amazon outfit on—at least that's how Serena thought of it.

She relaxed and put on a smile. "It's the weather."

Toni shook her head as she plopped down on the couch, her favorite spot. "Huh-uh. It's more than that. Come on, spill."

Serena grimaced before taking another sip of the ale.

Toni rolled her eyes. "It can't be that bad. Nothing in this place can be that bad, expect maybe Sandale's death. I just came back from the sculptor's pad. There is some serious talent here. It looks so real it's a bit eerie."

"Have they set a day for the ceremony yet?" She'd much rather talk about that than why she felt blue.

"Yup. Next week, on Hermday. That's the third day. At least, that's what I was told. I guess they haven't heard of hump day." Toni smiled, her pleasure in learning everything there was to know about Eden making Serena question her own curiosity.

She seemed more curious about the two men who loved her than the dream planet she'd come to.

"So, you didn't answer my question. What's with the long face?"

Serena smiled. "I don't have a long face. My father calls me his pixie for a reason."

"Nice try." Toni fixed her with a stare that said talk or else. "Come on. If you can't tell me, who can you tell?"

Toni did have a point. "Jahl and Khaos had a fight."

"So that's why I saw Jahl stomping his way past the sculptor's house. Did they physically fight? I didn't see any bruises on him."

"No." She shook her head. "But there were a lot of verbal hits that I know are just oozing inside them."

"Yeah, those two have so much baggage they're carrying around with them, it's amazing they can function at all."

Serena perked up. "What kind of baggage do you mean?"

Toni waved her hand aside. "You know, with Jahl, it's his family who seriously disowned him because I guess his ability wasn't up to par."

"True. He does seem to need to prove himself all the time, doesn't he?"

"Got that right. And then there's Khaos." Toni hesitated.

"What? What have you heard about him?"

"That's just the thing. What haven't I heard about him? We both heard Theron talk about his supposed lack of birthmark and ability, but the rumors surrounding him are ridiculous. Everything from he can vanish into thin air to he's really not alive."

Serena flushed as she remembered their time together in bed. "I can vouch for him being alive."

"I bet you can." Toni winked at her, causing her to heat even more. "But what seems to be consistent is because of his dubious Kindred, he was considered a freak by his family."

"What?" Serena sat up, her gut tightening. "What did they do?"

"That part is a bit muddy. All I know is it wasn't nice. I thought I had it bad with that abusive foster father, but these two have been put through the emotional meat grinder."

"That's it!" The little niggle in the back of Serena's mind finally connected.

Tony raised her brows. "What's it?"

"Oh nothing, you just triggered an idea I couldn't quite grasp. It's nothing." But it wasn't nothing. It was very important.

Both Jahl and Khaos didn't simply feel guilty over Sandale's death for one reason or another, they both felt unworthy and that happened long before they lost Sandale. That was what had bothered her about the argument. For two such strong men, their egos were mush. Sandale had been their anchor and now that he was gone, they were floating away on a sea of self-doubt.

So where did that put her in their lives? She didn't mind being an island, but she wasn't about to be an anchor. She had her own issues to contend with.

"So are either one of them coming back or are we on our own for dinner again?"

Serena smirked. "Hmm, I think we're on our own. I hope there's enough food in there to make something."

Toni stood. "No worries. I've got this. You, on the other hand, need to work on our hosts. I'm thinking they need a few lessons on what to do when having guests."

Serena shook her head as Toni strode into the kitchen. Hosting guests was the least of Khaos and Jahl's problems. The question was, was there anything she could do to help them or should she leave to avoid being their crutch? She wasn't Sandale nor did she want to be.

She stood and headed for the kitchen, feeling a lot more sure of herself. As much as she cared for both men, if they couldn't value themselves, there was no way she could love them.

* * * * *

Khaos approved the list of drinks to be served at Sandale's ceremony then ordered a drink of his own. Libations was quiet at the moment, but soon it would fill with men having finished their duties for the day.

He was impressed with Serena's idea to honor Sandale. She was not only beautiful and kind but smart as well. She was exactly what Jahl and he needed.

Jahl. He hated that they argued. He'd had no idea so much had happened in so few days. Yes, he'd been selfish, but at the time it was all he could do to function. He'd loved Sandale like a brother and never expected to lose him.

He loved Jahl as well and they both loved Serena. They *had* to figure this out.

The bar attendant brought his drink and he thanked him. Sipping the relaxing concoction, he stared out the open window. Rekah had filled him in on the lawbreaker sites, but when he inquired about Theron, he received no confirmation of Jahl's allegations. Then again, he wasn't about to ask outright. Filoz stood together.

He took a good look at the interior of the bar. Now that he had a chance, he could see a few improvements to the place. He'd been given a full report on the brawl and planned on visiting a certain filoz that contained four men. They would be restricted on their drink for a month if he had his way.

Two men entered the bar together, laughing at a shared joke. As they walked past him, their smiles faded and they nodded cordially.

Despite what Jahl said, while Khaos was gone he *had* thought about Loraleaf and wondered if it wouldn't be better off without him. Many of the men feared him and others distrusted him. Though to be fair, there were a few he could call friends.

But he had not thought it through as his need for Serena had pulled him in a different direction. He finished his drink and ordered another. He was prolonging the inevitable by staying at the bar. He'd have to go home eventually and face Jahl and Serena.

Another man walked into the bar and as the inside lights illuminated Jahl's face, Khaos tensed. No need to let others know of their argument. This may be the opportunity he needed. "Jahl."

At his voice, Jahl's head swiveled in his direction.

Khaos held his breath. Would Jahl come over?

Jahl nodded once and strode toward him. Khaos relaxed as Jahl took a seat at the bar and ordered a drink.

"I like Serena's idea for Sandale's ceremony." He started with the mundane. It might be the best way to feel out what Jahl was thinking. "I've ordered his favorite drink to be served."

Jahl accepted his clear drink from the bar attendant, but didn't take a sip. "Apple Fire?"

Khaos nodded. "I remember the last time he had too much of that. I couldn't believe we convinced him to kiss that feroon."

Jahl's lips quirked at the memory. "If I remember correctly, Konala was not pleased we'd caught that particular animal."

He shook his head. The feroon was known for having a very small mating window. Capturing it had delayed its season an entire month.

Jahl finally looked at him, a slight quirk to his lips. "I'm glad you're back."

"Me too." Relief poured through Khaos. No more needed to be said regarding their fight.

"We need to talk about Serena."

Khaos took another sip of his drink before responding. "That's my favorite subject."

Jahl shook his head. "I'm not sure I've helped our cause while you've been gone."

"I certainly didn't help it before you arrived." He chuckled. "Has she accepted that she's on another planet besides Earth?"

"Yes, but she is not willing to stay."

Khaos froze in the midst of lifting his glass to his lips, the light-blue liquid sloshing over the side. "What? She wants to leave?"

"She says she already has a *family*." Jahl sneered the last word. "She expects to leave in a few more days for some kind of reunion." He shook his head as if it were the dumbest event he'd ever heard of before taking a sip of his own drink.

They were so different in that aspect. Despite his family's rejection, Khaos still wanted one. "Maybe we need to make it clear she can still have her family and visit them as often as she wishes after we are bonded. That way she won't have to choose between us. We are still too new to her. If she is forced to make a choice, she won't pick us."

"Yes. If she can leave at any time, she might not be so anxious to go." Jahl contemplated his now empty glass. "But how do we get her to bond with us?"

That he didn't know. "Should we ask Wareson and Nassic? They were successful with their chosen one."

Jahl lowered his drink. "They may have bonded but she still wears clothes."

"She does?"

Jahl nodded. "And I don't think those two would welcome a visit. Wareson indicated we could bring Serena to talk with Erin only after we had bonded." He sighed. "I think Serena's friend Toni would stop wearing clothes but then we'd have a riot on our hands that far exceeds any bar brawl."

"True. And there would be no guarantee Serena would go naked just because her friend did."

Jahl ran his hands over his face. "I wish Sandale were here."

Khaos was about to agree, but stopped. "But he isn't. We had a plan that included him, but he's gone and wishing circumstances were otherwise won't get us anywhere."

Jahl looked at him with widened eyes. "So what are you saying?"

"We need a new plan. We need to work together to make Serena fall in love with us. I've already told her I love her."

"I have also."

Khaos nodded. "So she knows how we feel. What else does she need to have to be comfortable becoming our agapayto?"

Jahl frowned. "She wants to know about us. About our pasts, our goals and probably our abilities."

"Hmm, then that's what we must give her." He grinned. "And we need to pleasure her physically as well."

Jahl's face lightened. "I've done so once already."

"Good, so have I."

Jahl put down his drink hard. "When?"

"Last night." He had to ask, but hoped it didn't bring their argument to the fore again. "Where were you?"

"I had to check out the lawbreaker site Haven found. It's only a matter of time before they find us. Do you think…" Jahl looked away.

"Think what?"

He returned his gaze to his glass. "I was going to say it might be safer for Serena back on Earth, but even if that were the case, I don't think I could let her go now."

Khaos nodded. "I agree. So we need to concentrate on making it safe for her here. We need to work on this together, without Sandale."

Jahl straightened and lifted his glass. "Together."

Khaos clinked his glass to Jahl's. "Together." He smiled. "She won't be able to resist."

* * * * *

Serena looked out into the darkness, wishing she could see. The moon had not risen yet and it was pitch black. She'd bet one of those Kindred of Light men could see in the dark.

Toni had said the bonding was a physical as well as spiritual connection. Would a woman bonded to a man who could see in the dark then be able to see in the dark?

"I'm sure they're okay."

She turned toward Toni. Her friend was busy creating a new outfit from material she had sweet talked an Edenist out of. The bruise on her cheek looked awful in its yellow-green stage, but Toni said it felt a lot better.

"I'm not so sure. They were really angry at each other. What if they came to blows? They are both so strong they could do some serious damage."

"They are also filoz and I doubt—ouch. Shit. I'm done with this tonight." Toni threw down the material and the long sewing needle. "I'm going to bed. Let me know how it all worked out tomorrow."

Serena sighed. "Okay."

Toni walked over and put a hand on her arm. "It will be all right. Trust me."

Serena gave Toni a hug, a routine they'd started since being in Loraleaf. They were the only family they had on this planet and it just felt right. "Okay, I'll try not to worry."

Toni laughed as she pulled away. "Yeah, right. Have a good night."

Serena nodded and Toni disappeared down the hallway. She could be right. Khaos and Jahl could be busy doing completely different tasks, both avoiding the house, thinking the other was with her.

Moving to her favorite cushy chair, she plopped down and stared at Toni's pile of material. Maybe she should make herself another outfit too. But since she would leave in a few days, it didn't make sense. Of course, all she had was a purple bra and jeans to go home in. A top couldn't hurt.

She touched the material Toni had obtained. It was soft, but flexible in a rich green color that matched Toni's eyes perfectly. If Serena did make a top, she'd need a different color. Green made her skin look sallow. That was one thing the men of Eden didn't have to worry about. Between their dark tans and lack of clothing, color clashing was nonexistent. It certainly eliminated the decision-making process of what to wear to work in the morning. She smiled at the thought.

A noise outside had her jumping up and turning toward the doorway. It opened and Jahl came in, followed by Khaos. Jahl's face revealed nothing but Khaos wore a grin. She finally relaxed. "I was worried about you."

Jahl halted, confusion clear on his face. "Why?"

She put her hand on her hip. Were they really that clueless? "Because last I knew, you two were fighting. I didn't know if it had come to physical blows, if you were just busy directing people, or if you had been killed by criminals."

"We were drinking." Khaos smiled warmly.

She threw her hands up. "Drinking? Guess I wasted my time being worried then. Far be it for me to expect to be told what's going on." Exasperated, she turned from them, ready to go to bed without them.

Khaos grasped her from behind, his arm encircling her waist as he spoke against her ear. "Wait. We're sorry. We didn't know you were worried. No one has worried about us before."

His statement, made so matter-of-factly, was all the more heart-wrenching. She melted. Titling her head to see his eyes, she laid her hand on his cheek. "I do care about you."

He turned his head and kissed her palm.

"What about me?" Jahl came to stand in front of her, his face hard, his gaze shuttered.

If she'd just met him, she would think him cold, but she'd begun to understand the softness beneath his hard exterior. Looping her other hand around his neck, she looked into his eyes. "Yes, I care about you as well."

His dark-blue gaze flickered and his jaw relaxed, the only sign he'd heard her, but it was enough. He stepped closer, his hand snaking around her waist. "Serena." Her name as he spoke it was like a craving and desire ran through her.

Khaos entwined his fingers with hers as his lips touched her temple in a soft caress. Jahl pressed himself against her, his chest pushing her into Khaos' hard body. She let her head fall back upon Khaos' shoulder. He took advantage of her position to kiss her.

It wasn't the gentle kiss of the night before. His tongue swept into her mouth, demanding her surrender, even as Jahl's lips found her shoulder and he sucked hard. Desire sped through her body all the way to her toes.

Jahl moaned and pushed harder against her, his hard cock rubbing on her jeans, sandwiching her into Khaos' erection as it pressed against her ass. She sucked on Khaos' tongue in response, loving the feel of being desired.

Khaos broke the kiss. "You wear too many clothes."

"You're right." Her words came out breathy, a testament to her excitement.

Jahl lifted his head from her shoulder. "I can help with that."

Khaos nodded against the back of her head before Jahl stepped away. She bit back a moan of disappointment at the loss of his chest against her own, loving the feel of his dark hair rubbing against her body, but she did have too many clothes on. Prepared to take them off, she tried to disengage her fingers from Khaos' hand but he held on. Instead, he pulled her hand down behind her back. Before she could react to that, he'd grasped her other one and held it behind her too.

A jolt of excitement had her folds moistening. She'd never had two men before, never mind two Edenists who were built like fitness models. Her heart raced as Jahl slipped his fingers inside her jeans to work the button. She sucked in her tummy as he slowly lowered the zipper. Pulling apart the thick material, he revealed her purple panties.

Khaos pressed against her back, his cock pushing into her hands as he looked over her shoulder. "I think purple is my new favorite color."

Jahl grunted, ignoring the comment, and instead hooked his fingers around the waist of her jeans and pulled them over her hips and down her legs. As if she couldn't lift her own feet, he raised one at a time with his hand as if she were a piece of China. Their conversation about her not being delicate had her smirking. "I won't break, Jahl."

His head snapped up. "Maybe not, but it doesn't hurt to be careful."

She was about to retort but Khaos' cock jerked and he placed her hands around it, holding them to his erection. He was large and silky smooth, reminding her of what it felt like to have him inside her.

After throwing her jeans on the couch, Jahl knelt before her, his lips coming to the height of her nipples. He cocked his head as he looked at her bra, muttering something she couldn't make out. Leaning toward her, he reached around her back between her and Khaos and unhooked her bra. With his teeth, he pulled down on the center, causing the cups to brush against her already hard nipples. She inhaled at the stimulation. He continued downward until the bra wouldn't move any farther because Khaos held her arms.

Without a word, he let go of the material and grasping her hips, licked at each nipple.

She hissed at the feel of his tongue. She wanted to hold his head, but her hands were firmly attached to the pulsing cock behind her.

"You taste good." Jahl's simple statement made her shiver.

Khaos spoke from behind her. "You're making our love cold. Best you heat her up."

Jahl nodded as if contemplating a very important mission. Then he sucked one of her breasts into his mouth, as much as he could take. His tongue flicked across her hard nub, sending her to another whole plane of readiness. Unable to touch him, she let her head fall back to Khaos' shoulder, where he proceeded to kiss her neck.

As Jahl pulled back from her breast, he caught her nipple between his teeth and gently pulled. She moaned in delight and closed her eyes at the exquisite torture.

Finally, Jahl released her completely, and she took in a much needed deep breath, but her respite from stimulation was short-lived as he latched on to her other breast at the same time Khaos started to suck at her neck. The dual sensations curled her toes and she squeezed Khaos' cock. He pressed his hips tighter against her in response.

When Jahl finished giving her other breast equal attention, Khaos lifted his head. "Now you are branded by both of us."

Huh? If he meant by their attention to her, then she agreed. She'd never felt so sexy. She opened her eyes to find Jahl kneeling back, simply staring at her. Admiration and desire filled his gaze and she returned the favor. She wanted to feel the hair of his chest brushing her wet nipples, but even more, she wanted his large cock inside her. She wanted the cock in her hands as well. She was one greedy woman.

Khaos spoke against her ear, raising goosebumps along her skin. "Come on, Jahl, let's not take all night."

"Fine." He lifted his hands and placed his fingers just inside her panties on either side of her hips.

She held her breath, expecting him to slide them down her legs, but instead he pulled them up, pressing them against her already swollen clit. "Oh."

His facial reaction to her unexpected response was breathtaking. Every plane in his face hardened with desire and his nostrils flared. He leaned toward her and tongued the outside of her panties directly over her clit.

"Oh God, Jahl."

He groaned and inhaled deeply. Then he did what she'd thought he would do and pulled her panties down. She lifted one leg and he pulled them over one foot, but left them around her other ankle as he grasped her hips again and buried his face against her mons. His tongue flicked out, finding her clit and she opened her mouth to inhale.

No sooner had she done so then Khaos' tongue swooped in. She sucked on it, the only thing she could do with her hands behind her. But as Jahl's tongue pushed into her opening, she bucked forward, and Khaos' kiss turned fierce.

She was drowning in sexual tension as one man claimed her mouth and the other her pussy. Jahl's tongue moved to her clit and circled it, pushing her tension higher.

Khaos changed his grip to hold both her wrists in one hand and moved the other to her breast, cupping it. She arched upward, craving his touch there as well. As his thumb and finger began to twirl her hardened nub, something hard slid into her opening.

Somewhere in her consciousness she knew both of Jahl's hands grasped her hips, yet this hardness began to pump inside her. She moaned into Khaos' mouth as her orgasm loomed near, her heart racing at all the stimuli. Then Jahl sucked at her clit and her world exploded. Lights flicked behind her eyes as an inferno of satisfaction burst through her, jerking her body with ecstasy. The fire continued to burn as the men kept their attention on her, prolonging her pleasure.

As the fire inside died down, Jahl and Khaos removed their mouths from her body. Then Jahl released her hips and her knees buckled, but before she could hit the ground, Khaos had scooped her into his arms. His chuckle vibrated within his chest as he strode to the big comfy chair she'd claimed as hers. He sat in it with her still in her arms.

Jahl stood before her in his naked glory, looking more relaxed than she'd ever seen him, except for his still-rigid cock. So focused on the sensual vision before her and the strong arms around her, it took her a moment to notice the movement inside her pussy. "What the hell?"

Khaos laughed. "Jahl, don't scare her."

"Very well." He looked far too pleased with himself. "Serena, open your legs."

Huh? She looked to Khaos and he nodded. Feeling more than bit naughty, she bent one knee and moved it from the arm of the chair to the floor. She watched Jahl's body tense before she felt something pull through her sheath.

Her gaze flew to her legs. She stared as what could only be called a smooth wooden bullet flew from between her legs to Jahl's hand. She crossed her legs immediately, unnerved to see an object move through the air. "What was that?"

Jahl held it up. "I fashioned this after one of the sex toys found on Earth. It is made of wood, basically a piece of dead tree, so I can control it."

She stared at the object as all the possibilities started to float across her brain. With Jahl's abilities, he could create all kinds of toys from wood or even stone. Her body flushed with excitement. "Can it vibrate?"

His large chest rose with the deep breath he took. "Yes. I can make them vibrate, or pulse, or pump. I can make them hot or cold as well." He gave her a shrewd look. "I can even insert them when you are asleep and make them vibrate inside you when you least expect it."

Her breath caught and sexual need zinged through her. "Oh."

Khaos kissed her temple, switching her attention. "Would you like to remove the rest of your clothing?"

She looked down to see her bra still hooked on one of her arms. These men were such a distraction, she hadn't even noticed. Pulling it off, she threw it on the coffee table and it fell on Toni's sewing. "Oh shit." She looked toward the bedrooms.

Jahl looked behind him, then back at her. "What?"

She colored and pressed herself into Khaos. "Toni could have come out here and seen us."

Jahl looked at her as if she were a child. "If that is a concern, I will fuse her door."

She was about to shake her head but paused. They had more planned for her? Just the thought of having their hands and mouths on her body again had her nodding.

Jahl looked back for a few seconds then faced them again. "Done."

Again the thought that perhaps the bonding would give a woman certain powers floated before her, but Khaos stood, which had her grasping him about the neck, all thoughts of super human abilities fleeing.

He turned around and set her in the chair by herself, her legs dangling over one arm, her back resting against the other.

"I'm getting a glass of ambrosia. Anyone else?"

Jahl nodded and so did she, once again happy to watch the muscles in Khaos' back as he strode from the room. She was one lucky woman.

Jahl moved toward her. She enjoyed the sight of his thigh muscles as he crossed to where she was and sat on the couch Toni usually used. That she could see the movement of each part of his thigh had her silently sighing in pure feminine pleasure. These two men gave a whole new meaning to the term "eye candy."

"You are so beautiful without your clothes on." Jahl's remark caught her off guard.

"Does that mean I'm ugly with them on?" She smirked. She couldn't believe they were discussing this. With her other lovers, they didn't sit around with no clothes. Then again, those men didn't live in a naked town.

Jahl's gaze ran along her body, making her keenly aware she was nude. Oddly, it didn't make her uncomfortable. In fact, it turned her on.

His gaze locked with hers. "Yes."

Her eyes widened. "Really? I'm ugly with clothes on?"

He nodded.

She wasn't sure what to say to that, until she noticed a slight twitch at the corner of his mouth. Surprised Jahl would tease her, she reached for the pillow behind her and threw it at him.

His shocked face was so funny, she laughed out loud…until the pillow hit, right in her stomach. She grasped it to her and doubled over it.

"Serena?"

Without warning, she flung it back at him. He caught it in midair. Shit, not fair. She didn't have reflexes as fast as his.

The pillow came back again, this time smacking her knees.

"By the Poetess. What is going on here?" Khaos stood by her feet, staring at both of them.

She shrugged. "Nothing."

He set down the drinks. "It doesn't look like 'nothing.'"

As he stood straight again, she flung the pillow at him. Another followed, thrown by Jahl, and she laughed at Khaos' surprised look.

He squinted at her and threw both pillows back at Jahl without looking at him then pulled an ice cube from his drink with his teeth. The ice cube was round like a little snowball the size of a cottonball.

She watched in fascination as he leaned over her, expecting a kiss, but he didn't kiss her. He lowered his head to her breast and sucked.

"Oh shit." The ice in his mouth hit her warm nipple and she jerked at the sensation, but he held her shoulders down. Desire started deep inside as she wiggled beneath him. Finally, he lifted his head and grinned diabolically. "Thought you liked to play."

She shivered at his look before nodding, anxious to see what would be next.

"Good." Khaos pulled her legs until her hips rested on the wide arm of the cushioned chair.

Jahl came over and stuffed the pillows they had thrown under her torso, relieving her back from the awkward angle Khaos had created.

She grinned at him. "Thank you."

He shook his head. "Not yet."

She loved that they were so into her she didn't have to even try to entice them. Both sported hard cocks and their eyes never left her. Jahl brought over her ambrosia and lifted her shoulders while she drank. The multilayered drink tasted extra good after all their activity.

When she was finished, Jahl moved behind her head and she looked up at him. Unable to resist touching him any longer, she stroked his cock with one hand.

His intake of breath was more than rewarding, so she continued, happy to explore every inch of him with both hands.

Khaos spread her legs and she glanced over at him. He knelt on the floor on the other side of the chair. He grinned at her, showing the ice cube in his teeth.

CHAPTER TEN

"Oh no." She tried to move her hands down to stop him, but found them both in Jahl's hand in a tight, but gentle grip that kept them locked around his cock. She snapped her gaze to him and shook her head.

He simply nodded.

Oh God. She looked at Khaos as he bent forward, but with his free hand, Jahl tilted her chin to turn her gaze to him. It reminded her of her dream, but the men were in opposite positions.

Then cold hit her wet, warm pussy and her hips moved of their own volition. She shuddered at the erotic temperature contrast.

Khaos held her legs, each thigh in one massive hand as he opened her farther and began to push the round ice cube inside her with his tongue. He blew across her wetness, sending another shiver of pleasure through her.

Then she heard the ice in Khaos' drink clink. Oh no. She tensed, waiting for the cold, but instead of the ice, his tongue lapped around her opening. She relaxed while enjoying the view of the underside of Jahl's cock.

"Ach." Another cold ice cube pressed against her opening and her hips bucked again, but Khaos held her down, leaving her helpless against the icy sensation. Then as before, he pushed the ice cube into her. Her stomach heaved with delight and what inhibitions she had, melted away.

Jahl let go of her chin and traced his finger down to her nipple, lightly twirling it.

She wanted it all, the ice, the touch, and Jahl's cock. She stared into his eyes and licked her lips in invitation.

His cock jumped in her hands and she grinned. Jahl leaned forward, his balls within range. She lifted her head and took one gently into her mouth just as another ice cube pushed into her. She moaned against the ball, rolling it over her tongue.

Jahl finally let go of her hands and she stroked him, enjoying the hard steel of his erection.

He used both hands now to tease her nipples, alternately twirling them and then kneading her whole breast.

And another ice cube pushed into her sheath. Now she welcomed them, enjoying the spear of delight as each one entered her, while rising to meet the sensations Jahl sent buzzing through her.

Khaos licked through her folds with his tongue and she gasped as he hit her clit. Jahl took the opportunity to pull away from her, and she pouted.

He moved to where Khaos knelt and looked over his shoulder. "One more."

Khaos pulled another ice cube from his drink and held it between his teeth. This time she watched as he lowered his head. When he pushed the ice cube inside her with his tongue, she moaned. He must have filled her sheath because she could feel cold water dribbling out of her pussy and between her ass cheeks, creating another erotic sensation.

Jahl put his hand on Khaos' shoulder. "That should do it."

Khaos nodded and stood, giving way to Jahl. She watched as Jahl stood between her legs and her ice-filled sheath. Now he was going to enter her? The idea both titillated and confused her. Wouldn't the cold cause his beautiful erection to shrink?

Khaos came to the side of her head. "Jahl wants to enjoy you for a long time this first time. The cold will keep him from coming too soon."

"But won't it, well, you know…"

Jahl shook his head, staring intently at her. "Not with you."

She had a difficult time believing that, but then again, she'd had a difficult time believing she was on another planet.

Khaos took Jahl's old place behind her head and stroked her hair. "If at any time you want us to stop, just tell us."

She smiled at his thoughtfulness and then looked at Jahl. He stood between her legs holding his large cock, ready to enter her, melting ice and all. She'd never been more ready. "I don't think that's going to happen."

Jahl's nostrils flared at her answer. As the head of his cock touched her opening, her sheath contracted, forcing more cold water out and down her crack. She was contemplating that strangeness when Jahl pushed forward an inch, and she sucked in a breath at the pressure in her core. He'd hit the ice balls.

Khaos' fingers moved from her hair to her neck and jaw, gently stroking. She felt pampered and excited at the same time.

Jahl watched her and she gave him a small smile. Immediately, he pushed farther.

"Oh wow." The ice moved around him and more cool water spilled from her. As Khaos' finger began to stroke her lips, she sucked it into her mouth. She'd prefer his cock, but anything would do right now. He grinned and brushed her chin with his thumb.

Jahl pulled her attention from Khaos as his thumb flicked across her clit. Spirals of need flew through her abdomen and her sheath tightened. The look on his face made her heart race. He grabbed her thighs and pushed in another inch.

She sucked in her breath. Jahl's cock was stone hard inside her and the cold ice was no match for it, making her sheath widen. She wanted more, more of him, more of Khaos. She didn't care if she was greedy.

She looked up at Khaos. "I want to taste you."

His thumb stilled and his grin disappeared. She glanced at Jahl, whose face had taken on a hardness she'd only seen once before when he'd first appeared on Earth and told one of her attackers he would be dead. There was only one word for it—driven. He was going to fuck her until she came again and again. Her heart leapt.

Khaos moved around to straddle her torso, blocking her view of Jahl, and tingles of anticipation burrowed through her.

She studied Khaos above her, his abdominal muscles almost as rigid as his cock. His strong thigh muscles tensed as he settled into a good spot on the chair, careful not to make her uncomfortable.

He finally glanced down at her. "We are here to please you in every way."

She swallowed hard as myriad images sped through her brain of her sandwiched between them on a bed, kneeling to enjoy one while the other pumped into her, or spread over the kitchen table.

Khaos looked over his shoulder. "Ready." He turned back to her, smirking, spreading his arms out to his sides. "I'm all yours."

Now that was an invitation no woman could resist. Taking his cock into her hands, she brought it to her mouth and licked around the edge of the head. Khaos' arms came down fast and he grabbed the chair back with his left hand, his smirk gone.

She looked into his eyes as she slowly encircled the head with her lips, feathering the tip with her tongue. His eyes darkened to the steel gray she loved and air whistled between his teeth.

Encouraged, she pulled more of him into her mouth, licking along the hard ridge, learning every nuance.

"Shit, Jahl. Move."

She felt more than heard Jahl's chuckle just before he pushed farther inside her. Her mouth opened of its own accord as she gasped in more air. Her sheath tensed, sucking on Jahl and the coldness within.

Not to be outdone by him, she pulled Khaos into her mouth as far as she could and sucked. His right hand buried itself in her hair and grasped the back of her head just as Jahl pushed the rest of the way inside her, plastering his warm pelvis against her cold pussy.

She moaned against the cock in her mouth and Khaos' hand behind her head tensed, but he didn't pull her toward him, letting her do what she wanted. When Jahl didn't move, she tentatively scraped her teeth along Khaos' cock as she pulled back and then sucked him in again. She glanced up at his face, his eyes were closed and his jaw tense. She smiled, loving having such a powerful man at her mercy.

At that moment, the man between her legs decided to investigate her clit. Her suction on Khaos' cock became tighter as Jahl fingered her nub as if he'd never seen it before, stroking and circling, revving her core, causing her sheath to tighten around his cock as it remained deep inside her, still and full.

"So pretty." She barely heard Jahl's quiet words over her and Khaos' breathing. That the man enjoyed the view of her clit as he played brought her tension even higher. She could feel her orgasm lapping just beyond her reach. She wanted it. She wanted them.

She grasped Khaos' ass, aware Jahl would see her hands. Digging her fingers into his hard flesh, she pulled him deeper into her mouth, tipping her head back more to accommodate his length.

Jahl moaned behind him as Khaos growled. "My love, you play with fire."

She wanted to tell him she was an expert with fire, but the thought flew away as his hand left the back of her head and squeezed her breast. He held the globe in his hand while his finger and thumb pinched her hardened nipple.

Her hips tried to move against Jahl, but he held her to him and his fingers stopped exploring. Instead, he made deliberate circles against her clit.

Her body strained toward her orgasm as delight built all over. She rocked her head against the cock in her mouth, the same way she wished Jahl would rock into her, but he didn't, instead holding her still as he stroked her higher.

She wrapped her legs around Jahl and squeezed Khaos' ass harder, her eyes closing as she focused on the sensations in her mouth and clit. Then Khaos' cock pulsed against her tongue, her only warning before he came inside her mouth. She swallowed as he shouted and her orgasm burst through her, pushing her higher as every nerve ending screamed in pleasure. Jahl pressed his thumb against her clit, sustaining the waves of extreme satisfaction as her sheath clenched his cock.

Finally, Jahl removed his thumb, and she became aware of her jaw being stroked. She loosened her mouth and opened her eyes.

Khaos grinned down at her as he pulled his hips back, his cock leaving her mouth completely. His gaze turned tender as he ran his knuckles over her cheek. "Thank you."

Her eyes widened. He was thanking her? She didn't have a chance to say anything before he moved off her. She bit down to keep from whining at the loss of his body. When had she become so selfish?

Jahl squeezed her thighs and she looked up at him. He was still inside her, filling her and staying absolutely still. The man had to be made of granite not to have come. She felt a new appreciation for him fill her heart. While she was being selfish, he was anything but.

Khaos distracted her as he knelt beside her. He brushed her hair away from her eyebrows. "Are you ready for more?"

She moved her gaze back to Jahl, who stared intently at her, his deep-blue eyes almost black. Her gut told her he would leave her alone if she was done. Even if she felt that way, she couldn't do that to him. But she didn't feel that way. She wanted more. She wanted to feel him fill her with his own joy. He seemed to experience so little of it.

She gazed into his eyes. "I want more, Jahl. I want you coming inside me."

His chest muscles tensed at her words and his fingers pressed a bit harder on her thighs, but he didn't say anything, just gazed at her.

When he lowered his eyes to look at her breasts, she expected him to start the movement that would bring them to orgasm, but he didn't. He simply stared at her. How could he be so patient? She certainly wasn't. Her nipples were hardening again just from his stare.

She swept her hands beneath her breasts and lightly rubbed her thumbs against her hard nubs. They were more sensitive than she'd ever felt them and tiny flashes of excitement started in her belly.

Jahl's gaze flew to her face and she licked her lips. He watched her, as still as a statue, as if he couldn't move. But she needed him to. She glanced at Khaos, who remained at her side, a small grin on his face. He understood what she was doing.

With no interruption from that quarter, she refocused on Jahl. Leaving one of her breasts alone, she licked her finger before sucking on it. Jahl's whole body tensed, but his hips still didn't move. Damn ice.

Very well then. She moved both hands over her breasts, down across her stomach until her fingers brushed his thighs. Gently, she touched where his cock entered her opening. His eyes closed and his thigh muscles moved, but his pelvis remained stationary.

How the hell was he supposed to come if he didn't move? She couldn't help her grin when the answer came to her. He held fast to her thighs, but there was nothing he could do to stop her from moving her inner muscles. He may think she needed time to recover, but she was more than ready for him. It was time to prove it.

She moved two of her fingers to her clit and began a light rub against that very sensitive part of her. The erotic feelings immediately lit and her sheath contracted against Jahl's cock.

His eyes flew open and she grinned, but didn't stop her movement. Her muscles tensed again and she moaned, loving the feel of him inside. She looked over at Khaos, but his head was turned as he watched her fingers while she played with herself. That in itself ratcheted up her excitement and she squeezed again.

Jahl watched her fingers as if mesmerized. She wanted him to move, not watch. Moving her free hand back to her breast, she let her pants out, no longer caring if Toni woke up. She wanted Jahl. She wanted him now. She pulled at her nipple, breaking his focus and he finally reacted. A low growl formed somewhere deep in his chest before he clasped her thighs and pushed her legs just an inch wider before he gradually pulled out.

Cool water followed him, soaking her and the chair, but she didn't care. All she wanted was for him to come back. He slowly brought his hips toward her again, sinking his solid cock into her until the hair above pressed against her mons.

Her hands fell to the side as the sensations of his cock heated her. "Yes."

Jahl's jaw was tight but he didn't stop. He pulled back again and pushed in, back and in, a slow rhythm that had her desire climbing. She was too close, her playing with herself having brought her to the edge. She didn't want to come, afraid he would stop.

Khaos leaned over and kissed her. A deep, erotic kiss with his tongue mimicking Jahl's cock. She grasped his head to her, sucking on him, trying to stop the inevitable, but it hit anyway. Her sheath contracted around Jahl's pumping cock, forcing him to push harder as she cried into Khaos' mouth, wanting it and yet not. With the little sanity she had, she pulled her lips from his and managed one word around her panting breaths. "More."

Whether Jahl heard or not didn't matter because he kept pumping into her, his rhythm increasing, completely controlled. Her body started to rock against him as his strokes turned more powerful. He never stopped looking at her, his nostrils flaring, his thighs straining as he thrust faster and faster.

Her body having not come completely down from the last orgasm, didn't take long to rev up again. As she moved back and forth within the large chair, Khaos stood watching her, watching Jahl as he slammed into her harder, hitting her clit.

She needed him to know it was okay to let go. "Yes. Yes. Yes." Her hands curled into themselves as her body rocked, Jahl's hands securing her against him, not missing a single beat of the buildup. Her body tensed and she felt the titillating wisps of satisfaction coming. She didn't fight it this time. She let it come, the tiny hints of completion growing bigger, sweeping over her, engulfing every part of her body. She peaked. Throwing her head back, she screamed her pleasure.

Jahl yelled, his body stopping as he came inside her, delaying her come down. His hips rocked against her, though he never left her, just short pumps as he released all he had.

She opened her eyes to find Khaos looking at her, a wide smile on his face. She turned her head to look at Jahl, who was just opening his eyes. When he focused, he reached down and wrapped his arms around her, pulling her to a sitting position on the arm of the overstuffed chair. He held her tight, but not too tight and she wrapped her arms around him.

Khaos stepped next to Jahl and she reached out her hand. He took it and squeezed. For the first time she contemplated what it would be like to have a life with these two men who loved her by their own admission and just proved it. There were so many positives to the thought.

A banging coming from the hallway broke her reverie.

"Hey! Anyone out there? Is everyone okay?" Toni's voice filtered through the door.

Serena flushed and buried her face against Jahl's chest. His deep baritone rumbled from beneath her cheek. "We're fine. I'll let you out in the morning."

"Serena?"

Khaos used his fingers to move her chin. "You better answer her or we'll not have any peace all night."

She swallowed hard. "I'm fine."

There was silence and Serena had just begun to relax when Toni spoke again. "Don't do anything I wouldn't do."

Serena laughed before she yelled back. "That pretty much leaves my options wide open."

Toni chuckled and then there was silence. She looked up at Jahl. "Wow." She moved her gaze to Khaos. "That was wonderful." She yawned, unable to help herself. "Sorry, I didn't think I was tired."

She felt the chuckle in Jahl's chest but when she looked up, no smile lifted his lips. The man really needed to smile.

"I think we have tired you out." His gaze was soft, that special one only she received. He lowered his head and kissed her. A soft, loving kiss that made her heart melt, even as he left her body. He stepped away, holding her on the chair.

Khaos moved forward. "I think it's time we put you to bed."

She nodded. Lowering her feet to the floor, she hopped off and her knees gave way. Both men had her before she hit the ground and she chuckled. "Guess that took more out of me than I realized."

Khaos looked at Jahl. "I think some ambrosia may be helpful."

Jahl nodded. "I'll get it. You put her to bed."

Khaos effortlessly lifted her into his arms and strode to the bedroom. When they entered, the glass ceiling let in the moonlight, but it was a lot lighter than the night before.

She blinked at the brightness. "Guess we don't need a light to find the bed. With that bright a moon, I can see why you may darken the ceiling at night."

Khaos set her down on the bed and sat next to her. "Tonight is a double moon night."

"What?"

"There are two moons that circle Eden, Selene and Bendis. I know there is some pattern as to when we have a two moon night, but I've never paid much attention."

She made to stand, but he pulled her down.

"Wait. You need nourishment after all we did."

She put her free hand on her hip. "I'll tell you the same thing I told Jahl. I'm not delicate. I can handle a lot."

Khaos' face tensed and his eyes started to turn silver again. "That is why you are our chosen one."

She turned away, unable to handle that particular look from him. "I know you and Jahl have said this, but I need to go home in a couple more days. They expect me. I can't stay here forever."

He took her hand. "Yes, you can. You can visit your family anytime you want after we have bonded."

She faced him. "I thought you said I couldn't go home unless you and Jahl were here. So if one of you is gone, I wouldn't be able to leave."

"That's true. It takes two men with chips to open a portal. So as long as both of us are here, you can visit your family."

"Chips?"

"Yes. Jahl and I have the portal chips. They are the technology of the Crius and allow us to travel from here to anywhere."

She crinkled her forehead. "Then why didn't you portal Sandale directly to Haven?"

Khaos swallowed as guilt and grief seized his chest. He opened his mouth and took a deep breath. "Because we believe that Naralina has developed technology that allows them to track portal openings beyond the walls of the city. If we transported anyone directly to Haven, it could put the whole colony in danger. Once Naralina discovered there was one colony, they wouldn't stop until they were certain there weren't more."

"Because Naralina might attack you because they think you are criminals?"

"Yes." Her understanding of their culture pleased him.

"So if you were to bring me home, we would first have to travel by foot away from Loraleaf." At his nod, she continued. "So if I had to go home every month, as long as you two were here, you would take me, despite the danger in the jungle?"

He nodded, though the thought of subjecting her to such dangers had his gut tensing.

"How long could I stay?"

Jahl walked in, carrying three glasses. "That depends on whether we are with you or not. If we are with you, a week or more. If we aren't, then only a day."

Khaos' eyebrows rose at that pronouncement, and she had the feeling they were making this up as they went along. She'd have to talk to someone else about this. Maybe Theron. Then again, probably not, if what Jahl thought was true.

Jahl handed her a glass.

She eagerly took it. She may not be delicate, but she was damn thirsty. She really did love this juice. The spicy aftertaste between every fruity, nutty sip was heaven. When she finished, Jahl took the glass away and set it on a side table. He strode back to the bed and sat on the other side of her, taking her other hand.

Here she sat completely nude with two naked hunks holding hands under the light of two moons in a bedroom on the largest bed ever made. She shook her head. It was all so surreal.

Khaos lifted her hand and kissed the back of it, then Jahl did the same. Uh-oh, this looked serious.

Khaos gazed at her, his eyes no longer the silver she dreaded. "You know we want you to be our agapayto, our beloved in body and soul. You should also know that it is completely up to you. Though we chose you and have waited six Eden years for you, we cannot and will not force you. It must be your decision."

She couldn't believe her relief at those simple words. "Thank you. I was afraid you would try to coerce me into it."

Khaos' grin was lopsided. "Well, I wouldn't say seduction is out." He winked and she couldn't help laughing. "But it's against Dickinson Law to make you bond with anyone. Though we may be considered lawbreakers because we chose to leave our homes in Naralina, we still follow the laws of this planet because they have been critical to our survival."

Serena disengaged her hand from each man. "You need to understand something. On Earth, when we find someone we like, we get to know them. We go on dates. We do things each other likes. We talk to learn about each other's pasts and current interests and all this takes time. Lots of time."

Jahl stood and looked at her. "We already know you. You create explosions for science fiction movies because you like the idea of life on other planets. You refuse to work on any movie that portrays an historical war. You go to large events where humans dress up as aliens. You love pancakes and don't like champagne. You would rather stay home and watch a movie and eat popcorn than go rock climbing. And you miss having a pet but the people who own the building your home is in won't let you have one."

She stared at him, an eerie shiver going up her spine. "Exactly how much following me around have you done in six years?"

Khaos moved from the bed and knelt down before her. Oh no, he wasn't going to propose, was he? She placed her hand over her chest.

"Serena, we would never watch you in bed or in the bathroom, if that's what concerns you."

Hell, she hadn't even thought that far. "Well, that's a relief."

Jahl put his hand on Khaos' shoulder. "We only checked on you once a month unless Khaos sensed something traumatic."

Over the last six years? She hadn't been fired or physically hurt that she could remember. She did have one bad breakup though. She swallowed at the thought they may have seen that. "Then you must know how important my family is to me."

Jahl threw his hands up and walked to the window.

"What?"

Khaos laid his hand on her knee. "Actually, we didn't. We only check in for an hour or so before our duties here at Loraleaf claimed our attention. Sandale had the most time and related what he learned, but while he had a normal family with three fathers and five brothers, he was aware of our feelings about that. He never said anything."

"If he knew." Jahl spoke over his shoulder.

"Okay, so you know a lot about me, but I know next to nothing about you both." That wasn't exactly true because over the last four days she'd figured out quite a bit.

Khaos smiled. "We would be happy to help you learn, but you have to understand a woman who is not bonded is always in danger of being stolen."

What? "This is the first I'm hearing about this." She looked accusingly at Jahl. "I thought I was safe here."

He turned toward them. "You are, within Loraleaf." His gaze flicked away. He hid something.

"But what? What aren't you telling me?"

Jahl looked at Khaos.

"What? Is it that bad?"

Khaos squeezed her thigh. "We don't know exactly. The lawbreakers have been leaving strange markings in the jungle and there was one between here and Haven. They have never come so close to us before, so we are concerned about a future attack."

"So that's why Theron was spending so much time working on a type of explosion. But with all the abilities you have within Loraleaf, couldn't you protect it?"

Jahl nodded. "Yes. But our primary concern is you. The lawbreakers have no women. They would not care about Dickinson Law."

She shivered at that pronouncement. Going home was looking better and better.

Khaos stood and took both her hands. "You need not worry about that. We have been here for six years and they have yet to find us. We just want to bond with you so we can be sure you are safe. No man on Eden will touch a bonded woman in an intimate way."

Yeah, he hoped. She wasn't so sure.

"Enough talk." Jahl walked over and scooped her up from the edge of the bed and Khaos let go of her hands.

"Hey."

"You need to sleep."

She rolled her eyes. Sometimes Jahl could be such a Neanderthal. "Okay, okay, I'll sleep."

"Good." He gently lay her down on the bed. No sooner had her head touched the pillow than Khaos climbed in too and lay against her side. Jahl followed suit. Sandwiched between them she wasn't going anywhere without them, then again, why would she want to…tonight? She rolled to her side and put her head on Jahl's massive shoulder. Khaos moved against her back and pushed his leg between hers.

No one at home would ever believe this. Little Serena Upton sleeping with two gorgeous naked hunks who loved her. She was either crazy or had died and gone to heaven. Content to be in heaven for a while, she closed her eyes. "Good night."

"Good night." Both men's response at the same time made her smile. She could be in worse predicaments.

CHAPTER ELEVEN

Though they were in the meal room, Jahl kept his voice low, not wanting to wake Serena. "We're losing her."

"I know." Khaos put down his cup of kafez. "I had hoped after last night, after she experienced what we can offer her, she would be more open to bonding."

"It's not enough." He took a sip of the hot amber liquid. "She wants to know us."

Khaos smirked. "I don't want to know us."

"Yeah."

They sat in silence. Their first plan hadn't worked as they'd hoped, though just the memory of being inside Serena had Jahl's cock hardening. They had to find a way to convince her to stay.

"She wants to leave the day after next." Khaos' eyes were silver.

Jahl tensed. "Will she?"

Khaos continued to stare at nothing. Finally, he shook his head. "I can't sense anything. That must mean she hasn't decided."

"Then we still have a chance." Jahl's body relaxed. "We need to give her whatever she wants." He just wasn't sure what that was exactly.

Khaos took another sip of his kafez. "I have to go on patrol today. I promised Konala I would. I will get back as soon as I can, but I think you should plan to stay by her side all day. We have very little time to convince her to stay and need to be with her every minute."

"Agreed." It was good to have Khaos back. At least they could work together to keep their beloved. "She said it usually takes a long time to get to know each other. How can we make that shorter?"

"I don't know. We could use a Kindred of Mind to perhaps help, but I don't think that's what she wants."

"Then what?"

Khaos looked sternly at him. "She wants to know our pasts, our interests, what we like to do. You should show her your bali."

"But she's a woman."

"So? She wants to know you. Your expertise in bali is part of who you are. You trained hard to be so good. Then show her around Loraleaf. Point out the places you made with your ability."

"I can do that. Do you think it will help?"

"From what I've seen of Earth relationships, that seems to help." Khaos finished the rest of his kafez and moved to the sink.

"What about you? What will you show her?"

The brother of his heart grinned. "What she wants. I'll show her fun."

Jahl shook his head as Khaos chuckled softly and headed out of the room. He wished Sandale had written down instructions on how to woo an Earth woman. He was always scribbling and reading. It would have been nice if he'd left a book for them to follow.

Footsteps in the living area had him looking up.

"Hey, Jahl, fancy meeting you here." Toni's loud voice had him wincing.

"Serena is still asleep."

Toni headed straight for the pot of kafez, her new clothing making look out of place. "Really? Did you guys wear her out?"

Serena's insistence that she wasn't delicate came to mind. "No. But if she wants to sleep, she should."

Toni poured herself a cup of the hot liquid and sat across from him. The bruise on her cheek was almost gone, just a light yellowish tinge marked the spot. He was pleased she healed so well. She would make a good addition to a filoz.

She was Serena's best friend, so that meant she knew Serena like he knew Khaos. Maybe he did have a Serena instruction book after all. "What do we need to do to make Serena love us?"

Toni spit kafez across the table.

"Why did you do that?" Jahl rose and grabbed a napkin. "Here."

She took it from him and wiped her face. "Because of your question. You can't make someone love you."

Jahl shook his head. "I know that. I mean what would make her more disposed to love us?"

Toni studied him. "You really love her, don't you?"

"Yes." More than he could verbalize. "As does Khaos."

"Personally, I think she is very lucky. You two are so into her. You're not going to like what I have to say, but I'll give it to you straight. She's very attached to her family. Even if she were on Earth and met a guy who loved her, she would want her family's approval. Again I say a guy, not two."

Jahl's chest constricted. Scrat.

"But even if she got over the need to have her family approve of both of you, she would need time to get to know you, learn what makes you tick, what makes you happy, what makes you angry. My best advice to you is to let her go home. Let her miss you a little. Then show up and see if she wants to spend more time with you. That's how most guys do it on Earth. You know, take a break."

"That is not allowed."

"What isn't allowed?"

"We can't let her go back unless she is bonded to us. It is the only thing that will ensure her safety and ours."

"What do you mean?" Toni's voice grew loud. "Will the criminals follow her?"

"No." Jahl's own voice had risen in response and he consciously lowered it. "The lawbreakers can't follow because they don't have portal chips. Only those who leave Naralina of their own accord have them."

Toni blew air out between her lips. "Well, that's a relief."

"It is for our safety too because we do not want Earth to know we exist. It is for Serena's safety because if she tells anyone and they don't believe her, she could be considered unbalanced and put into an institution."

"Oh shit. You're right." Toni took a sip of her kafez. "But if Serena promised not to tell anyone, then everyone would be fine."

Jahl shook his head. "She could promise, but eventually she would have to share with someone. It's a woman's nature, but the bonding deadens the need to tell."

Toni eyed him skeptically. "If that's the case, then you have a problem."

That was an understatement. He had many problems, but Serena was the only one he would focus on. Talking to Toni hadn't helped as much as he'd hoped. Rising, he put his cup in the sink.

"Hey, Jahl, for what it's worth. I'm rooting for you."

He nodded and walked out. If he wanted Serena to fall in love with him, he needed to start now. Striding into the bedroom, he found the bed empty. He retraced his steps to the living area, bathroom and even checked Toni's room but all were empty.

Troubled now, he returned to the bedroom and noticed the door to the new balcony was open. Stepping through, he found Serena, wrapped in her blue table cover, gazing down below.

Relief flooded him until he looked down and saw Theron and Rekah talking. Jealousy shot through him like a meteor, causing his voice to sound harsh. "Would you rather be with them?"

Startled, Serena spun and lost her balance. She hit the side railing and tilted.

Jahl's heart skipped a beat as he sprung forward and grabbed her back from the sure brink of falling. He crushed her to him, his heart racing as he took deep breaths.

"Jll."

"Hmm." He closed his eyes at how close he'd just come to losing her.

"Jlll, I cn brth."

"What?" He opened his eyes and leaned back to look at her.

She took a deep breath and scowled. "I said I can't breathe."

"Oh." He cupped her face and kissed her.

She pulled away. "Hey, it's okay. It's not like I was going over the railing. Relax."

"You were. We can't lose you."

She pulled out of his arms. "Jahl, exactly why can't you lose me? It's not like I'm the sun that keeps you warm or the food that keeps you alive."

He shook his head. "You are more. You're our hope."

Instead of smiling, she scowled harder. What was wrong? He was simply being truthful.

"I'm sure there was more to your life before you discovered I existed."

No, there wasn't. Before they'd found Serena they had simply planned their escape from Naralina. Before that was basically survival, but something in her stance told him she wouldn't want to hear that. "Come." He held out his hand. "You must be hungry."

She folded her arms over her breasts. "Why? Because you two wore me out last night?"

His lips quirked at her defensive stance. Always denying her fragility was endearing. "No, because I need to eat breakfast and don't want to eat alone."

She unfolded her arms. "Okay, I can accept that."

She reached for his hand and her stomach growled. He turned away so she wouldn't see the amusement in his eyes. For a woman who had been loved thoroughly last night, she seemed to be in a dour mood.

Careful to keep his strides smaller, he led her through the new door off their room to the kitchen, which was now empty.

"Oh, I smell coffee." She pushed past him to the counter.

He leaned back against the cold box, understanding of her sour mood dawned. "It's called kafez."

She was already pulling down a cup and pouring the dark liquid in. Good thing he'd made a large amount.

"Do you have any sugar? I couldn't find any the other morning."

"No."

She turned at that. "Why not? Are you afraid you'll gain weight?"

He would have been insulted by her assumption, but the way her gaze flowed over his body made him feel complimented. "No. Sugar is a very rare commodity on this planet. At one point in our history we grew sugar cane but that was before the Fullamush. There are very few places left on the planet that can grow it, and they do so in small quantities."

"What was the Fullamush?" She picked up her kafez and sipped, her eyes closing for a moment before she focused on him.

He needed to remember to bring her a cup of kafez in the morning. "It was a period in our planet's history when the cities fought each other over women. We almost destroyed ourselves. It was thanks to the women and our first High Poetess that we were able to find peace and rebuild."

Serena's eyes glittered with curiosity and she sat at the table, her kafez forgotten. "How did they do that?"

He opened the cold box and pulled out henny eggs. If they were going to talk, like she wanted, he would cook too. "They gathered in one place and refused to have sex with any man until the heads of all the cities sat down and figured out how to get along."

"But how did they gather in one place? Isn't it dangerous to move from city to city with the criminals in the jungle?"

He pulled out the necessary pan and ingredients and broke the eggs into a bag. "No, because the cities use the portals. Every city has a security force that monitors all portal openings within its walls, so the women found a few men to help portal them all to the High Hall of Naralina."

She took a sip of kafez, her eyes wide. "So Naralina is like the capitol of Eden?"

He shook his head. "No. Every city serves as the Kif of Eden for two years and then it changes to another."

"Was that part of the peace agreement?"

He nodded, pleased she was so quick to take an interest in their planet. That had to be a good sign. "The women chose Naralina's High Hall because of its location and structure. It was forged by the Crius and has always been used as a place to keep what is most precious, even in the dark days at the beginning of the planets' cultivation. It sits on the peak of the mountain that is the base of Naralina."

"The Crius? Oh, that's right, they were the aliens who brought humans to Eden."

"Yes. They have never returned."

She took a sip of her kafez before asking another question. "So what happened once the women went on strike? Couldn't the men storm the High Hall?"

He added the other ingredients and shook the bag of eggs. "Yes, they could and they did as we had no Dickinson Law then to protect women, just Criuson Law. But the walls and doors held. Since the Hall had been created by the Crius, even the portals wouldn't work to transport someone inside. My ancestors didn't have a Kindred of Eden like myself, who could move stone and wood, only those who could control live nature, though in truth, I don't know if even I could get in. They tried wind and water too, but nothing could break the doors open."

She had turned in her chair and faced him, her kafez cupped in her hands. "So what happened?"

Jahl poured his mixture into the hot pan and carefully stirred. He'd never been a storyteller, but Serena's rapt attention had him prolonging the story. "Then the Kindred of Mind and Heart tried to persuade the women to open the doors, but the women were strong and had banded together. It is said that as soon as one woman started for the door, others would bring her back. Since the men outside were fighting amongst themselves, it didn't occur to them to work together."

Serena smiled. "I think I like your female ancestors."

He flipped over the breakfast in the pan and nodded. "I do too. They were strong against all odds. The ratio of men to women back then was close to twenty to one."

"It's larger now, right?"

"Yes. At least in Naralina we are at about a hundred to one, but that probably went down when those of us left to create Loraleaf, and more recently, Haven." He scowled at the thought that perhaps in leaving, he'd made it easier for his father to build his reputation. The man probably claimed to have exiled his worthless rogue son.

"So the women held strong against the men and…"

He held back a smirk at her impatience. "Then the women did something similar to the men. When a woman bonds with her agapaytos, a physical and spiritual bond occurs. It is different for every yenea, a filoz with a bonded woman. For some, the men and woman can feel each other's emotions, for others it is thoughts, for some it is energy, or it can be what the other imagines or dreams. There is a list of known bond connections. Our discoverists studied it for a while and then moved on to more interesting subjects, but one thing they were absolutely sure about was the bonding had less to do with the men's abilities and more to do with their personalities and how they melded with their woman."

Serena looked down at her cup and didn't say a word.

It was a lot to take in, so he finished making their breakfast and dished it out, setting it before her.

At the steaming plate, she snapped out of her reverie and looked at him hesitantly. "So if I bonded with you and Khaos, I wouldn't suddenly be able to manipulate stone or see into the future?"

"No, you wouldn't."

She sighed. "That would have been a nice perk."

That she thought about bonding with them and wanted their abilities had hope rising in his chest. Khaos was right. She liked it when they talked.

"What is this?" She had cut a piece of the egg mixture and held it on her fork.

"It's an omelet."

She looked at it and then at him. "It's a little different than the ones we have at home."

"It probably tastes different too. Though much of our food is similar to Earth's, we do have plants that are not found on Earth."

She shrugged and popped the bite of food into her mouth. He watched as she thoroughly tasted the eggy bit. She had just swallowed when she closed her eyes. "Mmmm." She opened them again. "I love this. You all cook this multi-flavored food, which has another whole taste that hits after a person swallows. It is amazing. Is it a spice, a technique, a food, or what?"

He shrugged. "I don't know. I just cook what I learned to cook, mostly from…Sandale."

She reached her hand across the table and laid it on his. "I know it's hard to talk about him."

He grasped her hand. "I want to talk about him. I don't want him to be erased from memory." He scowled. "That is my concern with this memorial. If everyone feels comfort by saying goodbye, then they will forget him."

She shook her head. "No. Those close to him, like you and Khaos, will always remember Sandale. In fact, I think you and Khaos should celebrate his life every year, maybe on his birthday. My younger sister still celebrates her first cat. Luckily, she doesn't do it for all the other animals she's owned." Serena rolled her eyes. "But my dad also celebrates his late dad's birthday with his mom, so they can spend a day reminiscing."

He couldn't help but notice how lively she became when she talked about her family. He wished, deep down in his soul, that someday that would happen when she talked about him and Khaos. "I like that idea. We will do that."

"Good." She pulled her hand from his grasp and he reluctantly let it go.

She did have to eat. He and Khaos should develop a large meal plan for her. If they were going to be as active together as he hoped, he didn't want her to get skinny. He'd seen a few women in Naralina who had obviously been well sexed but not as well fed. He cut into his cooling omelet and lifted a forkful.

"So what happened with the women?" Serena brought him back to his story.

He took the bite from his fork and chewed.

"You did that on purpose."

He smiled inside at her astuteness.

She pouted for a moment then took another bite of her food. Good, she needed to eat.

He started to cut another piece of egg when her hand shot out and stopped him. "Please, tell me what the women did to force the men to make peace."

He couldn't resist a plea from her. He set his fork back down. "Most of the women had bonded. The only ones who hadn't were the women from the Pleasure Temples, at least that's what we call them in Naralina. I think they have different names for them in other cities. It was actually these women who figured out what could be done. Since the men were fighting over having women, these women of the Temples, we call them Cythera or Cys for short, decided to have sex with the bonded women."

"No." Serena held a bite of food halfway to her mouth. She had no clue how seductive she looked with her eyes wide and her mouth slightly open.

"Yes. The bonded women thought it the perfect solution for a number of reasons. First, their men were so busy fighting a war, they had no time to pleasure their women. Second, having sex with another woman wouldn't be cheating on their beloved. And third, the women of Eden were so sought after by men that they'd never had sex with another woman and were curious. Personally, I think that was the deciding factor."

Serena took a sip of her kafez. "So they had sex with the women from the Pleasure Temples, who were experts in what pleasured a woman."

He nodded. Just thinking about that part of the story had his cock hardening. Not sure how Serena would feel about his erection, he took another bite of egg and concentrated on his food.

"So what happened when they had sex?"

He waited until he'd finished chewing, prolonging her interest. Her focus on him could be addictive. "Legend has it, they enjoyed it so much, they decided to really make the men feel what they were missing, so the giant female orgy went on for days."

She swallowed her final bite. "Days?"

"Yes, and when they opened the door to the High Hall, they found the men had masturbated so much, they were sore."

Serena giggled. "I guess the women must have communicated how much the men were missing pretty well."

"Before they came out, they received a written agreement from all the cities to lay down their arms and come to a peace table. The women actually brokered the peace and with the help of one of the women who had been visiting from Earth, they also created the Dickinson Law."

Serena sat back and eyed him skeptically. "Is that a true story?"

He shrugged. "Who's to say? It's the story we are all told once we are considered ready for the Pleasure Temples. It is even taught in our schools."

"What happened to the men who helped the women? Were they killed? Did they guard the outside or were they inside with the women? Oh boy, if they were inside I bet they were killed."

Jahl stood and took their empty plates to the sink. "Actually, they weren't."

"Why not?" Serena stood and poured the last of the kafez in both their cups. She stood with her cup in her hands, waiting.

"Because the men were the moral tribunal of Naralina and had remained celibate the entire time they were inside the High Hall."

"Wow." She took a sip of kafez. "But how did the men outside know this tribunal had been good?"

He bent and loaded the dishwasher with their dishes before turning to face her. As he did, he caught her staring at his ass. Khaos was right. They needed to spend every moment with her. "It was the bonding that saved them. Many of the bonded mates could feel what was happening inside the hall and they came to the tribunal's defense."

"So what is this tribunal?"

He took a gulp of the lukewarm liquid, his throat sore from so much talking. "It is a panel of three men who take an oath to never search out a chosen one. They judge each man based on his actions and determine if he should be invested with a portal chip."

"And what if they decide he's not deserving of a chip?"

Jahl didn't meet her gaze. Knowing his father's secret made it hard to answer. "He continues with his education and his training in whatever field he wishes to spend his life in, but he can't travel to other cities without two men who can open a portal, nor can he ever search out a chosen one on Earth. He can enjoy the Pleasure Temples as long as he wishes so he is not denied female companionship, he's just denied a beloved."

Serena finished her kafez and lowered her cup to the sink. "So who determines when you go before the tribunal? Do you need a sponsor? Does your family set it up? How did you do it when you were no longer with your family?"

Jahl held up his hands. "Too many questions and too much talking. I want to show you some of my favorite places in Loraleaf today."

Serena's mouth opened and her eyes widened but nothing came out. He took advantage of the silence to finish his own cup and added it, along with hers, to the dishwasher. "So will you come?"

"You're going to spend the day with me?"

He nodded. "Yes. Or did you want to do something else?" His immediate thought was Theron and he fisted his hands.

"No." She stepped up to him and placed her palms on his chest. Reaching up on tiptoe, she gave him a kiss on the cheek. "Thank you. You've been so busy, I didn't think we'd have any time together before I left. Just let me get on my shoes."

Before she left? His fists tightened. If he had his way that wouldn't be for a very, very long time.

* * * * *

She had a wonderful time with Jahl. He still didn't smile, but he was definitely more relaxed. He showed her a beautiful treetop hideaway he used when he wanted to gather his thoughts. Not wanting to risk her falling and breaking her neck, he'd simply had one of the dead vines bring her up.

The abilities of the men in Loraleaf did take some adjusting to, but she would be the first to attest they were pretty convenient. Jahl had pointed out a few kindred birthmarks, even stopping one man to show her the Kindred of Mind birthmark on the man's ass. He'd had an awesome ass, but then again, they all did. Jahl's was special though. She'd been able to watch that piece of his anatomy as he climbed up the tree to his perch before he brought her up with the vine. Yeah, his was special.

She wandered to the fridge to see if Khaos had left any ambrosia and found something else. Opening the bottle, she smelled it. Hmm, must be another type of ale. Taking the bottle with her, she walked to her favorite chair, made even more favorite after last night. She grinned. Toni was right, she was lucky.

Of course, she was also alone. Khaos wasn't back yet and Jahl had to leave for some kind of dispute, which tickled her. After seeing Jahl knock down at least a dozen men in his bali exhibition, she could just imagine how he handled a dispute. Knocking two heads together like he had in the bar brawl was the picture that came to mind.

She took a sip of the ale. It wasn't bad, though a bit heavier than the last one. She glanced toward the hallway. She hadn't seen Toni all day. It would be wonderful if Toni found a filoz here. If her friend was going to stay, she'd rather she'd be with men who adored the ground she walked on rather than in some Pleasure Palace. Toni had spent enough time in places she didn't belong. Either way, it would be difficult going home. Maybe Toni could have someone bring her to Earth for a visit now and then.

She would miss more than Toni. She'd miss Loraleaf, and wouldn't be able to talk to anyone about it. Khaos and Jahl may want her to become their wife, but that was not where she was with them yet and she didn't see that happening before she had to go home. If she didn't show up for the reunion, her family would freak. There was no way she'd put them through that. Maybe Khaos and Jahl could visit her.

She perked up. Why not? She could take a week off here and there and they could visit. She'd have to suggest that. Jahl certainly hadn't minded talking about Loraleaf, but the minute she mentioned his family, he went silent. It was so frustrating. Except that one eruption of information about his father burning his birthmark... She shivered. He hadn't said anything else about them. Even when she'd asked how he'd come to know Sandale and Khaos he'd been vague, his answers too short. He said they met at school.

She took another sip of ale. The whole idea that Eden existed was still an overwhelming concept. Jahl had been open about Naralina, its oligarchy government, how they found their chosen ones, and the two sets of law, but that was only one city. He said there were many cities, though he hadn't visited any.

She had just wrapped her mind around the fact she was on a different planet, but she still had the issue of Jahl's feelings for her. She may have learned a lot today, but she didn't learn anything else about Jahl. No, that wasn't true. She stared at the bottle of ale. To figure out Jahl, she had to read between the lines. It was what he didn't talk about or didn't say that was the key to who he was.

That was it. She put down her bottle of ale. Jahl would talk about anything but himself.

A noise at the front door had her standing.

"Serena?" Khaos' voice sounded like he was laughing.

"Yes?" A strange scratching sound came from the entryway that reminded her of one of Jaelene's dogs. She headed there to investigate. She just reached the archway when a creature on the floor peeked its nose around the corner. "Oh my God, it's a welchet."

At her voice, the animal spun around and ran. That's when she noticed the white bandage on one of its hind legs.

Khaos came through the arch. "He's for you." He didn't let her answer but swept her against him with one arm and kissed her soundly. When he finished ravishing her mouth, she grabbed his shoulder to keep upright. Shit, the man could kiss.

When she had her balance again, she noticed the leash in Khaos' other hand. "You caught a welchet? For me?" Her heart thudded at such a gift. Her sister was the one with animals, bringing them home or receiving them as gifts. No one had ever given her one.

He laughed as he tugged on the leash. "Yes, he's for you. Come here, you troublesome oaf. Your mistress wants to see what you look like."

The welchet resisted the pull on the leash with all his little might, but he was no match for Khaos' strength. She sat on the floor and scratched her fingers against it. "Come on. I won't hurt you."

Her fingers caught its attention and the welchet sniffed the floor until it reached her. With her other hand, she stroked its back. It started a high-pitched gurgling sound. She kept her voice low. "Why is it crying?"

Khaos stood with his arms crossed, looking down at her. "He's not crying. That's the sound they make when they're small. See his fake tusks? They've barely started growing."

She rubbed the small animal's back as she peered at his chin. Two little white nubs protruded out no longer than his fur. "Oh, he's adorable."

"He's lucky. Konala sensed his distress as we were out on patrol. His mom left him when he couldn't keep up. Konala says he has a broken leg."

She glanced at the leg with the bandage and could see there was a splint on it. "Poor baby."

Khaos chuckled. "That 'poor baby' was neck deep in feroon dung. He crawled in there to eat the undigested vegetable scraps and got stuck. Konala cleaned him up and bandaged his leg, but had nowhere to put him, so I asked if you could have him."

Slowly, so as not to startle her new pet, she rose and let him go back to sniffing the floor, rubbing his nubs against it. She turned to Khaos. "Thank you for thinking of me. I love him."

He opened his arms in invitation and she stepped into his embrace. "I'm always thinking of you."

His words seeped into her chest and she raised her arms to link around his neck. He lowered his lips to hers once again, this time giving her a sweet, loving kiss that had her melting.

A loud crash startled them both out of the moment.

"Now what?" Khaos moved around her to look into the living room where the welchet had wandered. He shook his head. "Jahl is not going to be happy about that, little one."

She peeked around Khaos to find the welchet on a side table next to the couch where he had knocked off a carving and broken it. "Wally, no. Off." She pointed to the floor and the little guy seemed to get the message, but when he jumped, he whimpered. "Oh, you poor thing." Carefully, she picked him up.

"Wally?"

"Yes. There's a character in a movie I like that was always cleaning up trash. So I'm going to call him Wally."

"Then Wally it is." Khaos smiled, that eye-crinkling smile that always made her catch her breath. "We're going to need a pen for him at night, which I'm sure Jahl can arrange."

"Is that so he feels safe?" She rubbed the animal's nose and it licked her finger.

"No, that's so *we* feel safe. Welchets are nocturnal animals, foraging at night. They usually sleep all day, but as youngsters they pretty much eat all the time."

She set Wally down, letting him continue his explorations. "What does he eat? How will I feed him?"

"He eats bugs and worms and grubs. But welchets love vegetables. I'm sure we can pull something together for him now. Is Jahl home?"

"No, he had to settle a dispute."

"Oh." Khaos looked at the door as if he wanted to help Jahl, but turned back to her.

"You can go if you want."

He shook his head. "I've been gone all day. Haven't you missed me?"

Actually, she had, but she wasn't about to let him know that. "I've been busy too. I learned about the Fullamush and the ruling council and bali and—"

"Come with me." He held out his hand.

"But what about Wally?"

His face fell, having obviously forgotten the critter was still attached to his wrist. "I'll tie him to the bar chair. That should keep him out of trouble for a while."

She watched as Khaos coaxed Wally over to the bar area and tested his knot. The sinews on the man's biceps were a pleasure to watch as he made sure all was secure. Seriously, what wasn't there to love about Khaos? Love? She meant like. He was a very likeable guy.

"I'll just get him some water and a snack. He's been traveling all day."

As Khaos left the room, she ran into the bedroom and grabbed her phone. Turning it on, she was pleased to see she still had some battery left. She opened the camera and snapped a picture of Wally sniffing at the arm of her favorite chair. She set her phone on the bar to be sure it was out of reach of her new pet, before sitting on the couch to wait.

Wally came over and sniffed at her boots. Absently, she scratched his back. Her feelings for Khaos had grown stronger. He was less hesitant around her, which put her more at ease. When he looked at her before he kissed her, she found such caring in his gaze that she felt like a fool for constantly keeping him at arm's length, emotionally.

Khaos strode out of the kitchen with a bowl of water and an orange vegetable that looked like a cross between a potato and a carrot. He put down the food and water where he tied the leash. She admired his taught backside as he bent while Wally waddled over to investigate.

The animal immediately started lapping at the water and Khaos gave him a quick pat on the head before he stood straight.

Shit, the man's body was to die for. She had to stop overanalyzing things and just enjoy the time she had left.

"Are you ready?" He held out his arm for her to precede him.

As she walked by, she grabbed his hand and smiled as his fingers curled around hers. Outside, the light from two moons was bright. She let him lead her to a platform with one of the vines Jahl had fused. He took the vine in one hand and grabbed her around the waist. "Are you ready?"

"What? No. Wait." She'd barely wrapped her arms around his neck before he swung them off the platform.

CHAPTER TWELVE

Her heart jumped into her throat and stayed there until they landed safely on a platform below. He let her go and looped the vine around a branch for someone else to use.

She turned on him. "Are you nuts? Oh my God, I could have died. Never mind a fall, my heart lodged in my throat. I could have had a heart attack." She breathed hard, feeling the rush of adrenaline dissipate. "Can we do it again?"

Khaos laughed. "Of course. Come on."

He grasped her hand and pulled her along. They ran to another platform. This time she jumped up on him and wrapped her legs around him. "This way you can use both hands."

He winked. "Good idea."

She was going to give him a setdown, but he grabbed the vine and swung.

"Yay!" She couldn't help yelling.

He covered her mouth with his, cutting off any other loud noises she might want to make, but with his tongue in her mouth as they swung through the air, she didn't care. When they landed on the platform, he let go of the rope and held her to him.

She didn't care that they stood on a platform in the middle of Loraleaf with the moons shining down on them. She didn't care that with her legs wrapped around Khaos, it opened the pareo so her pussy was bare to him. All she cared about at the moment was what he made her feel...loved.

Khaos backed up against the platform railing. He slid one hand through her short hair while the other held her ass, pressing her against his waist. His tongue played circles around hers and she grew moist. His smooth hard chest pressed against her breasts, making her crave him.

He broke the kiss. "Your joy is my joy."

"Khaos, make love to me."

At her words, he crushed her to him, his mouth on hers, his hard cock pressed against her belly, both hands holding her against him. After another devastating kiss, she caught her breath as he moved his lips to her neck. The moon shone on his dark hair and she pulled the tie that held it back, grasping the thick strands and forcing his head up. "I want you inside me."

His hands beneath her ass tightened before he helped her move back until his cock touched her opening. Her feet rested on the railing now, giving her leverage and some control.

His voice as he gazed into her eyes was ragged. "Ready?"

"Yes."

He started to enter her, but she was too hot, too ready to wait. Using her legs, she speared herself onto him. "Oh wow." Spikes of pleasure shot through every nerve and she shuddered.

Khaos' inhale was loud. "Don't move."

She couldn't if she tried, her body having gone from zero to off the charts in one movement.

Khaos stepped away from the rail and she quickly grasped his waist with her legs to stay connected. She felt so full, she wasn't sure she could detach if she wanted to.

He lowered his voice. "Someone comes."

No, not now. She didn't want to stop. Oh hell, screw it. She didn't care who it was, she would keep Khaos inside her. It's not like someone could see anything.

Khaos grinned and leaned back against the railing. "It's Jahl."

"Jahl?" She looked behind her, but the angle was wrong. She listened intently and could hear the faint sound of footsteps. As they came closer, they picked up speed. Had he seen them?

Jahl's footsteps slowed to a stop right behind her. "Serena, are you all right?"

His concerned tone made her feel guilty for worrying him, but Khaos laughed. "Jahl, she's fine, take a look."

What?

Jahl stepped to their side and gazed at her face.

"I'm better than okay." She smiled, still not totally used to having two men not be jealous of each other.

"I can see that. But you need more."

Huh?

Jahl stepped behind her and untied the pareo. As if he knew how the silky material would feel, he pulled it from between her and Khaos' body slowly. Its path against her sensitized skin left her breathless for a moment.

Jahl grumbled. "I don't know why you insist on wearing a table covering."

"A table covering? Is that what these are supposed to be?"

He nodded.

And here she was worried about how it looked with her boots, which rested on the railing.

Khaos shook his head. "Don't tease her, Jahl. She's still getting used to all this."

Were they really having this conversation while she was impaled on Khaos' very hard cock? She'd swear it grew harder when Jahl arrived.

"You're right." Jahl laid the material over the railing then turned toward them. "Let me see."

Khaos grinned at her. "Release your right hand and show him."

She caught the idea and let go, angling her body away from Khaos to show Jahl her breasts and Khaos' cock between her legs. Luckily, Khaos was strong or they both would have been on the floor of the platform.

Jahl's face tightened and she looked down to see his cock already hard. These two men were very good for her ego.

"Nice." Jahl stepped behind her and pressed his body against hers, his cock pressing along the line between her ass cheeks.

She grasped on to Khaos again, the feel of being pressed between the two men causing her heartbeat to race.

Jahl's breath caressed her ear. "Lean back against me. I won't let you fall."

Now that was an understatement. If there were two people in the world she could trust with her safety, it was these two. Wow, that was a revelation in itself.

"Serena?" Jahl's voice had her changing position.

She leaned back against his large chest, the spray of hair on it making a comfortable, though hard, back rest. She kept her hands on Khaos' shoulders so she could control her movements. She needn't have bothered.

Jahl's hand reached around her and found the spot where she and Khaos came together. Just seeing his hand there in the moonlight sent a shiver through her.

He spoke against her ear. "Relax and enjoy."

She looked at Khaos, who continued to grin. The man really liked knowing what was coming next when she didn't. That trait would be an irritant if he wasn't so damn hot.

Jahl's fingers began to play through her folds and around Khaos' cock. As Jahl found her clit, he kissed her neck. "We are going to make you come and you are not going to move at all."

Oh shit. Another burst of pleasure shot from her brain to her core. These men knew how to get to her.

Jahl's fingers lightly flicked across her clit. She let her head fall back against him, as delight sporadically sliced down her sheath. She was so intent on the feelings between her legs, she started when Jahl's other hand found her breast. Rubbing his thumb across her hard nipple sent pulses of pleasure straight to her pussy.

She tensed as her orgasm moved closer and Khaos whistled through his teeth. "By the Bendis, Jahl."

She agreed with Khaos and angled her hips to allow Jahl's fingers more room to play. He took the opportunity offered and slid one finger inside her with Khaos' cock. Her body exploded as her sheath contracted and her hips rose. Heat flamed between her legs, consuming her.

Khaos yelled and flooded her with his cum, sending her beyond the melting point. Red flashes filled her vision and she opened her eyes to find his head thrown back and neck muscles straining as he pressed against her, his fingers biting into her ass.

Jahl was a safe rock in her firestorm. Holding her steady as her orgasm faded and her body cooled. Khaos lowered his head and looked at her. His dark-gray eyes lightened and turned to silver before her eyes. She looked down, not willing to see what might be in that gaze.

Jahl gently wrapped his arms around her and pulled her away.

"Oh." She couldn't help her sigh of disappointment as Khaos' cock slipped from her.

Jahl picked her up in his arms. "I think we should take this inside."

A shiver of anticipation caught her by surprise. She'd just been completely satisfied by two men and she wanted more? They were going to spoil her for any other man on Earth.

She froze, the thought bringing her back to reality in a hurry.

Jahl walked at his usual brisk pace, across a bridge, around a tree and to a lift. Khaos followed and kissed her forehead before standing next to Jahl and throwing the lever.

The moist jungle air had cooled, which made her happy to be snuggled against Jahl's warm chest. His heartbeat was steady against her ear. As they rose, she enjoyed the view of Loraleaf in the double moonlight. The silver light gave the green leaves an almost supernatural glow and in a strange way reminded her of Khaos' eyes when he looked at her intensely.

The lift stopped and Jahl headed for another bridge. She and Khaos had swung quite far. She let her head fall back so she could look at him. He followed, but he wasn't paying attention, sensing the future maybe? He must have sensed her gaze because he looked up and grinned before he winked.

She flushed. Khaos was deviltry and insecurity. Jahl was responsibility and overcompensating, at least that's what she'd call it based on the daytime television show she watched in between movie jobs. She couldn't help thinking what it would be like to come back to Eden and live with them.

"Serena, are you asleep?" Jahl's voice was low. If she'd been asleep she wouldn't have woken.

"No, I'm awake. I told you, I'm not that delicate."

He squeezed her gently. "No, you're not. For that I'm very glad."

She glanced up, something in his tone caused her to think he might be smiling, but his lips remained in their usual position. Even in the moonlight she could see the shadow of hair above his lip from a long day.

As he carried her across the final rope bridge home, she had to admit she wouldn't find another man quite like these men.

Khaos opened the door, but he didn't turn on a light.

A whimpering noise had her scrambling out of Jahl's arms and into the living room. Khaos cleared the ceiling, allowing the silver light to brighten the entire interior.

"Wally?"

The whimper sounded again behind the couch. Moving slowly, she found Wally's leash tangled around the legs of the end table so he couldn't move and his water bowl had tipped over. "Oh, it's okay, sweetie, we'll help you." She sat on the floor and stroked his back to soothe him. She looked to Khaos. "We need to get him untangled."

Khaos nodded and headed for the bar chair.

"Why do we have a baby welchet in here?" Jahl scowled at the animal on the floor next to her.

"Because Khaos gave him to me."

Jahl looked over at Khaos, who had succeeded in untying the leash and approached. He shrugged. "She calls him Wally."

Jahl sighed. "If we're going to have a welchet, we need a pen. I'll gather some material and do a small one in here for tonight." Jahl headed for the door and Wally followed, tightening the partially untangled rope and tipping over the end table.

Serena cringed.

Jahl looked back and shook his head again before stepping outside.

She looked up at Khaos. "Are we in trouble?"

He grinned. "No. I think Wally will be good for Jahl. Maybe give him practice for when we have children. Can you see him with a baby in his arms?"

She smiled in return, but her stomach tightened. Children? These men were in a far different place in their lives than she was. She hadn't even given marriage a thought, never mind children. Though she was careful with her explosives, the profession did have one living life one day at a time.

Khaos untangled the rest of the rope and handed it to her. Wally finally gave up on Jahl and sniffed his way to her. She stroked him absently, her mind on Khaos' statement. She had a lot to think about when she returned home. She planned on having a long chat with Jaelene. Not about Eden, but about two men she'd met who wanted her in a forever relationship.

She could just imagine Jaelene's eyes going wide at that. Or at the little critter climbing into her lap. "Wally. Are you tired?" He curled up in a ball and sighed. She held back her laughter to keep from disturbing him. Oh, to have the worries of a little welchet who'd been rescued.

Jahl came in with logs, not in his arms, but floating in front of him. Serena couldn't help but stare. "Where should we put it?"

She took her eyes off the floating wood and looked him in the eye. "How about the bedroom?"

Jahl's gaze flew to Khaos, who was trying not to laugh. "I think maybe we should put it in the corner over here."

Jahl nodded and Serena watched in fascination as the little pen appeared to build itself. The scent of burned wood came to her nose. That had to be because Jahl fused it together.

When the pen was done, Jahl stepped to the door. Dirt floated through the room and deposited itself in the pen. Wally's nose started to go again and he lifted his head up. "I think he smells his new home." She held him to her until the dirt was done. "Is it okay to put him in now?"

Jahl came over and looked inside. "Yes. Khaos, see if we have any green vegetables."

Serena stood with Wally in her arms and placed him in the large pen. Then she unclasped the leash from his little collar. He immediately stuck his nose in the dirt and lay down. Her heart melted. The little guy was tuckered out, but now he was happy.

She gave Wally a couple more strokes and his eyes closed. She turned to Jahl. "Thank you for this."

He nodded. "I can deny you nothing."

His statement bothered her. It was too over the top. Surely he wouldn't let her sleep with another filoz or wander outside of Loraleaf by herself. Of course not. He was just in the moment and it was sweet.

Khaos came in with some green leaves. "I found this, but it might be a bit cold for him."

"Here." She took it from him and quietly laid it in the opposite corner. "Now when he wakes he'll have food and it won't be too cold. Why do we need the leaves in there if there are bugs and worms and stuff in the dirt?"

"Because there aren't." Jahl frowned. "I can't control those because they are living. I am only good with what is dead."

"Right, I forgot. So as you gathered the dirt, the worms and bugs stayed put. I have to admit this kindred ability stuff is hard to comprehend. On Earth we don't have anything like it."

Jahl looked like he wanted to argue, but his jaw tensed and he remained quiet.

Khaos stepped up to her and winked. "Now that the baby is asleep, I think it's time for the adults to continue their fun."

Again the reference to a baby had her thankful for her own implant that would keep her from getting pregnant. Jahl came up beside Khaos. "Or are you tired from our activity outside?"

He may very well be goading her, but she couldn't resist the bait. "I told you, I'm no lightweight. I can go as many rounds as you two—ach." Jahl swept her up and over his shoulder.

"What are you doing?" He started heading for the bedroom. She looked at Khaos. He shrugged and followed.

Jahl deposited her gently on the bed and stood looking down at her. "You've been naked since you were outside on the platform."

"So? Oh." He was right. She hadn't had a stitch of clothing on since Jahl took off her pareo. Wow. She must be really comfortable with these two.

Khaos came to stand next to Jahl and crossed his arms over his chest.

She studied them. Between Khaos' smug smile and Jahl's proud chin, they thought they had her. She couldn't help teasing them. "So I guess it's time to go to sleep then."

They looked at each other then at her, their frowns too funny to resist. She laughed. "Actually, I'm not tired at all." She opened her arms wide.

Khaos jumped on the bed, falling beside her and grabbing her to him for a body-hugging kiss.

Her insides turned to mush as he overpowered her mouth. When he gave her a moment to breathe, she rolled over into the arms of Jahl, who waited for her and gave her his own heart-stopping kiss that made her insides do somersaults.

When Jahl was done, he gave her a moment. She lay on her back and stretched. Yes, tonight was going to be great.

* * * * *

Khaos leaned against the counter and swallowed a mouthful of ambrosia as he waited for Jahl to come back from bringing Serena a cup of kafez. Yesterday had gone well, and last night even better.

He grinned at the memory of Serena on all fours, Jahl's cock in her mouth and his own buried deep inside her pussy. She had been so playful, issuing the challenge to see which of them would come first. Smart vixen. She had come twice before either of them let go and then she came again when they couldn't hold out any longer.

His grin disappeared. But the best of the entire night was lying next to her as she breathed in her sleep. To have her with them for the rest of their lives seemed too much to expect.

Jahl walked into the kitchen, his lips quirking at the corner. "Kafez definitely helps."

Khaos gave his friend a squeeze on the shoulder as Jahl sat down. "Maybe we should trade for another kafez pot and set up a station in the bedroom."

"If she wants one, I'll be happy to oblige." Jahl lifted his cup to his lips and drank.

They sat in silence, listening to the sounds of the shower, knowing their chosen one bathed. Khaos couldn't resist. "Do you want to bet on whether she comes in here with or without her clothes? I say she wears her clothes."

"No."

Khaos grinned and took another swallow of juice. Sometimes Jahl was no fun.

"We need to bond with her today."

"I don't think we will." Khaos lowered his glass.

Jahl's gaze collided with his own. "You sense something?"

"Yes. I sense she's not ready."

"I agree." Jahl stared at his kafez. "But we should ask anyway."

Khaos stared at the tree branches outside the window. The sunlight hit the greenery like rain drops, in tiny bursts of light. He focused on the future, trying to sense Serena's decision, but it wasn't there. "She hasn't decided yet."

"Good. We need to reason with her."

Khaos grimaced. He didn't see a lot of reasons for her to bond with them. Sure the sex was good, but to be honest, he and Jahl were not the filoz they had been with Sandale. She, on the other hand, was confident and sweet and friendly and—

"Good morning." Serena strode in wearing her blue jeans and purple bra.

"Good morning." He pulled her to him and gave her a kiss. The kafez flavor of her mouth tinted by her own sweetness was intoxicating. "Did you say hello to Wally?"

She poured more of the hot liquid into her cup. "Of course. He's so wonderful. Thank you again." She turned to Jahl. "And thank you for opening your home to him and making his pen last night. I know that wasn't what you planned to do when you arrived home."

Jahl shrugged. "It was better than mediating a dispute."

Khaos stiffened. "How did it go?"

"Not well." Jahl rubbed his hands over his face, a telling movement this early in the day. "I need to go back today."

Khaos heard the unspoken request for help loud and clear. "Mind if I go too? Maybe I could help."

Jahl's relieved expression told him he'd guessed right. "Yes, I'd appreciate that."

"Can I help?" Serena sat at the table between him and Jahl.

"No." Jahl's answer was immediate.

Khaos looked at Jahl. "Actually, maybe she could. The men are going to need to get used to seeing a woman."

Serena held up her hand. "Whoa, I'm not going to be here *that* long."

"If you bond with us, you will." Jahl's look was hopeful but Khaos' stomach tightened.

Serena lay her hand on Jahl's. "I really appreciate that you chose me to bond with, but I'm not ready for that kind of commitment."

"Tomorrow?" Jahl's face was perfectly serious.

Khaos interrupted before they heard a definite no from Serena's lips. "What is it about the bonding that concerns you?"

She contemplated her cup for a moment then looked straight at him. "You mean besides the forever part?"

He swallowed but nodded.

Serena raised her hand with one finger sticking upward. "Well, there is the fact I'd be living on another planet."

Jahl broke in. "But I thought you loved Loraleaf."

"I do, but it's not my planet. How would you feel going to Earth and having to wear clothes for the rest of your life?"

Khaos almost grinned at the shiver that ran through Jahl.

"Then there is my family." She raised another finger.

He had to speak up. "But we already told you, you could visit them whenever you wanted."

She waved that explanation away with her hand. "And then there is the L word." She raised a third finger.

They both looked at her in question.

"Love? You both say you love me, though I'm not sure how that can be." She held up her hand with the three fingers as they both opened their mouths. "Let me finish. The fact remains I have to love both of you. I've only known you existed for the last six days. People don't fall in love that fast."

Khaos wanted to disagree. He'd fallen in love with her the first night he spotted her. "Then stay longer."

She looked at him. "I can't. If I don't show up at the family reunion tomorrow, my family will worry. They probably already are because Jaelene and I usually talk a couple times a week if I'm not on location."

Jahl grasped her hand. "What about Sandale's ceremony?"

She squirmed and Khaos found hope. "Yes. Sandale would want you to be there."

She remained silent, torn in two directions, but his gut said in a tug of war between them and her family, her family would win. The idea was as comforting as it was heart wrenching. She would leave.

Serena took another sip of kafez as he and Jahl waited for her answer. Here was the turning point for them. Either they would have a future or there was little reason to keep going. His stomach tensed, rebelling against the juice he'd drunk.

Finally, she sighed. "I want to stay for Sandale's memorial." Her gaze moved to him and then Jahl. "I want to for his memory and for you two. But Sandale is gone and my family isn't. I can't put them through the fear that I was kidnapped or harmed, or knowing my mother, dead. I need to go home and I think I should leave now."

Khaos' heart dropped. "Why now?"

"I thought about it while in the shower. It's already been six days with no communication from me. My sister is going to be crazy with worry. You know I care for you both and sympathize with what you want to accomplish here, but my place is back on Earth."

Khaos' throat closed and he glanced at Jahl. The man was like a stone statute. He didn't even blink.

Serena's gaze implored him to understand, but he didn't, couldn't. How would he know what it was like to be worried about by his family? His family had wanted to transport their baby son to the jungle, to live or die as fate decreed. Only the moral tribunal had put a stop to that.

"No." Jahl's one word was said with such quiet authority, it pulled Khaos from his dark thoughts.

Serena's gaze whipped to Jahl. "No? You mean you won't let me go?"

Jahl stood. "I won't let you go. Sandale sacrificed his life so you could be saved and be our agapayto. If he hadn't done that, your family would have real reason to worry."

A flush stained Serena's cheeks as she followed Jahl's reasoning. "But I don't love you."

Bile rose in Khaos' throat at the statement. To guess she didn't feel for them what they felt for her was one thing, but to hear it stated so bluntly was another.

Jahl wasn't moved. "You will." With that pronouncement he strode from the room. The sound of the entry door slamming was the only indication Jahl was upset.

Serena sat and looked up at him. "You have to make him understand."

He shook his head. "How am I to make him understand when I don't?"

"Wouldn't your family worry?"

He laughed scornfully. "You mean the family who wanted nothing to do with the son whose birthmark had never been seen before? As humans would say, a freak?"

Her whisper was rewarding. "I didn't know you had a birthmark."

Turning his back on her, he pulled the tie from his hair and lifted it from his neck. "This is what I received as my legacy."

"And that's different from any Edenist on the planet? How do you know?"

He turned back, his self-loathing firmly in place. "All the cities have a book of every known birthmark. Mine isn't one of them. I am an aberration."

She frowned as her jaw lifted. "So because you and Jahl have had horrific families, you can't empathize with me. But Sandale would have. If Sandale were here, he would have let me go home."

"That's what we've been saying. If Sandale were here, you would want to stay. Without him, we are nothing but failures."

Serena stood, her eyes glittering with anger and hurt. "You said I could go home any time I wanted."

"After the bonding."

"How can I bond with men I don't love? How can I love men who can't love themselves? I'm not Sandale. I can't fix you!" She slammed her hand on the table then brought it up quickly and put it against her mouth. "I'm going home, somehow."

Khaos stepped forward, his heart disintegrating into pieces like Jahl disintegrated the infragilis vine. "Serena, don't. We need you."

"I get that. But you need me for the wrong reasons. If you ever need me for the right ones, come find me." The betrayal in her eyes stopped him from grabbing her to him as he wanted.

"Serena." He didn't know what to say. His heart was shattering and his brain wouldn't function.

She shook her head at him and turned away. He watched her leave the kitchen. Not so much worried she could leave the planet, but that she didn't want them. He'd been right all along. They weren't worthy of her.

CHAPTER THIRTEEN

Serena marched into the bedroom and put on her boots. She was going home somehow. When they were laced up she grabbed her cell phone and pushed it into her back pocket. She couldn't believe they'd gone back on their word. How many other promises had they made that they would break? Jahl had said he'd do anything for her. Bullshit.

She stalked out of the room and knocked on Toni's door.

A groggy, "Come in" greeted her.

Pushing it open, she stopped just inside. She hadn't been in the room since she presented it to Toni. Her friend had piles of small green paper on the dresser and handmade clothing everywhere.

Serena swallowed hard at the evidence that her friend would really be staying and moved toward the dresser.

"Hey, did you bring me some kafez?" Toni's question was punctuated by a loud yawn as she stretched in bed.

Serena picked up one of the small papers, each with one word and a check mark or more next to them, though some had none. "What are these?" She faced her friend.

Toni wouldn't look at her directly. "Just my notes."

"On what?"

Toni sighed and finally met her gaze. "Listen, I got to thinking. These men at Loraleaf haven't even seen a woman in five or six years. All the Pleasure Temples are in Naralina, which they can't go to, so that means they haven't had sex in a long time."

"Yeah." She wasn't sure she wanted to know where this was going now that Toni started.

"Well, I thought some of these men would have turned to other men, like we hear of in our prisons back home, but they haven't. They are totally fixated on women."

Serena nodded to show she was listening.

Toni shrugged. "I figure since I'm here and not in the market for my own filoz, I might as well help these men out."

"Hold on. Are you saying you are having sex with every man in Loraleaf?"

"Of course not. You have Jahl and Khaos and some of the men want to wait until their chosen one is here."

Serena shook her head. "But everyone else?"

"Yeah, pretty much." She held up her hand "But I still have quite a few to go."

Serena just stared. She may complain she wasn't a delicate flower to Jahl and Khaos, but after a night of sex with them, she was exhausted. Granted, Toni was bigger and had a hell of a lot more muscle mass and probably more energy, but shit. "Wow. I'm impressed."

"You are?"

Serena looked down at the slips of paper. They'd only been there six days and the first day Toni hadn't been with anyone. "Yes, I am. How do you avoid the bonding?"

She nodded. "We determine ahead of time who gets to come inside me, and I get the rest off in other ways. But I will go back to that filoz so a different man can be inside. Seriously, these men are so thrilled and they are so good, I could do this forever and be completely happy. They treat me like gold. No, more precious than that, like a delicate gold flower."

"When do you find time to eat?"

"Oh, don't worry, they feed me, and I'm getting plenty of protein and exercise." Toni winked and Serena closed down a visual that popped into her head. Nope, didn't need to see that.

"Nice love bites."

"What?" Serena clasped her hand to her neck. "I have hickies?"

"Yup. One on each side. That must have been some great sex that you forgot they sucked on you so hard. They look a lot better on you then those knife cuts. You can barely see those any more. So how's it going with your chosen ones?"

Serena walked over to the bed and sat on it. "It's not. I'm going home. I came to say goodbye."

Toni's face froze before she grabbed Serena and gave her a hug. "I'm sorry. I thought they were the ones for you."

Serena kept tears from forming by sheer willpower as she sat back. "I'm not the one for them. We are too different. They don't understand family, even within their own filoz. And they are so damaged. I don't know how to fix them."

"They may be damaged on the inside but they look pretty together on the outside." Toni wiggled her brows.

"But the inside is what matters." Serena held up one finger. "Khaos considers himself an aberration because his family didn't want him because he has a birthmark unlike any other one known to Eden."

"He has a birthmark? I'll have to tell the men. They are a little weirded out by him because they think he has none."

"That's part of why he thinks so little of himself. I mean, what if he is the next step in Edenist evolution? Maybe he is the beginning of a new race, like an advanced mutation?"

Toni cocked her head. "Back to the sci-fi again?"

Irritation flitted through Serena. "Maybe, but I was right the first time, wasn't I? There is life on another planet."

"Point taken."

Serena held up another finger. "Then there's Jahl. His family threw him out because his ability wasn't up to their standards. They couldn't think outside the box to see his ability would be a huge asset. So he's constantly on the defensive like he has to prove himself."

Toni's eyes widened. "Yeah, that explains him perfectly. Wow, you *have* been thinking about them."

Serena rolled her eyes. When hadn't she been thinking about them? "And then there was Sandale." She raised another finger. "He was their buffer and safety net. He basically became their enabler. As long as they had him, they functioned well."

Toni leaned back. "Oh, I see where you are going with this."

Serena nodded, dropping her hand. "Now they want me to be their stabilizing force, though I don't think they consciously see it that way. But I can't do that. I've had a loving family who has supported me and I understand my own value, but I sure as hell can't have those two dependent on me. I'd be a wreck within three months."

"They need to stand on their own two feet, so to speak."

Serena gave a slight smile, happy to have someone understand her. "Exactly. But I can't wait for that. I need to go home. The annual Upton family reunion takes place tomorrow and I *have* to be there."

Toni pouted. "That's right. I'm going to miss that. But yeah, you do have to be there. So what do Jahl and Khaos think about you leaving?"

"Jahl has refused to let me go."

"What?"

Serena nodded, fighting the tears again. "I have to find a way to get home. I'd hoped you might have some ideas."

Toni hugged her again. "Okay, let me get dressed while I think." She threw off the light material she'd used as a sheet and stood, completely naked.

Serena couldn't help but look. She'd always known her friend was in shape, but shit, she really did look like an Amazon. She was beyond toned, she had defined muscle. Why did everyone say women couldn't build muscle or they'd look bulky? Toni looked awesome.

"My first thought is Ware and Nase. I know they would get you back in a heartbeat, but it's too dangerous to go through the jungle to Haven. The scuttlebutt is the criminals are getting closer and leaving strange symbols in blood."

Serena shivered. Jahl had said a similar thing, but it was obvious he'd left out the gory details. "I'd rather leave that as a last resort."

Toni started to dress, throwing on a short white skirt and a halter top made of a deep-purple material. "Do you think Khaos would be willing to open a portal with another man?"

Serena was still admiring the halter. "What? Oh, I thought he had to open it with Jahl."

Toni sat on the bed and started crisscrossing straps up her calf on what looked like Grecian sandals. "No. Any two men who have chips can open a portal and I think everyone in Loraleaf has them."

Now that was a surprise. What had Khaos and Jahl said about waiting for the other one to send her home? It wasn't exactly a lie, but they definitely didn't tell her the whole truth. What else weren't they telling her? "No, Khaos won't help me go home. Though he recognizes it's wrong to keep me against my will, he won't betray Jahl. And I don't want him to."

Toni finished with her sandals and stood. "Okay, then we need to find someone who will."

Serena's gut tightened. It sounded wrong. She didn't want Jahl's men to betray him, but what else was she to do?

"So who here likes you enough to help you?"

"Unlike you," she paused and stared at Toni, "I haven't met many people."

Toni actually blushed, which surprised Serena. She expected to be teased back, but Toni didn't. That was interesting.

"Who have you met?"

Serena thought about her time at Loraleaf. "Only Theron, Rekah and Konala. Oh no. Will you do me a favor once I leave?"

"Sure."

Serena looked at the door to Toni's room. She was going to miss her new pet. "Khaos gave me a welchet yesterday. His name is Wally. Will you take care of him, at least until his leg heals? Konala should be able to let you know when Wally can go back into the wild."

Toni backed up a step. "You want me to take care of one of those critters?"

"Yes, and you can't forget to feed him no matter how busy your schedule is."

"Why not let the boys take care of him?"

She rose from the bed and strode to the window. "I don't know if they would. I know Jahl is going to be angry and for all I know Khaos will go missing again." She stared out at the beautiful greenery high in the tall trees. She would miss this. She turned back toward Toni. "Please."

Toni threw her hands up. "Fine, I'll take care of him. But first we have to figure out how we're going to get you back to Earth, otherwise you'll be caring for him and the boys, and your family will think you're dead."

Just the thought of what her parents and Jaelene would go through had her focusing. "Right. I have to go back to Earth for them, no matter what."

Toni moved to the door and put her ear against it. "What about Theron's filoz?"

Serena looked away. That would be so awkward and what would Jahl think?

"Serena?"

"I hate to ask him. Jahl thinks Theron is in love with me."

"Holy shit! No Edenist would ever willingly fall for another's woman. A filoz's chosen one is sacred." Toni moved away from the door. "But in this case it may work to your advantage. Theron, if he really loves you, may just be willing to go behind Jahl's back."

Serene clasped her hands together, her stomach nauseated at their discussion. "But even if he's willing to, why would Rekah or Konala do it?"

Toni smiled. "For Theron. Because if he is in love with you, getting you out of Loraleaf will benefit the other two. After all, they will be looking for their own chosen one soon."

"I don't know. It doesn't feel—"

Toni held up her hand "Shhh."

Serena kept silent as her friend listened against the door again. She hated that she had to sneak behind Jahl's back. Maybe if she talked to him again, he'd realize he had to let her go. She'd much prefer it that way. She looked up at the clear ceiling then at the room Jahl had built just for Toni. She would miss everything about Loraleaf.

"Okay, we're good." Toni stepped away from the door. "I heard Jahl telling Khaos he wants him to take a look at the last lawbreaker site. Something must be up."

There had to be some other way. Maybe she could lie and promise Jahl and Khaos she would bond with them if they took her home. Shit, she couldn't do that either. That would be too cruel and just plain wrong.

"So are you sure you want to do this?"

Serena shook her head. "No, I don't like going behind Jahl's back like this. Maybe I should wait and try to convince him one more time."

Toni stared at her. "Tell me this, if your family reunion was two weeks away, would you stay longer?"

Now there was a question. "I know I'd want to stay longer, but unless the two of them suddenly found value in themselves, the outcome would be the same. I don't think I could handle a relationship with one man whose ego has been decimated by his own family, never mind two."

Toni nodded once. "Okay, then let's go find Theron."

"Fine, but I want to say goodbye to Wally first."

Toni rolled her eyes, but opened the door.

Serena walked into the living room. "Wally, are you going to miss me?"

Scratching at the side of the pen brought her closer. She leaned over to find Wally covered in dirt, his water bowl tipped over and all the leaves gone. He looked up at her and tried to jump out of the pen.

She scooped him up, ignoring the falling dirt to cuddle him. "I'm going to miss you."

He buried his head under her arm and his high-pitched gurgle started.

"What the hell is that?" Toni put her hands over her ears.

"It's the sound he makes when he's happy." She stroked his fur and wished she could see how big he'd grow.

"If that's what he sounds like when he's happy, I'd hate to hear what he sounds like when he's upset."

Serena ignored Toni, her heart squeezing at losing her first pet so quickly. "Could you fill his water bowl and see if there's any green leafy vegetables for him?"

"Sure, why not." Toni sighed. "Might as well get used to my new role as nanny."

As her friend left, Serena buried her face in Wally's fur, letting her tears fall. She would miss him even though she had him less than a day, just like she would miss the men who'd given him a home, even though she had only known them a week.

If she felt like this now, she could just imagine how she would feel if she stayed longer. She'd made the right decision.

Wally lifted his head from beneath her arm and started to lick at her tears. If it was the right decision, why did it hurt so much?

* * * * *

"You shouldn't be here." Theron's greeting was so opposite of what Serena expected that she took a step back.

"Why?"

He turned back to his experiment. "Jahl wouldn't like it."

"Theron, it's just me and Toni. Jahl is out with Khaos reviewing the criminal site."

"I know." He didn't look at her.

She stepped a little closer and lowered her voice. "Please. I need your help."

He lifted his head and looked at her. His eyes darkened. Oh God, Jahl was right. Theron loved her. Then anguish flitted across his features and his eyes turned their normal brown. "I'm sure whatever you need, Jahl or Khaos would be happy to help."

He turned away again, but she could tell he hadn't really dismissed her. He kept rearranging the burn material on his counter.

Taking a deep breath, she touched his arm. "Please, Theron."

He jerked his arm away as if burned.

God, she hated putting him through this. Too bad he hadn't been the one to save her, but the truth was, it wouldn't have changed anything. There was something about Jahl and Khaos, beyond their heart-wrenching past, that spoke to her.

Theron wasn't looking at her. Instead he half turned away from her as if being in her presence was too painful. She looked back at Toni, who motioned with her hand to continue. Taking a deep breath she dumped it all out.

"I need to get back to Earth by tomorrow and Jahl has refused to let me leave."

Theron's head snapped up. "What? He can't do that."

"But he has. I have to go home to my family by tomorrow or they will think something terrible has happened to me. I just can't put them through that."

Theron's body could have been a statue for how still he stood. "Why wouldn't Jahl allow you to visit your family? That seems odd."

Theron deserved the truth if he would risk Jahl's wrath. "I told him I wouldn't bond with them. I want to go home for good and he won't let me leave."

Theron studied her face. "Do you mean you will *never* bond with them?"

"Not unless they can change significantly." Her eyes started to tear at the chances of that. "And I don't think they even realize they need to."

"You love them."

She shook her head. "No, but I will if I stay any longer and if I bond with them, I'll be miserable."

Theron continued to look at her, his expression unreadable. She hoped he wasn't thinking she might turn to him. She did care for him as a friend, but nothing beyond that.

"Why me?" His fingers curled into fists and uncurled. "Why do you ask me?"

She held her hands out to the sides. "I don't know anyone else."

He finally moved, gathering up his materials from his experiment and sweeping them into a box. Turning off the light over his work area he faced her. "I still need another man to open the portal."

A squeal of delight threatened to erupt before it was overtaken by a hiccup of sorrow. God, she wished she had more time. For the first time in her life, she silently cursed the family reunion.

Theron held up his hand. "We will go to Rekah. He can read emotions and he will know if this is the right course of action for you. If he agrees, only then will I betray my leader for you."

Serena clasped her hands together as much from consternation as to keep from touching Theron in thanks. "What will happen to you if you do this?"

He shrugged. "I don't know. I could be banished or given constant patrols in the hope I don't come back one day. No one has betrayed the leaders of Loraleaf before."

She couldn't resist asking. "What did they do in Naralina?"

"Traitors are exiled."

If Theron was exiled, he'd be out there on his own with the criminals. She couldn't allow that. "Never mind. I'll find another way." She turned to leave.

Theron grabbed her arm. "Wait. What other way?"

She shrugged, not willing to look at him. "I don't know. Maybe I'll try to convince Jahl one more time. If not, I can travel to Haven and ask them for help."

"Serena look at me."

She finally turned, despite the growing knowledge that she should never have come here. She met Theron's gaze and flinched. He looked at her with such love that it made her feel like a worm. What a mess she'd created.

He still hadn't released her arm, which was so opposite of all the times they had any physical contact. "You know how I feel about you. I will do whatever will make you happy."

She pulled her arm away, not able to bear him touching her when she wasn't worth his love. "But it won't make me happy. It won't make any of us happy. It would only make it hurt less now than later and save my family from heartbreak. It's not worth you risking your life."

Theron's lips turned up on one corner. "There is one way to be sure I don't get exiled."

"What?" She didn't see how anything could keep Jahl and Khaos from taking their anger at her out on Theron.

"Toni can tell them that you didn't want me to be thrown out of Loraleaf. Just the fact that you said it, will keep them from doing so."

She stared at him. "They'd only throw you out faster."

"No, he's right." Toni, who had been unusually quiet decided to pipe up now?

She turned to her friend. "How do you know?"

"Because once you're gone, the only thing they will have left is your request."

None of this felt right.

"Please Serena. Let me do this one thing for you." Theron's dark gaze stabbed at her heart and her throat closed. She couldn't deny him.

All she could do was nod before she turned to leave. She passed Toni, whose face was serious, another sign that Serena's whole visit to Eden had become a complete disaster.

* * * * *

Jahl's thoughts buzzed around him like the Daemond honey bee. He couldn't let Serena go, but he was wrong to make her stay. He didn't care about her family, but the look of betrayal in her eyes had pierced his gut.

He glanced at Khaos as they walked through the jungle. Khaos didn't agree with his refusal. It was against Dickinson Law for a filoz to force a woman to bond. He hadn't exactly broken the law, not that it mattered in the jungle, but he came pretty close. If his men heard of what he'd done, it would set a bad precedent.

But how was he supposed to let her go? Without her, life would be motions with no happiness, no love. There had to be some way around this and he was going to find it. He'd been in worse positions before and come through it. Hadn't he proved his father wrong, even if Grandall couldn't see it?

Khaos slowed as they approached the site. He hadn't seen it before and it was gruesome, even with the feroon buried and the blood a brownish-red on the trees. "This appears ritualistic, like they are marking their territory."

"That's what I thought. My concern is how close it is to both settlements."

"Both?" Khaos crouched to view the dried blood on the ground. "You worry about Haven?"

Jahl sighed. "Yes, only because I know it to be filled with Naralinians like us, only there they are ones legitimately exiled for false reasons. Depending on the size of this group of lawbreakers, these two settlements may need to band together."

Khaos looked up. "That's true. We might have to do that if Naralina discovers us as well through portal tracking."

Jahl's heart constricted. "If we knew for sure that Naralina hadn't finished a system for tracking portal openings outside the walls, we very well may have been able to save Sandale by bringing him to Haven. But it has been six years now. They must have figured it out by now."

Khaos stood. "We need someone inside. We need a spy. I wish we could make contact with someone there."

"I agree." It had frustrated him for years that they didn't know what was happening in the city that could affect them. "If we had a Kindred of Mind strong enough, we might be able to make something happen."

Khaos moved next to the tree with the circular marking on it. Now that the blood had dried, it was clearly a symbol. "Why did you tell Serena she couldn't go home? If we aren't good enough for her, we can't make her stay."

Jahl started at the sudden change in topic. "I know." He rubbed his hands over his face. "I just didn't know what else to do at that moment. All I know is we can't lose her too. We deserve her. We built Loraleaf for her. She's ours."

Khaos leaned his shoulder against the tree and folded his arms. "She was meant for you, me and Sandale. From the moment he was gone, the match was no longer compatible."

Jahl sneered. "According to whom? Naralina? Our parents?" He spit on the ground. "We left Naralina to be free of all that. We deserve Serena."

Khaos shook his head as he uncrossed his arms and moved away from the tree, brushing dried blood off his shoulder. "That's true. But even if we deserve her, she has decided against us."

Jahl focused on the spot on the tree Khaos had leaned against. Something shone in the dappled sunlight. Moving closer, he investigated.

Khaos continued. "We have to bring her back to Earth when—"

"Khaos, come here." Jahl peered at the shiny object. It looked like a ring made of cyndistone. The polish on the teal color reflected the light.

"What is it?" Khaos grasped the object and pulled it free from the tree trunk it had been embedded in. "It's a ring."

Jahl's breath caught. "Is it Sandale's?"

"What?" Khaos' eyes widened before he looked down at the round object in his palm.

Jahl reverently picked it up and brushed off the bark debris. He peered at the outside. A small heart with shaded lines was engraved in the center. On one side were diagonal lines mimicking a scraping or a burn scar. On the other side of the heart was a horizontal line curved downward then upward with a dot in each curve and a tiny spiral at the front of the line. A unique symbol only found on Khaos' neck.

Jahl fell back against the tree. "It's Sandale's."

Khaos grabbed the ring and peered at it.

Jahl remembered when Sandale had shown them the ring. It had been his way of proving to them he would always be part of their filoz even though he had a wonderful family and a place within Naralina society. The ring symbolized his acceptance of them as they were, Jahl's birthmark erased by the burn and Khaos' mark out in the open for anyone who wanted to really look at the ring, though no one had except them.

Khaos speared him with a silver stare. "How can this be? You said he was dead."

He was, wasn't he? "He is, but…"

"But what?" Hope shone in Khaos' eyes as his intense gaze grew almost white.

Could he have been wrong? Was Sandale alive and had he been near, or had a lawbreaker left the ring here to twist the knife of anguish? "I don't know." He rubbed his hands over his face as he remembered the night only a week past when he'd found the mound of dirt. "It was a grave. I found his grave and I lost it."

Khaos' squeezed his shoulder. "Tell me what you remember."

"There isn't much to tell. Haven's healer, Jerumbala and I were tracking Sandale's blood when we came to a mound of recently disturbed dirt. It was like the burial practice of Earth, an insult. When I saw it, I whipped it away, digging down, determined to pull up Sandale's dead body, but I lost control."

He looked straight into Khaos' eyes. "I blacked out." He moved his gaze. "I'm not sure if it was from the strain of pulling up trees and roots and boulders or if something I spun out hit me on the head. I remember a rumbling and the ground shaking and then nothing. When I woke, Jerumbala told me Sandale was gone. I refused to believe it and crawled to the opening I made, but it was half filled with ground water."

Khaos' gaze moved from Jahl and stared into nothing. "Then this ring could be all that is left of Sandale or it could be a sign he lives."

Jahl's own hope flared, like a match in a dark cave. "Can you sense anything?"

Khaos didn't answer immediately and Jahl's heart sped at the possibility the brother of his heart was alive. Khaos tensed before whipping around. "We must go back." He started running.

Jahl followed, the look on Khaos' face, sending a surge of adrenaline through his body. "What is it?"

"She's leaving."

"Who? Serena?"

"Yes and she's leaving very soon."

Jahl increased his speed. "How can she? She needs two men to open a portal."

Khaos was on his heels. "She found two men who will."

Jahl's anger flared to life. *Theron.* With renewed strength, he charged forward. They were a half day's leisurely run away. They had to get there in time.

* * * * *

Serena's heart was breaking as they walked into Theron's house to find Rekah.

"Wait here." Theron had them stay in the entryway. She looked over at Toni apologetically.

Toni shrugged. "Hey, if it's what we have to do to get you home, we deal with it."

"You're right. I just feel so bad about all this."

Toni put her hands on her hips. "Do you want your family to think you're dead or not?"

"No." Her heart skittered at the idea. "She could see her mother crying while her father held her, swearing at fate while Jaelene grasped their mom's hand as silent tears fell. Her younger sister would try to support her parents in every way, but inside she would be hurting so much. Serena banished the image. Family came first. "I want to go home."

Toni searched her eyes and seemed satisfied. "Then buck up."

Sure, easier said than done. There was so much on Eden she would miss. Earth would seem boring in comparison, but it was where she belonged. She'd probably skip working for the sci-fi movies any more. She knew too much now. She had experienced the true wonder of another planet with another race of amazing men.

She pictured Jahl as his lips quirked and Khaos with his dazzling smile, and almost moaned.

Rekah entered with a scowl, Theron right behind him. "You want to go home."

She nodded. "Jahl says I can't."

Rekah waved away that serious issue as if it were no more than a rebel attack on a deathstar. "You have strong feelings for Jahl and Khaos and they for you."

"Yes, but if I bond with them we will all be miserable, they have no self-worth. I can't give that to them."

Rekah's face lightened. "This is true. I have a question for you. If Sandale were alive, would you have consented to being their agapayto?"

That was the hardest question she'd been asked yet. "I don't know. I don't even know how I would feel toward Sandale. I only knew him for a matter of minutes and you ask me if I could spend the rest of my life with him."

"True." He continued to stare at her. "Your family ties are strong."

She nodded. That was a given.

"They won't fill your empty heart."

Startled, she frowned. "What do you mean?"

"All the feelings you have for Khaos and Jahl and even Sandale fill a place in your heart. When you have no contact with them, you will feel empty and lost."

"But if I stay I will suffer and make their lives worse, not better."

Rekah remained silent and she held her breath. Answering his questions had made her more determined than ever to return to her family.

"Very well. We will help you go home."

A surge of relief swept through her, almost buckling her knees. "When?"

"Right now. We need to leave Loraleaf to do so. While we can open a portal anywhere on Eden or Earth, if Naralina is tracking them beyond the city walls, they will find Loraleaf. We should get started and run directly toward the city before opening one."

Her heart hitched at that. It was dangerous in the jungle, but she'd be safe with Theron and Rekah.

"I'll come along. I could use a good run. I feel a bit couped up in Loraleaf." Toni stretched her arms as if she hadn't moved in days, when she'd actually been rather active...in bed.

Serena was secretly relieved. She didn't want to say goodbye any sooner than she had to.

The four of them made their way to the hatch. Theron sent a man to tell Konala he was in charge for a few hours before they all exited.

She was aware of the men on the pathways watching them. If she'd had any doubt that Jahl and Khaos would know it was Theron who helped her, that was crushed. She looked at him, still unhappy that he insisted on helping her. It would be one thing if he gave her safe travel to Haven, but to actually open a portal for her… Her gut twisted.

Once outside the tree trunk entrance, Theron faced her. "I know you have reservations, but I promise you, I will be safe. Now to keep you safe, you need to jump on my back so we can get as far as possible from Loraleaf."

She opened her mouth to suggest he take her to Haven, but he held up his hand. "I'm going to see you safely home, so do not argue."

She snapped her jaw shut and nodded.

Theron turned around and she climbed on his back. It was strange to be so close to him, but she had little choice.

Within seconds they all headed out, Theron leading the way and Rekah behind Toni.

Serena had no idea how long they ran, but she could hear Toni breathing hard. They hadn't stopped once and she was about to suggest that when Theron slowed to a stop.

"This should be far enough." Theron bent and Serena slid off his back.

Rekah laid a hand on Toni. "We will go slower on the way home."

She nodded, still taking in big gulps of air.

Rekah moved to Theron's side. "We are ready when you are."

Serena turned to Toni. "I'm going to miss you."

Toni grinned. "I know."

She hugged her friend, thrilled Toni was so happy, but incredibly sad she'd never see her again. She pulled back with tears in her eyes. "What do they say? If you love someone let them go? I guess I love you enough to see you are happy here, but I will be miserable without you."

Toni cocked her head. "Hey, who knows, maybe I'll come by for a visit one day."

"You better." Serena wiped the tears from her eyes and turned to Theron. "I don't know how to thank you."

His gaze turned dark. "Like you said, if you love someone, their happiness is all that matters."

Oh God. Hesitantly, she opened her arms. He stepped forward and gave her a fierce hug. "Return to your family. They will be your comfort."

When Theron let go, she nodded and took a deep breath to stop the flow of tears. She needed to focus on where she was going—home. "Okay, what do we do?"

Rekah frowned. "Because we are not your agapaytos we cannot simply find your home based on your feelings. We can get you to Earth, even to America and anywhere there that we have traveled, but to pinpoint your home will be difficult. Can you describe it?"

As far as she was concerned, getting to the right planet and country was huge. She could figure stuff out from there. She may not have her wallet, but she had her phone and she could get help. She was about to say that was close enough when Toni spoke up.

"Serena, don't you have pictures of your family's house on your cell phone?"

"Of course." Her excitement increased. Pulling the phone from her back pocket, she mentally crossed her fingers and turned it on. Relief flooded through her as it lit. The low battery message came on so she scrolled quickly through her photos, thankful she had them organized in albums. Finding one of her parents' house, she showed the two men. "Does this help? They live in Iowa."

Rekah grinned. "That will work. Now when we open the portal, make sure we are on the ground before you step through."

She nodded, her excitement building. "Oh, thank you." She threw her arms around him and after a split second he hugged her back. When she stepped away he still smiled.

"Ready?"

She looked over at Toni, who waved her away. "Tell Jahl and Khaos I said goodbye. Oh and be sure to tell them I said not to banish Theron." She looked at Rekah. "I'm ready now."

Theron and Rekah stood side by side facing her but moved about three feet apart. Both men reached across their body and under their arm. The space between them began to shimmer and her parents' house came into view.

Rekah spoke. "Try to go through when there is no one near."

A car drove by so she waited, but other than that, it was a quiet evening in June. Taking a deep breath, she walked through.

The smell of freshly cut grass filled her nostrils and she inhaled. She turned back to see if the portal was still open, but it was gone. For a moment she panicked. What if she'd made the wrong decision? She wasn't delicate. Maybe she could have been an emotional stabilizing factor for Jahl and Khaos. Pain sliced through her gut at her thought.

"Serena!" Her sister's voice brought her attention back to Earth and she spun to see Jaelene running down the front steps. "Didn't you get my messages? I've left five. Holy shit, where's your shirt?"

Chapter Fourteen

Khaos ran up the steps behind Jahl, the closer they came to entering Loraleaf, the faster his heart raced. They were halfway up when a vision of Serena leaving Eden flashed before him. He stumbled as pain seized his chest and he fell forward, getting his hands out to catch himself before his head hit the stairs.

Jahl stopped above him. "What is it?"

He knelt on the step beneath him "She's gone."

"No!" Jahl ran upward, bursting through the hatch of Loraleaf.

Khaos slowly picked himself up. His chest remained tight, causing him difficulty breathing. He'd never had a future vision flash before him like that. Not even Sandale's danger had cut into his consciousness. He'd already developed some kind of bond to Serena and now she was gone.

He forced one foot in front of the other, up until he reached the hatch, feeling like he moved in slow motion. He had to catch up to Jahl for some reason, but his brain couldn't wrap around the loss of their beloved.

The sound of a door ripped from its hinges had him peering ahead. The door to Theron's house flew down the path and Jahl stood in the threshold. "Jahl!"

Jahl didn't move, his chest heaving.

Was it from the run or the pain? Khaos forced himself to traverse the distance to Theron's house. When he stepped up behind Jahl, he laid his hand on his shoulder, but couldn't find any words.

Jahl shook him off and entered. "Theron!"

"I'm right here, Jahl. No need to yell."

Jahl stomped into Theron's living area. Khaos joined him and stared at the tableaux. Toni sat on the arm of the couch, an ale in her hand. Rekah sat on the couch, a glass of water on the table before him. Theron stood in front of a large chair as if he'd just risen.

Jahl addressed Theron. "Where's my chosen one?"

Theron didn't flinch. "She returned home."

Jahl started for him, but when he reached the chair, there was no one there. It had been a reflection.

Khaos had to admire the man for his guts. But the fact was, he stole their beloved. With anger he didn't know he had, he swung toward the door they had just come through and slammed his fist into Theron's jaw.

Theron went down.

Khaos scowled. "Not smart."

Toni ran over as Jahl approached. "Oh no you don't. This isn't his fault. You two are the ones who screwed up." She stood bodily in front of Jahl, who had death written in his gaze for Theron.

"Move." Jahl barely ground out the single word.

"No." Toni put her hands on her hips.

Rekah spoke from where he was on the couch. "Toni, don't push him. He's beyond reason. You don't want him to break another Dickinson Law and hurt you."

Jahl whirled toward Rekah. "I've broken no laws."

"You told Serena she couldn't leave Eden."

Khaos cringed. Jahl's back muscles tightened, then his shoulders slumped. "There is no law that says a filoz can't deny a woman going back to Earth."

"Not that specifically, but if she turns away the bonding, you cannot force her."

Khaos spoke to Theron. "We would never force her, but it was our decision when she returned, not yours."

Theron lay on the ground rubbing his jaw. "No, it was her decision. You don't deserve her."

Khaos opened and closed his hands. Now that his anger had surfaced, he wanted to hit something, anything. He stepped closer to Theron, who simply watched him. Then he threw his fist into the wall. Pain smacked into his hand and radiated up his arm, stunning him. He pulled his hand from the dented log and turned his back on Theron. He couldn't look at him again and not hit him.

Toni moved in front of Rekah now as if she could protect him.

Didn't she realize nothing would stop him and Jahl from killing someone if they wanted to? He looked at Jahl. "Death?"

Jahl's eyes widened, the reality of what was possible registering, but instead of the nod Khaos expected, Jahl shook his head.

At the disappointment blooming in his heart, Khaos shivered. He'd never been a cold-hearted killer, even in the back streets of Naralina where he'd met Jahl. What was happening to him?

Rekah must have sensed their troubled emotions. He finally stood. "Theron, you can get up now."

Khaos heard Theron move behind him, but he didn't turn around.

"I know you are both angry."

Jahl opened his mouth and Rekah held up his hand.

"Don't. I sat here and felt your anger and worry and guilt and loss and love. That's why I couldn't stand when you entered. It was overwhelming, coming from both of you."

Khaos felt a certain amount of satisfaction in that. He hoped it hurt.

"I helped Theron open the portal, but before I did, I searched Serena's emotions."

Khaos tensed, sensing a similar reaction in Jahl.

"She is not in love with you, but she cares very much for you. She left because she was afraid she'd bond with you."

"What?" Jahl's exclamation married Khaos' thoughts.

Rekah held up his hand again. "But she recognized if she bonded with you, she wouldn't have lasted long."

Khaos couldn't keep silent any longer. "Why? We would have taken care of her."

Rekah nodded. "Yes, you would have, but you also would have depended upon her psychologically like you did with Sandale and she isn't Sandale. She has no special abilities."

Jahl shook his head. "What are you talking about? We don't need Serena for psychological dependence. We need her to love."

Khaos' stomach flipped over as understanding crept into his conscience. "Why do you say we would depend on her?"

Rekah looked relieved. "The two of you have gone through the worst childhood anyone here in Loraleaf can imagine. You both became adults by building defenses and have become leaders. You have great strength, not just physically, but mentally. But you have gained deep scars along the way."

He stared at Khaos. "You have a sense of unworthiness because of your unique birthmark."

"How do you know about my birthmark?"

"I told him."

Khaos looked at Toni. "Why?"

She threw up her hands as she walked back to the couch. "Because half your men were afraid of you because they thought you didn't have one at all. I simply told them the truth. That you do have a birthmark that's unique. Shit, you should have seen how relieved they were. The news spread across Loraleaf like wildfire."

He didn't know what to think. The men preferred that he had a unique mark over having no mark? It was too much to grapple with.

Rekah turned to Jahl. "And with you and your family's dismissal of your abilities as beneath them, you have striven to prove yourself in everything. This makes you quick to feel attacked so you are always defensive."

Jahl's jaw jutted. "I am not."

Rekah's lips quirked before he addressed them both. "Unless you two can overcome your scars, Serena is better without you."

"I've heard enough." Jahl turned on his heel and stalked out.

Khaos looked at each person in the room. Theron who loved Serena. He fisted his hands to keep from hitting the man again. Rekah, who seemed to know his emotions better than he did himself. Toni, Serena's best friend. He looked at her feeling betrayed and yet wanted to talk to her.

Finally, he took a deep breath and turned to leave.

"Oh Khaos, I almost forgot."

He looked over his shoulder at Toni.

"Serena asked me to ask you and Jahl to take care of Wally."

He closed his eyes as new pain permeated his heart. His throat closed and his hands fisted. He managed to nod once and strode from the house.

* * * * *

"So tell me who he is."

Serena opened one eye, looked at her sister and rolled over. Unfortunately, Jaelene didn't take the hint and instead hopped over her and lay down next to Serena. For a twenty-eight year-old, she could be such a teenager at times.

"I know you're not sleeping, so might as well open your eyes."

She grumbled and rolled over again. She didn't want to get up yet. Her eyes were swollen from crying and she needed coffee before she'd move.

"Your coffee is sitting on the dresser." The singsong voice told her she was being set up.

She opened her eyes and looked over her shoulder. "Are you lying?"

Jaelene shook her head, her long black hair flowing over her shoulders.

Serena focused on the dresser across the room. Sure enough, a steaming cup of coffee sat among her knickknacks, a picture of her family, and a stuffed extraterrestrial better known as ET. "Okay, if you bring it over here, I'll spill."

Jaelene jumped off the bed, her thin hips swaying in her faded blue jeans as she picked up the cup and set it on the nightstand.

"You left it way over there on purpose."

"Of course. I didn't just fall off the turnip truck." Jaelene's blue eyes sparkled in delight. The little minx.

Serena rolled her eyes and took a sip. Wow, it tasted sweet. She must have become used to drinking it black. She may just start drinking it that way.

Jaelene sat on the side of the bed. "Okay, so who is he? I know there is a he because for all your smiles yesterday, you showed up with no shirt, you have two love marks on your neck and you cried yourself to sleep last night. So what happened?"

She stared at her sister like she'd just dropped out of a starship and told her she was from the future. "Since when did you get so observant?"

"Since my big sister didn't return my calls for five days. I had very important things to discuss with you."

"Really? Like what?"

Jaelene shook her head and crossed her legs under her. "Uh-uh. Nice try. I want to know what the bastard did. You owe me for getting you a shirt before Mom or Dad saw you."

Serena took another sip of the sweet coffee, more to stall for time than because she wanted it. Who knew a person could switch to black and get used to it so fast?

"So…"

"I met a man."

"Well, no shit, Ms. Live Long and Prosper. I already established that."

"Right, but you didn't establish that it was actually two men."

Jaelene's eyes widened. "So you had two men fight over you and in the process one died and the other dumped you?"

Serena crinkled her forehead. "You watch too many movies."

"Maybe, but at least I watch a variety. They're not all science fiction."

Serena took another swallow.

"So what happened exactly?"

"Exactly? Well, they made mad passionate love to me together multiple times and fell in love with me, but then I had to leave because of our family reunion."

Jaelene studied her for a minute. "Holy crap, you aren't lying."

Serena spit some of her coffee out. She'd hoped to throw Jaelene off but that backfired.

"So why didn't you call me? Didn't they let you come up for air?" Jaelene tried to hide it, but she was hurt about the calls. They were as close as sisters could get.

"I'm sorry. I was in South America in the jungle and they didn't exactly have a lot of cell phone towers."

"I thought you were filming in Nevada."

The skeptical look Jaelene gave her warned her to stay as close to the truth as possible. This was a lot harder than she expected. "We were, but that's where I met these guys and they whisked me off to the jungle. What can I say, they were two serious hunks."

Jaelene grinned. "So were they bisexual?"

"No." At least she didn't think so. "No, they were totally focused on me and we actually did more than just have sex."

"Yeah? Like what?"

"We stayed in a treehouse that was really high above the ground and it had its own bathroom and kitchen."

Jaelene waved that away. "I've seen those on television. So what else?"

"We swung on vines like Tarzan. It was scary at first, but they knew what they were doing."

"So what happened?"

Serena took the last gulp of coffee and held the cup out. "Do you think you could fill me up again?"

"Sure, after you tell me what happened." Jaelene crossed her arms over her Love Me, Love My Goat t-shirt, a sure sign she wouldn't budge.

"I told you. They wanted me to stay, but it wouldn't have worked out." She looked away, not willing to share the pain of leaving Jahl and Khaos.

Jaelene's hand on her shoulder surprised her. It reminded her of Khaos. "You cared a lot about them."

Serena shrugged. "I only knew them for about a week. How much could I really care?"

Jaelene studied her face again and she had to look away.

"Jaelene! Where are you? I need your help with the potato salad."

"Coming, Mom!" Jaelene looked back at her. "I think you're going to have to find your own cup of coffee. I live too close to be special so I have to help in the kitchen, but you'll have to keep the relatives entertained."

Serena groaned as Jaelene jumped off the bed and padded out of the room in her bare feet.

One day at a time. That had been the mantra she'd started since giving her mom a big hug and almost breaking into tears. Since she came home every month, a teary, "I'm back" would have been suspect, but it was so hard. Her dad had been just as happy to see her and showed her some new tools he was trying out for the hardware store they owned. Everything was so normal, everything but her.

As if missing Khaos and Jahl wasn't enough, hiding her whole experience added to it. If only Toni had come back so she could talk to someone, but that was selfish. Toni was happy and that was all that mattered. Throwing off the covers, Serena rose and padded down to the bathroom. Guess there'd be no automatic shower today.

* * * * *

Jahl swallowed another Cinn Cream shot and threw the glass against the wall, stopping it before it hit and setting it down on the bar to join the other eight glasses. Khaos hadn't come back yet. Probably disappeared again. Damn.

A bang and a whimper from the bedroom had him growling. "Wally, what the scrat are you doing now?" He forced himself to rise, though his balance was a bit off. He would be miserable tomorrow, unless of course he drank through the night.

Stumbling into the bedroom, he found Wally curled up on Serena's pareo that he'd pulled from the drawer of the dresser he made her. "I know, little guy. I miss her too."

He grabbed the pillow from the middle of the bed where Serena had slept and inhaled. The scent of vanilla had him weaving with pleasure. He threw the pillow on the floor, intending to sit on it when he noticed a piece of paper on the bed where the pillow had been.

Jahl picked up the paper, but focusing wasn't easy. *Come slowly, Eden! Lips unused to thee, bashful, sip thy jasmines, as the fainting bee, reaching late his flower, round her chamber hums, counts his nectars—enters, and is lost in balms!* Sandale's favorite poem.

He dropped the paper as if burned and sat down hard on the pillow next to Wally. The animal lifted its head and whimpered and Jahl absently stroked it. First Sandale and now Serena. How much more would he have to suffer before his own burning ceremony? If they had listened to Sandale, to this very poem's words, they wouldn't have lost Serena. That certainty pierced through the alcohol's haze and he gasped.

A high-pitched gurgling started and he focused on Wally, all they had left of Serena. The critter was probably pretending Serena stroked him. He didn't blame him.

He heard the front door open, but didn't move. There was no reason to. It was probably just Khaos.

"There you are." Toni's loud voice had Wally opening his eyes.

"Don't worry, he's fine. I'm taking care of him like Serena asked." Jahl continued to stroke the welchet.

Toni shook her head. "I didn't mean him, I meant you."

He raised his gaze to her but didn't see a need to comment.

"What are you doing in here?"

Couldn't she see he was stroking Wally? He ignored her and returned his focus to the welchet. Maybe she'd go away and leave him in peace.

"Are you drunk?"

He shrugged. What did it matter?

"I was hoping I wouldn't have to do this, but…" Toni untied her yellow halter top and dropped it on the floor next to him.

"What the scrat are you doing?"

"I'm getting ready to have sex with you." She started unbuttoning the green skirt she wore.

He rose, a bit unsteadily. "Why would I have sex with you?"

"You lost Serena so now you want to drown your sorrows in drink and sex, right?"

He stepped back. "No, wrong."

She dropped the skirt and stood naked before him. For all her womanly curves, he felt nothing.

"What? Are you going to be celibate for the rest of your life?"

He shook his head, not sure what she wanted from him, but pretty sure it would be better if he got away from her. He started out the doorway.

"Where are you going? To find Sandale?"

He spun and faced her. "Sandale?" He tried to make his brain function. He needed to remember Sandale. No, he needed to remember something about Sandale.

Toni huffed. "I can see now why Serena didn't think she'd last three months with you two. The ring. Sandale's ring that Khaos has. You remember that right?"

Damn, he needed a drink. Weaving toward the bar, he brought a bottle to his hand and opened it. Was she supposed to know about the ring? Wasn't that a secret?

"I think you've had enough already." Toni made a grab for the bottle and he jerked it away. "Get away from me, woman." He took a hearty swallow and felt the fog clearing from his brain, but with that came the hurt. He set the bottle down hard on the bar. Not sure he wanted more clarity.

Toni sat on a barstool. "Listen, Jahl. You can't just wallow in here for days on end."

"I've been here one night."

She waved that away. "You know what I mean. You need to make a decision."

What he needed was for her to leave, so he pasted on an interested look and didn't say a word.

"You can't stop living. You have to make some decisions. If you don't want to lead Loraleaf any more then you have to hand it over to a filoz that will."

"Like who?"

"Theron, Rekah and Konala."

Jahl grabbed the bottle and walked away from her. "No." He took another swallow, his balance returning but the pain of Serena being gone growing stronger.

Toni just wouldn't stop talking. "You know, if you really loved Serena you would have let her go if that's what made her happy."

He froze, his gut tightening at her observation.

"That's what she did for me. She could see I was happy here and didn't even try to get me to go home with her though I would be the only one she could talk to about this place."

"By the Crius, woman, what do you want from me?"

"I want you to take responsibility and get control of Khaos. Need I say he's causing chaos? You have to figure out what you are going to do about Sandale, and whether you are willing to do whatever is needed to win Serena back."

He faced her, hope rising in his chest. "Win her back?"

She jumped off the chair and sauntered toward him in all her naked glory, but all he saw in his mind was Serena.

"Listen, Jahl. If you really want her, you have to change and there is only one person who can help you with that."

"You?"

"Shit, no. I have enough on my plate. Rekah."

"No." He took another swallow then sent the bottle to the bar. "He's a traitor."

Toni put her hands on her hips. "No, he isn't. What he did was right and if it had been another filoz with another woman you would have supported him. You need to put to rest the catastrophe that was your childhood. If you can do that, Serena will come back to you."

He grabbed Toni by the shoulders. "Did she say that?"

"Yes. It was the only thing that kept her from the bonding. You know, she really cares about you two."

He'd once told her he'd do anything for her and he'd failed. He looked at Toni. "What do I have to do?"

First you need to find Khaos and get him to agree too. Last I saw, he was swinging on the vines and he wasn't watching who he might hit.

* * * * *

Khaos left the sculptor and headed for Rekah's. He hated this. Rekah set up multiple scenarios during the day with different men, all to help him "overcome his past." Last he knew, he *had* overcome it, which is why he was still alive today.

What he hated about all the "testing" was he kept failing. He never knew when a conversation was real or another test. He was supposed to be valuing himself. He knew exactly what he was worth. He was part of the leading filoz of Loraleaf and he helped protect them, what happened in his personal life was his own problem…except Serena would be his personal life and that was a problem.

He took a lift down a level. He used to love the vines, but they reminded him of Serena. Besides, Jahl thought it best if he stay off them after he had knocked three men off one of the bridges, and one of them was still recovering. He should never have had those Apple Fires in his mental state that day. He grimaced.

Tomorrow was Sandale's memorial. It felt strange having it after what Jahl and he found, but they'd agreed not to give false hope. The only one who knew about the ring was Toni and that was only because she saw it and figured it out. That woman was too smart.

He grinned as the lift came to a stop and he crossed another bridge, nodding at those he passed. Toni was a handful. She had talked to Jahl and him about setting up her own Pleasure Temple in Loraleaf, but with so many men wooing their women, there would be little need for her services very soon. But he did appreciate her thoughtfulness. The men were much happier then they had been, especially those who still hadn't decided upon a chosen one.

Khaos stepped into one more lift and headed for the ground level. Below he could see Jahl leaving Theron's. From his angry gait, Khaos guessed Jahl had failed his tests too. Khaos didn't hold out much hope for himself. He could think of four times today when he'd undercut himself to someone and his guess was that those were Rekah's tests.

As he walked across the bridge, he met Toni heading to Rekah's as well.

"Hey, Khaos, how did you do today?"

He shrugged. "Don't know yet. I'm heading there now."

"Mind if I join you?"

He opened his arm to let her precede him and they entered Theron's home, except Theron wasn't there. He was still working in the lab, which was for the best. Both he and Jahl were still angry with him and in truth, Khaos didn't know if he could ever forgive him.

Rekah greeted them. "Toni, so good to see you. Will you be staying tonight?"

"If you want?"

Rekah took in Toni's short skirt and half top. "I think that would be pleasant."

Toni sauntered by the man. "I'm hoping for a bit more than pleasant."

Rekah smiled goodnaturedly.

Khaos stepped inside as well. "I'm here for my report."

Rekah led the way into the living area where Toni lounged on the couch. Khaos stood, already knowing the bad news. He'd been doing this stupid test routine for three days. It obviously wasn't working.

The other man picked up four papers and shook his head. "Still no change."

"What?" Toni sat up straight. "No change?"

Khaos shook his head. "I knew that. It's not like I can change my entire way of thinking about myself. This is wasting everyone's time. I suggest we give this up."

He turned to go.

"Wait." Toni ran up to him. "Can I speak to you outside for a moment?"

He nodded and they went back outside. Toni made a project out of closing the door to Rekah's home and hooked her arm in his. Now what?

When they had crossed the bridge to the lift that would take him home, she stopped. "Listen, I really need you to view yourself differently, not in front of others but inside yourself. Serena deserves you two and you have to make her happy. Right now, she's not happy."

"You've checked on her?"

Toni ignored his question. "She needs you and Jahl, but not as you are now."

He fisted his hands. "I'm not sure what you want is possible. I am who I am. Sandale accepted me for who I was. I can't change overnight, even if I want to for Serena."

"You know, Serena had an interesting theory about your birthmark."

"She did?" He was thrilled to hear anything Serena had said.

"Yes. She thinks your birthmark is different because you are the first of this race to evolve to a new level. Like a new mutation that will be better Edenists."

A better Edenist? That hadn't occurred to him. What if she was right?

"And just think. If you and Serena have a baby, your son could have the same mark as you with new abilities that can help all men on the planet. You never know."

Khaos' mind stuck on the word "son." A son by Serena. A warmth filled his chest. He hadn't thought that far into his own future, ironic as that was. A son with new abilities, maybe better than his own. He stared over Toni's shoulder and sensed happiness, a new beginning and hope filled his soul.

"Okay, Khaos, your eyes are glowing. You're freaking me out now."

He blinked and refocused on Toni. Grabbing her by the shoulders he gave her a kiss. "Thank you."

Her eyes widened. "Don't thank me, thank Serena."

"Serena. Yes." He ran past her and jumped on the lift. He needed to talk to Jahl.

Striding along the rope bridge to his house, he imagined so many new possibilities. They had a future. They could bring Serena back.

He stopped at the door as a new pride in himself filled him. This is why he was different, not because he was a freak, but because he was the new future for Eden, and his sons would be leaders of some kind in this transition. Sons?

He shrugged as he opened the door. Why not? He himself had four brothers. Why not? Maybe a son for each city. "Jahl!"

"I'm in here.

He found Jahl in their bedroom, or rather on the balcony of their bedroom.

"We need to get Serena."

Jahl turned. "You've sensed something?"

Khaos grinned. "Oh yes. I've sensed my son."

Jahl scowled. "How can that be? Serena won't bond with us."

"But she will."

"This doesn't make sense. Why will she suddenly bond with us when she refused to last week?"

Khaos felt doubt creep into his mind and confidently pushed it away. "Because something is going to change."

Jahl studied him in silence.

"What?" He looked behind him to see if Wally was there. "You've changed."

"No I'm the—" Jahl was right. Something had changed. It was as if a lift lever had been switched up instead of down. "You're right. I have. I think we need to try again with Serena. And if she won't have us now, then we try again. But I'm confident she will bond with us eventually." He grasped Jahl's shoulder, willing him to see what he could see.

Doubt clouded the other man's features but he nodded, willing to put himself through her rejection again. A man couldn't have a better brother of his heart.

"When should we try again?"

Khaos wanted to try now, but they still had Sandale's ceremony to complete. He removed his hand from Jahl. "The day after tomorrow. That will give us the time to celebrate Sandale's life and recover from it." He smirked.

"What if we discover Sandale is alive?"

Khaos fingered the ring on his third finger. "Then we can have a celebration of his life. In the meantime, the men will have closure and we'll be the only ones shouldering this burden of hope."

"That and our hope for Serena."

Khaos grinned. "Yes. We will need time to prepare the house for her as well."

Jahl turned. "What do we need to prepare? I already made the changes to the bedroom." Jahl headed that way and Khaos followed, his step lighter than he ever remembered it being.

"I think we need more table cloths for one."

Jahl looked back at him, his lips quirking at the corner. "Any particular color?"

Khaos laughed. "Don't worry, I'll get them."

They both stopped as they entered the living area. It looked like a windstorm had come through. Jahl growled. "That welchet will be the death of me."

Not likely. The welchet had been sleeping at Jahl's feet ever since Serena left. "Maybe it's time for a full-size pen. What about off here, so he can have a safe place to grub but still see us when we come home?

Jahl eyed the large window that looked out upon the rope bridge to their home. "If I keep it short we won't lose the view, but the dirt I bring in won't have grubs."

"What if you brought it in in buckets instead of directly? Have a couple men dig it up instead of you and then you can transport the wooden buckets."

Jahl nodded. "That will work. We don't want Wally to starve before Serena comes back to take care of him."

"In the meantime, I'll clean up this mess if you want to test the smoke dissipater for the ceremony. Unless you don't think you can speak to Theron without hitting him…again." Jahl had run into Theron the other day on a bridge. He couldn't even walk past him without giving the man a black eye.

Jahl's jaw tensed. "I better stay here and clean up after the critter. Speaking of, where the scrat is he? Wally!"

Khaos took that as his cue to leave. He'd just made it to the door when he heard Jahl and a high-pitched gurgle.

"Wally, what in the Crius name have you done?"

Making his escape, Khaos strode across the rope bridge. Eschewing the lift, he walked to a convenient vine. He unhooked it from the branch holder and swung across Loraleaf. Though he was headed to talk to Theron, there was nothing that could spoil his day as long as the reflection and air smoke dissipater worked.

He dropped down onto the next level, hooked that vine and grabbed another. If Sandale's ceremony was delayed, they'd have to delay finding Serena.

As he swung down to another level, he grinned. They could always bring Serena beforehand. His confidence in her commitment grew.

CHAPTER FIFTEEN

Serena thanked the policeman and left the station. There was no money left in her purse, but at least her wallet with her license and credit cards was inside. When she came back to Earth, she'd expected to start all over with new everything, but a message in her voice mail told her they had it. Luckily, she had a passport she'd obtained when she had to work on a film in Mexico last year, so she was able to fly to Las Vegas to retrieve her belongings.

It would be hard working on the new film without Toni around, but at least the fantasy film paid well. She would stay away from science fiction films for a long while, too, afraid she'd blurt out something about how they had it all wrong. For all she knew, they might not if it was based on a different planet than Eden. Her belief in life on other planets had grown exponentially now that it had been verified.

Serena jumped in her car and headed for home. She finally understood why Jahl said they couldn't let her go unless she was bonded. Keeping the secret of Eden was difficult. After a week with her family, she couldn't take it anymore and had accepted the fantasy film job.

It wasn't that her family was any different, it was that she was different. She couldn't tell them where she'd been, what she'd seen or felt and it created a distance that wasn't there before. It had become too stressful and her sister had come close to the truth too many times. Halfway through the week, the questions had focused on animals in South America. Not a surprising topic, but it was as if she knew something. It was probably just Jaelene's inherent curiosity about animals. Now even *their* relationship was different. It was ironic that though she hadn't bonded with Jahl and Khaos, she still lost a precious bond with her family. Would it have been different if she *had* bonded?

She shook her head, tired of second-guessing her decision. She would simply go to work and return to her apartment to avoid contact with others as much as possible until the whole experience seemed like a dream. The problem was, it wasn't and her heart ached. Maybe it was simply the idea of not appreciating something until it was gone.

Her gut told her she'd made the right decision, but her heart yelled at her every day. If only her men could have seen how valuable they were. Hell, they had saved her from certain death. She'd think they would recognize how important they were just from that.

She'd given a description of the four men who had attacked her on set by phone while still in Iowa, the detective insisting she not wait because her memory would change the facts as more time passed. She told him Toni was missing as well. If they could nail Toni's disappearance on those lowlife, she'd be thrilled. It wasn't quite the truth, but she had to have it on record that Toni existed and was now missing. Her friend had spent too much of her life with no one caring if she existed or not.

Pulling into her apartment complex, Serena turned off the car. Her next job had no extras working on it, so that made her feel a little safer, but she may have to think about moving to California. Chances of the police finding her attackers were pretty slim.

She climbed the stairs to her second-floor apartment and opened the door. Maybe she should adopt a cat or a dog. Something she could come home to at night. Something like Wally. Ugh, she needed to stop. Maybe she should get hypnotized. But how would she explain what she didn't want to think about?

Closing the door behind her, she glanced at the full wine bottle on her counter. No, she wouldn't resort to that. She'd suffer through this. It had to get easier. The clock on the stove told her she had just enough time to change and head to the new set.

Throwing her purse on the couch, she walked by Toni's room and stopped. Shaking her head, she ignored the closed door and continued to her own. There would be time enough to pack up Toni's stuff. Toni had promised to visit so she might want some of it on Eden.

Quickly changing out of her sundress and into a pair of black jeans, she threw on a black Terminator t-shirt over her red bra and pulled on her combat boots. She laced them up and grabbed her work bag. Lastly, she stuffed her newly recovered wallet into the back pocket of her jeans. With her cell phone in the other pocket, she left her place.

A strange feeling of being watched had her walking faster. Just in case, she looked around for a portal. Jumping into her car and locking the doors, she started it up. Khaos said they had watched and waited, but she never felt their presence. Maybe it was just wishful thinking on her part.

Following the GPS voice in her car, she headed out of the city. She was pleased the location they were shooting at was far from the other set. Different people, different genre movie, no extras and a different location should make the odds of running into the lowlife that had attacked her before pretty low. Still, she was glad this movie was shooting in Texas in a couple weeks. Staying out of Vegas for a while as the police investigated would make her feel safer.

Pulling into the building parking lot, she relaxed. It bustled with activity and a giant mechanical dragon sat mounted on the roof. Oh yeah, this would be a fun shoot. Just what she needed to take her mind off the men she left behind.

Within the lot she could see what looked like a mermaid fountain, a tall Buddha-type statute that had to be two stories high, and bales of hay. Along the lot fence was a row of desert senna bushes in full bloom. They must have been watering those for weeks for them to be so luscious in the middle of the Vegas summer. She watched as a very large bumble bee flitted around the yellow flowers, fully indulging in their nectar.

A phrase echoed in her mind at the sight. *Reaching late his flower.* Where had she heard that? There was more too. *Round her chamber hums, counts his nectars—enters, and is lost in balms.* Where had she heard that poem? Pulling her cell phone from her pocket, she searched for the phrases. Emily Dickinson's picture popped up. Oh God. Sandale. It was the last thing he said as she left him. She looked at the bee again, now joined by another. On the next bush were more. That's what Sandale meant. He was telling her they would be healed through her.

"Shit!" She stuffed her phone back in her pocket. Now she was seeing things in a simple bumble bee. "Serena, you have seriously lost it."

Exiting the vehicle, she grabbed her small bag with one hand and moved to her trunk. She unlocked it and pulled it open. The large bag had her set-up canisters, so she hauled it out too. Slamming the trunk down, she headed for the side entrance. Again that feeling of being watched had her slowing. She stopped and looked around, but she didn't see any large naked men, nor any openings in the air.

She shook her head at herself and continued inside. Maybe being back on Earth just had her a bit uptight. She needed to focus. Explosives were not something to daydream around. Throwing down her bags, she headed off to find the director.

* * * * *

Jahl watched as they tested the smoke dissipater again. The air portion worked fine, but the reflection wasn't working at all. "Theron, what is the problem?"

The man glared at him, his yellowing skin around his eye making him look evil. "Maybe it's my concentration lately."

Damn, so now it was his fault Sandale's ceremony had been put off? "Fine. Let me know when you have it working." Turning on his heel, he strode back toward the bakery, where Khaos was overseeing the storage of Sandale's favorite biscuits. The delay was grating on his nerves. Since he and Khaos had decided to contact Serena and try again, he'd been itching to go.

Khaos was just leaving as he approached.

"Will they last another day?"

Khaos nodded. "Yes. What about the dissipater?"

He shook his head. "I was plainly told my presence was causing the delay because someone couldn't concentrate."

Khaos laughed, a sound too often heard lately. He shouldn't begrudge the man his good mood, but he did.

Khaos slapped him on the back. "Come. Maybe an afternoon kafez will help."

He doubted it, but he had nothing better to do except watch Wally sleep. "Fine."

They'd just started for their house when the hatch opened and the men sent on patrol, including Konala, returned.

Konala held up his hand. "Jahl, we bring news."

He stiffened and looked at Khaos. Lawbreakers?

Konala strode up to them. "We were on patrol and ran into patrollers from Haven."

Interesting. So Haven finally took his advice and started to be proactive. He'd been surprised they hadn't been looking to their own defense besides the walls they'd built. "What is it?"

Konala nodded to Khaos, but addressed him. "They had a message for you."

"Me?" He looked at Khaos. "This should be interesting."

"Yes, they said one of their leaders, Nassic, requests your help."

Jahl looked in disbelief at the man. "Nassic? Are you sure he didn't say Wareson?"

Khaos turned toward him. "Why are you questioning which leader it is?"

"Because I consider Wareson a friend, but Nassic and I don't see eye to eye."

Konala's cocked his head. "Really? From the way this man spoke, it sounded like you were well thought of. He said Nassic had seen what you'd done in their waterhole and had heard how you'd slipped through their defenses and hoped you would come and help them strengthen theirs. They are pretty worried over there about the lawbreakers."

Jahl tried to grasp the idea that Nassic wanted *him* to help with their defense. It was almost unbelievable.

Khaos elbowed him. "Hey, they must like your work."

"It could be a trap."

Konala shook his head. "I don't think so. The man went on and on about all the ideas Nassic had that you might be able to help with."

It didn't sound like a trap.

Khaos laughed. "Don't look so shocked. Look at what you built here. How can you doubt others would value your abilities?"

He did look at Loraleaf, the bridges, the houses, the vines and he was proud of his accomplishments here, but to have someone like Nassic, who hated him, appreciate his ability made it real outside of himself.

The slap on his back broke him from his thoughts and he scowled at Khaos. "I will think about it."

"Don't think too long. I'm supposed to meet this man again at the Savinstone in two days' time and it will take me a day to get there."

Jahl nodded, and Konala turned for home.

"You have a lot to think about, so I'll leave you be." Khaos turned back the way they'd come.

Jahl remained where he was, the scent of yeast tickling his nose. Haven wanted his abilities. No, Nassic wanted them. The man who had knocked him unconscious and dragged him into a stone storehouse that had been the easiest of all places to escape from, at least for him.

One of his men brushed by him and apologized. He didn't acknowledge he'd heard.

A new feeling of confidence permeated his soul. His ability to control natural things that were dead wasn't such a hindrance after all. It was a strength and a damn good one.

His father's angry face floated across his mind and he swiped it away. What did that man know? He didn't even have a portal chip.

* * * * *

Serena shook her head at the cut wire between the trigger and the explosive charge. Now how did that happen? One of the crew must have rolled something over it. She examined the two ends. No, that was cut.

She looked around the scene set up for the take. All the other explosions had gone off but this one. The director was not happy with her. Did someone cut the wire not knowing what it was for, or did they cut it because they did?

A shiver ran up her spine. She'd have to figure it out tomorrow because everyone was heading out and if there was one thing she'd learned from her last movie, it was not to be the last one to leave.

She pulled her camera from her back pocket and took a picture of the cut, then dropped the line. After taking a photo of the line between her trigger and the explosives she pushed her phone back in her pocket. She'd look at the scene at home.

She heard cars exiting the lot and hurriedly packed up her small bag and strode toward her car. Once turning the corner around the mermaid fountain, she had the feeling again she was watched. She picked up her pace. It had become a daily occurrence and if it wasn't Jahl and Khaos then she could be in trouble. Maybe she should call the detective who had taken her statement.

She'd just reached her car when an arm wrapped around her waist and the butt of a gun dug into her ribs. Fear sliced through her. This couldn't be happening again.

"Don't scream or I'll kill you right here." The rough voice was muffled against the back of her head.

She nodded to show she understood, wishing she was Toni for a change and knew how to head butt backward.

"Now get in the car."

She didn't want to leave the set. She'd be dead for sure and the guy would get away with it. Her keys were already in her hand so she fumbled them as she reached toward the car door and they fell to the ground.

"Bitch." He spat and dug the gun into her ribs. That tone. It was the leader of the attack on her and Toni. She clamped her jaw tight, trying to keep her teeth from chattering.

"Fine. I can kill you here just as well."

That was true, but at least there was a security guy on duty. Maybe he would hear the shot and call 9-1-1. Oh God, she didn't want to die. She loved Jahl and Khaos. She needed to tell them that. There had to be a way out of this.

"Come on." He backed her toward the fountain and out of sight of the people climbing into their cars after a long day on set.

She wanted to scream, the sound rising in her throat, but the gun digging into her ribs made sure she didn't let it out.

Slowly, he walked her back behind the statue and around the building to the outdoor scene they'd been shooting. Blackened set pieces from her explosions had been pulled aside to allow the crew to start set-up for the next day while they refilmed the one explosion that didn't go off.

"This is far enough. Now we wait until everyone leaves."

She swallowed hard and unclamped her jaw. "Why are you doing this?"

"Because you had to go and tell the police. I don't know where you disappeared to with those macho men, but all was well with you gone. Then you had to come back. They've arrested the rest, but I'm a lot smarter. I know when I'm being tailed."

"You've been following me." Her teeth were chattering at warp speed but she didn't care.

"Of course I was. Needed to find out which movie you were working on. It wasn't hard. There aren't a lot of female pyrotechnicians who work on movies in Las Vegas."

Duh. As far as she knew, there was only one other woman and she wasn't that good. Why hadn't she waited for a job to surface in California? Or why hadn't she just bonded with Jahl and Khaos? She could have gone to her family reunion and then back to Loraleaf.

The sound of a car door slamming in the parking lot and an engine starting had her clamping her jaw down. She didn't want to die. What if Khaos and Jahl came back for her and she was dead? She closed her eyes. *Please. Please. Please. I need you.*

The arm around her waist tightened. "Ah fuck."

Opening her eyes, she didn't believe Khaos and Jahl stood in front of them. She closed her eyes and opened them again. They were still there.

"Serena." Jahl's whisper of her name sent a shiver through her.

"Stay back, or I'll kill her."

Khaos cocked his head. "Isn't that your intention anyway?"

Her attacker didn't seem to know what to say to that.

Jahl looked at Khaos. "So after he kills her, we kill him, right?"

Khaos nodded.

Kill her? They would let him kill her? Khaos crossed his arms over his chest like he always did when he was teasing, but he scowled and made it look like he couldn't wait to kill Tommy. So they were going to save her, but how?

"Maybe we can trade." Her attacker sounded assured, but she felt a tremor ripple through his body. Hadn't Jahl come down on him pretty hard last time?

Jahl looked bored. "Like what?"

"I give you the girl and you let me go."

The two Edenists looked at each other before Khaos addressed him. "But then you would come back and kill her anyway, so why not simply get it over with?"

The man holding her stiffened. "Because I could not kill her and then— " The grip around her slackened and her attacker fell to the ground, a giant rock lay next to him.

She looked up at Jahl and her knees buckled under her.

"Serena." Jahl ran to her but wasn't fast enough. She hit the ground in a heap. He knelt and hugged her to him.

Khaos sauntered over and crouched, running his knuckles across her cheek. "Are you all right?"

She opened her mouth but her teeth chattered.

He grinned. "It's okay. You're safe now."

She was. They'd come. "K-Khaos, you knew?"

"I'm the next evolution of Edenists. I can do anything." He winked and her heart filled.

"Come." Jahl lifted her up, but didn't let her stand on her own. Good thing because she'd probably collapse again.

"I didn't think I'd see you again. I didn't tell anyone anything, I promise. I'm so sorry I left."

Jahl squeezed her. "No, you were right. If you hadn't, we would have never realized we were depending on you. Rekah explained it to us. We don't need that anymore."

Her eyes widened. "You don't?"

He shook his head. "No, all we need you for is to be our beloved."

She looked into his dark-blue eyes and glimpsed a confidence she hadn't see there before. It filled her heart to bursting to see them this way. "Oh good. Because I love you both."

Jahl pulled her into a passionate kiss that didn't help her knees at all, but there was no worry because as soon as he stopped kissing her, Khaos swept her up in his arms and kissed her, completely melting every limb in her body.

When he let her up for air, his dark-gray gaze held her. "Ready to come home?"

She looked over at Jahl and scowled. "On two conditions."

The man froze. "Anything."

"Really?"

He had the grace to flush. "Yes."

"I want to bond with you and become your beloved and I want to be able to visit my family anytime I want for as long as I want even if I want to go tomorrow."

Jahl looked at Khaos before meeting her gaze. A slow smile spread over his face and her heart thumped hard. The man had a beautiful smile.

"We agree."

She scrambled out of Khaos' arms and threw herself at Jahl. He hugged her to him tightly but gently.

Khaos put his hand on her shoulder. "Now can we go home? I know Wally is anxious to see you."

She squealed as she nodded. She just couldn't help it. Her heart was bursting with love for these two Edenists. Who could have guessed she would fall in love with two men from another planet? How unexpected and absolutely wonderful.

Jahl and Khaos stood side by side leaving a space large enough for her and opened the portal. As she walked between them, she took each of their hands in hers. "Let's go home."

EPILOGUE

Serena clenched her sheath tight as her nipples were pinched lightly. She tried to roll over in her sleep, but her legs were caught in the covers. Not wanting to open her eyes and totally leave her dream, she pulled at her right hand, but it was held. Her eyes snapped open.

Khaos held her hands above her head. "Good morning."

She smiled. "Good morning. What are you doing?"

He shrugged, his muscular shoulders attracting her attention. "Just holding your hands."

Another pinch to her nipple had her looking to her breasts. She stared at the clamps attached to each one. It wasn't the first time she had nipple clamps on, but they didn't usually move.

"Good morning, beloved." Jahl knelt at the foot of the bed. In each hand was one of her ankles.

Heat surged through her. Laying on the bed between her legs was a smooth wooden penis with ridges. She met Jahl's gaze. "Yours?"

He smirked, a sight that had her toes curling below his hands. He shrugged.

Her men liked to shrug when they didn't want to give away their plans. She pretended to study the dildo. "Hmm, doesn't look quite as big as you, but it will do."

Jahl's smirk turned devious and her folds moistened.

She looked up at Khaos. "You're just going to watch, aren't you?"

He nodded, his own grin as he looked down at her breasts caused her to take a deep breath.

"Aren't we having guests this morning?"

Jahl answered. "This won't take long."

"You are far too sure of yourself."

He nodded. "Yes, I am."

She took another deep breath at that. They had bonded as soon as they'd returned to Loraleaf yesterday afternoon. She didn't feel any different, but they said it would come soon enough. She couldn't wait to discover what connection she would have with them.

Her nipples pinched again and her gaze flew to Jahl. It was so weird and so stimulating to have her men holding her while items mysteriously played with her body.

Movement on the bed had her watching the dildo as it slid toward her opening.

"Bend your legs." Jahl punctuated his request by pushing her feet closer to her. She did as requested and the dildo touched her.

"Does this take a lot of effort?" Her voice was breathy with anticipation.

"Not at all."

She opened her mouth to make another comment, but her nipples were pinched again, this time a little harder. "Oh." She couldn't help her comment as the feeling sped right to her core.

The dildo started to push inside her and she lifted her hips, letting her knees fall to the sides. Khaos stood above her, holding her wrists together and watching.

She loved the look on his face as the dildo penetrated her completely and she sucked in a breath.

The nipple clamps pinched again, harder still and her sheath contracted around the hard wood inside her. It really gave a whole new meaning to the old term "a woody." She couldn't voice her thoughts as her body was on edge, but she did grin at her thought.

Khaos bent over her and gave her an upside down kiss, his tongue thrusting in her mouth like she wanted Jahl to thrust the sex toy.

When Khaos broke off the kiss, she was so wet she was sure the dildo would fall out, but it stayed in place.

The nipple clamps pinched and her pussy contracted in response, grasping the wood. The dildo started to move smoothly in and out but the stimulation to her nipples became uneven, not allowing her to predict the zings of pleasure that flowed from one point of her body to another.

Then the wood inside her started to vibrate, speeding its thrusts in and out of her pussy. Jahl focused between her legs and the sight was too erotic. She closed her eyes and let the feelings build, knowing she could trust the men who held her.

Her hips began to push against the sex toy, wanting it deeper, harder. The vibrations sensitized her clit. Nipple pinches were like sparks that set her fire blazing and she hung on the edge of satisfaction for a long moment when a vision of what she looked like from above flashed clearly across her mind. She could see her body and Jahl and it sent her over the edge.

She yelled, arching her back as the sex toy pumped into her, the nipple clamps falling to the side as she held her hips up for the final thrust. When her orgasm subsided, she opened her eyes and stared at Khaos. "I saw it."

"Saw what?" He continued to hold her hands.

"I saw your view of what was happening to me."

He let go of her arms and looked at Jahl. "The bonding."

"Really? Does that mean you can see what I'm looking at?"

Khaos sat on the bed next to her. "I don't know, but we will test it out."

She pushed herself up on her elbows, curious as to why Jahl still held her ankles. "Are we done?"

"Almost. Allow me." Slowly, he retrieved the dildo from her sheath.

"That was so… I don't know what it was, but I liked it."

Jahl grinned. "Good. Then you'll like this as well." He placed a large bullet on the bed. Unlike the toys on Earth, there was nothing attached to it that she could tug on to pull it out. It would only leave her body when Jahl decided to retrieve it.

She shook her head. "Not now."

"Yes. Now."

Before she could protest, Khaos had laid her back on the bed and kissed her. As his mouth tangled with hers, the bullet entered her all the way to her cervix.

Khaos finished the kiss and sat up.

Shit, she was ready to come again already.

Jahl let go of her ankles. "Better get ready for our guests. You have time to take a quick shower if you want."

She blushed as she remembered the shower they'd taken yesterday evening. All three of them had enjoyed washing one another until she found herself pressed face forward against the glass and pumped into twice in a row by her beloved. They had told they did so just in case the first bonding intercourse didn't take. But they didn't need an excuse. They could make love to her anytime in any way and she was more than happy.

After Jahl gave her a sweet morning kiss, she hopped into the shower. Jumping up, she hit Jahl's shower program. The warm rain setting felt great, but she didn't waste time. Jahl and Khaos had changed for the better. It wasn't a huge change, but there were the little things like Jahl's smiles that still caught her off guard or Khaos' new stride. She couldn't wait for her family to meet them.

Toweling off, she ran into the bedroom and opened the top dresser drawer. A vibration inside her sheath had her grasping the furniture. Oh, that was so not fair. Moisture filled her folds and she quickly dried herself again. What if Jahl did that while they had guests? Excitement zinged to her core at the thought. Shit.

Finally looking in the drawer, she found pareos in a rainbow of colors neatly stacked within, or rather every color but blue. The blue pareo had been commandeered by Wally and they let him keep it in his new pen.

Hearing voices in the living area, she chose a pink pareo and quickly put on her new Eden sandals. She loved them. They were so soft and it looked like she wore nothing at all, but the soles were thick yet flexible. Just another example of the strange combination of Crius advancement and Edenist ingenuity.

By time she walked into the kitchen, everyone was there. She ran to Toni and gave her a long hug. To Theron, Konala and Rekah, she gave a nod, well aware she was bonded now, even if she didn't know what her link to Jahl was yet. She looked at Theron. A yellow bruise beneath his eye and a fading one at his jaw made her wince.

Khaos set cups of kafez on the table. "Thank you for meeting with us. I must reiterate, what is said here can go no further. No one is to know. Do you understand?"

Serena walked around the people seated at the table. They all nodded. She sidled up to Khaos, picking up a cup of her favorite hot liquid. Jahl moved closer, sandwiching her between them, exactly where she wanted to be.

"What is it?" Konala put down his cup. "How can we help?"

Jahl took a deep breath. "We have hope that Sandale yet lives."

Rekah stood, his body tense. "Why?"

Khaos held up his hand. "We found Sandale's ring at the last lawbreaker site between here and Haven. Either they put it there to mock us with his death…"

"Or…" Jahl finished. "He left it as a way of letting us know he's still alive."

Rekah slumped into the chair. "But you said he was dead. Today is his ceremony."

"I know." Jahl looked over her head at Khaos and back to Rekah. "I followed a trail of Sandale's blood that led to a grave. In my anguish, I dug beneath the mound and threw up all that lay beneath it. I lost control, digging trees as deep and as wide as I could. I destroyed it all. The healer I was with said if there had been a body, it was in pieces. It still could be, but we need to know."

Konala nodded. "Yes we do, but you tell *us* this for a reason."

"We do." Khaos gave her hand a squeeze. "As you know, Haven has asked for Jahl's help. Next week, after we visit Serena's family and she takes care of things on Earth, we will go to Haven. Serena will be safe there while she talks with the leaders' agapayto. Jahl and I will pursue the original path the lawbreakers took with Sandale to see if we can find anything."

Theron spoke for the first time. "Will you be gone long?"

"No." Khaos looked at him. "We don't want to leave Loraleaf for too long. If we find nothing, we will leave it in Haven's hands. We tell you this because we would like your filoz to oversee Loraleaf while we are gone."

Konala and Rekah nodded, but Serena noticed Theron gave no indication.

"So what do you need *me* to do?" Toni held her cup up for more kafez. Jahl reached behind him and lifted the pot. As he poured the liquid for her, he explained. "We ask a very big favor from you, but only if you are willing."

Toni's face turned serious, reminding Serena of how her friend looked when she took instruction from the stunt coordinator on where to fall when jumping off a high building so she hit the air bag perfectly.

Jahl put the pot back in its holder. "We would like you to enter a Pleasure Temple within the city and communicate with us about what goes on there."

"You want me to spy for you." Toni put her cup on the table and leaned forward.

"Yes. You are the perfect person as no one would suspect a woman and you have the ability to handle yourself well."

"Thank you." Toni preened under Jahl's compliment and Serena noticed a sparkle in her friend's eye. She did like to be useful. Still, Serena felt the need to speak.

"You don't have to do this. It could be very dangerous as you'll have no one inside that can portal you out if you need to escape."

"I know, but for this place and Haven I would be happy to." Toni's serious face disappeared. "Besides, think of all those men

I could educate on what a woman likes." She wiggled her brows and Serena felt better that Toni was comfortable, but she still had reservations.

Khaos added to the mission. "We'll set up regular times for communication. Konala, I'm hoping you can help with this."

The man looked startled, then his eyes widened before he grinned. "I do think I have a few winged friends who could help us out, and if Toni doesn't mind, a few small furry ones who can find their way into anywhere."

Serena hadn't thought of Konala's connection to animals as being able to help with communication, but now that he mentioned what he could do, she felt a lot better about Toni going inside the city. "Hold on. How will we get Toni inside?"

Silence filled the kitchen. Maybe Toni wouldn't be going to the city after all. Serena wouldn't mind that at all as she much preferred having her friend close by.

Theron broke the silence. "If we can get very close to the city, as in next to a wall, we could portal her in. If they have developed the technology to track portals outside the city, the closeness of the portal may make it seem like a bad reading, or a slightly off-the-mark instrument."

Konala nodded. "That could work. Toni's story could be that she is new to Eden but was dropped off from another city after she chose a Pleasure Temple over the filoz who brought her here. That's how women usually become cythera."

"Oh, I like that name. Toni, the cythera. I can get into that." She grinned.

"We'll need two men to open the portal. I'll go." Theron volunteered and Serena wanted to kiss him, but she kept that to herself."

"I can go too." Konala looked at Toni. "Then I can instruct you on how to work with my animals."

Toni nodded. "That sounds like a plan. I'm ready to leave whenever you are."

Rekah stared at Theron in the strangest way. Suddenly he spoke. "You aren't coming back." It wasn't a question.

Everyone's gazed moved to Theron.

"No, I'm not."

Konala's face fell and Serena was reminded of Jahl when he knelt over a bleeding Sandale. These men were close. "Why, Theron?"

Theron looked directly at her and she caught her breath. "I can't stay at Loraleaf any longer. I will go to Haven or take my chances out on my own."

Her heart broke at his unspoken confession. Theron was leaving for good because of his feelings for her. Everyone at the table knew it, but no one said a word.

Toni finally interjected. "I know you men have nothing to pack." She gave Theron and Konala the once-over. "But I do, so if you'll excuse me, I need to decide what to bring. I may be starting a naked profession, but I'm new to Eden. I need to look the part. Just let me know what day you want to head to the city and I'll be ready." She stood, breaking up the gathering.

After people left, Serena sat on her favorite chair while Jahl cleaned up the kitchen.

Khaos came in and lifted her into his arms before he sat, her on his lap. She couldn't resist confiding in him. "It's my fault Theron's leaving."

"No, it's not. He fell in love with you. It's not something any of us can control. The first time I saw you I fell in love with you, and I didn't even know your name."

She looked him in the eye. "I find that hard to believe. When was the first time you saw me?"

He grinned. "You were standing in line at the movie theatre with Toni, who didn't look thrilled to be there."

"What movie? I've seen tons of movies over the years."

"*Avatar.*"

"Oh my God, I remember that night. The guy I was seeing refused to go, so I dragged Toni with me. What would you have done if I was there with a man?"

Khaos kissed her temple before he answered. "I told you. I fell in love with you the minute I saw you. If you were with a man, it wouldn't have mattered. I would have simply wooed you away."

"Wooed? Really? But you didn't even know—ouch!"

"What is it?"

She stared at her hand, which looked completely normal. "It felt like I just burned my hand."

"Khaos!" Jahl yelled from the other room. "I need ice."

Serena looked at Khaos and he shook his head. They both stood and ran into the kitchen.

Jahl stood at the sink, his hand in cold water. Serena looked at her right hand and checked to see that Jahl had his right hand in the water. "Oh wow."

Khaos laughed as he opened the cold box.

"It's not funny." Jahl scowled. "That kafez was hotter than the helios center."

Serena sighed. "No, Jahl, he's laughing because I just discovered the results of our bonding."

Jahl's blue eyes darkened, his focus complete. "What?"

She held up her perfectly healthy hand. "When you burned yourself, I felt it."

His eyes widened. "I've never heard of that."

Khaos brought the ice over. "No one had ever seen a Kindred of Eden able to control dead nature either. You are unique, just as I am."

Serena looked at them. "I hope this new connection is only for very extreme touches, otherwise we are going to drive each other crazy."

Jahl's mouth quirked up on one side and a devilish gleam entered his eyes. "Maybe we should test this."

"How? I'd rather not burn myself or cut myself." She frowned.

Khaos grinned. "I'm thinking a bed might be in order."

Jahl wiped his hand off. "No need for a bed when we have a perfectly good table right here."

"Here?" She looked at the table and then back at them and then at her hand. Curiosity got the best of her. Better to find out now. If she felt Jahl come and saw Khaos' view, she was in for the orgasm of her life.

She gazed at her two gorgeous, confident men. How lucky was she to have stumbled into this unexpected Eden? A vibration in her core had her eyes widening and her folds moistened. Oh, she was very lucky.

Jumping up to sit on the table, she opened her arms. "Ready when you are."

The End

ABOUT LEXI POST

Lexi Post is a New York Times and USA Today best-selling author of erotic romance. She spent years in higher education taking and teaching courses about the classical literature she loved. From Edgar Allan Poe's short story "The Masque of the Red Death" to Tolstoy's *War and Peace*, she's read, studied, and taught wonderful classics.

But Lexi's first love is romance novels. In an effort to marry her two first loves, she started writing erotic romance inspired by the classics and found she loved it. Lexi believes there is no end to the romantic inspiration she can find in great literature. Her books are known as "erotic romance with a whole lot of story."

Lexi is living her own happily ever after with her husband and her cat in Florida. She makes her own ice cream every weekend, loves bright colors, and you will never see her without a hat.

Lexi enjoys hearing from readers. She can be contacted at lexi.post@yahoo.com or through her website www.lexipostbooks.com

Here's a peek of *Cowboy's Never Fold*, the first book in the
Poker Flat series.

Cowboys Never Fold

Wade Johnson slowed his Chevy Silverado and stared at the
wooden sign with burnt-in letters hanging above the dirt road:
POKER FLAT NUDIST RESORT.

It swung between two weathered posts, the sign's newness
jolting the senses against the Old West background.

Stopping his pickup, he hesitated to make the left turn. His
best friend had called in a big favor. Nine years ago, Wade had
been blinded by love and almost made the worst mistake of his
life. If it hadn't been for Dale's instincts and a paternity test, Wade
would have been shackled to a selfish sorority girl and left with
another man's kid. Shit, he could have been a country song.

He owed Dale and he'd never back out on a friend, even if it
meant working at a nudist resort for three months. "I *am* doing
this." The sound of his voice gave him the boost he needed. With
his commitment firmly in place despite a dozen misgivings, he
turned the truck down the dirt road.

At least the pay was outstanding, and he could choose his
own horseflesh and set up the stables as he felt they should be run.
Just the thought of starting a new operation had him stepping on
the gas a bit harder, his truck throwing up a cloud of dust that
could probably be seen in Wickenburg.

After a good mile of nothing but desert, a wooden barrier
declared the end of the road. To the right was an overly large garage
with only three sides. He brought the truck to a stop underneath

the shelter. It could clearly house a couple dozen cars and the massive metal structure was tall enough for RVs too. The roof had to be at least twenty feet high.

Exiting his vehicle, his boots hit concrete. Nice. If this is how the owner built the garage, he couldn't wait to see the new stables. Dale's voice in his head dampened his enthusiasm. *I've sent three men out there to set up this woman's stables and all three quit. This could kill my temp agency's reputation. I need someone I can trust to find out what's going on. If she is a cranky old bitch who expects miracles, I don't need her as a client. But if it's something else, I want to know. If her resort takes off, I plan to be the one filling her staffing needs.*

Wade straightened his black Stetson and walked toward the old man sleeping on a chair in the relative coolness of the structure. It was August and days in the desert usually hit three digit degrees. The sound of his boots hitting the floor didn't wake the man, so he shook him.

"What? What? I don't knows nothin'." The man's eyes were a bit glazed and his chin showed a few days of beard growth.

Wade tipped his hat. "Afternoon. I'm Wade Johnson. Dale Osborn sent me to set up the stables here."

The man stood and teetered before steadying himself with the folding chair. "I'm Billy." The smell of alcohol was faint but definitely there. Billy thrust out his hand as if suddenly remembering his manners.

Wade shook, taking in the faded blue jeans, ripped sneakers and dirty t-shirt. He sincerely hoped Billy wouldn't be the one greeting the guests. "Where would I find the owner?"

The short man stared at him for a few moments. "Right. Right. Come on. I'll takes you down."

Down? Wade followed Billy to a tan golf cart and got in. As they proceeded out of the garage, he looked everywhere for the supposed resort, but there was nothing but desert for miles, and no butte stood out to hide it.

Then they drove past the wooden barricade and after a few minutes he recognized the edges of what must have been a hundred-year-old ravine that had weathered away to create a small canyon. As they drew closer to the ledge, the resort came into view.

"Wow." It was an ingenious design. One that had him rethinking a few of his own plans for a spread.

Billy smiled a toothy grin. "Yup. That be what everyone says."

Wade shook his head in astonishment. Across the ravine, near the top was a natural shelf of land where a large building, pool and stables sat surrounded by green lawn and narrow pathways for walking. Below that shelf was another that was home to small cottages sporadically placed among the natural desert landscape. There were more walking trails going farther into the small canyon. At the bottom was a creek with a strip of green growth on each side.

"How long did it take to build this place?"

Billy frowned. "If you counts the stonewallin' from the county, two years. But when the permits was in place and legit, the construction took a year. The stables is the newest building." He pointed to the white structure.

Wade's stomach tensed with excitement. A new barn, corral and soon horses of his choosing without spending a dime of his own money was too enticing to pass up, not that he would. Dale's company was new and he needed a good reputation if he was to succeed in Phoenix. Wade owed him and he would stay long enough to discover why the other stablemen left. That Wade would enjoy the job he was hired for was a bonus. He could already see possibilities for trails down to the creek. How far did it go?

"We could has opened sooner if we has reli…help we can depend on. I hope you plan to stay longer than the last horse man." Billy spat over the side of the cart. "We needs someone we can count on out here."

He looked at Billy and his excitement dimmed. "Was the stable manager quitting the only thing that held everything up?"

"Nah. We gots a nosey sheriff and stupid stuff breaks every day." Billy slowed the cart as they drove around a switchback. After the cart rumbled across a well-made wooden bridge that spanned the creek, Billy pointed at the road. "This here path were designed for the wagon and stagecoach. Only the employees gets to drive those. The golf carts, them is for the guests."

"Stagecoach?" Wade scanned the resort as they drove closer, expecting to see the oddity sitting on the verdant lawn.

Billy broke into a big grin, revealing a missing tooth on the left side. "You betcha. Prettiest darn thing I has ever seen. It's a repro…copy of one of them Old West ones. You be in charge of it. Maybe you can give me a ride in it? Miss Kendra don't lets me drive that one."

Wade silently agreed with Miss Kendra's decision. There were a lot of the woman's decisions he agreed with, so why did she have such a hard time keeping staff when she hadn't even opened? It couldn't be because of the nude clientele. She didn't have any yet. He would never have taken a job at a nudist resort if Dale hadn't needed him. People walking around nude in public wasn't his thing.

Oh shit. What if the resort was the owner's retirement dream come true and she ran the place nude? Now that was a sight he wasn't in a hurry to see.

"Here you be. Miss Kendra through that there pavilion. At least, that where I sees her last. She were bossing over the buildin' of some water thingy by the pool. Whatever it are, I sure when she be done, it will look good."

Wade stepped out and tipped his hat. "Thank you." As Billy drove away, Wade shook his head. How could the old man obviously idolize the owner and yet others quit on her? He strolled in the direction Billy indicated. He appreciated the view the resort presented, but he mentally braced himself for encountering a naked old woman.

As he turned the corner at the end of the freestanding pavilion, he found the pool, its crystal-clear water actually making him thirsty. The large rectangle had a curvy pool coming off it that imitated a winding river. Every eight feet or so a concrete high-table broke the surface of the water. Talk about an enticement to drink. Whatever kind of personality this woman had, he would be the first to admit she was smart.

He approached a group of three men with Desert Pool Design emblazoned on their shirts. They rested in the shade, chowing down on sandwiches. "Good afternoon. Could you tell me where to find Miss Kendra Lowe?"

One of the men pointed, his mouth full.

"Thanks."

Wade strode toward the bar. It was under another pavilion, but this one attached to the main building and its far side was supported by stone columns. The sleek wood bar top was at least three inches of ironwood. The rattling of glasses came from behind it but he couldn't see anyone.

"Hello there. I'm looking for Miss Kendra Lowe?"

A young woman stood up from behind the bar, her disheveled dark brown hair caught in a clip behind her head. She wiped sweat from her brow with the back of a dirty hand. It seemed everything was clean but the workers. She gazed at him, no curiosity whatsoever in the deep blue of her eyes. "I'm Kendra Lowe."

Wade couldn't help staring in disbelief. Out of habit, he wiped his hand on his jeans although it was probably cleaner than hers. "Good afternoon, Ms. Lowe. I'm Wade Johnson. Your new stable manager."

She studied him as she shook his hand, her expression revealing nothing.

He, on the other hand, didn't expect the owner of such a pristine spread to be so young, maybe thirty or so, almost his age. Her mouth was wide with a straight nose above it. She had very high cheekbones, but her face held none of the lines of a woman used to manual work, which she appeared to be doing. Her arms were toned, almost muscular as revealed by the modest black tank she wore, though nothing could truly hide the substantial chest it covered. But she was too thin by half, as his grandmother would say.

She placed one dirty hand on her waist and jutted out her hip, giving it a curve that wasn't there before. "So, Cowboy, it appears Dale was successful in finding me another stable manager. Good. I don't have much time left before we open and the trails still need to be chosen, the horses need to be purchased and transported, feed needs to be ordered and a ton of other details I have no clue about.

I must have someone who is going to stay at least three months. Can you commit to that, no matter what?"

A surge of adrenaline shot through his body again when she mentioned picking horses. He could pretty much stay however long she needed for a chance to do that. "Yes, Ms. Lowe, I can."

"Good. I can't be worrying about that side of the operation, so you just tell me what you need, Cowboy, and we'll make it happen." She turned toward the main building. "Lacey!"

Wade stared at his new boss. This was a dream job to any cowboy worthy of riding, which made it harder to understand why so many before him quit. Maybe she was really a micromanager and pretended not to be. Or maybe she was too hard to read. Her eyes, a nice royal blue, were anything but windows to her soul. There was no smile of welcome or satisfaction. Even her tone of voice didn't give away anything.

A petite blonde woman came through the glass door of the building and smiled warmly as she approached. "Howdy, I'm Lacey."

Now that was the kind of greeting he liked. He shook her hand, careful not to squeeze too hard.

Kendra leaned on the bar, her substantial chest supported by the dark wood. "Lacey will show you your living quarters. Then become familiar with the stables, corrals and your office. We can meet around nine tonight to discuss next steps."

"Nine, yes Ms. Lowe." He nodded, not sure what to make of the late hour, but she was the boss.

Lacey hooked her arm in his. "Right this way."

"And Cowboy." They'd only taken a couple steps, when Kendra stopped them. "Don't call me Ms. Lowe. It makes me sound like a teacher or something. Kendra will do."

He tipped his hat. "I can do that if you can call me Wade."

Kendra's face didn't even twitch. He waited for a sign from her that she understood. Finally, she nodded once. "Fair enough. See you at nine, Wade."

Kendra watched Wade leave, his tight butt impossible to ignore. Once he was through the glass door into the main building, she let herself slither back over the edge of the bar to sit on the floor. Damn, the man was hot. Why had Dale stopped sending her old codgers? The last thing she needed now was a distraction.

And Wade Johnson was definitely a distraction. His clean-shaven chin could serve as artwork. His brown eyes, which matched his short hair, reminded her of milk chocolate and his voice had her muscles wanting to melt. Thank God she'd been behind the bar because what really had her libido revving was his broad shoulders. Only a muscular man could be that thin at the waist and have such broad shoulders. Dammit. She hadn't had sex since she bought Poker Flat and she'd be damned if she'd have it now with some hunky cowboy employee. The odds were stacked against that working out well.

Refocusing, she pulled the small cooler back into place, assuring it would drain through the floor and not all over it. At least she wouldn't have to worry about the cowboy being underfoot. He had his domain and she had hers. She just needed to make it through their meeting tonight. After wiping her hands on her work jeans, she picked up the glass washer and set it in the sink. The plumber would be in tomorrow morning to take care of installing the final pieces of the bar according to code. Luckily, she had the liquor license from the last owner of the Poker Flat Bar, which had been located where her garage now stood. That license was worth every penny she'd paid for the ramshackle building she tore down.

And having Adriana as the bartender of her new bar should keep the liquor sales high, *if* the woman kept her clothes on. Kendra wiped her hands on a bar towel and shook her head. She had quite the crew here, but she knew all of them and their weaknesses. All she had to do is discover Wade Johnson's weakness and she could feel comfortable because right now he seemed too perfect and that would never work here. She threw the towel over the towel rack and stepped out from behind the bar.

Thankfully, she'd instituted the rule that all employees must be clothed while on shift. She'd found that tidbit in her research on nudist resorts. There was no way she'd be able to keep her hands off her new cowboy if he decided to get naked. And there was no way Adriana would be able to keep her legs closed with that man around. A former prostitute, Adriana still loved sex, but she also loved not having to do it for the money.

As if she'd known she was being thought of, Adriana pushed open the glass door to the outdoor/indoor bar. She held a tray of glasses filled with what appeared to be iced tea. Her skimpy jean shorts and red-checkered halter had her looking like a Mexican Daisy Duke. Kendra admired the woman on that level. Her comfort with her sexuality was impressive. As a teenager, Kendra's own substantial chest had simply added to her aura of trailer trash so she kept it well covered most of the time.

"Hey, boss, I thought the pool workers would like a refreshing cold drink." Adriana raised her hand. "All non-alcoholic, of course."

"Fine, but then they need to get back to work. They've been eating their lunches for an hour. I'm not paying them to take a siesta."

"You got it." Adriana's smile was wide as she tossed her straight black hair over her shoulder and sauntered out beyond the pavilion.

Kendra shook her head and sighed before heading inside. She could tell Adriana was much happier than she'd been when Kendra met her in Storey County, Nevada, during a small poker tournament. She hadn't planned on playing that one, but at the last minute had skipped Reno to avoid a possible awkward meeting with her ex-husband. When she decided to open a nudist resort, Adriana had come to mind immediately as someone who wouldn't care about a bunch of naked people running around.

Striding through the large gathering room with its twelve-foot-wide stone fireplace, Kendra allowed herself a secret smile. The contractor had thought the fireplace would be too big, but even he acknowledged how awesome it looked in the great room. It had become the centerpiece of the main building.

Walking through one of the cozy dining rooms, she pushed open the batwing doors to the kitchen. The spotless, stainless steel area was the domain of her cook, Selma, who was, as usual, muttering to herself in Spanish.

Kendra opened the refrigerator and grabbed a protein shake. She hadn't had lunch, but she didn't have time to stop for it either. Walking over to the shiny dishwasher, she listened to the hum as it sanitized its contents then crouched and looked beneath it to be sure everything was draining properly. Two nights ago, that had not been the case. If it was having issues, she would add it to her list for the plumber tomorrow. All appeared fine, so that meant one less task for the man.

She stood, then walked to where Selma cut vegetables on the stainless steel counter. She went at the food like a lumberjack at a tree, but Kendra couldn't fault the results. "Selma, any other plumbing problems I need to have the plumber take a look at tomorrow?"

The older woman didn't stop slicing. "Yeah, the hand sink is clogged. There's no fucking reason why it should be that way. I only wash my hands there. I take as good care of my kitchen here as I did of my girls in Carlin. I'm telling you, either there is a curse upon this place, or someone is messing with us."

Selma's brothel had been the best on Interstate 80 until, according to the ex-madam, a curse had been laid upon it. So it was no surprise this was her latest theory regarding the many hiccups they'd encountered in getting the resort ready, but Kendra honestly believed it was simply how things went these days. Faulty products, ignorant installers, cracks due to shipping, etcetera, had easily explained the hurdles she'd had to jump over. "Okay, I'll have him look at it tomorrow. Hopefully, that will be the end of it."

Selma grumbled something unintelligible that Kendra had a feeling wasn't meant for her ears, so she grabbed up her shake and took a swallow as she exited the kitchen. Striding toward the front desk, she noticed Wade and Lacey getting into a golf cart. Now why did Lacey have to show him where the stables were? Couldn't he see them for himself?

Irritation had her taking another swallow. Pushing open one of the tall tinted doors that welcomed visitors to the resort, she stepped out into the heat.

Lacey was explaining. "Don't worry, it's actually a rule that we keep our clothes on during our shift. Just be forewarned, Adriana does like men, so you may want to be on your guard with her."

Wade smiled. "Good to know."

Kendra gritted her teeth. The cowboy didn't need a personal escort to the stables. Her bookkeeper/receptionist had a lot of work to do. "Lacey, did you show Wade his casita?"

The pretty girl started as if she'd been caught doing something she shouldn't. "Oh, I didn't know you were here. Yes, I did. I was going to explain the stables to Wade, but I need to reconcile the bedding shipment with what we received."

Kendra's muscles relaxed. "Go ahead and do the shipment. I'll point out the way. We're shorthanded as it is and your abilities are critical to Poker Flat."

Lacey blushed. "Okay. Thanks."

As Lacey walked into the building, Kendra studied the cowboy. He considered her with equal interest, but it wasn't admiration. He appeared puzzled and that gave her a certain amount of satisfaction. She never revealed her hand.

Strolling over to the cart, she took one more swallow of her shake. "Have you ever driven a golf cart?"

The brim of his hat shaded his face, but his expression was easily read. "Yes, actually. I helped my little sister with a few of her golf tournament fundraisers."

Oh boy, this cowboy was far too good for the likes of Poker Flat. One more reason for her to stay away. "Good. Then take the path marked with the horse's head. We made all the signs easy for guests to follow."

He looked at the sign, putting his face in profile again. Shit, he was as handsome from the side as from the front. She had the unusual urge to nip at his jawline.

"That's smart. I wish all vacation spots did that."

His compliment surprised her, and she shifted her weight to her right leg, jutting out her hip. "I had to do that because our employee base isn't large and I didn't want to waste staff positions on golf cart drivers."

He turned back to her and smiled. "Another smart idea."

Completely uncomfortable with his praise and inviting smile, she ignored his comment. "In your office you should find enough to get started. Make a list of anything there you need as well as anything else for marking trails and suggestions for horses. I plan on having guests chauffeured from the garage to the resort in a wagon and I want to offer trail rides for those who are more adventurous. Remember, all guests will be nude, so if there are any special supplies we need in order to make sitting a horse comfortable, write them down too."

His smile disappeared. "Wait, you want people to ride horses while naked?"

"Of course. This is a nudist resort."

"I'm sorry, but you can't do that."

She opened her mouth to tell him she could do whatever she wanted, but he kept talking.

"If a person rides naked, they will have burns not only on their legs where they brush the saddle, but also in other areas that I guarantee you they will not be happy about."

She pondered that for a moment. Maybe that was why no other resort offered nude horseback riding, why Buddy and Ginger had longed for that experience so much. So if she could figure it out, it would make her place even more unique than it was. "I'm sure we can come up with a way around that. We'll go over it tonight."

He frowned and her stomach tensed. "Dinner is at six. Don't be late. You don't want to miss Selma's cooking and you don't want to make her mad at you either."

"Why Ms. Lowe?"

"Trust me. I was late one night and I found my quesadilla riddled with hot pepper sauce so fiery it burned my mouth for two days. You're better off not showing up at all."

He grinned and her stomach relaxed. "Okay, I'll be on time."

"Good, and Wade…"

"Yes."

"I'm not high society and I'm not married anymore, so as I said before, we can drop the Ms. Lowe."

He bowed his head and she could have sworn he was hiding a smile, but when he looked at her, he was dead serious. "I'll remember that, Kendra."

Her throat closed as he spoke her name, a strong rush of heat invading her body. Nodding once, she turned around and strode back to the building, throwing her empty shake can in the trash outside before stepping into the coolness of the resort.

Damn, she liked the sound of her name on his lips. Staying away from that cowboy was going to be very, very hard.

Cowboys Never Fold (http://www.lexipostbooks.com/cowboys-never-fold/)

www.ingramcontent.com/pod-product-compliance
Lightning Source LLC
Chambersburg PA
CBHW060938120726
47910CB00002B/382